Praise for Gina Robinson's
DIAMONDS ARE TRULY FOREVER

"A fast-paced and exciting thriller. Jam-packed with funny dialogue and hot sex, Staci and Drew couldn't be more different and yet so alike. Secrets, dead bodies, and pure good luck follow Staci wherever she goes. The characters are funny, loveable, and extremely clever with all their anecdotes. There's never a dull moment . . . [this] is one book you definitely will NOT lose interest in; instead you will be unable to put the book down. Excellent and innovative read!"
—*Fresh Fiction*

"Readers are in for a fun, rollicking read with *Diamonds Are Truly Forever* and you'll be chuckling at the funny scenes—and hoping that Drew and Staci get back together. Gina Robinson is a new author to me, but one I can't wait to read more from. If you love a romantic suspense that is long on funny situations and romantic to boot, then you'll love *Diamonds Are Truly Forever*."
—Patti Fischer, *Romance Reviews Today*

LIVE AND LET LOVE

"Secret agents, mysterious identities, and a love that just won't die make for a sweet, clever escape from reality."
—*Kirkus Reviews*

"Robinson's action-packed tale doesn't shy away from the fact that the hero is an assassin. Featuring plenty of interesting gadgets for spying and killing, as well as some delightful dogs—and a good dose of humor and suspense—this book ensures readers will race to the perfectly fitting finish."
—Susan Mobley, *RT Book Reviews,* 4½ stars

"Gina is a talented writer . . . if you are a fan of her stories and you find a book gift card in your stocking, this book is worth adding to your wish list." —*Night Owl Romance*

THE SPY WHO LEFT ME

"This first Agent Ex novel is good, old-fashioned fun. Full of laughter, intrigue, and, of course, steamy spies, it's a great weekend escape. Robinson knows how to balance a book with lighthearted romps and serious romance."
—*RT Book Reviews*

"At times laugh-out-loud funny, Robinson's foray into the world of James Bond has its poignant side, assuring that readers will be back for more." —*Booklist*

"Punctuated with Bond-worthy downhill car and bike chases and near-death surfing parties, Robinson's clever concoction of lust and longing is a refreshing tropical cocktail." —*Publishers Weekly*

"Mystery, mayhem, sexy spies, and lots of laughter. Gina Robinson writes a damn good book!"
—Christie Craig, award-winning author

ALSO BY GINA ROBINSON

The Spy Who Left Me

Diamonds Are Truly Forever

Live and Let Love

License
to
Love

GINA ROBINSON

St. Martin's Paperbacks

This is a work of fiction. All of the characters, organizations, and events portrayed in this novel are either products of the author's imagination or are used fictitiously.

LICENSE TO LOVE

For information address St. Martin's Press, 175 Fifth Avenue, New York, NY 10010.

ISBN: 978-1-250-03300-0

Printed in the United States of America

St. Martin's Paperbacks edition / September 2013

St. Martin's Paperbacks are published by St. Martin's Press, 175 Fifth Avenue, New York, NY 10010.

10 9 8 7 6 5 4 3 2 1

To the courageous men and women who serve our country, clandestinely and otherwise, at home and abroad, and the spouses and families who wait for them.

PROLOGUE

A LUXURY HOTEL ON THE STRIP
LAS VEGAS, NEVADA

Disappearing on her husband in the middle of an expensive Vegas magic act would be considered rude. By almost everyone. Especially given that undercover CIA agent Lani Silkwater was performing on stage with her husband of less than a day, premier illusionist Rock Powers. As his exceptionally able-bodied assistant.

She'd shown him just how able-bodied too many times to count, on stage and off. But particularly last night, on their wedding night, when she'd played contortionist just for him. The memory should have made her blush, if she'd been prone to blushing.

Damn, Rock, she thought as she waited in the dark just offstage for her cue.

He'd gotten her drunk and taken advantage of her, plying her with romantic sweet nothings and shuffling her off, still in her stage costume, to be married by Elvis before she came to her senses. Being duped by Rock was the truly embarrassing part. She wouldn't be surprised if she discovered he'd drugged her drinks.

If she'd been sober, she never would have signed the license. And he knew it. But he was as smooth a manipulator, as charming a rogue, and as big a liar as any spy or foreign agent she'd ever known. And she'd known plenty. In his favor, he worked magic with his hands, and she didn't just mean in the show. You had to love a man skilled at sleight of hand.

Worse still, she'd been so sloshed, she'd signed the stupid document, Lani Silkwater, which was her real name rather than the cover name Rock knew her by, Lani Torres. A fact she'd only realized in the morning when she woke and spotted their signed commemorative certificate of marriage sticking out from the breast pocket of the jacket he'd tossed on the floor by the bed.

Blowing her cover was a major, major violation of the trade, a total lapse in spycraft. And probably made the damn thing legal. Hopefully, Rock hadn't bothered to check her signature for authenticity and noticed the name she'd used. He'd been nearly as drunk as she was.

Fortunately, he wasn't the only one in this relationship with sticky fingers. She knew a thing or two about pickpocketing, too. She'd lifted the certificate and stuffed it beneath the insole of the three-inch-high white pumps she wore. The stupid thing would probably give her a blister when she made her stage entrance and danced into Rock's arms.

First thing when she got back to Langley, if she got back to Langley, she'd have to tinker with the marriage records and get her name replaced with her stage name before it became public record. She'd love to just delete the marriage, wipe it off the books altogether. But that type of operation required higher clearance than she possessed. She knew guys who could do it, both in and outside the law. But the fewer people she involved, the better. The *last* thing she wanted was to call her blunder to the chief's attention. CIA National Clandestine Services Chief Emmett Nelson would not be happy. He'd be furious.

Chay, the show's choreographer, rested a hand on Lani's

shoulder. She jumped. He'd sneaked up on her with those graceful, quiet dancer moves of his.

"Sorry!" Chay laughed. "Got a case of jitters to-night?"

Jitters? Fear of being executed on stage, more like. Assassins are such harsh critics.

Lani faked a nervous smile. Fortunately, she was good at faking just about anything. She felt confident the smile looked genuine enough to fool Chay. "I was lost in thought. I didn't hear you."

"A great performer always concentrates on the show." He leaned in and whispered in her ear, "You'll do fine. You're always brilliant."

Empty promises and false assurances. If Chay knew the stakes involved and the men I've angered, he'd be preaching a different message. Like run for your life.

Chay gave her shoulder a squeeze. "One more minute. Are you ready?"

As ready as I'll ever be. She nodded. Being an adrenaline junkie helped.

Rock had inadvertently put her in an especially uncomfortable bind. Joining in holy wedlock, or even questionably holy wedlock performed by the King, violated the Agency's unwritten rule, particularly without the blessing of her boss. Fortunately, she worked for the good guys. Emmett would merely bench her and assign her to desk work at Langley when he found out.

Merely. If she hadn't been about to go on stage with the eyes of the crew on her, she would have rolled her eyes. Desk work would kill her. Which is why she intended to rectify the situation before the boss got even the smallest inkling of her mistake.

She took a deep breath and tried to get her head in the show. She should count her blessings. If she'd been an enemy RIOT agent, she'd already be dead instead of planning a run for her life before the end of her act.

A valuable piece of top-secret intelligence, intel she'd stolen just before the show, information that would save Hoover Dam from being blown to smithereens in an attempt to bring down the Western power grid, rested between her breasts beneath the tightly corseted white bodice of her costume. Which was, ironically enough, a wedding gown with a diaphanous skirt that would catch the laser light bouncing around the stage. The sheer material showed off her tan legs and the tiny white-sequined bikini panties she wore underneath.

Rock had supervised the design of the costume, and constructed the illusion himself to be spectacular and bend her mind to his will—convince her to marry him. His reasoning had been that if she played his bride night after night she'd eventually acquiesce and actually marry him. After all, he was a world-class master of persuasion and mind-bending. When she hadn't, he'd done what he did best—resorted to trickery.

The music on stage rose to a crescendo. That was her cue. Chay gave her a gentle shove. "You're up. Break a leg, beautiful bride girl."

A broken leg *would* be lucky compared to the danger she faced, namely death by sniper bullet and a broken heart.

As Lani glided seamlessly into the act, her long dark hair blew in the breeze created by fans at the other end of the stage. This was the most dangerous part of the performance for her. Blinded by the stage lights, the audience before her disappeared, becoming a clapping, cheering, dark mass housing a Revolutionary International Organization of Terrorists, or RIOT, agent who wanted his intel back and her very dead. With any luck, he wouldn't try to kill her until he was close enough to search her body and retrieve what she'd taken.

But RIOT agents were unpredictable and often crazy. A single shot and she'd crumple, a wilted, red-stained white bridal flower bleeding out before the audience's eyes.

As she strutted toward Rock and his outstretched hand, playing the seductive part of the eager bride, her breath caught at the sight of him.

His long, dark bangs fell forward over his forehead. Stage makeup emphasized his sexy five o'-clock stubble. And his brown eyes sparkled beneath the heat of the stage lights with lust and challenge, with showmanship and desire. Rock claimed the spark between them gave the show the magical quality it needed to thrill audiences and made his life complete. If that were really the case, she was about to do the unforgivable—betray the man who was her magic.

She'd violated still another of the most important rules of spycraft and fallen in love with her target. Now she had to pay the price and do her duty. She'd been sent not only to save the dam from the RIOT scum, but to steal an extremely valuable illusion from Rock.

Magic thrummed through the air, created by Rock's magnetic presence and sheer force of personality. By the music and the lights. The stage. The curls of smoke wafting up. The illusions he created were so powerful and complete, an extension of his mind that she almost believed them. And she knew his secrets.

Her spy senses on high alert, Lani swore she could feel her enemy draw a bead on her as she took Rock's warm hand and felt the spark his touch always elicited. She sensed her stalker calculating the risks and odds of success.

As the volume of the music rose, she guessed her hunter knew he didn't even need a silencer. Every eye in the

audience would be on Rock. No one would see the RIOT
bastard shoot her. He'd be the magician of the moment.
But he wouldn't get what she'd tucked between her breasts.
That was her only safety net right now.

She smiled at Rock with her heart breaking. She was
planning to ruin his life.

"Ladies and gentlemen, behold my beautiful bride."
Rock squeezed her hand. "Isn't she lovely?" His voice
boomed through the theater, silken and husky. "I married
this girl last night. For real, folks."

Lani's heart stopped. He wasn't supposed to make a
public announcement.

Even the most cynical heart loved a real-life love story.
The theater resounded with the audience's approval,
drowning out the panicked beating of her heart in her ears
as adrenaline kick-started her back into action. Rock
squeezed her hand again, reminding her of her role. Lani
inclined her head toward the crowd as Rock had taught
her and turned to face him.

Dressed like a disheveled groom after the ceremony
and grinning like an idiot, he looked pretty much as he
had last night as he carried her over the threshold of his
mansion. Tight black tux pants. His gauzy white shirt falling open to his waist, revealing a hard, defined chest with
every muscle glistening beneath the lights. It was tucked
into a small, stylized vest, a wide belt really. His bow tie
was untied, hanging loose on either side of his chest. The
look in his eyes said he couldn't wait to ravish her.

Just looking at him turned her on and broke her heart.

I hate to leave you, baby.

He may never believe it, but she loved him. He and his
crew had made her feel as if she belonged, like only the
Agency had before. She hated to leave him. But she
couldn't stay and she couldn't tell him she was going or
why. If she lingered much longer, she'd be dead.

He pulled her into his embrace. "They say that love makes you feel as if you're walking on sunshine. As if your feet don't touch the ground."

Slowly, they began to levitate together. But the audience wasn't impressed. Not yet. Not until another sexy, scantily clad assistant tossed him a shiny silver hoop and he spun it all around them to prove there were no strings attached.

He lied, of course. But the audience gasped and applauded, believing him.

She wrapped herself around him. She touched his cheek, ran her fingers through his hair, and stared into his eyes, trying to memorize every detail of them.

She mouthed, "I love you, Rock."

And then she kissed him. It was supposed to be a stage kiss. A faked tongue-down-the-throat affair. But she made it the real deal. Pressed up against him. Opened her mouth to him. Kissed him as if they were doing a repeat of their wedding ceremony. As she did, they levitated higher into the air.

The crowd went wild.

During the months Rock had been honing her magic, he taught her the secret to the coin drop. He told her to practice by holding a coin in her hand and staring at it so that when she performed the trick and was in reality staring at her empty hand as if it held the coin, she'd be convincing. She took his advice now, and kissed him as if she were staying, coiled herself around him as if it would be impossible for her to disappear.

But, of course, that was the magic of this trick—making just her disappear, leaving him, the sexy, mournful, frustrated bridegroom dangling and holding empty air. The timing had to be perfect. She prayed her assassin didn't see her disappearance coming. Just a second more . . .

Rock gave the signal. *Now.*

"Bye, baby." In one swift, confident move, she swung behind the black curtain behind her. She motioned for the stage crew to let her down and unhooked herself from the wires as the audience roared with approval. From their vantage point, it looked as if she had disappeared in a puff of white smoke. Vaporized.

She landed on the floor behind the curtain with a thud that the music drowned out.

The stagehand nearest her frowned at her. She was going off script and he was confused.

There was little time. In an instant, Rock would call her back.

She had just moments to escape, but she couldn't leave him to fail. "I'm not feeling well. Clara!" She motioned for her double, who waited in the wings, to take her place. "Quickly."

Clara was the same height, age, body type, and general appearance as Lani. They doubled for each other in acts that required teleportation or being sawed in half. With enough makeup, they could pass for each other on stage. Not on camera, but they were close enough to fool a theater audience. Fortunately, there were no cameras for this trick.

Clara realized something was wrong and came running.

Lani pulled her veil and tiara off as Clara rushed to grab them from her and pin them on. With luck, the audience wouldn't notice the difference between the two women and would assume Lani had reappeared in a siren's dress meant for after the ceremony.

She tried not to think about what Rock would think.

Before anyone on the crew could protest, Lani ran off the stage, through the backstage area, and down the hall toward freedom, her high-heeled bridal shoes clicking on the vinyl floor as she sprinted off to save the world.

On second thought, disappearing for good with their marriage certificate in her shoe, less than twenty-four hours after the nuptials? Simply popping out and not re-appearing at his command during the middle of his successful act—yeah, that *was* heartless. Even for Lani, who was used to disappearing on people.

CHAPTER ONE

LAS VEGAS, NEVADA
TWO YEARS LATER

Out of costume and dressed inconspicuously in a show T-shirt, jeans, and a silk-screened black hoodie to hide his distinctive tattoos, Rock Powers leaned against the crowded casino craps table and placed the bet he'd been cryptically instructed to play, Hi-Lo. The house edge on this placement was just over eleven percent. The payout fifteen to one. So far he hadn't won. What else was new? He was beginning to wonder whether he was wasting not only his money, but his time. He wondered the same thing about his search for Lani nearly every day.

On his own, he'd never play these lousy odds. The house always held the advantage. Just like fate seemed to. He preferred to stack the deck in his favor, which was why he was banned by the Vegas casinos from playing any card game. Too good at sleight of hand, and palming and counting cards. Anyone as good at the ambitious card trick as he was was bound to be suspect. Hazard of the magician's trade. The mysterious person who'd instructed him to play craps and wait to be contacted knew a thing or two about him. Which was reassuring, in a strange, creepy way. At least the guy had done his research.

Rock was a gambler, but only on stage, and in his bid to find his missing wife. Much more of this futile betting and he'd lose his favorite Rock Powers Faith Unseen show T-shirt right off his back. Hey, it was a limited edition.

Where the hell was the bastard who'd given him these ludicrous instructions to place this bet and wait for him to identify himself? The mysterious contact that either had a Jason Bourne complex or was some kind of an espionage nutcase.

I know where your wife is.

The words on the missive slid beneath his dressing room door two nights ago, on the last night of his show's run until it picked up again in November, haunted Rock. He might have ignored it; turned it in to security so they could catch the guy the next time he slunk by. Except for the enclosed QR code. Which when Rock had snapped a shot of it with his cell phone, took him to a video of a living, laughing Lani. A hypnotic video Rock had studied until he felt as if his eyes were going to fall out.

Lani, two years older? Different hairstyle. Wearing up-to-date trendy fashions and makeup. A newspaper in the background with a current date. But then anyone could print one of those up, right? Her fabulously rich laugh. He couldn't get enough of hearing it over and over again. When was the last time he'd laughed like that, really laughed from the heart? The night he'd married Lani.

The way her shiny, straight, nearly black hair fell over her face as she moved. The distinctive gesture she used to sweep it back and tuck it behind her ears, out of her dancing, barely perceptibly almond-shaped eyes. The curve of her full lips as she smiled.

There was only one way to describe Lani—exotic. One quarter white, one quarter African-American, one quarter Japanese, one quarter Hispanic, Lani called herself the great all-American mutt. Everyone else found her looks arresting.

A picture could have been Photoshopped, altered in any number of ways. A video? That was a trickier deal. Then he spotted the unique silver ring on the pointer finger of her right hand and his heart stopped. He noticed every detail, as he was trained to do. She wasn't wearing the huge diamond-and-platinum wedding ring he'd given her.

Whether that was really Lani, or a very convincing double in the video, whoever had made it knew something about Lani's disappearance. Nutcase contact aside, desperation drove Rock to look into it. No rock unturned. Only himself, Rock Powers, completely upended.

Tell no one about this missive or the deal's off.

The note gave the instructions he was now following. He'd spent two days in silent hell, thinking of nothing but this meeting.

Two days in hell were nothing in comparison to his years of torment. He'd been looking for Lani for two horrifically long years, enduring all the humiliation and frustration that came with her disappearance and the never-ending search. Offering a standing hundred-thousand-dollar reward to anyone who provided a tip that led to her. Or her body. Checking up on crackpot leads and greedy individuals who sought to trick him out of the reward. Being offered tips by supposed psychics. Didn't these people pay attention? He was Rock Powers, debunker of psychic phenomenon.

There were two camps of magicians, both of which performed "psychic" tricks or mentalism. One camp practiced, claiming they had authentic supernatural abilities. The second camp performed just as convincingly, but let people know they were being tricked, duped by lies and modern magic. Rock was in the second camp. He could bend spoons with the best of them, but he never claimed it was anything other than sleight of hand.

For two years, the rumors had flown, mocking him, making fun, and hurling ridiculous accusations as he tried to contain his grief and worry and just find Lani.

"Great illusionist's wife dumps him before the honeymoon even began. Magician Rock Powers can't keep the magic in his marriage for even a day; claims he's brokenhearted."

"Drunk, Rock Powers marries on a whim without a prenup. Millions of little motives for murder? Where are you, Lani Powers?"

"Has illusionist Rock Powers performed the perfect crime and disappeared his beautiful bride for good without a clue? Stumped police demand he reappear her."

"Rock Powers initiates a brilliant publicity stunt. Audiences pack his show, waiting for the ultimate prestige, the reappearance of beautiful Lani Torres Powers. Bring her back, Rock."

For Rock it was no publicity stunt and he obviously hadn't murdered her. That left only a few options. Either someone had abducted or murdered her. Or she'd decided she'd made a mistake by marrying him and disappeared as a way of rectifying it.

Running out on him neither made logical sense, nor jibed with what he knew of Lani. Logically, she would have stood to make a pile of money in a divorce, just as the gossipmongers proclaimed. He *had* married her on the spur of the moment and been incredibly reckless—no prenup. In addition to the money, the publicity from a split with him would only have helped her career.

And the Lani he knew? If she'd wanted a divorce she'd have come right out and asked for one. She was dedicated to the craft. None of this disappearing in the middle of an act crap. Finally, she loved him. He knew she had.

Which left the darker alternative the more likely, and frightening, scenario in Rock's mind.

Ironically, the mystery, the sense that it could all be an act, the dark aura of suspicion that hung over him, and the desire to be in the crowd if he actually reappeared Lani combined to shoot his act to the heights of success. Professionally, he'd never done better. Personally, he was darkly driven. If he hadn't been addicted to magic, he'd have long ago overdosed on something worse.

He pushed himself, worked until he dropped. Created dark tricks and acts spun from the turn his imagination and psyche had taken since she'd vanished. The reviews raved about the deep, disturbing nature of his tricks, saying he'd finally found his magical voice, his theme. Dark worked for Rock Powers. Dark was Rock Powers. His sense of naïveté gone, his act was true magic.

Women wanted him. They threw themselves at him. He had groupies, fan clubs full of them. Starlets and strippers. Porn stars. Nice girls with soft hearts. He could have had just about any woman he wanted. The ladies loved a tortured hero. He ignored them all. Which, ironically, only ratcheted up his appeal.

Work was the only thing that dulled the pain and kept him sane.

He'd known Lani just over six months, been married to her less than a day. But he wouldn't rest until he found her. He wouldn't let her down. If she needed rescuing, he was her guy. If it took him the rest of his life, he'd discover the truth of what had happened to her.

Then that note showed up beneath his door. Hope, as they say, sprang eternal.

Rock was just about to give up on craps and his mysterious contact and pick up his chips and go home. He gave a mental shrug.

One more bet, what the hell could that hurt?

He slapped the chips on the table. Once more and he was leaving with what was left in his wallet and of his pride before anyone recognized him. Before anyone realized he was a sucker for believing he'd finally find Lani.

The shooter, a cocky young guy, held the dice out for his tipsy girlfriend to blow on for luck. He shot. The dice bounced against the back of the table. The table erupted in applause.

The dealer surveyed the table. "Hi-Lo wins!"

Rock had just won something in the magnitude of fifteen thousand dollars. In a single toss, he'd recouped everything he'd lost, plus about five grand.

As the dealer handed him his chips, Rock felt a hand on his shoulder. "Excellent play, boy. You were about to give up, weren't you?"

Rock turned and stared into the steely brown eyes of a distinguished man who could have been anywhere between thirty-five and fifty-five. Despite the steel in his gaze, his lips twitched as if he were fighting a smile. But his stance and attitude said he was a fighter and not to mess with him. There was something lethal about him.

"The impatience of youth," the newcomer continued. "If you'd walked, you'd have lost the advantage of having already sat through the first few rolls where the house held the definite statistical advantage. In my business, we know how to play the odds to our favor."

"Worried I'd lose the reward money?" Rock said. "That's why you're here, isn't it? I'm not easy to fool."

The man laughed. "Hardly. I'm in no position to accept it. The ethics committee would have a field day. Come with me." The man squeezed Rock's shoulder. "It's too crowded to talk here. Too many ears."

The guy wasn't making any sense. Probably another loony.

Rock tipped the dealer, took his payoff and, ignoring his better judgment, followed the stranger as he wound his way through the crowd and the neon art in the hotel.

His contact had the good grace to allow him to collect his cash before leading him out of the casino into the bright, flashing neon magic on the Strip. Rock pretended to stash his payoff in his wallet and put it in his jeans pocket. In reality, he used sleight of hand to stash it in a concealed money belt.

"Paranoid?" Rock asked the man as they walked out of the casino toward the street.

The man shrugged. "No more than you are, stashing your cash in a money belt."

Rock stopped and stared at him. How the hell had he seen that? Rock's diversionary sleight of hand tricks never failed.

The man laughed and kept walking. Rock rushed to keep up with him. Rock was a world-class magician. If this guy hadn't been distracted by the motion Rock made of stuffing the wallet in his pocket, this guy was something else. A formidable foe. A danger. Rock's heart raced.

"Don't look so worried," the guy said as he kept walking. "I know a bit of magic myself. When I was a small boy, John Mulholland taught me my first trick or two."

"You knew the great Mulholland?" Mulholland had been a magician for the CIA. The hairs stood up on the back of Rock's neck. This guy really was a spy buff.

Rock grabbed spywannabe's arm. "What game are you playing? What do you know about Lani?"

"Everything," he said. "But here's not the place. Trust me when I tell you that you have too many enemies here. Far too many enemies. You've stirred up trouble, boy. In more quarters than you know." He shook off Rock's hand and led him away from the hotel, down the street, and into a shadowy back alley.

Rock had to be crazy, certifiable to follow this guy. But he did. It was a balmy evening. A nice night for a walk if you weren't out with a crazy. Finally, his contact stopped in the shadows upwind from a garbage Dumpster and leaned casually against a brick wall, studying Rock.

The guy wore an expensive suit. Rock wouldn't have touched a thing in that alley, let alone risk staining or snagging his suit. But his contact wasn't so finicky.

It was warm, almost too warm for the hoodie Rock wore. But he didn't take it off. And he didn't lean against the wall, either. "What do you know about Lani?"

"Direct and to the point. I like that." As the guy smiled, his teeth gleamed white in the shadows. "But it's generally considered polite to make introductions first, before delving into business." He stuck out his hand, offering to shake. "Emmett Nelson, chief of National Clandestine Services. Recently appointed head of domestic spying for the top-secret antiterrorist task force. You can call me Emmett or Chief. Or Mr. Nelson, if you prefer. Pleased to meet you."

When Rock hesitated, Nelson laughed.

"Don't trust me?" Emmett said. "Afraid I have something lethal up my sleeve?"

Rock's eyes narrowed. "I've never heard of National Clandestine Services."

Nelson sighed. "What? Never heard of the spying arm of the Central Intelligence Agency?"

"CIA? What the hell?" Rock didn't trust him, but he shook Nelson's hand to humor him. Nelson had a firm, confident, calloused grip, the grip of a man who knew how to take care of himself, and who fired a gun often.

"Yeah, I know," Nelson said, releasing Rock's hand. "Sad how many Americans don't know the official title of the spying branch of the Agency. Too many people don't realize the Agency is made up of many divisions, most of them desk jobs, analysts, and eggheads. The spying part is just the most fun." His eyes twinkled. "I have the best job in the world."

Rock shook his head, still wondering whether to believe this guy with his spy complex, or brush him off as a loony. He decided to run with it a while. "What does the CIA know about Lani? Why are *you* involved, Em?" It was hard to keep the scoff out of his voice. If this guy wanted to play James Bond's boss M, Rock would go with it.

With a movement so quick, Rock didn't see it coming, Nelson's hand shot out and grabbed Rock by the throat, squeezing his larynx in a crushing way that only a professional thug would know. "No one calls me Em unless I invite them to, got that, showman?" Nelson locked eyes with him, his gaze decidedly unfriendly.

Shit! This guy is crazy and *dangerous.*

Rock considered fighting back, but he needed Emmett. For the moment. He nodded.

Nelson grinned and let go. "Good, now that we have that straight, I could ask you the same question."

Rock rubbed his throat, hoping Nelson hadn't damaged his vocal cords. They were insured with Lloyd's of London for their hypnotic quality along with his mesmerizing eyes. But still, what was a magician without his commanding voice? How could Rock perform magic without uttering the magic words, *abracadabra!* Not that he'd ever really said abracadabra since he was about ten. "Me?" The word came out as more of a croak than anything. Rock cleared his throat.

Emmett stared at him without pity. "Yes, you! Why were you involved with Lani? What business did you have marrying one of my spies behind my back?"

Spies? Rock's senses reeled. *Lani, a spy?* And yet, it made a warped kind of sense. He stared at Nelson, trying not to gape. "Lani's a spy? That's ridiculous."

Nelson ignored him. "Everyone in the biz knows my agents don't marry without my blessing." He grinned, evilly. "Which I deny in almost every case. I like my agents to remain single. So many fewer complications and less baggage that way. Spouses are liabilities, security lapses and blackmail opportunities waiting to happen. My people know that when they sign on.

"Married people, especially women, want children"—he rolled his eyes—"don't even get me started on the dangers of spies with children."

Was it Rock's imagination, or did Nelson hiss the word *children*? Speechless, he stared at Nelson as if he were crazy.

"What? Do you want proof, magician? A skeptic, are you?" Nelson shook his head again. "Need to see a badge or something?" He paused, studying Rock. "Sorry to disappoint. Secret agents don't carry badges. They tend to give us away."

"Why *should* I believe you?"

Nelson crossed his arms. His eyes narrowed as he watched Rock. "Because if you don't, you'll end up dead. Very soon, I suspect."

Rock took a step back. He should run the hell out of here.

Nelson's laugh stopped him. "Oh, not by me. I don't want to kill you. But our enemies do."

"Enemies? I don't have any enemies, other than the nuts who want to steal my tricks." Rock squinted at him, wishing, not for the first time, that he really did have psychic powers. Nelson looked deadly serious and suddenly not at all crazy.

"But our country does and you've attracted their attention." Nelson paused. "The way I see it," he said, "without my help, you'll be dead within the week. Possibly tortured in the process." Nelson shrugged. "You can never predict what those RIOT bastards will do. Or . . ."

Speaking of showmen, this guy was an ace. His pause was pure dramatic effect.

Rock broke first. "Or, what, spook? And who the hell, or what, is RIOT?"

Nelson laughed softly. "Impatient again. Should you accept my offer, all will be revealed in due time." He shook his head as if amused. He seemed easily amused.

"Or we help each other out, magic man. Turns out, the Agency and I are in need of a talented magician. We rarely recruit from the magical realm. The last one was Mulholland in the fifties and the director got all kinds of grief for that.

"In the seventies, Congress and the press accused the Agency of using too many showboaty shenanigans. That failed assassination incident with Fidel Castro and the exploding cigar was unfortunate, but you have to admit it was creative. Too bad it put the final nail in magic's coffin." His eyes were devilish. "Richard Helms, the director at the time, ordered all copies of Mulholland's classified magic manual destroyed. More's the pity."

For an instant, Rock wondered if the Agency really had given up on magic in the intervening years. Nelson's tone left room for doubt.

"But, you know," Nelson continued, "our R and D came up with some exceptionally clever devices because of Mulholland's input. The Agency learned more about escapology, misdirection, change blindness, and creating cognitive illusions than most people can imagine.

"Saved our butts more than once, I can tell you. And then of course, there was the unfortunate incident where one of the manuals was discovered still in existence and published a few years back.

"And now"—Nelson waved his hands in an all-encompassing gesture—"we find we have need of magic again. Which brings me to you and the proposition I have for you. You have skills we need, my boy. And we have something you desperately want—your wife."

Without thinking, Rock made a fist and took a step toward Nelson. *The bastard has Lani.*

"Step down and stop looking at me like that," Nelson said. He shrugged again. "She's not my prisoner. As I said, she's my agent.

"And, you, Rock Powers, crave excitement and challenge. It's a match made in heaven."

Rock stared at him in disbelief. *The CIA wants to recruit me?*

This conversation kept taking one bizarre turn after another.

"I see you still don't believe me. I guess it's not every day the layman runs into a spy." Nelson laughed. He looked as if he was having the time of his life at Rock's expense. "Or maybe it is. Maybe you entertain spies unaware all the time. But seeing that you need proof . . ."

With a flourish, he produced a document out of thin air. He caught Rock unaware. He didn't see how Nelson did it, but he was good. Must have had it up his sleeve the whole time.

Nelson held the document out for him. Rock snatched it from his hand and scanned it. He swallowed hard when he saw Lani's handwriting and signature at the bottom, next to his own. Although her last name was different. He'd been too drunk and in love to notice before, but she'd signed her name Lani Silkwater, rather than Lani Torres, as he'd known her. He'd had no idea Torres was her stage name.

Rock's heart crashed into his stomach. The commemorative certificate of marriage he and Lani had signed after the ceremony trembled in his hand. "How did you get my original certificate of marriage?"

It had been missing since the night Lani disappeared, and was obviously authentic, down to the tiny smudge of Lani's lipstick in the corner.

"Lani took it with her when she left. Hid it in her shoe."

Rock attacked Nelson, grabbing him by the lapel of his suit. "Where's Lani?"

Nelson shook his head. There was no fear in his eyes as he stared Rock down. In fact, he somehow managed to look both lethal and amused at the same time.

"Not until we have a deal, Rock. Surely you can see that if I give you that intel, I lose my tactical advantage. A good negotiator never tips his hand."

Rock released him and ran his hands through his hair. He couldn't believe he was even considering Nelson's bizarre offer. "How would this work? Will I have to train at the Farm? Would I have to give up my show? I'm on hiatus now, but I'll be back on stage in a few months."

I'll never give up my show. Not even for Lani.

"No, we'd never ask you to give up your show. And yes, we'll give you some training, but not at the Farm. Nothing about your involvement is *official,* you understand." Nelson paused. "But let me be clear about this, once you accept my offer, there's no going back. We know everything about you, including how to destroy you if you betray us.

"And just so you're clear, betraying us, giving out our national defense secrets, is treason and punishable by death. The highest offices of government are aware of this operation.

"If you have any doubts, any hesitation, now is the time to walk away, Rock Powers. After this, there's no going back."

Rock took a deep breath. Espionage, that had to be an

adrenaline rush, a new frontier for magic. And Lani. Damn his weak soul, he had to see her. Plus there was that little matter Nelson had mentioned about someone killing Rock within the week.

"We're in a bit of a time crunch," Nelson said. "But if you need a day to think it over—"

"Hobson's choice, but I'm in."

Nelson extended his hand.

Rock didn't take it. "With one condition—I get my wife back. I get a chance to work things out with Lani." Rock stared him in the eye.

Nelson dropped his hand and studied Rock. "I can give you the opportunity to see her, the rest is up to you. No guarantees. The decision to remain your wife is ultimately Lani's."

Rock nodded. "Fair enough. What do we do now? How does this work?"

"We shake on it. I'll get you the details later." He grinned. "And so you know, we'll pay you handsomely. This deal will be worth your while."

Rock didn't give a damn about payment. He shook Nelson's hand without hesitating when Nelson extended it.

"When do I get to see Lani?" Rock's heart raced as he asked the question."

"I'm going to have to train this impatience out of you." Nelson shrugged and snapped his fingers. "My girl, reveal yourself."

Then, right before Rock's eyes, a woman dressed in skintight black and carrying a pistol stepped out of the shadows from behind the Dumpster. She raised her gaze to look him in the eye.

Rock's heart caught in his throat. "Lani?"

Even in the twilight, her beauty took his breath away. She'd played up her Hispanic side, so much so that she looked like he imagined a hot Havana night felt—balmy, lusty, sexy with heat.

"Classic misdirection." Nelson laughed. "She was there all along, watching my backside."

She may have had Nelson's back, but knowing she was going to see Rock, she'd dressed for him.

CHAPTER TWO

Lani stared at Rock, trying desperately not to let her emotions run away with her as she watched surprise, relief, desire, and hurt light his eyes in rapid succession. Rock still turned her insides to mush and vaporized her common sense. She'd hoped she'd gotten past that. Apparently not.

He grabbed her and pulled her into him, tipping her face up for a kiss before she could utter any of the ridiculous canned phrases she'd rehearsed as her opening lines. How did she apologize for disappearing on her husband and leaving him to dangle in the mist of mystery and suspicion for two years? How did she keep her most important secret from him and not let her heart rule her head again while she was around him? And yet encourage him to help her on a mission fraught with intrigue, double-crossing, and secrets of his magic revealed? Rock might not realize it yet, but their reunion was doomed to be short-lived.

Emmett had used the worst kind of deception to entice Rock into this mission—false hope. *Damn him.*

Lani simply stared into Rock's eyes, willing him to forgive her for what she'd done and what she was about to do to him.

"Lani," he whispered and crushed her against him so

tightly she felt the hard contours of his body as her body reacted to his.

He stared back at her with his heart in his eyes, almost daring her to crush it again. And then he lowered his lips to hers and kissed her with so much intensity, he took her breath away.

He tasted the same—like Rock, the man she'd loved. The man who'd tricked her into marriage and nearly ruined her career.

Despite all that, she kissed him back. At least, she was almost sure she did. As his tongue probed her mouth, she lost her senses. Would she behave so civilly if she'd been in his position? More likely she'd spit on him and call him names. Shove him away. Demand answers.

She hoped he didn't make the same realization and suddenly bite her tongue. As it was, he was bruising her lips. And she had no intention of stopping him.

She wondered how long it would take for the shock and joy to wear off and the accusations and questions to start flying.

Emmett cleared his throat, and not subtly. If throat clearings can have tones, his was reprimanding and hinted that they should get a room. Lani wasn't getting a room with Rock. Not anytime soon. Not ever, if she could help it. Emmett had duped Rock into believing this was going to be a *happily ever after* type of reunion rather than just business.

"It isn't wise to lurk in dark alleys," Emmett said. "The walls have eyes."

Breathless, Lani pulled out of Rock's kiss, rather too reluctantly for her own good. Her heart wasn't behaving the way she'd trained it to, traitorous thing.

Down the alley a tomcat screeched and hissed. Lani nearly jumped as she cocked her ear, listening for what had provoked the cat.

She turned and surveyed the area, feeling Rock's gaze on her as she did.

A second later, another cat hissed back and a fight broke out between the two toms. *Boys!* Lani relaxed.

The commotion, and Rock's nearness, dulled Lani's senses. She almost didn't hear the scuttle of a pebble as it bounced against the wall behind them.

We aren't alone.

Almost didn't catch the motion of an arm raising a gun in the shadows at the end of the alley in time. Fortunately, Emmett was on his game and totally undistracted by her charming husband's animal magnetism. He shoved Rock to the ground just as a bullet ricocheted over his head. Lani dropped to the ground with them. She saw the flash of gunpowder from the barrel, pinpointing the shooter's position.

Another shot bounced off the wall to their right. It was only a matter of time before the gunman honed in on them. She didn't dare to hope he was as bad a shot as movie gunmen.

She glanced around wildly, looking for cover as she spun around on her knees and aimed her pistol at the shadow. Beside her, Emmett had his gun trained in the same direction as she did. Both of them waiting for a kill shot in the dark. On her other side, Rock was totally unarmed. Or so she thought.

With a movement so small and subtle Lani almost didn't notice it, Rock pulled something from his pocket and tossed it into the alley. An instant later, they were surrounded by thick, black smoke.

Flash powder. Genius. Just the magic we need.

"This way," Emmett whispered. He grabbed Rock's arm. Rock grabbed her.

The three of them tumbled out of the alley under the cover of smoke into the neon light that overwhelmed the streetlight on the Strip. Emmett led them to a waiting car, unlocked it, and waved at them to get in.

The trio jumped in. Emmett in the driver's seat, Rock and Lani in the back. So not a good idea. She had a sudden hero worship thing going on with Rock. She was utterly amazed. He'd saved them. Good thing her boss was in the front seat or she might have let go and acted out her fantasies of showing Rock just how much she appreciated what he'd done.

Then again, that would probably give him the wrong idea about things.

Emmett peeled out, burning rubber and doing some high-speed evasive action down the Strip, dodging drunks as he went.

"That was impressive back there," Lani said to Rock. "Do you always carry flash powder on you?"

"Never leave home without it." He grinned and squeezed her hand, holding it in a grip so tight it was clear he didn't intend to let go. "You never know when you're going to need to make a stealthy escape. I learned that from Houdini and from confronting all the nutcases and greedy bastards who've been trying to collect the reward I've had out for your return."

His grin turned into a modest smile and he became self-deprecating. "And that was nothing. That was just standard flash powder. Medium noise, plenty of long-lasting smoke. You should see what I can do with Pyromaniac X14 sparkle flash powder. Now that's impressive."

"Sparkles remind me of unicorns. Not exactly your thing, Rock. Doesn't fit your image." She was hoping to distract him from talking about her absence.

He laughed heartily, squeezed her hand again, and looked her fully in the eye. "The way I use it, baby, no one's going to think of unicorns. Trust me."

Unable to hide the tide of desire and longing rising

inside her, Lani looked away. She couldn't afford to unleash her heart and let Rock back in. Love made her weak and foolish. There were too many opportunities for this mission to stop RIOT from stealing top-secret technology from Area 51, or Dreamland as some called it, to fail as it was.

Rock swiveled around and peered out the back window. "Think we lost them?"

"If we hadn't, there'd be gunplay." She laid a hand on his arm. "You'd better turn around and keep your eyes on the road. Emmett's driving tends to have a negative effect on even the stoutest stomach."

"I heard that," Emmett said from the front seat. "I'll have you know I'm certified to teach high-performance driving."

"You know what they say about teachers," Lani shot back. "People who can't do, teach."

"I'll remember you said that when your next job performance review rolls around."

"Who was shooting at us in the alley?" Rock asked, interrupting their banter.

"One of the enemies I warned you about earlier." Emmett took a turn without signaling. First rule of evasive action—never signal your intentions.

"Damn opportunists," Emmett muttered. "He followed you from the casino, sneaky bastard. Probably thought taking you out in a dark alley and making it look like robbery was a good cover. And he'd get fifteen grand for his trouble. Not a bad payoff." Emmett looked in the rearview mirror and scowled so Lani could see him.

"How did we miss him, Lani? How?" He sounded pissed. Which wasn't particularly unusual for him, but still made Lani cringe.

She didn't like being reprimanded by the boss in front

of her husband, even if she planned on their marriage being short-lived. "No idea, Chief."

Rock put his arm around her to comfort her, nuzzling her ear with his nose. "Baby, I've missed you."

His words and his breath in her ear conjured that magical, involuntary ripple of desire inside her.

"You'd better get an idea and soon." Emmett glanced back at the road.

She could always count on the boss to put a damper on passion.

Rock grabbed Lani's chin, and tipped her face to look into her eyes. "Why did you run from me? Was it because of a mission?" His voice broke with emotion and he looked too damn hopeful.

"To avoid being killed by this same group of terrorists. Lani was a hero. She saved Hoover Dam." Emmett was *not* helping matters.

"They had their sights trained on her in the middle of your act. If she hadn't popped out when she did, she'd be dead. Probably along with your career.

"Death tends to kill an act. The audience likes to feel safe while they watch people get sawed in half. Go figure."

"He wasn't sawing anyone in half," Lani interjected.

"Then again," Emmett continued, ignoring her, "you may have gotten lucky and merely been known as that magician whose assistant was murdered on stage. Still, not real good for business or your image, whether it was your fault or not. *'Other than that, how did you like the play, Mrs. Lincoln'* is not how you want the reviews to read.

"The enemies of the U.S., the terrorists I mentioned in the alley, want you permanently silenced. You have information they want contained. Stick with us and we'll protect you."

Rock frowned, obviously puzzled. "*I* have information?"

"You'll tell him later, won't you, sweetheart," Emmett said to Lani.

Rock scowled at Emmett's use of the endearment. Rock didn't know there was no such thing as sexual harassment at the Agency, not in NCS, anyway. Hard to claim sexual harassment when sometimes your orders were to sleep with the enemy. Or your husband. This was just Emmett's way of reminding her who was in charge.

"Why do you think they were aiming at you?" Emmett said to Rock. "I'm a much more valuable target." Emmett laughed. "Wipe that frown off your face, Lani, dear. You are, too."

Distracted by Rock and the "happy" banter of conversation, Lani hadn't been paying attention to Emmett's circuitous escape route to Rock's mansion. Her heart sank when he turned another corner and she realized what street they were on. She thought she'd have more time to get control of her emotions and fortify herself against Rock's charms.

Emmett pulled into the driveway of Rock's multimillion-dollar estate, paused at the security gate, punched in a code, put his thumb on the touch screen, and watched the gates swing open.

"You should change your code more often," he said, conversationally. "Don't worry. We've taken care of it. Starting now, you'll need to use a thumbprint to get in along with the password. I'll give you the password when we get inside."

"Wait a minute!" Rock said. "If I'm the target of a group of terrorists, why are we going to my house? Wouldn't I be safer someplace else? Like deep in hiding?"

Emmett shrugged. "If you go into hiding that tips our hand that we've either turned you or someone's clued you in to the real danger you're in. And that runs contrary to our plan—"

"Your plan?" Rock nearly came off the seat. "What about my plan to live for another fifty years or so?"

Emmett ignored Rock's outburst. "For now we don't want RIOT to know we're on to their latest plan. Don't worry. You're a valuable asset. We'll protect you with our lives."

"You keep mentioning RIOT. Who are they?" Rock asked.

"The Revolutionary International Organization of Terrorists, the boys who want you dead," Emmett said. "For now, what could be safer, and more comfortable, than home sweet home?"

Lani could think of about a million places. Almost anywhere, maybe even that stupid dark alley, was safer for her than here, with all the memories of the time she'd spent here with Rock. She'd never officially lived with him. She'd kept her own place. But for all intents and purposes, she'd moved in with him just weeks after starting in his show.

"Seventy-seven percent of all accident-related injuries happen at home, Chief," she said, just to tease him and show him she had spunk and wasn't easily cowed. "And that doesn't even count the nonaccident-related ones, the intentional ones, like those initiated by RIOT agents."

Emmett chuckled. "Not to worry. We've installed security measures."

"Did I give you permission for that?" Rock sounded mildly peeved, much less indignant than Lani expected.

She kept wondering when the shock of seeing her again and the shooting in the alley would wear off and Rock would begin to question the validity of their relationship. When the time came, she wondered whether she'd actually have the strength to lie and tell him it had all been an act.

"We're NCS, since when do we ask permission?" Emmett pulled to a stop in the middle of the circular drive, in front of the main entrance.

"What kind of security measures are we talking about?" Lani had her suspicions and discussing security diverted her thoughts from how good it felt to be sitting next to Rock again and how hard it would be to keep her distance. "Invisible walls, switch-activated nets, fireplace smoke screen?"

Beside her, Rock smiled, probably at the apparent absurdity of her suggestions. What in the world did he think they were bringing him on board for? They were looking for magic.

"Don't laugh," she said. "Emmett is capable of anything."

"I didn't bother with the fireplace smoke screen," Emmett said as he got out of the car. "As he so ably demonstrated, Rock seems perfectly capable of creating a smoke screen on his own."

Lani rolled her eyes as Rock stepped out of the car, pulling her along with him. Apparently afraid she'd vanish into thin air again, he refused to let go of her hand. And she had to admit, she'd given him reason to be leery.

Rock pulled his keys from his pocket and held them up. "How do we get in? Do these still work?"

"Unlock away," Emmett said. "I'll take it from there."

Rock unlocked the door. Emmett showed him how to get past security. And they were in.

As always, the sight of the grand entryway of Rock's seventy-five-hundred-square-foot villa-style mansion took Lani's breath away. And for good reason. She remembered all too well Rock carrying her up the carpeted curving staircase with its dark, hand-carved cherry railing to the master suite. And the ravishing that followed.

Memories I really should forget, she thought as she stared up at the sparkling crystal chandelier above. *In case the mission goes wrong.*

She glanced over at Rock. He was eyeing the staircase, too. She'd have to disabuse him of the notion that things were going back to the way they were before she disappeared. Her entire relationship with Rock had been a mistake. She'd inadvertently given RIOT the weapon they'd been looking for for years to use against both Rock and the Agency.

Emotional attachments were hell on spies. She'd been warned to avoid them. She'd been trained how to avoid them. The spying life was filled with deceit and trickery, things that usually killed relationships. You had to be able to fool all kinds of people, the innocent ones along with the bad ones. Sometimes, you even had to fool yourself, tell yourself that what you felt wasn't real. And that even if it had been, it had been a dangerous mistake.

Hers had been an even worse mistake—she'd made a baby on that drunken wedding night. She had the faint scar left from a tummy tuck by one of the world's top plastic surgeons to prove it. The tummy tuck she'd had to get her pre-baby body back. Rock's baby. Which he knew nothing about. Nor could he unless . . .

If Rock noticed the scar, and he noticed everything, explaining the tummy tuck would be tricky. Back in the day, he'd hired her for her stripper's body. How likely was he to believe she'd suddenly developed a belly bulge and saddlebags that needed immediate removal?

There were other changes to her body, too. Changes plastic surgery couldn't hide—the wider spread of her hips, and breasts that weren't quite as perky as they used to be. Rock knew her measurements down to the millimeter. He had to so he could fit her into the tiny hiding spaces of his illusions. Another man in another profession might not have noticed such subtle changes, but she feared Rock would. And that would be disastrous.

As for her precious baby, he was currently in the care of an NCS agent aptly code-named Nanny. Nanny was good with children and one of the Agency's best bodyguards. Nanny had cared for the children of kings, potentates, spies, double agents, and informants. Nanny had a perfect record of keeping charges safe and kidnap-free.

But none of the other children had ever been quite as big a prize for RIOT. A son of a secret agent and a magician they had been courting for years was a plum the terrorist organization would go after with the full force of their evil to get to Rock. *If* RIOT ever realized her little boy existed. For that reason, Rock couldn't be allowed to know that he had a son, either. Not unless, or until, RIOT no longer had a use for Rock or a need to make him do their bidding. In this situation, what Rock didn't know could save him and the mission.

In any war, there are casualties and sacrifices. That's what she told herself when she was rationalizing. It wasn't much comfort.

Rock turned to Emmett. "Are you going to tell me what this mission is about?" His tone was impatient. He obviously wanted to be briefed and left alone with Lani as quickly as possible.

"Not here in the entryway. Someplace more comfortable, maybe?" Emmett said.

Rock nodded and led them to his living room with its floor-to-ceiling windows, grand piano in the corner, gas fireplace, built-in flat-screen TV, and groupings of dark-brown leather furniture and equally dark wood furniture. The only softness in the room was the large bouquet of fresh flowers on the oversized coffee table.

Rock pulled Lani to the deep, overstuffed, polished

leather sofa and tugged her down next to him, situating her so she was practically in his lap. He kept staring at her as if she'd disappear again, as if he couldn't believe his good fortune in getting her back. Lani had the feeling a pair of handcuffs would be less restrictive than his possessive optimism.

Emmett took a seat in a leather chair opposite them as Lani fought not to slide off the slippery leather couch. It was so deep she felt like a kid, her feet barely touching the floor, even with high-heeled boots on. She was five feet seven inches. No shrimp by any means. She hated feeling small. Fall off that thing onto the hardwood floors, even with the plush area rug beneath her, and she'd probably get a concussion.

She stared at Emmett and tried to ignore the intimate way Rock stared at her. "Sitting in here I feel as if we need the Rock Powers, Chief, and Lani silhouette shades."

Emmett laughed, but her reference to *Get Smart* was lost on Rock. He'd never been in on her spy humor before. And why would he have been? Until tonight, he hadn't known she was a secret agent. He gave her a quizzical look as if there was something about her he didn't know and was still trying to figure out.

Oh, there was plenty about her he didn't know. Despite their married status, he knew nothing about her really. Practically everything she'd told him had been a lie or a stretch of the truth. She wondered whether he would still love her if he knew the real her.

"We'll be fine," Emmett said. "I'll bring them next time."

Lani looked around. There were a million places to hide a bug inside and another million for a sniper to hide outside. "Are you sure this place is clean?"

"Our guys swept it while Rock was gambling earlier this evening. We're good."

Lani shrugged. The Agency boys were experts. Were they expert enough? She was jumpy these days. Jumpier than she'd been when she had only herself to worry about. Emmett had good reason not to want his agents to form attachments. She was living proof of that.

Emmett cleared his throat. "Is it just me, or has it gotten thirsty in here?"

Rock reluctantly let go of Lani's hand and jumped up. "Where are my manners? Can I get you anything? I have a fully stocked bar."

"Whiskey, neat." Emmett smiled at Rock.

"Lani?"

"Bottled water will be fine." She needed to keep her head about her and she didn't trust Rock not to lace her drink with the stuff he'd used on their wedding night. The stuff that made her cast aside her convictions, inhibitions, and good sense and marry him. She was definitely going to check the cap and seal on the water when he handed it to her, even though, deep down, she had the feeling it was the strength of his love that had drugged her.

"Neat and water, I can do," Rock said as he poured Emmett and himself a drink and opened the minifridge for a bottle of water. "Peach or lemon flavor?" he asked Lani.

She should have been touched he still stocked the water she loved and remembered her two favorite flavors. Instead, he was just making it tougher on them. "Peach."

"The help's out tonight," Rock said as he handed Emmett his whiskey.

"I know," Emmett said.

Lani was sure he did. For all she knew, he'd given them the night off. If the help was out, she'd be left all alone with Rock. Not good. Not that having the help around had inhibited them in the past, either. But this was too convenient. And she still wasn't comfortable with his apparent calm. Last thing she wanted was to have to stun-gun him.

She thought about drugging him, but Rock would probably notice in the morning. The man held his alcohol like he was born in a distillery.

Rock handed her the water. "Would you like a glass?"

She shook her head. No use giving him easy access to her beverage.

Rock sat down beside her as she screwed the cap off her bottle. "So, this nefarious mission?"

CHAPTER THREE

Think what the two spies with him would, Rock was no idiot. He was acting calm and unsuspecting, the eager husband, for his own reasons. Not that he wasn't dying to get Lani into bed. Sexual tension practically crackled in the air between them. Whatever kind of woman the real Lani the spy was, she hadn't faked, and wasn't now faking, their chemistry. Rock had been fantasizing about their reunion for the last two years. He wasn't going to blow things now, even if that meant he had to wait a few days for his fantasies to become reality.

Rock wasn't a great illusionist and good mentalist for nothing. He read people for fun, and sometimes profit, and always for the upper hand. Which right now Rock needed if he was going to win his wife back. If she was indeed the woman she'd pretended to be when she married him and not some coldhearted femme fatale or Mata Hari.

As for Lani, the signals he was getting meant that beneath the surface of her breathtakingly beautiful and tantalizing exotic exterior, an inner conflict and emotional war roiled. She was holding something back from him. He felt her desire, the old desire he knew so well. But she was reining it in subtly. He felt the restraint in the slightly tepid way she held his hand. Or maybe he was simply fooling himself. *She's a spy, idiot. Did she ever really love me?*

Yes, he answered himself. He couldn't have been wrong about that. She may have been on a mission, but she'd fallen in love with him, even if she hadn't intended to. He knew she had. But now, after two years? He couldn't say for sure whether she still loved him.

If she was the woman he thought she was, he could woo her back. Make her feel the force of his love again. Convince her he was the man for her. He would.

But he had to proceed carefully. He couldn't let this chance to get Lani back slip away. He put on his best poker face.

Being *unofficially* in NCS's employ had to mean something dangerous and risky. Something like he'd take the fall if the operation went south. Something like if he ever found himself in deep shit, they wouldn't be bailing him out. Was finding out if he really wanted this Lani back worth the risk?

He knew the answer to that question, too. *Yes*.

Two years ago Lani had bailed on him in the middle of a performance to save her life and his career, so NCS claimed. Rock understood self-preservation as well as the next guy. But in the intervening years she'd never found time to drop him a text, send him a coded message, maybe call him on a secure line to let him know she was alive? She'd never thought to mention to him during their affair and almost laughingly short marriage that she was a spy? As if he, of all people, couldn't keep a secret. Now that stung.

He had the feeling that if it weren't for this mission, she would have let him dangle for the rest of his life. And yet, despite the danger, she had come back. She sent mixed messages. What did the real Lani want with him?

He squeezed Lani's hand and smiled at her encouragingly. *The art of misdirection*, he thought.

Sitting across from Rock, Emmett Nelson smiled and set his whiskey on the coffee table. "From now on, you're sworn to absolute secrecy. I won't tell you more than you need to know, but if you spill a word of it, we *will* take you out. We have a license to kill." He grinned. "Understand?"

"License to kill, like Bond. Got it." He thought Nelson was being a touch overdramatic. Citizens still had rights.

Emmett nodded. "We have an enemy of the state, of the world, really, that citizens of this country and the rest of the planet are totally unaware of. As I mentioned in the car, they call themselves RIOT, an acronym for Revolutionary International Organization of Terrorists.

"RIOT is headed by genius megalomaniac Archibald Random. His goal is to take over the world."

Rock had to fight to hide a smirk. "You do know how melodramatic that sounds?"

Nelson sighed, looking unsurprised by Rock's reaction. "Yeah, we get that a lot. Which is why we've kept his ambitions a secret from the American public and the rest of the world. Their reaction would be the same. The public, if they know of him at all, recognize him only as a fierce businessman who'd just as soon make his money off a bear market as a bull one. He likes to see others suffer.

"People may think he's a crackpot. But he's terrifically wealthy, well funded, and dangerous. His goal is to bring down the world's governments, starting with the United States and the rest of the economic world leaders.

"The list of his terrorist plots we've thwarted is long and classified."

"What does this have to do with Lani and me?" Rock wanted to goad him into revealing as much as possible.

Nelson leaned forward and spoke in a solemn tone. "As I alluded to earlier, it was his men who tried to kill

Lani two years ago. RIOT had a plan to blow up Hoover Dam, take out the Western power grid, and cause mayhem and panic.

"Lani gathered vital intel that allowed us to stop RIOT before they could act and innocent lives were lost. And fortunately for Lani, and us, she got away and we took out any RIOT operatives who could identify her.

"Whether you believe me or not, she was incredibly brave to step out onto that stage with you at all, given that it made her a sitting duck for a sniper's bullet." Nelson smiled, speaking as pleasantly as if he were talking about a recent family hike in the desert rather than a group of maniacal madmen.

A shiver ran down Rock's spine at the reality of Lani crumpled on stage, dying before his eyes. He turned his attention to her, shaken by the actuality of what she'd done. She was a hero, no doubt about it.

A jumbled maelstrom of emotions played through him. She'd betrayed him to save others. *Very admirable*. And hell on a relationship. Could he live with the thought that he'd never be first in her life?

He squeezed her hand again, reassuring himself as much as her.

She shrugged, looking at him as if what she'd done, and what she'd sacrificed, were no big deal. That cut Rock, too. Had he misread her feelings for him?

Rock felt Emmett's gaze on him. "RIOT is back in Vegas," Emmett said. "This time they're targeting the magic community."

Rock raised a brow. This was getting more interesting by the minute. "Really? What do they want with us? The secret to making the Strip disappear? I've done that before. On television, anyway." He was being lighthearted, but that TV special had been a ratings phenom and the illusion a huge success.

Nelson remained serious. "Close. They're planning to penetrate Area 51 and steal a piece of top-secret technology we're developing."

Rock shook his head. This was ludicrous. He didn't see how he fit in. "That's your ball of wax. I can't create a magic force field to keep them out, if that's what you're hoping. Besides, I thought Dreamland was impregnable. In fact, hell, I thought it didn't even officially exist."

Nelson smiled. "You speak too soon, about that force field, anyway. You haven't heard their plan. Or our counterplan."

"A force field?" Rock may as well leave his brow cocked for the duration of this conversation. It just got more and more bizarre. "Intriguing. All right, I'll bite. What's the plan?"

If believing in illusionary force fields was the state of the world's best intelligence agency, the free world was in deep trouble.

Nelson didn't crack even the slightest of smiles. "They're going to stage an alien attack."

Rock sat back and studied Nelson. *He's dead serious.* "What?"

"It'll be an illusion, of course. The kind of thing the U.S. did in World War Two. Ever hear of the Twenty-third Headquarters Special Troops?"

Rock shook his head. Great, he heard a history lesson coming. "No."

"No, most people haven't," Nelson said. "During the war even most of the regular troops didn't know they existed. They were actors, sound engineers, special-effects specialists from the movie industry, writers, designers, camoufleurs, and engineers. Deception and secrecy were their stock in trade. They never wore their own insignia. Instead, they impersonated other battalions and other troops, sometimes even the enemy.

"They reported directly to General Omar Bradley, the ground commander in Europe. Their mission was to feed the enemy false intelligence and lead them away from where the Allies were planning to attack. To get the enemy to amass their troops in the wrong locations, leaving the gate open for our campaigns.

"The actor Douglas Fairbanks, Jr. was instrumental in leading them and designing some of their campaigns. They were brilliant, using inflatable tanks and dummies to stage what appeared to the enemy as our troop movements. They created chatter, sonic illusions they called them, that fed the Germans false information and also simulated the sound of large companies of men moving through the countryside.

"They were mostly unarmed, exceptionally brave men who helped win the war with deception." Nelson cracked the slightest of smiles. "I can see you're starting to get the idea that we have need of a deception specialist and a little countermagic.

"RIOT is going to stage an alien attack, using the tactics of illusion, sometime during the upcoming National UFO, or NUFO, convention. Their goal is to send a panicked crowd streaming into Dreamland past the gates, overwhelming the camo dudes and security. Dreamland isn't even gated.

"RIOT's counting on us not bombing or shooting into a crowd of our own civilians.

"We can, of course, use tear gas and other riot-control techniques. But with a large enough crowd in the open-air environment?" Nelson shrugged. "How effective will it be to stop the chaos?

"RIOT will have agents in the crowd, egging them on, and ready to sneak into the secure area during the mayhem." Emmett clenched his fist. "I will not allow RIOT to breach our facility on my watch."

Rock's mouth went dry and his pulse raced as he thought of the possibilities. He had an ominous feeling that he knew where this was headed. "They'd need an accomplished magician to plan, orchestrate, and pull something like that off. Who . . ."

Emmett didn't reply, just smiled knowingly, looking as if Rock would eventually figure it out on his own.

"Shit!" Rock pounded the arm of the sofa and squeezed Lani's hand so tightly she grimaced. "Sol Blackledge?"

As Rock eased up on his death grip of Lani's hand, he cursed Sol. He and that ass went way back to magic training at the Magic Castle in Los Angeles.

To think they'd actually been friends then. Until Sol stole the plans for one of Rock's most creative illusions, performed it, and passed it off as his own before Rock could perform it. Since that defining moment, he and Sol had competed for everything. Including Lani.

Lani gave Rock's arm a reassuring squeeze. Or maybe she was simply trying to calm him down.

Emmett nodded. "They've been backing Sol financially for years. Who do you think financed that illusion Sol stole from you, the one that made his career?"

Rock went cold as realization dawned on him and a memory from a decade ago came back to him. "That group of financial backers approached me first. I turned them down because I didn't want to sell out and give up my creative control. They were terrorists?"

"Yes. RIOT," Emmett said.

Lani sat silently beside Rock, letting Emmett deliver all the bad news.

Rock shook his head, trying to grasp the situation. "Sol doesn't have the creativity, the talent, or the skill to develop an illusion that complex. Especially not on the fly," Rock said. "A trick like that takes years of planning."

"Yes, it does." Emmett looked Rock in the eye.

Beside Rock, Lani tensed. Rock got a very bad feeling.

Emmett paused and then spoke slowly. "Does the name Outlandish Marauders mean anything to you?"

"F—" Rock let go of Lani, jumped to his feet, and resisted the urge to punch something as he ran his fingers through his hair. "But how? That's my illusion. Very few people other than me even know about it. After Sol stole that first illusion from me, I've kept Outlandish Marauders closely guarded." He stared Emmett down.

"How do you know about it? How do you know it's mine, not Sol's?" A sick feeling burned in his stomach. He turned to Lani. An involuntary look of guilt crossed her face so quickly a layperson would have missed it.

"One of our agents got the intelligence from a RIOT informant," Emmett said, lying like the pro he was.

But it was too late. Rock knew the truth. Lani hadn't just been sent to save Hoover Dam two years ago. She'd also been sent to spy on him. Rock didn't know what was real with her or not now.

"RIOT has been spying on you for years, Rock." Emmett's voice was smooth and calming, almost hypnotic.

Rock knew the technique and put up his guard. "My studio and house have been broken into and subtly tampered with over the years. I thought that was just Sol.

"RIOT is very good, and scary, if they managed to get past my security for Outlandish Marauders." And so was Lani.

Rock's emotions were tightly wound as he turned and looked at her. His gut clenched. She was trying to mask her expression, but excitement shone through subtly. The thought of a mission of magic excited her. And him.

At least they had something in common. Despite everything, he still wanted her, more than ever, damn his weak soul.

Through the shock of the past few hours, a thrill and

an adrenaline rush built. Best Sol. Perform Outlandish Marauders, a trick he'd been dreaming of doing since he was young. With the CIA's help, could it really be done? Show the world that an alien attack could be faked. And find out exactly who the woman he married really was and what she really felt for him.

For two years, he'd wanted to know the truth. Here was his opportunity.

Lani gazed back at him with heat in her eyes. Unfortunately, given what he'd learned about her in the past hour, everything she did, and had done, was suspect. Even, maybe especially, marrying him.

On the other hand, she was a professional liar. Liars and deceivers turned him on, especially beautiful ones.

"Outlandish Marauders is an illusion, a television special that, if I'm ever able to perform it, is supposed to be the pinnacle of my career. I make an alien attack appear out of nowhere before a live audience. No computer-aided graphics like in the movies. Then I make them disappear just as quickly.

"You're telling me Sol and RIOT have co-opted it and are going to use it to create terror?" Rock was so angry at the thought, his stomach burned.

"Yes," Nelson said.

"What do you want me to do? Perform it before they can use it against us? Does the technology I need even exist?" Rock took a deep breath as he thought through the logistics.

"It does. Trust me," Nelson said.

Rock rattled off his thoughts. "Ginning up the publicity for an illusion like that, booking the venue, selling the tickets, getting the equipment, and shit, just practicing, will all take time. The NUFO convention is in what, a few weeks?

"If we're going to beat Sol to the punch . . ." Rock shook his head. "You're asking the impossible."

Nelson finished his drink. "You misunderstand, Rock. We're not booking any venue. You're not performing this on stage or on television. You're orchestrating it, setting it up to look like a real invasion at the gates of Area 51. And doing the reveal at the last minute to stop the crowd from storming the perimeters."

"I don't understand," Rock said. "Isn't that risky and unethical? Why panic people? Why take the chance of someone getting hurt or killed or the plan backfiring?"

Nelson's look was penetrating. "Because we have reason to believe some high-profile RIOT agents will be involved. Terrorists high up on our pack of RIOT playing cards, our list of most wanted. We want this chance to draw them out, apprehend them, and cripple their organization.

"We'll create some intelligence deception of our own and let it slip that NUFO, with its list of heavy-hitting, wealthy backers, has hired you to perform a surprise secret show for them during their annual picnic at the black mailbox near Area 51. We'll trot out a few details of Outlandish Marauders. And then we'll see who bites." Nelson grinned.

"As for impossible, all of our resources are at your disposal. As you probably suspect, we've been making preparations of our own since we first discovered RIOT's plans. But we've lacked the master illusionist's touch and knowledge. Lani can fill you in on where we stand."

Rock stared at Lani again. "Good. Damn. My act is in hiatus. Reappearing her would be the perfect way to reintroduce her to the world. The perfect act of showmanship—"

Nelson cleared his throat. "About that. We have another plan for Lani.

"Your shared history and competition with Sol presents

us with an opportunity to place Lani exactly where we need her to keep an eye on Sol so she can tip us off to any details of RIOT's plans—"

"No!" The word exploded out of Rock's mouth involuntarily as he realized exactly what Nelson had in mind. "I will not put Lani in danger, or let Sol have my prestige to reappear her and humiliate me again."

He shook his head, sat, and grabbed Lani's hand as if he wouldn't let them whisk her away again. What the hell? They weren't giving him time with her? How was he supposed to discover the truth about her and how she felt for him now?

"I'm sorry," Nelson said. "It's part of the deal. Getting revenge on you will distract Sol while we make preparations for our strike. And Lani will be in an ideal position to gather intelligence to see whether RIOT's biting. Who they're planning to send, how they'll be disguised, that kind of thing.

"Even in the midst of the chaos, it will take a specially trained, skilled agent to get all the way into the secure area. Catching him will be a big prize worthy of the risk."

"It's too dangerous for Lani." Rock was vehement.

Nelson arched a brow and shook his head. "For one of my agents? You underestimate our abilities, especially Lani's."

"She may be a damn fine agent," Rock said with his heart hammering in his throat. "But Sol is ruthless. He takes too many risks. He doesn't pay attention to safety. And these RIOT people you describe . . ."

Nelson cocked his head. "We'll take that under consideration. But it doesn't change the facts—we need Lani in Blackledge's inner circle."

"And you think you can just insert her there?" Rock was dumbfounded. Was Nelson some kind of idiot?

"Sol's been advertising for new assistants. Don't you

think he'd jump at the chance to bring your wife back to the stage? To steal your prestige. Maybe even collect that reward?"

Rock swallowed hard and looked at Lani, who gazed back at him coolly. "I thought—"

He cut himself off before he said too much and revealed his vulnerability.

Rock cleared his throat as he composed his thoughts. "I thought Lani and I were going to get a chance to reconnect and work together again." That sounded neutral enough.

"Yes, of course. While you engage in a public battle with Sol. It'll be delicious fodder for the gossip rags. And, as I said, distract everyone from what's really going on." Nelson pushed his glass back and stood, taking the cue that he was intruding too long on Rock's hospitality.

"Lani will spend the night here, just in case there's trouble. But she can't be seen leaving in the morning. Blackledge must think he's found her himself.

"Lani will fill you in on the mission details and the other agents who will be involved. You're going to love Tate. Everyone does. I should be going." He looked Rock in the eye and smiled.

Rock made a move to stand.

Nelson held up a hand. "Don't bother. I'll show myself out."

Rock watched Nelson walk to the door, where he paused. "We'll be in touch. Expect your handler to be contacting you in the morning."

"I don't need a handler. I have Lani."

"All new spies get handlers, Powers. Impartial handlers who plan the mission without letting bias and emotions come into play.

"Your handler won't give a damn whether you come

out alive or dead. He'll only care whether you accomplish what we ask. Lani, here"—Nelson nodded toward her—"is not what I'd call impartial. She's too concerned with the state of your precious hide."

Rock's heart leaped with hope, but the rational part of him wondered whether Nelson was just leading him on to get his full cooperation.

"This isn't fun and games, Powers. Remember that." Nelson let himself out.

Lani stood and walked to the window, watching him drive off.

Rock came up behind her. "You stole more than our certificate of marriage when you ran off. You stole the plans to Outlandish Marauders."

She turned to face him. The corners of her mouth turned up slightly at the edges in a faint smile. "I don't suppose there's any point in denying it now."

She seemed almost too cavalier with her admission. Rock recognized a skilled diversion when he saw one and he was being intentionally diverted now. What else was she hiding?

"I should be pissed. I am pissed. Betrayal is such an ugly thing."

"I wouldn't call it betrayal. I like to think of it as commitment to cause and country, which includes you."

"Do you?"

"It was all for the greater good."

He ran his hand lightly along her arm and caught her hand in his. "So it was all just an act?" He made his voice low and sultry, laced with the hypnotic tone that won audiences over and created the perfect diversions for his illusions and magic.

This was a diversion and an illusion, too. A test to find out whether their chemistry and her desire for him were real. He was certain she hadn't faked that. There was one way to find out for sure.

He could see desire welling up and sparkling in her eyes now. The pattern of her breathing had changed, too. He took a step into her, standing so close his chest brushed hers, sending waves of need through him. "Do you want to talk about Outlandish Marauders?"

"There's time for that later." She looked into his eyes.

Though he should have been furious and hurt, standing so near her, he wanted her. He loved her. He couldn't help it. He wanted to plunge into her and make her cry out in ecstasy. If she didn't love him, he at least had to know she was attracted to him. Then maybe there was hope. This new, treacherous, dangerous, deceitful Lani grew more enticing and intriguing by the minute.

One way or another he was going to break this Lani and find out for sure whether she ever had, or ever could, love him.

Lani's pupils dilated.

He pulled her into him, tugging her against his chest until she braced against him with her hands. He leaned down, lifted her hair, and kissed her neck, sucking as he went, hard, as if branding her with his desire and hurt.

He sucked and kissed his way over her collarbone to the tops of her bustier-clad breasts, breathing hard, barely controlling himself from taking her right there in the living room.

He reached to swoop her into his arms, envisioning carrying her up the swirling staircase to his room for a repeat performance of the fireworks they'd created there before.

She wrenched free with startling strength and speed and took a step back from him. "Not tonight, Rock." Her voice shook.

He'd rattled her. Good. It was a start.

"Our marriage was a scam, really." She didn't back down from him. He admired her courage. "Our relationship is purely business now. Our mission is *everything*."

Her emotional emphasis on the last word threw him. It was almost as if she was sending him a coded message. He stared at her, hoping she felt his gaze burning into her. "A scam? I have a certificate of marriage in my pocket that I got from Emmett that says otherwise. I'm entitled to my marital rights."

She laughed softly and stroked his cheek. "Marital rights? What century have we just stepped back into, Lord Powers?"

He gently tucked a strand of hair behind her ear. "Come on, Lani. I don't remember signing any divorce papers. Can't we mix business with pleasure? You did before."

She eyed him warily and sighed. "About our marriage. Don't get any ideas about it being a permanent thing. We're magicians in our own right. We can expunge any records we choose, make anything disappear as efficiently as you do, including marriage records."

His hopes soared. "But you haven't yet?"

She could have at any time during the last two years, but she hadn't.

"Because of the publicity and because of the mission, no. But when it's over . . ." She held his gaze.

"Come on, Lani. When it's over, you may as well try to divorce me and collect a big share of my millions as pay-off for putting up with all of this bullshit. As the gossip blogs have reported for two years, there is no prenup."

"*Try* to divorce you?" She arched a brow. "Are you challenging me? Is that a dare?"

He leaned in close to her. "What do you think?"

"I think if you want a public spectacle, I can give you

one. Tell me this, Rock—what did you drug me with the night we got married?"

"What?" He was stunned. He hadn't seen that right hook coming.

Her eyes narrowed and flashed with anger. She pointed at him. "If I hadn't been under the influence of whatever you doped me with, I would never have lost my professional control and defied orders."

He couldn't believe what he was hearing. "You're serious? You think I drugged you? That's low." He leaned into her, grabbed her accusing finger and kissed it lightly, boyishly. "You married me of your own free volition, Mata Hari.

"We may have had a few drinks, but it was your love and desire for me that shot your professional control, as you call it, to hell, Agent *Silkwater* Powers." He used what he supposed was her real name on purpose to rattle her.

She stared back at him with that damned veiled expression again. "You read my signature on the license Emmett showed you. Very good. That was an unintentional slip." She wrenched her hand free from his. "And don't call me by your last name again."

"If you want to keep your maiden name I can live with that." He took a strand of her silky hair between his fingers and thumb and let it slide through. "Some might say signing with your real name was a subconscious effort to make the marriage legit."

"Some would be wrong. I made a mistake and violated Agency policy. Spouses and families, long-term partners, love interests—they're all weak links, a way to get at agents. Liabilities. And ex-spouses, well, they're simply security leaks waiting to happen."

"I'm the exception. I'm a master at keeping secrets." He grabbed her arm. "Consider this. Magician or not, hypnotic powers or not, I can't force you to act against your will. Never could. Even if I *had* drugged you, I couldn't get you to recite the vows.

"I didn't brainwash or coerce you into marrying me. There was a part of you that wanted to, whether you'll admit it, even to yourself, or not."

She shook her arm free from his grasp and took a step back from him. When she spoke, she stared past him, not at him, looking over his shoulder out the window.

"Spies lie," she said simply. "Innocent people sometimes get hurt by friendly fire. Sad to say it's an occupational hazard of keeping the free world free."

Her voice became soft, sounding more like the Lani he knew. "I never wanted to hurt you. I never *meant* to hurt you. We had fun together. Let's leave it at that. I haven't returned to make things worse for you—"

"Then why *did* you come back?" Call it vanity or denial or instinct, but he didn't believe she'd never loved him. He didn't believe her now. He knew his business well enough to recognize real magic when he saw or felt it. What he and Lani had had was magic pure and simple. The electricity rippling between them now, heated, frustrated, and denied, was simply more evidence of it.

"To save the world, Rock, just as the chief said."

"And I'm collateral damage." He stepped away and turned his back to her, setting his jaw as disturbing images from the night she'd disappeared came flooding back to him. "Do you know what that night was like for me?"

"I can imagine—"

"You can't." He took a deep breath, trying to wash the visions away. "No one can." He swung back around.

She started. Good, he'd caught her off guard.

"Do you know how worried I was when Clara showed up in the prestige? I nearly botched the act. Something in

her eyes told me she was worried about you, too." He shook
his head. "Clara wasn't reassuring, Lani. You scared her.
I had to finish the show worried sick about you. I was
crazy trying to figure it out, thinking maybe a sudden case
of food poisoning, or hell, nauseous headache. I don't
know.

"I didn't in my wildest worries think for a minute
you'd disappeared on a dangerous mission for the CIA."
He ran his hands through his hair.

Her laughter stopped him short. "Listen to yourself,
Rock. You're implying I'm all about my career, but *you
had to finish the show.*

"It didn't occur to you, I suppose, to take a quick break
to check on me? Your beloved new bride who for all you
knew might have been mortally ill." She shook her head,
looking almost as bitter as amused.

Her expression caught him up short. Maybe there *was*
hope.

"Good luck for me, I suppose." She leaned forward
and whispered. "Or was it? Maybe I knew you well enough
to know you'd finish the show, even if you were the one
dying. And I was in no danger of being caught as I escaped and ran for my life. You wouldn't leave that stage
until the last encore was over. Not even if the world was
ending."

"Damn it, Lani!" He clenched his fists again to keep
from grabbing her. He wanted to pull her to him, make
her see reason. Hold her to his heart. Make her his again.

She was staring at him, but it was his turn to look past
her for fear of giving himself away. "Don't accuse me of
putting my career before you. I *was* concerned about you,
but I trusted my staff to take care of you. You of all people
know how well-trained they are. You know I have medics
waiting in case of an accident. I believed you were in good

hands. The best." He took a deep breath, struggling to maintain some control over his ragged emotions and hang on to his dignity. What was left of it.

"You left me in the worst possible state a woman can—not knowing what's happened to you. Imagining the worst. Nightmares so terrible—"

He swallowed hard. "Unable to move on with my life. The moment the show ended, I rushed backstage, screaming to the crew, asking them about you, wild for information. The police stopped me. Pulled me aside. Delivered the news.

"A member of the hotel staff had seen you run out the back door by the loading dock. Someone else reported hearing gunshots near there and called the cops.

"They found puddles and a trail of blood. One of the cops held the scraped, bloodied, broken heel from your white shoe, the one you wore in the show, out to me in an evidence bag. *'Recognize this?'* he said.

"My heart stopped. I went cold. I couldn't piece it all together for a second. And then I realized you were missing, presumed murdered or kidnapped, and even though I'd been on stage at the time you disappeared, I was suspect number one."

He made himself look at her, watching her closely for any sign of regret or sympathy. "That's just the beginning of the nightmare for me. They found tire skid marks in the lot, but no body. It looked to the police as if a car had peeled out in a hurry.

"They interviewed the crew, stagehands, and Clara. They all said the same thing—you looked frightened, as if you were running from someone. For your life. And the natural assumption was it was me. That I'm a monster. A wife killer. A Bluebeard who disappeared his wife for good.

"A sample of the blood came back as yours. And then the rumors started to fly. I'd mistakenly gotten drunk and married you without a prenup. The crew was lying for me. I had you murdered to protect my assets." He snorted. "As if I'm that kind of man."

He imagined his eyes were bores and he could somehow pierce the truth out of her. But Lani remained placid and unreadable.

"What really happened that night, Lani?" he said. "I deserve to know that much."

CHAPTER FOUR

This mission is going to be harder than I thought.
Lani hadn't anticipated that hearing what Rock had
gone through the past two years from his own lips would
tear her up so badly or bring up such an almost irresistible
urge to reach out and comfort him. And she'd forgotten
that next to a crack secret agent, Rock was probably the
most observant and intuitive man on the planet. Which
was partly why she fell for him in the first place. And now
might lead to their downfall.

Lani forced herself into spy mode and composed herself as she sat down on the sofa, still wondering what
magic Rock had worked to convince her to marry him. If
it wasn't drugs, what was it?

She changed tactics. It no longer suited her purposes to
be professional and distant. Better to beguile and charm
the enemy, if that's what he was. "Yes, I suppose you do
deserve to know as much of the truth as I can tell you.
Most of what happened that night is classified, but now
that you're with us, I can give you the basics."

They were still standing. She walked to the sofa and
took a seat, patting the cushion next to her.

He took the chair perpendicular to the sofa.

But at least he sat, leaning forward and resting his el-
bows on his thighs as he watched her with his magician's

eyes that missed nothing. Good thing she wasn't going to try to pull a rabbit out of a hat. Well, not literally. Maybe humor would work?

"As it turns out, I didn't quite make the clean escape of it I'd hoped for." She put a smile in her voice and spoke lightly, trying to diffuse the tense mood. "RIOT had the hotel covered. An assassin waited for me as I came out of the building."

She didn't care to remember the details and she didn't want to shock Rock too badly. Surprisingly, she didn't want him to believe she shot at people without conscience. But she had to be honest.

"I had a fellow agent, a sharpshooter, covering my back and waiting for me with a car in the lot out back. Unfortunately, he'd been shot at and fired back, killing one of RIOT's men.

"Originally, I was going to leave before the show. I swiped the intel just prior. Until I realized I was being followed and there was no way out except to go on with the show and make a break for it in the middle, hoping I threw them off my scent. That's the beauty of magic. It's all a gorgeous diversion, isn't it?"

She'd said it playfully, but he didn't smile back.

"You should have come to me," Rock said. "I do gorgeous diversions better than anyone."

What he said was probably true, but—

She shook her head. "I did what I did to protect you. You have to believe me. Besides, how crazy would you have thought I was if I'd come to you seconds before the show with some crazy story about terrorists chasing me? And that I'm a secret agent working for the CIA? You'd have had me committed." She smiled at him.

Rock shook his head, but he looked less angry. "Maybe not."

"*Maybe not* isn't good enough. I only take reasonable

risks. Too many lives hung in the balance. Besides, terrorists can't torture out of you something you don't know." She paused to let the seriousness of the situation sink in with him. "Come on, Rock. I'm not the bad guy. Give me a bit of a break here."

He scowled. "What happened next?"

She shrugged. "The usual spy stuff. Murphy's Law. As I came out of the building and sprinted for the car, I hit a pool of the dead terrorist's blood at full speed. Didn't even see it until I nearly slid onto my ass in it. Tunnel vision. No one expects a dead terrorist in her path, right?" She tried to coax a smile out of him, but he remained stone-faced.

She shrugged again. "Hindsight. Anyway, bam! I was suddenly windmilling and skidding in the blood slick." She made a face and pantomimed the motion, trying to get a smile out of him. "And do you know what I was most worried about right then?"

"Your lovely hide?"

She shook her head. "Nope—my costume and how blood would never come out of that skimpy white dress that you'd specially designed just for me. And whether I'd gotten blood on the marriage certificate tucked in my shoe." Her voice broke unexpectedly. Since she'd become a mother she'd gotten emotionally soft and sentimental.

But she had Rock's attention now. He stared at her with something like hope in his eyes. "Stress does strange things to a person. Is that when you broke your shoe?"

"No. I tripped over the body and came down hard on my heel and that's when it snapped off. As I bent to retrieve it, another of the bastards fired at me and I accidentally kicked the heel and didn't have time to find it.

"It was sloppy spycraft, leaving part of a white wedding slipper behind like Cinderella on a bad night and

I'm not happy about it. But I didn't have much choice. In that white dress, I was too visible, a sitting bride, so to speak. I ran for the car, firing back at that RIOT jerk as I went.

"The bastard grazed my arm and it gushed." She was still mad about being hit at all. She'd almost gotten a tell-tale scar.

At the mention of gushing blood, Rock flinched.

She'd forgotten for a minute he wasn't used to real blood and gore like the spies she was used to hanging out with. To distract him, she mimicked the motions of her story as she spoke, just like she had when she'd related the incident to her buddies at the Agency. "So there I was—running with a distinct hobble because of the broken shoe, applying pressure to my gun arm, and trying to fire over my back. It was quite the scene. And funny, too, in retrospect."

He scowled. "Not funny, Lani."

"The guys at Langley laughed when I told the story."

"I'm not the guys at Langley. I don't see what's funny about you being hurt."

"Oh, come on. It's a bit like something out of Funniest Spy Videos." She mimicked the actions again. "The hobbling and the running and the slipping—"

He shook his head.

"Well, to each his own, I guess. You'll get used to spy humor. But to continue the tale, I guess I didn't do a fantastic job of stopping the bleeding, which is why the police found my blood along with that villain's."

"Did you kill him?" Rock asked. There was no smile in his voice, either.

"Just nicked him. But then, being wounded, I was at a disadvantage. I'm usually a crack shot." It was important he knew she was competent. "My fellow agent hit him with a clean kill shot. Which is what he's paid to do, of course." She still felt the sting of indignity in having to mention another agent had had to bail her out of trouble.

"We meant to clean up the site before the cops got there. We called our cleanup crew to take care of it. But the body was gone before they arrived. RIOT must have removed it, but missed the heel of my shoe. They didn't want to be discovered any more than we did. There, does that comfort you? Or will you have more nightmares now?"

Rock stared at her with his head in his hands, his jaw set, his eyes hard. "So all this pointing at me and throwing suspicion my way—was that the CIA, too?"

So that's why he didn't warm to her story—he was mad about being slandered? He was quick on the uptake. A little too quick, maybe. But his intelligence was part of what made him attractive to her.

"Suspicious minds," she said, shaking her head. But of course the Agency was behind them. Partly. "Rumors will fly. The public loves a scandal."

He frowned. Opened his mouth. Shut it again as if he'd reconsidered what he was going to say. He paused and then continued. "There's something I don't understand—if these RIOT bastards saw you, knew it was you who took these plans, won't they be suspicious and looking for you now? Aren't you in danger? And why would one of their allies, Blackledge, take you into his company when they think you're an enemy spy?"

She couldn't help laughing. He looked so solemn. But he was right. And she was touched by his concern. "I'm always in danger." She shrugged as if it didn't matter. She was used to it.

"But to answer your question, we're better than you think. The RIOT bastards have no idea I work for NCS.

Any of their agents who could identify me as the spy who stole their Hoover Dam intel, or a spy period, are dead."

"But they know Lani Torres isn't dead," Rock said. "So what's their theory?"

"If anything, they think I was running from you. Running from something, in any case.

"Vegas showgirls, even magician's assistants, generally aren't pure as the driven snow." She laughed. "There are all kinds of scenarios. Like I was in some kind of gambling or drug trouble and had to leave town in a hurry. Or I had escaped with a large chunk of your change, money-grubbing little me."

"Yeah, I know. The cops went over and over my bank accounts." He didn't sound happy about it.

"Sorry about that, Rock. Really."

He squinted at her and frowned. "Yeah, I know, collateral damage." He scowled. "That's all these RIOT people believe about you?" He didn't look convinced she was in the clear.

"Not exactly. That damn broken heel." She resisted, not for the first time, cursing beneath her breath. "It announced I was in that alley. They think I saw something I shouldn't have." She shook her head. "I'll never wear cheap shoes again."

"Hey! Those shoes weren't cheap. I paid a boatload for them. They were custom designed." Rock tried to smile at her, but she could tell he was shaken and defensive because he felt responsible.

She laughed at his indignation. "Then I suggest you hire a better designer next time, one with some engineering and structural expertise. A woman in my position needs to be able to count on her footwear, both on and offstage."

She studied him with his penetrating stare. "Back to the original topic. RIOT believes my fellow agent stole their secrets. He's a famous assassin in clandestine circles and his signature was all over those two kills. They aren't concerned with him. They know they'll come up against him again. It's part of the game.

"But RIOT will welcome me into Blackledge's crew easily enough. They want me where they can keep an eye on me and learn what I know. They can't have a leak. Of course, they'll never find out what I really know. I'll convince them I know nothing." She grinned. "When they clear me, I'm good to go."

That was a lie, too. They'd try to kill her either way— whether she convinced them she knew nothing or spilled all the Agency's secrets. They weren't the kind of thugs who took chances. Her best insurance policy was to string them along until the completion of the mission. Not that she'd tell Rock any of this. It would only make him jumpier.

"And if not?" His gaze was penetrating.

"I'm dead. They don't suffer leaks." She shrugged as if it were no big deal.

But Rock came out of his seat and onto his feet. "What!"

Yeah, she'd been right to keep the whole truth from him. "Calm down. They don't know who they're up against. I can take care of myself."

"Yeah, obviously. Because you're an ace shot when you're not windmilling in blood slicks, tripping over bodies, and no one's nicked your gun arm."

She nodded. "Exactly right. Anyway, that's a once-in-a-career bad luck situation. It won't happen again." She didn't tell him stuff usually went wrong. Murphy's Law was an integral part of the spy biz. The general rule in the Agency was that you should expect to fail half the time.

"You're the one who needs to be careful," she said to divert his attention away from her and remind him of what was really what. "I've come back to make sure you're safe."

He stared at her. "Thanks, but I can take care of myself."

"Can you?" She stared back. "A little flash powder won't save you next time."

He studied her. "We'll see about that."

An uncomfortable silence followed.

Finally Rock shook his head. "This whole situation's a little awkward, isn't it? Is this the part of the conversation where I ask what you've been up to these past few years? I'm sure you know my every move so there's no point discussing me."

That sounded more like the old Rock, the one who had a sense of humor and irony.

"There's not much to tell," she said. Which was an out-and-out lie. She wished she could tell him about her pregnancy, and the birth of their son, congratulate him on being a daddy, and see his joy. Tell Rock how he'd given her the best gift of all and made life worth living. Share Stone's first smile and steps. But the revelation of that secret hung on the mission. And could only ever be told if she were successful.

"That's not classified, that is. Mostly I spent my time in hot water, confined to desk work and playing nursemaid to a recovering agent who was blown up in the field." She couldn't keep the grumble out of her voice.

"You'll be pleased to hear, though, that I kept up my skills. As part of his therapy, I taught that agent a bit of magic."

"None of my tricks, I hope." Rock's voice held the slightest hint of a teasing edge, which was encouraging.

"Of course not! What do you think I am?" On second thought, that was a bad question. She had a pretty good idea what he thought she was and it wasn't pleasant. "I know how to keep a secret."

"Yeah, I gathered that."

"I suppose I deserve your sarcasm, Rock. But really, put this in perspective—I saved thousands of people. Thousands. How many people can say that?"

He didn't answer. How could he? She had him fair and square.

"Now," she said. "Have I satisfied your curiosity sufficiently? Can we get down to the mission? We only have a few hours left until daylight and I have to scram."

"Not so fast." He sprang out of the chair and sat down on the sofa disturbingly, enticingly close to her. "I have a condition, a term of agreement." His voice was hypnotic, like the one he used to engage a crowd.

She didn't trust him or herself. It would be so easy to drop her guard and melt into his arms. And so dangerous. "Don't worry about terms. NCS will be paying you handsomely. And if they balk, you can blackmail them. You have leverage." She laughed, but it came out nervously.

He shook his head. "Those are my terms with your boss and the government. I mean terms between us—you and me." He took her hands in his warm, tight grip.

"Terms between you and me—what are you talking about?" She eyed him warily, too stunned to pull free from his grip. As usual, he had something up his sleeve.

"Give us a real shot at making our marriage work. If that means waiting until after the mission to genuinely get to know each other, so be it." The look in his eyes was completely pleading and hopeful, so smoothly seductive.

He almost made her believe in the dream that they could make things work and live happily ever after. But that was Rock, the king of illusions.

Her heart hammered. "Rock, you don't even know who I really am," she said as reasonably as she could. And when he found out, would he ever forgive her or be able to live with who she was and what she did and had done?

"You only saw a small part of the real me during the time we were together. The part I let you see. The part I played. You have no idea what you're asking."

"I think I do." His tone was uncompromising and confident.

She took a deep breath. "If I don't agree?"

"I walk away now and your mission is toast."

"You do realize that if you walk away you're a dead man? RIOT wants you dead because, to their knowledge, you're the only other person capable of performing Outlandish Marauders and thwarting their plans?

"We're here to protect you. Once we're done with this mission, you'll be safe again. Until then—"

"I don't care, Lani. Those are my terms. Take them or leave them." He squeezed her hands and stared deeply into her eyes.

Why did she get the feeling she was almost playing a game of chicken with him? Show no fear or duplicity. She squeezed his hands in return. "Deal. But I'm only doing this to save you from yourself."

He held on tightly when she tried to withdraw her hands from his. "You agreed much too quickly," he said. "Don't forget. I'm a magician and just as used to fooling people, lying, misdirecting, and pretending as you are. Don't think because I don't have a notarized legal document you can get out of this. If you renege on your promise, I'll talk and damn the consequences."

"And be tried for treason," she retorted just as reasonably.

"The damage will already be done." He smiled, suddenly pleasant and released her hands as he settled back in the sofa. "Now, tell me all about the mission, my handler, and my new best friend Tate. And while you're at it, the details of how you're going to get Sol to take you on."

She slipped off her shoe and pulled a small data card out. "It's all on here, the entire mission brief and cover dossier." She held it out to him.

He took it reluctantly. "You really need a new hiding place." He stared at the data disk.

"Study it carefully. You only get one read of it and then the data self-destructs."

He looked as if he didn't believe her. "Like in *Mission: Impossible*."

"Well, yeah. Only the actual disk doesn't disintegrate or go up in smoke, just the data."

"You're hedging," he said. "What's in here that I'm not going to like?"

She may as well tell him. "I'm going to go to Sol and offer to split your reward money with him if he'll take me on as his assistant."

"My reward money?" His tone was frighteningly neutral and calm.

"Well, the government will pay it. You won't be out a thing, but we do have to keep up pretenses."

"And then you feed him my illusion secrets?"

She shook her head. "No."

He cocked a brow. "But you publicly humiliate me by reappearing in Sol's act."

She blew out a breath. "I have my orders. My hands are tied."

He stared at her. "And what's the story behind why you didn't come back to me?"

She shrugged. "Money. Cowardice. I'm afraid you won't take me back. Like I said, it's all in the brief."

"I'd rather hear it from you."

He was just being obstinate now. "I'm not the storyteller that the Agency cover life developer is. Now he can really spin a tale. Reading his briefs are like reading a best-selling thriller. Believe me—"

"Lani—"

"Okay, fine. What do you want to know?"

"If we're estranged, how are we going to report to each other and get to know each other, for real, as you like to say? Won't that involve a lot of sneaking around?"

Rock wasn't going to like what she was about to tell him. "That's where Tate comes in."

"Tell me about this agent Tate. Tate who? And why am I going to love him?"

"Tate Cox." She waited for his reaction.

Sure enough Rock's eyes got big. "*The* Tate Cox? Software billionaire, son of the former senator, international playboy?"

She nodded. "The very one."

"He's a spy?" Rock sounded astounded.

"Yes, and now that you know, if you tell anyone I really will have to kill you."

"Is he really a billionaire? Or is that faked?"

"Oh, yes, he certainly is. And a brilliant spy. There's only one problem with Tate—he can't seem to go undercover. Not that his real life isn't cover enough. It allows him to go anywhere and do just about anything. But if he's ever found out, he'll be useless. And for all his spying ability, I've always said Tate has more of a James Bond complex than anyone I know. Besides which, he's hard on cars."

She'd done a good job describing Tate. Rock was momentarily diverted.

And then he set his jaw again, looking as if suspicion was dawning. "Wait a minute—international playboy?"

"And gambler, with a taste for showgirls."

"And magicians' assistants," Rock finished for her.

"Probably, but not in this case," Lani said, wanting, against reason and logic, to reassure him of her fidelity, in her own warped way. Even now she couldn't wipe away the desire that coursed through her for Rock. On him, jealousy was incredibly sexy, if inconvenient. "You may not know it, but I'm a master of disguise. I'll appear as one of Tate's women whenever I need to go out in public or meet with you."

He stared at her. "Is that safe? Someone could recognize you."

She shook her head. "I'm talented. Even you won't recognize me." She paused, feeling the need to reassure him about Tate.

"Most women find Tate incredibly hot. I'm not one of them. And, of course, his money and lifestyle only add to his allure. But I've known Tate for years. He was married to a friend of mine, as a matter of fact. I know all his dirty laundry. You don't have to worry about anything real *ever* developing between Tate and me."

She couldn't tell whether she'd succeeded in reassuring Rock or not. His jaw was still set and his eyes steely. But that was only a diversionary tactic. He slid next to her, grabbed her head between his hands, and kissed her.

She was so startled, she didn't move. This was the second time he'd kissed her, but this time was different than the first—gentler, more seductive, loving. It took her a moment to remember she was supposed to pull away.

He broke the kiss, keeping his lips only inches from hers so as he spoke it was almost as if he were breathing his words into her. The look in his eyes was hypnotic and dangerous to her common sense. "I've missed you. There's been no one else since you. Spend the night with me. My bed's much more comfortable than the one in the guest room. Just because you're going to be Tate's girl tomorrow, doesn't mean you can't be my wife tonight."

Her heart stopped. She reached up and gently pulled his hands from her cheeks and clasped them in hers between them. She couldn't sleep with him. Not yet. Not until she was certain she wouldn't give her secret away.

She shook her head. "It's too soon, Rock." She kissed his hands. "Give yourself some time to get to know the real me first."

CHAPTER FIVE

G*et to know the real her?*

Rock knew the real her, or at least the woman Lani was pretending to be, well enough to know he wanted to make love to her. The old Lani would have taken him by the hand and led him to the bed. So what was up with this "real" Lani?

She had to have a reason to be keeping him at arm's length when at least one thing was certain—the air between them fairly crackled with desire. But he wasn't going to force her so he ended up spending the night alone.

Thinking about all that had happened and Lani sleeping alone in the room next to him had made for a restless night. Accessible after all this time, but not available. She probably slept with her gun beneath her pillow. He had a lot of magic up his sleeve, magic he'd like to show her, but stopping a speeding bullet? The bullet-catch was just a parlor trick. He was defenseless against the real thing.

But not against the machinations of NCS. Did they really think he was going to quietly endure the humiliation of handing over one hundred thousand dollars to Sol Blackledge, even if the money wasn't really his? And watch Sol pull Lani out of his hat, upstaging Rock? Or idle in the background while Lani put her life on the line?

As for Lani and her little secret, last night after Lani

had gone to bed, Rock had texted Davo, the PI who'd been working for him trying to find Lani the last two years. Despite Davo's lack of success in locating Lani, Rock had faith he could get this job done. If anyone could. It was hard to go up against the resources of the CIA. Rock gave Davo Lani's real last name and instructions to find out what she'd been up to since she disappeared. If she was hiding something from him, Davo would find it.

As for that mission brief, Rock had read through it. He'd never performed Outlandish Marauders partly because the technology he needed wasn't yet up to the task. Or so he'd thought. NCS, however, had a few things up their sleeves that the public knew nothing about. Now Rock was itching to get busy working on the performance.

Right now, though, Rock needed coffee. He slid out of bed, ran a brush through his hair, checked his messages— a confirmation from Davo that he'd start digging—and threw on a pair of pants before heading downstairs.

The door to the guest room was open, the room empty as he walked by. It looked as pristine as if no one had slept there for years. Lani was already gone, as he'd known she would be. She couldn't face him in the harsh reality of a sunny morning in Vegas. Rock cursed to himself as he headed downstairs to the kitchen.

He stopped short in the kitchen doorway. A large man, powerfully built, with dark hair and caramel-colored skin, who looked like he could have been a tight end in a not-too-distant life, sat at the island, sipping a steaming mug of coffee and working a crossword puzzle. A gray plastic case, a gun case, sat on the counter in front of him. "What's a six-letter word for stir that starts with P?"

Next to him a latte-skinned beauty dressed in a tight, bright orange halter top nibbled on a piece of toast. As she rolled her eyes upward in thought searching for the answer, she looked familiar to Rock.

Halle Berry, Rock thought. With her short, spiky hair, smoky eyes, and high cheekbones, she reminded Rock of the popular actress.

"Pother," Rock said before she could answer. "P-O-T-H-E-R."

The man looked up and stared at Rock with startlingly blue eyes, making no move for the gun. "Morning, sleepy-head. Evidently *early to rise* isn't part of your act." He filled in the answer.

"Who the hell are you two and how did you get in here?" Rock wondered whether he should be afraid. Was this guy and his lady friend, friend or foe? Friend was a bit of a misnomer. So far no one in the Agency, who were all *supposedly* on his side, had been overly warm and cozy. Lani in particular.

Now that he was dealing with spies and enemy agents, Rock should have thought to keep a few weapons handy. For situations like this where people broke into his kitchen to do a crossword puzzle. What had happened to the Agency's new top-notch security system? Had it failed already? These spooks really were like ghosts—they walked through walls. Maybe what he really needed was a proton pack and a containment unit.

The guy laughed. "And here I thought you were expecting me." He shook his head as if amused. "I'm your handler."

The woman laughed. "Calm down, Rock. I let Tal in. He knew the code word of the day. And unlike some people, I recognize my colleagues and friends."

Rock froze. He fought to keep his mouth from falling open. How in the world had he not recognized Lani? Damn, she was good with disguises. And she'd gotten him good.

"*Klaatu barada nikto.*" Rock's uninvited guest grinned. "Satisfied?"

"Yeah, sure," Rock said, still trying not to gawk at Lani, and recover his dignity. Now that he studied her, of course it was her. The mission brief Lani had given him last night had instructed him to wait for those magic words that would identify his handler as the real deal. "I guess this means you want me to save the world now. But I was hoping for à la peanut butter sandwiches. It has more pizzazz."

"I prefer Walla Walla, Washington. But you're the showman. You know best. I'll recommend the Amazing Mumford's line for next time." Tal waved Rock over. "Don't just stand there lurking in doorways. Come on in and join us. Have a cup of coffee. If you can't even recognize your wife, you must need one desperately."

Damn. Rock was never going to hear the end of this and there was no defense.

Tal turned to Lani. "You really did a number on the poor guy last night."

Not as much as Rock would have liked. Or maybe he should say, not the number he'd been dreaming of.

Lani smiled. "Me? I think it was being shot at in the alley that did him in."

"I did just great in the alley." Rock approached the kitchen counter and put a cup pack in his single-cup coffee machine, yawning as his coffee brewed.

"I'll vouch for that," Lani said. "That flash powder saved our lives. Rock assures me he's even more lethal with sparkle powder." She winked.

Cruel woman.

Tal laughed. "Sparkle powder, eh? We have our work cut out for us."

"Sparkle powder is highly effective in the right illusion." Rock grabbed his coffee and changed the subject. "What should I call you? Tal?"

His handler shrugged. "Whatever you like. I answer to almost anything."

Rock pulled his coffee cup from the machine, and arched a brow. "Anything?"

"Don't get any wiseass ideas. Tal will do. Short for talent because I handle the talent."

Rock grabbed a Danish to go with his coffee, even though he'd pay for the pleasure at the gym, and pulled up a stool across from Tal and Lani. "So what's the plan? When do I get my spy trench coat, my top-secret gadgets, and learn the secret handshake, the dead drop, and the move that can kill a man with a single karate chop?"

"Vegas spies don't wear trench coats. Too damn hot for that. The rest's advanced stuff." Tal took a sip of his coffee. "Let's start with the basics, spycraft one-oh-one." He shoved the hard shell gun case toward Rock. "Know how to use a firearm?"

"He shoots blanks in his act," Lani said, still teasing and obviously amused, and smug, that he'd mistaken her for a stranger.

Rock gave her a hard, deadpan stare, and said to Tal, "Just blanks, like the wife says." Tease him and he was going to fight back. She bristled as he called her the wife.

"Not the same thing. Top priority—get you to the firing range. Not that I'm real eager to let you loose on the unsuspecting public." He studied Rock, who was shirtless. "You're in shape."

Rock should say so. He worked hard to maintain his six-pack.

"He has lovely abs." Lani ran her gaze slowly down his body, obviously trying to get a rise out of him.

And succeeding.

"You have an edgy style." Tal sounded distinctly less than impressed. "You like to look tough."

He probably meant Rock's tattoos. His big, heavy silver rings. The chains Rock liked to wear in his act. "It's my stage persona."

"Can you fight?"

"I don't have to. I travel with bodyguards when necessary. And if that fails, I know how to disappear."

Tal cocked a brow. "Showbiz bastards. Don't want your pretty show face ruined by getting your hands dirty! You think you walk on water."

"You haven't seen my act—I do walk on water."

Tal laughed. "Very good. But RIOT knows how to disable bodyguards. And magic tricks." He reached into his pocket, pulled out a silver ring, and handed it to Rock.

Rock took it reluctantly. When he saw what it was, his eyes went big. "This is a replica of mine." He flashed a look at Lani. She'd given him the original as a birthday present when they were together. Had that been a setup, too?

She nonchalantly took another bite of toast.

Rock pulled a ring off his right pointer finger and held it next to the new one for comparison, unsure whether he should be angry or flattered. "You were expecting me to say yes to this mission."

"We know our subjects. We *are* in the intelligence business. We don't gamble unless we're confident we can win. There was no doubt you'd agree."

Rock looked at Lani again, but she'd turned to stare out the window as if avoiding him.

Rock turned the ring over in his hand, examining it as he hefted it. "Heavier than mine. Nice. It has a secret compartment, maybe two. They're cleverly concealed." He smiled at his handler. "You've given me a spy ring. What does it do?"

"Tracks you."

"That's not very flattering."

Lani turned from the window and smiled sweetly at him. "We need to know where you are in case you get into trouble."

"It has other features, too," Tal said, interrupting before Rock could reply. "A panic button. If you need us, you press right here." Tal showed Rock. "This will put a call in to us and we'll come running. Use it sparingly. Don't cry wolf. We don't appreciate that game."

"I'm not a coward."

"That remains to be seen." Tal took the ring back and held it up for Rock to see. "It has one more special feature. See here? Alakazam!" He pressed a ridge on the ring, twisted something, pressed again in a rapid series of movements. A miniature, gleaming razor blade popped up.

"A weapon? It's not quite a death ray, but it'll give someone a hell of a scratch."

"Ye of little faith. This is a murder weapon. Think like a spy." Tal held the ring up to the ray of sunshine streaming into the kitchen, catching the light so the ring gleamed. "Surgical steel. As sharp as a scalpel. And tipped with one of the fastest-acting, most deadly poisons in the world. Handle this with care."

He performed the sequence of movements again and the blade retracted. "There's enough poison for one swipe, maybe two. Three if you're real lucky and precise. It looks easy, but the sequence must be performed exactingly. We don't want the blade accidentally popping out at the wrong moment."

He handed the ring back to Rock. "I assume a man with your sleight-of-hand skills can manage it. It won't be easy to do while you're fighting for your life. And, of course, it only works in hand-to-hand combat, which can be a disadvantage."

Rock nodded, still marveling at the ring.

Tal pulled one more thing from his pocket. "Your new magician's secret utility device."

Rock laughed as he recognized the device and reached for it. "A new rubber thumb. Just what I always wanted."

"It was Lani's idea." Tal nodded toward her.

She grinned.

"This one is an exact replica of your real thumb," Tal said. "It was made by a prosthetic artist to match your skin color. It's even calloused like your thumb and has your thumbprint on it. Just don't work on your tan until this mission is over."

Rock had a pretty good idea of who had gotten his thumbprint and thumb measurements. "Measured me in my sleep?" he said to her. "What else did you measure?"

"Wouldn't you like to know?" Her gaze dropped to his crotch.

He sure as hell hoped no one had developed that kind of gun yet. He wasn't strapping one on no matter who ordered it.

"Okay, you two, stop flirting. Try the thumb on, Rock," Tal said.

Rock slid it on his right thumb and tilted his head side to side as he evaluated it. "Not bad."

"Not bad? That thumb's genius. A real bit of magic."

Rock was in a contrary mood and offended anyone who would think he didn't already have the best for his act. So far he saw no real advantage to this new rubber thumb. "Mine's pretty damn good, even without my thumbprint. That's just over the top."

"You think so?"

Rock pursed his lips. "This one is a bit heavier. Clunkier."

Tal laughed. "Clunkier? You mean has more features. Like a single-shot gun in it."

Rock couldn't hide his surprise. "No shit!"

"One shot, magic man. For emergencies only. Use it wisely." He held out his hand for the thumb.

Rock reluctantly handed it over.

"The safety's on now. You disable it here." Tal showed

him how to use the secret trigger. "Think you can remember all that?"

"Piece of cake. Watch this." Rock grabbed a paper napkin from the counter. "Here it is, just an ordinary paper napkin. Nothing special about it. Until I make it disappear."

He made a fist with his left hand and began stuffing the napkin into it. When he was finished and none of the napkin showed, he blew on his fist. He opened both hands for Tal and Lani to see. "Vanished."

"Not bad." Tal studied Rock's right hand. "The fake thumb looks natural. Maybe a shade longer than the left if you look closely enough. You're going up against one of your colleagues. He'll be looking for tricks, though probably not for thumb guns. What do you think, Lani?"

"He's pretty good at disappearing a napkin. And the thumb looks real." Lani glanced at the clock. "Look at the time. I have to run." She slid off her stool and grabbed a bright yellow purse from the counter. "Off to see a man about a job."

She wore tight short shorts and heels that made her legs look long and turned Rock on.

"Looking like that?" Rock said.

She struck a pose with her hand on her hip. "You don't like?"

She was just taunting him now.

She laughed. "This is just my leaving the house disguise. I'll change before I get there." She pulled a set of car keys from her purse.

"You have a car?"

"The Agency left one for me yesterday." She turned to go.

"Lani?"

She paused and looked at him.

"Be careful."

She grinned back. "Always."

Rock and Tal watched her leave.

When she was gone, Tal stared him directly in the eye. "A word of caution—forget about Lani. Don't let her mess with your mind or the mission. She's a danger to you. More dangerous even than Blackledge and RIOT because she's your Achilles' heel and everyone in magic and clandestine circles knows it."

Tal shook his head and mumbled beneath his breath. "I don't know what the chief was thinking bringing a layperson into this mission, magician or not. Especially one whose vulnerability is tattooed on his chest. Someone should have warned you—never ink a broad's name on your body. That one's going to be hell to erase."

"Erase?" There was no damn way Rock was ever having Lani's name removed. If for nothing more than to remember the lesson. "She's my wife."

Tal laughed. "See what I mean? Point made. Lani screwed up by marrying you. A weak moment in her mission, or maybe she just couldn't figure a way to get out of it. Either way, not good spycraft. Don't make the same mistake. Don't let her get to you again." Tal paused and took a sip of his coffee. "Cold."

Rock wasn't sure whether he meant Lani or the coffee.

"If all goes according to plan, Blackledge will reappear Lani in his act within a week. We're already working on prepublicity for the show where he does it, getting a slew of reviewers and media types in the crowd as soon as we know the exact date. Blackledge won't be able to resist this opportunity to show you up.

"We've also deposited the reward money in a special account for you. Blackledge will come calling for it soon enough.

"Tate will be in Blackledge's audience when Lani is reappeared. But before that, this afternoon, you'll run into him in the hotel lobby where he'll profess a fondness for your act. You'll show him a few magic tricks, help him out at the card tables, and the two of you will become fast friends."

Rock shook his head. "I'm banned from the card tables."

Tal shrugged. "Tate isn't. And his money talks."

Rock crossed his arms. "I don't have time for cards. If I'm going to carry off this illusion, I'll need a cast of magicians. And a place to rehearse. Plus all the toys, props, and supplies."

Tal laughed again. "If your mission planners tell you to play cards, you have time for cards. As for the other, Tate's working on getting your magicians. All in due time." Tal grinned.

"Wait until you meet Tate. He can charm the skin off a snake or the most valuable intel out of the most tight-lipped terrorist. You'll have fun playing cards and hanging with him. Enjoy it."

If alien beings actually popped to Earth and were presented with Sol Blackledge and Rock Powers, odds are they'd pick Sol as the good guy. Of course they'd be wrong. Sol had all the clean-cut good magician looks of a David Copperfield or Lance Burton while Rock was often compared more to David Blaine or Criss Angel. And if the hypothetical aliens had the sense to look deep into Sol's eyes, as Lani was forced to do in his penthouse suite at the luxury hotel on the Strip where he performed night after night, they'd see the dangerous drive and greed in them. But as is so often the case at first glance—good appears evil and evil as good.

Sol sat in a plush leather chair facing the 180-degree view of downtown Vegas with his shoes off and his legs crossed, a glass of Scotch in one hand. He was mindlessly bending a spoon with the other as he studied Lani with a look meant to pull the truth out of her.

"So the errant, disappearing Mrs. Powers is back," he said in the mesmerizing stage voice he'd cultivated over the years.

It had little effect on Lani, who knew most secrets of magic and who'd trained to steel herself against all interrogation techniques, including hypnosis. Only Rock was able to penetrate her guard.

"I must compliment you—you're exceptional with a disguise." His gaze raked over her. "I didn't recognize you at first. Even now that I know you're you it's hard to grasp."

He's impressed. Good.

Lani shrugged. After leaving Rock's mansion, she'd changed and played up her Asian looks. And yes, she did look very different from the Latin beauty she'd shown Rock.

"Talent and genetics. I can be any race I want to be. Be anyone, except a Nordic blonde." She stood with her hip cocked, not quite comfortable enough to sit yet. Besides, she was still strutting her stuff.

Sol grinned and stared at the bustier top she wore which pushed her breasts up to the point of almost tumbling out. Two and a half years ago, Sol had wanted her for more than his act. If the hungry look in his eyes was any indication, he still did.

"You haven't lost your figure," he said, appreciation practically oozing in his voice.

She smiled, stretched, arched to show off her form to even better advantage, like a *Playboy* playmate in a spread. "I haven't lost a lot of things." She bent over so he got the full view of her breasts, and rested her palms flat on the floor, even though she was wearing three-inch heels.

"Impressive," Sol said.

She stood erect. Did a backflip, landed, and twisted

herself into the tiniest of pretzels, a ball so small she could fit herself into the tightest of magician's cabinets.

Sol clapped. "Indeed you haven't lost a thing, Lani."

"I've been staying in shape. Doing some yoga. I'm delightfully limber." She let the suggestion hang in the air and unfolded herself, stood, strutted to a leather sofa across from Sol, and slid onto it, crossing her legs provocatively and smiling.

Sol released the spoon he'd been toying with. "What do you want from me, Lani?" It was clear he was intrigued and trying to maintain control; his voice had a breathless edge.

"I want to be your main assistant. I have the skills, the chops, the drive."

"In case you haven't noticed, I have an assistant. Several, in fact. Damn good ones."

"My mistake, but I thought you were advertising for a new one?"

He grinned. "Not a new main assistant."

She grinned back. "Can any of them upstage Rock like I can? I want *you* to be the magician who reappears me and steals Rock's thunder."

Sol laughed again, but his eyes were hard and intense as he studied her. "You know I'd like nothing better than to upstage Rock, baby. But running out in the middle of a show, and only mere hours into a marriage, that's hardly reliable behavior."

They'd reached the delicate part of negotiations. "I had to run, Sol." Lani put just the slightest bit of pout and feminine frailty into her voice. There was nothing like a damsel in distress to stir ardor in the male breast, even in a black heart like Sol's.

Sol cocked a brow. "In the middle of Rock's trick? It couldn't have waited until, say, after the show?"

Lani looked casually down at her long, manicured

acrylic fingernails as if she was nervous. Which she was. Nervous and excited. She had her cat on her string. Sol was interested. It was time to swing the ball of yarn and keep him batting at it, gently reeling it in until she had him in her lap right where she wanted him.

She looked up at Sol, rotated her foot to show off her sexy, strappy sandals, another feigned nervous gesture, and met Sol's eyes. "I've always had a flair for the dramatic."

She smiled slowly. "You know my motto—if you're going to do something, do it all the way and make sure you generate the most attention possible." She paused and shrugged. "Besides, I had no choice. I was running for my life."

The truth, as far as you can tell it, is always more convincing than a lie. Just as a smile must reach the eyes to be believed, so must anger, bitterness, and fear.

Sol took a sip of Scotch. "No choice, baby?"

"Do I have to explain?"

"You do if you want me to hire you."

She shrugged again. "My ex was in the crowd. With a gun. That jealous bastard—"

She cut herself off for effect and paused. When she spoke again, she lowered her voice and made it shake with rage. "Why do you think I was in Vegas in the first place? I was running from him. It only took him six months to find me even though I'd covered my tracks and been clever with my disguise and new identity . . ."

She took a deep breath, acting as if she had to calm down. "That bastard was there to kill me. As he'd promised to do a dozen times before. He said that if I ever left him . . ."

She shuddered on cue and took another breath.

"I have no doubt, none at all, that if I'd finished the show and tried to leave the hotel, he'd have found and killed me. And Rock. Probably after beating the shit out of me first. And torturing Rock."

She shook her head, keeping her eyes steely. "It was foolhardy of Rock to announce our marriage during the show." She didn't have to feign her bitterness.

"It practically sealed his death warrant. Or would have if I hadn't disappeared. Fortunately," she hesitated as if she were about to trip on a name, "the ex took off after me immediately and left Rock alone. I barely escaped out the back . . ."

She paused again and shuddered, remembering slipping in the dead RIOT agent's blood. "He was already after me."

She stared at Sol, trying to give him the impression she was deciding whether to trust him or not. "That was the worst night of my life. I ran out the back into the dark of the back parking lot and right into a dead body."

She shivered again. "It was so dark I didn't even see the bloody thing. I tripped over it, slid in the pool of blood, broke my heel, and kept running." She took a deep breath.

"You didn't see anything else?" Sol seemed more interested than a casual observer. RIOT of course wanted to know what Lani the magician's assistant knew.

When she laughed it wasn't pleasant, but harsh, cynical. "Like the murderer? No." She shook her head. "But I was scared, really scared. I had a raging ex after me and I'd just stumbled onto a murder scene. It could have been a gang execution, for all I knew. You know this city. No way I was getting in the middle of testifying in something like that. That's a death warrant." She took a deep breath. "I ran, just ran."

She uncrossed her legs and leaned forward as if imploring Sol to understand. "After that I couldn't come back. The cops would want to talk to me; keep me around as a witness. I'm as civic-minded as the next person. But I didn't see a thing, just a dead body. I had other things on my mind." She studied Sol. He appeared to be buying her story.

"Leaving in the middle of the show was the only way I could think of to escape. And protect me, Rock, the crew. That bastard ex didn't expect me to run in the middle of a trick."

She laughed as if delighted with herself that she'd pulled one over on him. "When you think about it, it *was* very clever of me."

Sol was still studying her and, though he prided himself on his inscrutable expression, she could practically see the wheels of his little criminal mind turning. He wanted to believe her.

She was telling him just enough truth to lead him on.

"Does the ex have a name?"

She studied her nails again, admiring the pretty flowers on them before glancing up at Sol from beneath her false lashes. "Not that you need to know."

"I see," Sol said. "So hiding out for two years, that was to avoid this jealous bastard and any questions from the cops?"

She nodded.

"Now that you're back and ready to reappear, I assume the problem's been taken care of."

She met his eyes and let her grin spread organically. "He won't be bothering me, or anyone, again."

"So the fewer questions asked . . ." Sol's eyes had an evil, admiring twinkle in them. He looked almost turned on.

Lani smiled in reply and winked at him.

"Well, that answers the big question—why you haven't come back to divorce Rock and capitalize on his fortune. The papers have assured the public there was no prenup involved with this quickie wedding." Sol picked up the spoon and wove it through his fingers, disappearing it up his sleeve.

"But why me, your husband's nemesis, Lani? There are other magicians on the Strip, not to mention Rock himself." Sol acted cool, but his eyes gave him away. He wanted this opportunity to show up Rock so badly it hurt.

"You're the best. Rock pulls his punches. Doesn't take the risks he should and could to create the best illusions. Now that I'm unencumbered I want fame. And fortune. Plenty of it. My own with no strings attached and no one's permission to get to spend it. I want to be my own woman.

"After the experience with my ex, you could say I'm a bit burned. The independent life has become much more attractive than being saddled with a ball and chain. You never know when a ball and chain will suddenly decide it can be a weapon."

She put a touch of seduction in her voice. "I'm sorry, Sol. I made a mistake choosing Rock over you the first time. Who knew he'd get so possessive? I belong to no one but myself. I think you and I are a lot alike that way."

"We all make mistakes, baby."

She couldn't tell whether that was an acceptance of her apology or not. She simply babbled on like a nervous showgirl. "Let me join your entourage, Sol. You have to admit, it will make for superior showmanship. And isn't that what this is all about?"

"And Rock? Your marriage?"

She snorted as if cynically amused and shook her head again. "The marriage was one of those get-drunk-and-get-married things that happen in Vegas. Usually to tourists. And women stupid enough to think they've found a steady man who can protect them." She straightened and sat back on the sofa. "The marriage was over the moment it began. Rock is too possessive. It scares me."

"Yes, babe, but how will you be dealing with it?" Sol set his glass on the end table next to him. "This is tabloid fodder of the finest kind."

She studied Sol, grinned, and nodded. "Yes. And if we're smart, which we are, we can make a few bucks by tipping the best of them off to my reappearance."

Sol laughed. "You are a mercenary bitch." The words rolled off his tongue like flattery. "There's the matter of the reward money, too."

"Oh, I haven't forgotten that. Rock will be mad as hell at having to pay it to you. As for you and me, we split it fifty-fifty." She grinned. "See? I've just paid for myself. How many girls can say that? You're getting me for a steal. How can you turn down an offer like that?"

Sol's eyes gleamed with avarice and lust. "You still haven't answered my question—how are you going to play Rock? What will you tell the tabloids about why you've come to me? The public loves Rock. They'll hate you for betraying him."

"They love you, too, Sol. Don't forget that."

Sol laughed. She'd properly stroked his maniacal male ego.

"I'll tell the press you and I were always friends and I came to you for help because I feared Rock wouldn't take me back."

"Were we friends, baby?"

She laughed. "We could be." She leaned forward again. "Think of all the lovely PR we'll get, Sol. I'll string Rock along. If he's smart, and we know he is, he'll play along with us and fuel this competition to new heights.

"The public loves love triangles and scandal. And magic. And professional competition played out in the public arena. Our shows will be *packed*. And of course I'll want my cut."

Sol didn't object so she rushed on. "As an added

bonus, I'll do my best to get into Rock's confidence again. Find out what he's up to with his new illusions. With your permission, we'll feed him a few of your new ideas for tricks. This could be the magical feud of the century, with you and me raking in a king's ransom."

CHAPTER SIX

Midnight or noon, the lighting was the same inside the best hotels—neon and fluorescent. Lots of it. A trick, a misdirection of time to keep the gambler guests up all hours and at the machines and tables. Opulent tile patterns ran through the floor. Arches and sculptures provided visual interest. Chihuly glass sculptures, urchins, and sea anemones in every heavenly color imaginable, hung from the ceiling. Gold and glitz sparkled as accents on walls and handles. The feeling of luxury everywhere pervaded, adding to the scent of money that hung in the air—the making and the losing of it. And in the background the din of the slot machines and gaming tables rattled on incessantly.

Tal had instructed Rock to "bump" into Tate in the lobby at precisely 2:03 p.m. Evidently NCS agents were sticklers for details and timing. Conveniently, Rock was well known for wandering through the hotel lobby and taking his magic to the streets, showing off for randomly selected guests and bystanders. He was prepared to do so now, fully decked out with playing cards and all manner of tricks up his sleeve. Including picking Tate as his random bystander.

Rock glanced at the clock on the wall of the baggage storage room where he sat waiting for his cue. A bored

baggage handler held court over the sea of luggage surrounding them, totally unimpressed by Rock and not at
all interested in him. Which made Rock wonder—NCS
bodyguard perhaps?

Rock had a few minutes yet before he burst into the
lobby, seemingly from nowhere, appearing out of a puff
of smoke. He planned to disappear Tate and him together
the same way. There was no taking the showman out of
Rock.

Nor was there any taking the art of misdirection away
from the magician and that's what had Rock stymied,
frustrated, and feeling foolish, lamebrained, conned,
duped, bamboozled. Whatever word you like. Misdirection is the soul of magic. And apparently of clandestine
missions and operatives. Somehow the CIA had out-
misdirected him.

As Rock thought back over his brief time with Lani
before she disappeared, he looked for the misdirection
that had been applied by NCS to him. By Lani to him to
make him believe she loved him. But damn if he still
couldn't see it.

Was he suffering from what magicians call inattentional blindness? Falling for the old crossing-the-gaze
technique cleverly applied by the CIA as smoothly as if
the Agency were a master magician? Rock used the technique all the time to appear a coin apparently out of nowhere.

It worked like this—the magician holds his empty left
hand palm out to the audience, pointing to his palm with
his right hand. The magician looks at his audience, di-
recting their gaze to his eyes. He then gazes at his empty
palm and the audience follows suit. During that quick instant of time, the magician holds out his right hand in a
gesture that says *hold on, wait for it* with his right palm,
and a coin, in full view of his audience. But no one sees it

because they're looking at his empty palm. Inattentional blindness. Classic misdirection.

What had Lani done to make him believe she loved him when she was just doing her duty for her country and advancing her career? Since she'd disappeared, he'd gone back over their romance too many times to count, relishing and reliving every detail, trying to figure out where he'd gone wrong. *If* he'd gone wrong. Wondering whether he'd been mistaken about her feelings for him. Wondering whether she'd simply run out on him or if there'd been another reason for her flight. And whether she'd been abducted in that alley because she'd literally stepped into the middle of a murder.

He still didn't see the misdirection. Maybe he didn't want to. Or maybe he'd inadvertently rewritten their history by replaying it too many times and replacing it with what he wanted to see. All he knew was that despite everything she'd said and done even since returning, against his better judgment, his logical self, and yes, even his conscience, he still loved her. Even now she was probably misdirecting him. But two could play that game.

There was more CIA misdirection than just Lani. How had Rock missed Lani's mission? How had he not seen her associations? Clandestine meetings? Dead drops? Fear?

The woman was damn talented. If he could go back and determine the truth, see the tricks, he'd have power, over both Lani and NCS. Power he wouldn't hesitate to use when it suited his purposes.

Even now he was looking for the misdirection they must be applying to him and the situation. He'd be a fool to believe everything, maybe anything, they told him. This time, he was going to be in the driver's seat.

Hell, that attempt on Rock's life? That could have been manufactured by NCS just to get him in their camp. Scare the shit out of him and keep him dancing on their string as he looked over his shoulder for shadows. That little shooting was so perfectly timed and orchestrated and effective in bringing him and Lani together, getting them to work with each other when Rock otherwise might have been tempted to tell Emmett Nelson and the Agency to go to hell, that Rock couldn't help thinking it had been scripted and planned.

Rock focused on a spot on the wall as he thought about the mission. It was dangerous and tricky sending Lani back in. There would be all kinds of questions regarding her and tons of publicity that would shine a spotlight on the operation. It was a huge risk to take, planning a mission in the public eye with the paparazzi watching. NCS must want the publicity, was all he could think, though it seemed to go against the CIA's code of secrecy and operating in the shadows.

As for Sol, it was hard to believe they'd once been close friends, buds, blood brothers. They met at the Magic Castle in Hollywood when they were both crazy college kids taking magic classes and dreaming of stardom and magical feats beyond the ordinary. Even the fact of their previous friendship flew in the face of a smooth mission. They were rivals now, but when it came down to it, Rock feared their former friendship still tainted him. He had a damnable soft spot for Sol even though Sol had screwed him over one too many times. If ordered, could Rock kill Sol?

Tal had posed the question bluntly to Rock at the shooting range earlier in the day. "Think you could kill the bastard?" Tal had said.

"Depends," Rock had answered truthfully.

Tal had pinned him with a look of disgust. "Shouldn't. The world may seem gray to you, magic boy, but Sol's aligned with RIOT, which makes the situation completely black-and-white.

"We're white. He's our mortal enemy. If you get the chance, kill him. If you have a soft spot for him, kill him quickly and painlessly." There'd been no humor in Tal's voice or expression.

It all sounded like so much melodrama. *Mortal enemy.* Hadn't that gone out with Snidely Whiplash? Rock might have sneered if he hadn't been so deep in thought.

What the Agency didn't know, couldn't have known, what no one besides Rock and Sol knew was that Sol had saved Rock's life when they were young, up-and-coming magicians. Straightjacket escape gone wrong. Rock had had the brilliant idea to try it while water-skiing. Outdoing Houdini and all that. The fearlessness of youth. He and Sol had gone out on Lake Tahoe at dawn to practice. Sol drove the boat. Rock put on the straightjacket, a pair of water skis, and they were off.

Rock took a tumble before he could get out of the jacket. He hit a ski as he went down and was knocked unconscious, still in the jacket. He couldn't move and didn't have a life jacket on, no flotation devices at all, just that damn heavy straightjacket and a pair of swim trunks. Rock sank like a 180-pound rock.

It's foolhardy to water-ski without a spotter. It's even crazier to ski with a straightjacket on without a spotter. Fortunately, Sol knew how to handle a boat and was damn observant. He saw Rock go down the instant it happened and circled back for him.

They'd been young and cocky enough to bring one safety device along in case things went wrong—a grappling hook to retrieve Rock's body. Heavy metal thing. Sol tossed it out, miraculously hooked Rock on the first throw, hauled him in, and performed CPR. The hook took a big chunk out of Rock's right thigh. It bled like hell. Sol had said it was a good thing Lake Tahoe wasn't shark-infested. Rock had to have a dozen stitches to close it up. But he and Sol never told anyone about the straightjacket or the grappling hook.

They told the emergency room doc who sewed Rock up that Rock had slipped while hiking and gotten the gash. Didn't even mention the near drowning. The doc didn't question them. They tabled the trick until further notice, as in they got more experience.

Escaping from a straightjacket isn't an illusion. It's pure escapology. Rock could escape with ease now. And he'd gotten better at water-skiing, too. But he'd never performed that trick again. As he'd learned the hard way— too many things beyond his control could go wrong. Rock took risks, but they were calculated risks. As for the scar, he'd gotten his first tattoo to cover it—*Expect the Unexpected*. Words to live by. So why did he feel so stunned by the current situation?

An analog clock hand clicked off another minute of Rock's life. He glanced at the clock: 2:03.

A man came to the counter. "Wickstrom. I have two bags." He pulled a ten from his pocket as the baggage clerk jumped to find the man's suitcases.

There's my signal. Right on time.

Rock got to his feet, pulled his flash powder out, eyed the tile where it should land for perfect placement, and tossed it. Good thing he had a good arm and precise aim from playing baseball in high school. An instant later, he slid into place just as the smoke cleared and there stood Tate Cox, international playboy, dressed casually in obviously expensive slacks and a dress shirt, Italian leather shoes.

Tal's right. Cox looks like a dandy.

Tate had the kind of rugged jawline, dark hair, and

athletic build a majority of women found attractive. Rock gave him that. And of course he had a buxom brown-eyed blonde, a real stunner, on his arm. The blonde was wedged into a tight red dress so short and low cut only the tiniest scrap of material held it together in the middle.

Rock realized with a start that the blonde was Lani in disguise in a blond wig. She looked so patently all-American white bread it was startling. Where had all her ethnicity gone?

"Why if it isn't Rock Powers." Lani laughed with delight. "Did you arrange this just for me, Tate? You know how much I *love* magic." She stroked Tate's arm as she cooed the words. Then she smiled and winked at Rock. "I'm always telling Tate he has the magic touch."

Rock balled his fist as a wave of jealousy crashed over him. Despite her earlier denial, Lani's attraction to Tate seemed genuine. She was either a damn fine actress or an impressive liar, or both. Rock wondered again how much Lani had faked with him. And why the hell hadn't anyone bothered to tell him to expect Lani to show up with Tate?

Rock had to force himself into action. Before Tate could answer her question, Rock reached behind Lani's ear and pulled the diamond tennis bracelet the Agency had given him for the trick from behind her beautiful lobe with a flourish. "What's this? Diamonds?"

She took the bauble from Rock's fingers and fixed a sultry smile on Tate. If Lani had aimed that smile at Rock, it would have been enough to make his toes curl. Instead, he wanted to punch Tate out.

"It's beautiful. Help me put it on, Tate." She grabbed Tate's chin, pulled his face around, and planted a deep-tongued affair on him as Tate simultaneously fastened the catch of the bracelet.

Was Lani trying to torture him? Show him she could pull his chain at will as she had in the past? Or was this some kind of test? It took all his stage training not to lose his professional cool.

"I produce the jewels and he gets all the credit." Rock cocked a brow and held his hands out for her.

She laughed, giddy with the attention, took his hands, pulled him to her, and planted one directly on his lips. It wasn't the tongued affair she gave Tate, but it was good enough to distract her. A flash went off from somewhere. The paparazzi had arrived. Just as quickly, hotel security stepped in to ward the guys with the cameras off.

Rock squeezed her hands, let go of one hand as he squeezed the other more firmly, and deposited a tiny playing card between one of her beautiful breasts and her dress.

So this was the only feel he was going to get of his wife. He would have tucked it into her bra if she'd been wearing one. Rock was so deft with his movements and his distraction she didn't seem to notice he'd ever let go of one of her hands.

Or maybe Lani was just letting him do the trick and playing along.

"He's a wonder, Tate. A treasure." Her eyes sparkled. "Do some more magic! Please." She made perfect pouty lips.

"I think she's hoping for the necklace that matches that bracelet." Tate winked.

"Sorry to disappoint. No more diamonds up my sleeve." Rock produced a pack of cards out of thin air. "Just ordinary street magic."

"Magic is never ordinary. Show it to me." She clapped and laughed like a delighted teen. She was so convincing, it was hard to believe she was really Lani.

A crowd grew around them. It may have been Rock's imagination, but he felt a gaze more intense than a common crowd's watching him. The hair on the back of his neck stood up as he kept up the act and tried to determine where his sense of unease was coming from.

Rock shrugged easily. "Card tricks are the soul of street magic. Every card tells a story." He held the deck out to Tate to inspect with the joker faceup. A warning, *someone's watching us*. "Look it over. Verify for yourself that it's just a regular deck."

Tate took it, hefted it, and examined it for any sign of marking. "Looks all right to me."

"If your reputation is accurate, you know cards. You're sure?"

Tate nodded. "I'd stake my golden reputation on it."

Rock fanned the deck out. "Excellent. Take a card, any card."

Tate grabbed a card.

"Don't show it to me! Memorize it." Rock pulled a pen from his pocket and held it out to Tate. "Write your name on it on the face. Good. Now put it facedown back into the deck." Rock did some more fancy shuffling, throwing the cards out and pulling them back. Then he had Lani cut the deck.

"Are you concentrating?" he asked Tate.

Tate nodded.

Rock closed his eyes and frowned in apparent thought. He was supposed to look as if he was concentrating, but he could perform this trick in his sleep. He was really listening to the crowd and trying to pick up on the vibe. Something still wasn't right. After a few seconds had elapsed, Rock slid a card from the deck without looking. He opened his eyes and held the card up with a flourish for Tate to see. "Is this your card?"

The audience gasped.

Tate grabbed the card. "Well played."

Rock bowed his head in a falsely humble gesture, holding his arms out, palms up like a showman. "Wait."

He smiled at Tate's blonde. "Is that a card I see peeking out of your dress?"

The audience followed Rock's line of sight right to Lani's lush cleavage.

She gasped and reached to pull the card out of her dress, but not before Tate grabbed her hand. "Allow me."

Damn him, Rock thought.

Tate pulled the miniature card from the fake blonde's dress with a flourish and a leer, every bit as much of a showman as Rock. "I'll be damned."

He held the card out for Lani and then the rest of the crowd to see. "My card, shrunken. The amazing shrunken card trick."

"And that's your signature, too, I presume?" Rock pointed to the card.

Tate grinned. "No shit. It is indeed. If I find any charges I didn't sign for on my bill, I know who to come after."

Lani shook her head so that her platinum highlights fell around her face, her bountiful breasts bounced, and the bracelet on her wrist glistened under the neon lights. "You are a smooth one," she purred to Rock. "I generally feel it when a man slides something beneath my dress."

Rock winked. "The ladies only feel me when I want them to." And he wanted her to feel it.

"And I imagine you're very good then, too," she said with enough seduction in her voice to make Tate reach out and put his arm around her.

Rock resisted balling his fists, smiled, and nodded toward the card. "That's your lucky card."

Tate pulled her close. "She's lucky with *me* tonight, magician. Very clever show. Now, keep your hands off my woman." Tate's eyes danced with challenge.

The man had nerve and a sense of humor and irony.

"Join us in the casino," Tate said. "Drinks are on me."

"Generous guy." The very strong feeling they were in

the crosshairs hadn't left Rock. "Drinks are free in the casino and I'm banned from the tables."

"I'm not and I have cash. Plenty of it. And a seat at a private high-stakes table. Come and watch us play. I could use someone watching to make sure the game stays clean. No dirty tricks." Tate held his gaze. "Know anything about Texas hold 'em?"

"A thing or two," Rock said. "That's a game that requires a lot of luck. The odds favor the house."

"Not if you have the right skills," Tate said as the crowd dispersed.

Rock wondered whether Tate was all bluff. "And those would be?"

"A knowledge of human psychology and probability," Tate said as he ran his hand up Lani's waist and rubbed her bare arm with a challenge to Rock in his eyes.

"You're talking to a man who counts cards. I'd love to watch. I can't play, of course. But how about a friendly wager?"

Tate cocked his head. "What are you thinking?"

"I'll watch you play and write down what I would have done in your situation. The lovely blonde here—"

"Gillian," Lani said and winked.

"Gillian," Rock repeated, "will keep track and announce the winner at the end."

"What are we playing for?"

"Honor's enough for me," Rock said. "And a bottle of the house's best champagne. Loser buys and toasts the winner."

Tate held out his hand for a shake. "Game on."

Rock shook and stepped aside to follow Tate and Lani through the casino to the private back room.

Tal had given Rock the mission details. Rock was to play bodyguard to Tate the great secret agent. Keep an eye out for dirty dealing. Watch to make sure no one poisoned

Tate's drink. Or reached for a gun. Guns shouldn't be a problem. Security checked for them, and knives, big sticks, and heavy belt buckles, anything that could be used as a weapon, as the players arrived. Piece of cake duty, really. Except for the poison. To Rock's knowledge the casino had never checked for that.

Once again, Rock wondered how Tal could have forgotten to mention Lani. This had to be a test. Lani was Tate's real backup.

Clyde Bancroft was one of the high rollers who'd be playing. Bancroft had gained some notoriety as an ambitious and talented online gambler looking to make his way in the real world of high-stakes poker. He was also a financier for Archibald Random, a name Tal had spoken with hatred, and other bad dudes whose names the Agency determined Rock didn't have a need to know.

Bancroft's MO was to invest his clients' funds in short sales of successful companies. In the current economic climate, with so many previously profitable companies either failing or faltering, short sales had been a good bet in general. But Bancroft liked to put the odds in his favor. If inside information, blackmail, and corporate espionage failed him, he orchestrated terrorist attacks on the companies to ensure their stock fell and he made an exorbitant profit.

Unfortunately for him, both the Agency and Homeland Security had become wise to his scheme and better at predicting and preventing terrorist attacks. They'd thwarted one too many of his attempts at terrorism and now Bancroft was bleeding money. His investors, none of them exactly nice guys, were getting nervous and demanding their money back. On pain of torture. Or death. Or both.

Bancroft had the brilliant idea to win back the money he owed his investors at a high-stakes game of hold 'em.

Tal was certain he wouldn't play fair there, either. Tate, who apparently was the best gambler in the Agency, was charged with stopping Bancroft from winning. And preferably, to further bankrupt him. In his public persona, Tate had a reputation as a gambler. His presence at the table wouldn't be suspect.

The Agency had the same goals as Bancroft—make sure the risks they assumed were minimal. With taxpayers wanting an accounting of every dollar spent, the Agency didn't need the embarrassment of Tate losing the fifty-million-dollar bankroll they'd given him. NCS wanted the return of both their money and their most glamorous agent, whole and alive.

Tate's job was to concentrate on the cards and game and Rock's was to watch for funny business and threats. Just watch and signal Tate should anything look shady. Yeah, Rock had excellent powers of observation. Which didn't mean he was going to simply sit on the sidelines as instructed and let Tate handle everything.

NCS hoped by applying enough financial pressure to Bancroft, they could turn him and get him to spill what he knew about RIOT's plans in exchange for protection.

For the scheme to work, no one could suspect any connection between Rock and Tate. No friendship. No reason for Rock to help him play. Which is why NCS staged the public first meet.

At the door to the private room, the bouncer patted them down. Fortunately for Rock, he didn't pat down Rock's hand. Rock was wearing his thumb gun. It was a tiny one-shot wonder. But then again, in a pinch one shot might just be the difference between life and meeting the great magician in the sky.

"Is this standard procedure?" Lani asked Tate as the bouncer ran his hands down her curves.

Does every man in town get to feel up my wife except for me? Rock wondered.

"I couldn't fit a weapon in this dress if I tried." Lani as Gillian laughed prettily. "I couldn't even fit in any underwear." She winked at the guard. "I'd be happy to go through the full body scanner, like at the airport." She shrugged. "I'm used to it. For some reason, I'm always picked for that duty anyway."

"Everyone just wants to feel you up, baby," Tate said.

The bouncer patted Tate down and gave him the all-clear. Rock remained unimpressed with the bouncer's weapon-detecting skills, certain Tate wouldn't walk into that room unarmed.

The dealer looked up at them. "Mr. Cox, welcome. You're just in time. I believe everyone else has arrived." He pointed to an empty chair. "We held number five for you. At your request."

Tate nodded. "Thank you."

Tate had chosen a seat just past the midpoint of the deal. Interesting choice. Usually the later in the deal, the more information a player had and the greater the odds of winning the pot. Which meant the later players played more hands. Generally poker games at casinos played nonstop with players constantly joining and leaving the game, not beginning at once, as was the case for this game. In the case of joining an in-progress game, accepted strategy was to wait for the big blind to get to you before beginning. That gave you plenty of time to watch how the others play before you had to bet.

The same could have been said with this game. Either Tate was exceptionally cocky in his ability to read the other players, or someone else had more clout to get the prime position.

The most commonly accepted winning strategy was to play tight-aggressive, meaning you played fewer hands very aggressively. That, too, could have accounted for Tate's choice.

Bancroft, who was in seven, apparently thought knowledge was power and opted for late in the deal. Since the deal button rotated from player to player, the advantage was eventually lost. That is, if one survived the game long enough.

The casino dealer frowned at Rock. "Mr. Powers. I believe the table is full. And you're—"

"Banned from play. That's right." Rock laughed. "I'm just here to watch and keep the lady company." He took Lani's elbow, glad he finally got to touch her even innocently. "We'll be at the bar."

Rock led Lani to the bar. When she walked, every male eye followed her. At the bar, she seated herself in such a way as to draw as much attention as possible to herself, sitting with her legs crossed facing the table, the short skirt of her dress all but disappearing. The men were probably thinking about her beautiful, panty-less body beneath the scanty sheath. Rock sure was.

Tate, my man. I have to give you credit. Using Lani to create a diversion is brilliant.

Even if it was driving Rock mad with desire and jealousy.

Rock got Lani one of those girlie drinks made with chocolate vodka and a name like Chocolate Desire and turned his attention to the group of gamblers, ignoring her rapturous murmurs about the scrumptiousness of chocolate.

He was convinced she was just trying to torment him again. It was hard enough keeping his hands off her as it was.

Bancroft sat two down from Tate, looking cool and urbane, like anything but a thug. Expensively dressed, midthirties, clean-cut. He was the kind of guy you pictured on Wall Street in a high-rise corner office. Rock recognized Bancroft by reputation, but had never seen him in person in a casino before. Bancroft was big in online poker and had his own fan club and Web site.

Bancroft had two thugs positioned behind him, or Rock missed his guess. They looked more like junior law partners than strong arms, but as uninterested as they tried to appear, they were definitely Bancroft's men. Rock noticed Lani subtly watching them as well.

One of them fiddled with a touch screen tablet very near Tate. Probably keeping the fans up to date about the live-action play. Rock noticed the stylus the guy used was unusual, a little thicker than normal, and from the way the guy handled it, heavier, too.

A stylus was the biggest implement allowed near the table. Anything bigger could be considered a weapon. Rock wondered briefly whether it was some kind of mini baton and made a note to keep an eye on it and the bean counter wielding it. He was also going to make sure the guy wasn't using the tablet to somehow signal Bancroft the cards Tate held.

Next to Bancroft in eight sat a dark man known as the Cuban in gambling circles. He must have had a real name, but damn if Rock could remember it. He was a regular in Vegas, almost a celebrity. He looked hard, like the streets of Havana. Which may have explained how he'd outmuscled Bancroft for the last position of the deal. Or maybe it was his reputation. The Cuban was fearless, cockily so. And known for being reckless, too. A bad, hotheaded combo. But it made for exciting poker for the spectators. Even with the Cuban's superior table position, Rock wouldn't place any bets on him walking away with the big pot. More likely he'd end up a victim of his own ego.

A middle-aged couple, obviously husband and wife, sat in one and two. Rock hadn't seen them in the casinos before. He wondered whether they had more money to burn than they knew what to do with, or were looking for a thrill, or were simply desperate for quick money and cash.

The woman had sharp eyes and angular features and flashed a ferocious gaze at Lani when she thought her husband wasn't looking. Her husband was the nervous, cautious type. He'd scare easily and wouldn't hold his head unless his wife held it for him. They'd probably be first out. Maybe second.

The woman in three was late thirties, graying, men's haircut, lean and muscular, no bust. The complete opposite of the way Lani played Gillian. Her eyes were intelligent and hard. She looked like she was used to kicking boys' butts. As Rock wondered where she'd come from, he gave her even odds of hanging in.

The guy in four had perfected a poker face. He was probably late fifties. A longtime pro with a solid reputation. He was a wild card. It would all depend on whether he could remain calm and not panic as play began.

The kid in six was young, a nerd, probably had a system all worked out and a pile of money from some Internet start-up to blow. Knew the mathematical odds down to the tenth decimal point and would try to fool the casino into thinking he wasn't counting. Rock didn't recognize him and figured that was intentional. The kid had probably waited for this minute to strike with his system and bring home a big killing. If his system was too effective, he'd be banned from the casinos. This might be his one big shot. But the kid's weakness would be his inability to read people.

"What are you thinking?" Lani whispered in Rock's ear.

"That Tate has excellent taste in women and wisely chose you as a distraction," Rock whispered back. "You're distracting me, at least."

She laughed. "Keep your head in the game."

The dealer made introductions around the table and the game began with the married woman in number one in the button seat as dealer. Random chance runs medium to high in hold 'em. But players like to believe they're in control.

Watching the first few rounds, Rock developed a sense of respect for Tate. He knew what he was doing and played every hand just as Rock would have. Rock borrowed a pen and paper from the guy behind the bar and recorded every move he would have made and showed them to Lani as play continued.

Tate played with enough skill that Rock was pretty sure he was counting cards and damn good at reading people. Not to mention he was a lucky bastard. There was no denying that some people were born with lady luck on their side.

"Did Tate ever take a course on probability and statistics?" Rock asked Lani.

She gave a seductive shrug of her shoulders. "I suppose so. He's a software genius. But I've never really asked. It's not what excites me about him."

Either Lani was really good at staying in character, or she just couldn't resist tormenting Rock.

"Want to see my predictive powers of prestidigitation at work?" he asked her.

"Love to. What do you have in mind?"

"I'm going to predict the order in which the players drop out of the game." He had to do something to impress his wife and get her attention back on him. He wrote his predictions on a napkin and showed it to her before placing it facedown beneath another napkin. "For safekeeping."

Not. If Rock's educated guesses were wrong it was a simple matter to switch the list out. Lani had barely glanced at it. If he wrote the order down as the players fell out and replaced the list, she'd never be the wiser.

"You're a gambling man," Lani said. "I like that."

"Do you like gambling enough to place a wager yourself?"

Lani arched a delicate brow. "What do you have in mind?"

"If I guess the order the players fall out of the game correctly, you appear in my act after I come off hiatus."

"Very clever, Rock," Lani whispered in his ear. "I've always wanted to appear as a blonde in a magic act."

Rock returned his focus to the game and watched the play. *Tate should take another card,* he wrote and showed it to Lani just as Tate did just that.

Tate bet aggressively and took chances. He won when the rest of the players folded and took in a large pot.

"You're good," Lani said.

He couldn't be sure whether she was stroking his ego. "Yeah, that's why I'm banned."

As the hours slid by, the stakes rose higher and higher, the losses mounted into staggering millions, and the jovial mood dissipated into nervous tension. The room smelled first of expensive cologne and perfume, and gradually more and more like a gym in the heat of a vicious basketball game.

One by one the players fell out—first the married couple. Then the Cuban who'd started out in the prime position got cocky and irresponsibly reckless and was out.

Lani's cell phone buzzed. She pulled it from her purse and checked her messages. Her eyes lit up and she smiled as she read a text.

Not above eavesdropping, or whatever you call reading someone else's messages, and obviously not above spying, Rock read the text over her shoulder while pretending not to. Magicians were skilled at many things, including reading upside down, sideways, mirror images, and in dimly lit casinos with the victim covering the message for privacy. How else did a good magician get valuable magical intel?

"Good news, I hope," Rock said, acting as if he hadn't the slightest idea what it said when, of course, he'd read the entire message. Sol had just offered Lani the job as his main assistant.

"I just got an audition for a part I've been dying for!"

"Congrats." Rock raised his glass to her in a toast, hating that she'd be working with Sol.

She clinked his glass with hers.

Rock was growing tired of watching poker. "What do you say to speeding the game up and making things interesting?"

"I'm all for interesting," Lani said.

"Good. Make eyes at the nerd every time before he bets," Rock whispered to Lani. He may as well use his wife for the good of the mission. "He's nervous and his lack of composure is beginning to show. He's exposing his tell. See the way his hands shake when he'd got a good hand?

"The other players have certainly noticed that. Make him nervous. Give him a false shake tell. We'll see who that shakes up and causes to make a mistake. Maybe we'll even get lucky and cause the sweet little nerd to lose concentration and screw up."

"You are devious." Lani cooed the words with completely plausible admiration.

"Diversions, darling."

"Isn't that cheating?" Lani said, but her eyes danced.

"There's nothing in the rules that prohibit making eyes at a player. Just as long as Tate doesn't get jealous. Then again, Tate's savvy enough to realize what you're doing."

"You're just trying to cheat now and make that list of yours come true." She smiled seductively at him.

He felt himself growing involuntarily hard. "I did pull diamonds from behind your ear."

"Are you saying you could do it again?"

"Is that blackmail?"

She winked. "Let's get this show on the road."

Rock grinned as Lani turned her gaze on the kid. With the kid's next hand, which Rock was certain was a bad one, he shook like a junkie going cold turkey and was breathing so rapidly it looked as if he might hyperventilate. Rock's little trick was enough to spook the woman with the buzz cut. She folded to cut her losses and lost everything she had in the pot. Which was everything she had left. She'd held the winning hand, but now she was out of the game.

And, yes, Rock was cheating, making sure the players went out of the game in the order he'd predicted.

Luck next turned against the kid and he was out, too. So far Rock's guesses were right on the money. Next the pro fell, going for gusto when he should have held.

And then there were two.

There's no time in a casino, but judging by the way bed was beginning to beckon, it had to be the wee hours of the morning. Rock liked to stay up all night, but in truth he needed his sleep to be sharp in his act.

Bancroft sat in the dealer. The dealer dealt—two cards apiece for Tate and Bancroft. Five on the table, faceup. Tate placed an outrageous bet, enough to bankrupt him, and the U.S. taxpayers, if he lost.

Ah, yes. Tate must be able to count cards. By Rock's reckoning the odds that Tate held the winning hand were in his favor.

Bancroft looked desperate. His stash of cash was running low, but he anted up, looking subtly ashen. If he lost this hand, and the money, which was probably largely his clients', he was a dead man.

Tate's turn again. But before he could place his bet, a funny thing happened. Bancroft's goon with the stylus unobtrusively stuck it in Tate's back between two ribs at an angle that from Rock's point of view looked as if it was aiming directly for Tate's playboy heart.

Rock's mouth went dry. The way the guy held the stylus it looked as if he had his finger on a trigger. *On a trigger—what the—*

And then it hit Rock—that damn stylus wasn't a club. *It's a cleverly disguised gun. Damn.*

The room buzzed around Tate, but no one besides Rock, not even Lani, seemed to notice Tate's dilemma. Except maybe Bancroft, who'd ordered it and had had a change of attitude, as if the winds of fortune had shifted. He looked pleased and as if he was particularly looking forward to his upcoming win.

As Tate considered his next move, Rock watched Bancroft's man. His lips were moving. Rock had learned how to read lips years ago. It was part of the magician's bag of tricks.

The guy with the stylus was quietly counting down from ten into Tate's ear. Now, sure, most people could read lips well enough to recognize someone counting, especially if the counter enunciated clearly. This guy was being subtle, counting for Tate's ears only. Unless Rock missed his guess, which he never did, educated guessing was his trade of craft, Bancroft's buddy was urging Tate to fold on penalty of death. Hobson's choice—lose his life or the hand. And the taxpayers' fifty million.

Rock resisted the urge to look at his thumb gun as the countdown continued. He pointed his thumb like an eager hitchhiker at Bancroft's man. Damn, the woman with the butch haircut obscured his shot. Rock tried another angle. Still no good. It was as if the woman was hell-bent on getting in the way.

Maybe she was. For all Rock knew, she was part of Bancroft's team. Even though she was about as soft and cuddly as a steel-toed boot being wielded by a three-hundred-pound construction worker, Rock couldn't take the chance he'd hit her by mistake. He made a mental note to get some practice with the thumb at the firing range.

Even if Rock were successful in hitting his intended victim, how would it look to shoot Bancroft's thug in public view? This mission was supposed to be hush-hush, not *Famous Magician Rock Powers Kills a Man With His Thumb* headline material.

Rock had his spy ring, but he was too far away for its lethal razor blade to be of much use and he sure as hell wasn't going to hit the panic button.

Rock could signal Tate and alert him to the danger he was in, but it was pretty much a given Tate already knew he was in a precarious position. No, now was the time for magic, in the form of a little diversion. Rock was certain all Tate needed to take care of the situation was an instant to recover the upper hand.

Six, the guy mouthed.

Rock had no time to think so he reverted to boyhood pranks. Tore off a corner of a napkin, rolled it into a ball between his fingers, and stuck it in his mouth.

Five.

Damn, his mouth was dry as cotton. Why did he have so little saliva when he needed it? He took a gulp of his Scotch to soak the spit wad with.

Four.

He raised his straw to his mouth and took aim. He would have preferred a pen barrel as his method of delivery. Pen barrels were more rigid, making for a more accurate shot. But time was of the essence and he didn't have a pen on him.

Three.

He took aim at Bancroft's guy's neck and blew.

Two.

Bancroft's stylus-wielding thug slapped at his neck, momentarily diverted.

Yes! Direct hit.

Tate seized the advantage and shoved his chair back, knocking the stylus out of the man's hand as Tate toppled over backward, taking the chair with him. Lani moved into position. A gunshot went wild. Tate kicked the stylus toward Rock with power and accuracy worthy of a soccer player.

"Tate!" Lani rushed to Tate's side along with the others who'd been at the table, probably to provide backup.

"Baby, are you okay?" Lani crooned to Tate, creating a diversion for Rock.

No one seemed to notice the stylus. While Lani and the others hovered over Tate, who'd fallen back in his chair with the panache and showiness of a stuntman, Rock scooped up the stylus and slid it into his pocket. Stylus concealed, Rock twirled the spitball straw and slid it back into his drink. The spitball worked fine, but think of the damage he could have done with a marshmallow shooter.

"Sorry. Sorry," Tate was saying as he looked appropriately embarrassed and Lani squatted next to him in her teeny tiny dress. Evidently he wasn't going to call the goon out, either. "Yes, I'm fine. Leaned back a little too far in the chair. Had a bit too much to drink, I guess," he looked apologetically at Lani, "and lost my balance."

The Cuban gave Tate a hand up and righted the chair. Lani ran her hands over Tate and through his hair as if checking to make sure everything, most importantly his head, was intact.

"No, I think we're fine to continue," Tate was saying as the rest of the group peppered him with questions and Lani clutched his arm. "Yes. Carry on." He straightened the lapel of his jacket, readjusted his chair, and kissed Lani lightly.

Rock led Lani back to the bar, glad to get Tate's hands off his wife as Tate looked at his cards and placed all of his chips into the pot.

"You're sure, sir," the dealer asked.

"Perfectly." Tate grinned.

Bancroft paled until he looked as paper white as a vampire facing daybreak. "All in."

Each man flipped over his cards for the showdown. The crowd gasped. Tate had somehow managed to compile an unbeatable hand.

"Winner takes all," the dealer said. "Congratulations, Mr. Cox."

Tate scooped up his chips. Shook hands all around the table, playing amiable winner. Bancroft refused to shake. The atmosphere was decidedly tense. It was time to blow this joint in a hurry. Tate left a large tip for the dealer, came to the bar, and slid his arm around Lani. "I think it's time we leave."

Which was one of the great understatements of the century. As if it was wise to hang around with a hundred million in chips and a terrorist bent on killing you.

Tate calmly turned to Rock as if he hadn't a care. "Powers, coming with us?"

Hell, did he have any choice? Rock had a bull's-eye on his back now, too. He walked with them toward the door. The feeling of Bancroft's henchman itching to kill them prevailed, along with the eerie feeling of another unseen evil watching them that had haunted Rock all night.

Rock leaned into Tate. "It's not safe for us to take the usual route out of here. There's a service entrance just to your right. It's time we simply vanished into thin air. Fortunately, I'm good at disappearing.

"See that table, the one with the couple laughing and having drinks? I'm going to give them a little show and perform the old pull-the-tablecloth-off trick. When I flourish the tablecloth like a cape, grab Gillian and run like hell for the service door. You'll only have seconds to disappear."

"You mean that table loaded with drinks and flowers and the lady's purse? That tablecloth?" Tate said. "How about an easier target?"

"Worried? This is my area of expertise. If I can't do the old pull-the-tablecloth-off trick, I should lose my membership in the Academy of Magic."

"Then go to it," Tate said.

Rock reached for the tablecloth. "On my count. One." He grabbed the edge. "Two." He gave it a huge tug. "Three!" He flourished the tablecloth like a cape and ran for the service exit.

CHAPTER SEVEN

The three of them tumbled into the service hallway, laughing as if they'd pulled off the caper of the century, or at least the evening, in high spirits because they'd lived to die another day and pulled one over on RIOT.

Rock locked the service door behind them.

"Great job, simply fabulous!" Lani said. "I was worried about Tate carrying all that hard, cold cash—"

"Million-dollar chips," Tate interrupted. "Worried, hell. There was a time you would have helped Mal murder me."

Lani laughed. "Bygones." Lani turned to Rock. "Saved by magic and disappearing tricks again. We're making a habit of this."

Rock leaned in close to her and whispered in her ear, "The key to successfully disappearing is knowing where the nearest secret exit is."

"And a diversion helps. Like pulling a tablecloth off without spilling things everywhere," Tate said, drily.

"I rather imagine spilling cocktails everywhere would create more of a diversion and takes a lot less skill," Lani said, reverting for a second back to playing Gillian. "But pulling the cloth off was brilliant and showy."

She turned to Rock. "Speaking of tricks and magic, what about our bet? I don't suppose you grabbed the napkin, did you?"

Rock pulled it from his pocket as Tate shot them both a quizzical look.

Lani explained. "Rock bet me he could predict the order the players would fall out and who would win."

"I hope he was betting on me," Tate said.

"Who else?" Rock showed them his empty hands, made a fist, and pulled the napkin out from between his curled fingers.

Lani clapped delicately, almost mockingly, and pulled the napkin from Rock's hand, holding it so she and Tate could read it together. When she finished, she turned her gaze on Rock. "You'll have to teach me this trick."

"I've taught you too many of my secrets already." Rock meant it as an indictment.

Tate watched, apparently amused by their banter. He nodded toward Rock. "What did you wager?"

"She said she'd appear in my act," Rock said. "As a blonde."

Lani shrugged. "When I can work it into my schedule."

"I'm guessing you need a little help negotiating these corridors," Rock said to the two spies. "Where can I take you?"

"To my suite to celebrate," Tate said with a grin. "I'll call the casino manager from there and make arrangements to cash in and deposit my winnings. And then we'll order one of everything from room service and celebrate my good luck."

Rock wound them through the catacombs of the service hallways, which seemed like another universe from the glamour of the hotel and casino the guests saw to the service elevator. They got in along with a blue laundry basket full of dirty towels and rode to the penthouse floor.

"You tempted to keep some of that cash?" Rock asked Tate.

"I have enough money of my own." Tate laughed. "But

it was fun to play with. Kind of gives a new meaning to play dough."

"That was a bad pun," Rock said.

Tate laughed and changed the subject. "Thanks for the help down there," Tate said. "Good thinking. You saved the day without giving us away."

"That's high praise coming from a man of your reputation." They were in an elevator that probably had a camera to keep tabs on the staff. None of them were going to speak directly about the mission.

The elevator dinged. The doors opened. Rock led the way to Tate's suite. Tate let them in with his key card. The room was dark, but the curtains were open, letting in the glow from the neon of the city and the sparkling lights of downtown.

Lani pulled off the blond wig and shook her hair out the moment the door closed behind them, glad to be free of the hot thing.

"That was some performance," Rock said in a hard tone that made it clear he was jealous and angry with her.

She plopped into a chair and kicked her heels off. "Don't go all possessive on me, Rock. You wanted to see the real Lani, and that's what you got. That's what I do. Play roles. Play up to men. Use my sex appeal to distract them. If the mission calls for falling all over my good friend's ex-husband and sticking my tongue down his throat in front of my husband, that's what I do."

As much as she would have enjoyed seeing Tate squirm, he was a seasoned pro. He simply laughed. "Don't drag my ex into this. Thank goodness Mal isn't here."

Rock frowned. "Wait a minute! Aren't marriages and exes strictly against NCS policy?" He flashed Lani a hard, angry look as if she'd betrayed and lied to him again.

"Tate's one of the exceptions. He was married to one

of our own, the Agency's cover life artist, Malene, Mal as we call her, so all the secrets remain in the family."

"Cover life artist?" Rock looked confused.

Tate gave Rock a brief explanation of Malene's job, how she set up cover lives for spies—picked their clothes, set up their homes, decided which kind of car they'd drive, that kind of thing. "Why do you think I never go undercover? If Mal ever got a chance to get her hands on my cover, she'd make my life miserable.

"Besides, I believe in the great spy Dusko Popov's philosophy. He said, 'Your life as a spy is your cover life. If your cover is a dishwasher, you're a dishwasher. If your cover is a playboy, you're lucky.' I'm one lucky bastard."

"Yeah, Tate was born under a lucky star." Lani couldn't resist poking at Tate for Malene's sake. "I, for one, though, would love to see Mal get her hands on you."

"I bet you would," Tate said, drily.

"If you weren't such a favorite of Emmett you'd be in deep trouble." She shrugged. "Though Mal might spare you from complete slaughter for your daughter's sake. Too bad it would take something extraordinary to get you undercover."

"You have a kid, too?" Rock looked really angry now. About to burst.

Tate rolled his eyes. "That was definitely against policy. But accidents will happen."

"She's five and a beauty." Lani smiled.

"She certainly is. No doubt she'll cause me a pile of trouble once she hits her teens." Tate dumped his stash of chips on a nearby table. "She's enough trouble already."

Lani's and Tate's cell phones buzzed at the same time. They grabbed them in unison, like gunfighters going for the draw. "The FBI picked up Bancroft as he left the casino," they said in stereo.

"Good job, boys." Lani pulled off the diamond tennis

bracelet and held it out to Tate. "Better deposit this, too. It's gorgeous." She watched it sparkle in the light. "Is it real or paste?"

"Real. On loan from a jeweler friend. I'll make sure it gets returned." Tate took the bracelet from her and called the house banker to arrange to deposit his winnings.

As they waited for the banker to come to the suite, Rock pulled the stylus from his pocket and showed it to Lani. "A souvenir from the mission."

As she took it from him, she spotted the trigger. "A gun. Very clever." She frowned. "And observant of you to notice Tate was in trouble and improvise. Tate's never going to live down being saved by a hundred-proof spit wad." She paused. "You didn't use your thumb gun?"

"And blow the mission?" Rock stared directly into her eyes with that hypnotic stare of his.

She looked away. If he thought she was going to let him look into her soul, he was mistaken. He couldn't hypnotize her, except by his touch, and his laughter, and his sense of cunning. "And you didn't have a clear shot. Nor did I."

It was just like Rock to think of using a diversion rather than risk lethal force, even in a desperate situation. She was still peeved and embarrassed that Rock had noticed Tate's situation first. Rock could read people and situations with uncanny accuracy. She was good, but not as good as he was.

Rock hadn't known it, he would never know it, but he'd helped her crack the Hoover Dam case. She'd listened to his observations of people, followed the leads he'd inadvertently shown her, and stopped the worst from happening.

She'd never met a man outside the Agency with powers of observation as strong as Rock's. It was part of his attraction. She'd never considered having a relationship with one of her fellow agents. Office romances carried too much risk. But Rock was another matter. Being on the outside and part of a mission with a fixed end date, he'd seemed safe. Until she completely lost her heart to him.

Rock was merely competent with a gun. His self-defense skills left something to be desired. But his mind was the most agile and imaginative she'd encountered. He couldn't actually read minds. He'd be the first to tell you that. He debunked psychics for sport. And yet, he was so observant and intuitive he may as well have been able to.

Lani felt Rock watching her, but refused to meet his gaze. "You take too many risks, Rock." She stared out the window at the winking lights.

"I never wager on success when it counts unless the odds are heavily in my favor."

"Stop being a mother hen, Lani. Rock was brilliant," Tate said.

She was too concerned about Rock's safety and it wasn't good for the mission.

The casino banker arrived, interrupting their discussion. He performed his duties quickly. When he left, they resumed their conversation.

"How about you, Lani?" Tate said. "When do you start rehearsing with Sol?"

"Day after tomorrow. Sol needs a day to pull things together. The big reveal is in five days. Not much time to rehearse, but then I'm good. I got you two tickets. Not front row, but close enough. Rock, you'll be Tate's guest now that the two of you are bosom buddies."

Rock crossed his arms. "I'm not going to Sol's show."

"Oh come on, don't be like that, Rock. This is all great showmanship. Like in *The Prestige*. You show up in his audience to keep tabs on him. He shows you up by reappearing me and the game is on. It's trick for trick."

"Does Sol know I'll be there?" Rock was still frowning.

"It was his idea." Lani stood and went to the console table by the door. She picked up a ticket envelope. "Who do you think sent these tickets to Tate's suite?"

"But how does he know Tate will invite me?" Rock's jaw ticked.

"He issued a challenge, of course. That's the first part of the PR campaign." She read the note that accompanied the tickets. "'I heard you were hanging with Powers at the casino this afternoon. Bring him with you and come see how real magic works. I have a little surprise for Powers. A pleasant one, I hope. You won't be disappointed.'"

Rock's frown turned into a scowl. "Cocky bastard. He really thinks I'll come?"

"He knows you recognize a good business opportunity when you see one. And with that bait, how can you refuse?"

Rock's look remained murderous for an instant before he smiled. Like the devil.

Lani didn't trust him. "Rock."

He smiled at her.

"Don't do anything stupid," she said.

"Stupid." He laughed. "What do you mean?"

"Like trying to upstage him during his show. Like performing some magical feat. Or sabotaging a trick."

"Now why would I do that?" Rock sounded too innocent. "It's not like he's putting a move on my wife."

Lani tried not to flinch under Rock's steady gaze and hard tone.

"Or trying to ruin my career and life or anything," Rock continued.

Tate intervened. "Kids. Play nice." He turned his attention to Lani. "Did you find anything out from Sol?"

"Not yet." She looked frustrated. "But I'll get him to talk."

Rock's eyes narrowed as if he was suspicious of the *way* she was going to get Sol to talk.

Tate nodded and yawned. "It's late and we have plenty of work to do"—he glanced at his watch—"today. Time for some shut-eye. This is a two-bedroom suite. I have the master bedroom. Lani, you take the second bedroom. And Rock, the pullout sofa is yours."

"No, thanks. I think I'll head home to my own bed." Rock pulled his keys from his pocket.

"Not tonight." Tate grabbed Rock's arm. "Too dangerous to be out. Take the sofa. In the morning we'll regroup and go over strategy."

Plush pillows, scads of them. Thousand-count Egyptian cotton sheets. The bed in Tate's suite was as close to heaven as a bed on earth got. As she sunk onto the mattress, Lani could only imagine the scrumptiousness of the master suite. If it outshone this one, it must have simply been the highest level of paradise, like sleeping on a cloud next to the angels.

Tate really was the luckiest agent on earth. Born into money, he got the most expensive, most exotic, most everything cover of any spy in the service. It would serve him right if he did get assigned the cover of a dishwasher.

Not that it will ever happen, Lani thought. Tate Cox was too high-profile and recognizable for the mundane. Still, Lani would pay to see Tate live like the rest of us.

Although many would say that her cover as a magician's assistant wasn't too shabby, either. There was the excitement, the danger, the prestige, the fabulous costumes, the fancy hotel rooms, the money, the fame. Better than being a dishwasher, right?

She flipped off the light and stared at the ceiling. She'd been prepared to spend the night and had brought her skimpy cotton lace nightgown. The hotel provided soft cotton robes. The nightgown was one of her favorites, but she couldn't deny her subconscious had somehow picked it knowing she'd be close to Rock.

And then there's Rock. No matter how hard she tried, she couldn't scrub him from her mind.

She'd never expected to find the perfect man and fall in love. Rock wasn't perfect by any means, not at all. But he was right for her on every level. That is, he would have been right if she were an ordinary woman and not a spy, a spy who'd made the mistake of falling in love.

On the one hand, her attraction to him was completely understandable—women all over the world fell for Rock. He was athletic, built, exotic, tall, and exuded a cute sense of danger. Cute because Lani knew real danger and saw through Rock's façade. On the other hand, Lani dealt with really dangerous men on a daily basis. Well-built, handsome, powerful, cunning men. And none of them, not even the good guys, the NCS agents, thrilled her like Rock did.

For these past two years while she was fruitlessly trying to forget Rock, she'd tried to analyze it. If she could pinpoint what made Rock special, she could develop a counteroffensive on her feelings. That's basic operation training and it may work for love as well as counterterrorism operations.

Rock made her feel part of a group, made her feel like she really belonged somewhere. That was certainly part of it. But so did the Agency. They were a group of like-minded people, thrill seekers and adventurers, who admired and envied her exotic mixed-race ancestry that gave her chameleonlike qualities. So that wasn't the whole thing with Rock.

She pictured him towering above her wielding a

chainsaw as she lay strapped in a box ready to be sawed in half. The stage lights dancing and highlighting the hard planes of his face, the dark eyeliner, the excited light in his eyes. The music blaring. The sense of danger. There was always a chance something could go wrong. And the very real sense of magic that exuded from Rock. Rock the showman who could make magic happen.

And then he'd look at her and the corners of his lips would turn up in the slightest private smile just for her, totally at odds with the hard look of concentration on his face for the audience's sake. And it struck her—Rock was the only man she'd ever truly trusted. She didn't worry that he was a double agent, or an enemy spy, or an agent who had his own career aspirations first and foremost in mind and would sacrifice her if need be.

As he lowered the saw and began cutting through the box, he worked with the utmost, gentlest care. He wouldn't slip. He'd never hurt her. Rock would sooner saw off his own arm than scratch her.

She wouldn't put herself in a vulnerable, unarmed position for anyone but Rock. Trust. Utmost loyalty. Those were qualities she couldn't buy, couldn't manufacture, and almost couldn't fathom. *And that's why*, she thought, *I love him*.

She hadn't been looking for more than a fling. She hadn't been doing more than her job. And then Rock had changed everything.

When she auditioned for the part of one of his assistants, he'd grinned at her and her heart melted. "Don't look so scared. I don't bite.

"I saw women in half and lock them in with tigers. I cuff and chain them. I set them on fire. And levitate them and disappear them. But I don't bite. Despite my somewhat gory reputation, I'm really a very sweet guy at heart."

"Maybe I'm not scared," she'd said. "Maybe I'm just

excited by the thought of all those dangerous situations."
And she was.

He laughed and snapped his fingers. A Monarch butterfly appeared sitting in his hand, delicately perched and
absolutely gorgeous and calming.

She'd gasped and stopped just short of clapping like a
small girl. He really was a marvel. "It's beautiful."

She loved butterflies, loved watching them in her
grandma's butterfly garden. Butterflies were beautiful
and girlie. They were black and white and yellow and tan,
just like her. They floated on fragile wings that a single
touch could destroy. She often felt like that herself.

But they fought like true warriors. Swooped and de-
fended their territory. As strange as many people might
find it, butterflies were her mascot. Rock couldn't have
known that, but it was as if he somehow had read her mind.
He'd materialized the very thing that was guaranteed to
calm and impress her. This man known for his piercings
and tattoos, for cutting his skin in his act and appearing
to draw blood, for his heavy metal music, was at heart a
true gentle spirit and romantic.

"Is it real?" she'd asked.

Rock had held his hand out to her. The butterfly flut-
tered.

She was sure her eyes went wide. "It is." She looked
deeply into his eyes, her voice full of wonder. "But how?"

Rock had grinned. "Magic. Come." He nodded toward
the stage door. "Like all of us, it deserves to be free."

She followed him past the stage, through the lobby,
and outside. He lifted his arm, gave his hand a gentle flip,
and the butterfly flew off in the sunshine toward the bub-
bling fountain. As the butterfly drifted toward light and
water, Lani began falling in love with Rock. And now the
question was, how did she fall out of love? What magic
spell would release her?

A grunt followed by a thump as if someone was thrashing around and struggling cascaded over the soothing hum of the air-conditioning.

Rock!

Lani grabbed her gun, threw the covers back, and bolted out of bed.

CHAPTER EIGHT

Rock struggled and thrashed against the bonds of his sheets wrapped around him securely enough to bind him. He finally broke free and sat bolt upright on the sleeper sofa, breathing hard, his pulse racing, sweat beading on his brow as he tried to come to grips with reality.

The nightmare. The damn recurring nightmare again.

He punched his pillow and fought for breath against the strong involuntary response to hyperventilate. His lungs burned, still held hostage by the emotional power of the dream. Drowning again. An illusion of his mind's own making as potent as any he performed on stage.

He cursed as he gasped for air and willed his pulse to slow. He wasn't some two-year-old in the throes of night terrors, but it sure as hell felt like it. Ever since that accident on the lake when Sol had saved him after he'd been knocked unconscious by his skis, and now with Sol back in Rock's life and Rock's suspicions about just how Lani was planning to get intel out of Sol—

The door to the guest room burst open. Rock jumped and looked up. Lani appeared wearing a gossamer white cotton nightgown that showcased her gorgeous long legs and creamy cappuccino skin.

Damn. There goes my pulse again.

And that was before he saw her nipples budding and poking through the thin cotton. And the gun.

From the top of the stairs, she studied the exits, traced the room with her pistol and drew a bull's-eye around his crotch.

"Geez, Lani, don't shoot! I'm unarmed." He held his hands up as if surrendering. He wasn't about to give her any reason to fire. Especially not at the jewels.

She moved off target and kept the gun up, poised to shoot any intruder as she glided down the stairs, a beautiful, lethal white moth lit by the neon light filtering in from the city below through the open curtains.

He supposed he should have stopped her, told her there was no need for her precautions. But he was too intrigued by her spy routine and the sight of her body beneath the thin gown as she cased the room and peeked behind furniture.

"All clear. Are you all right?" She lowered her gun and sat on the edge of the sleeper sofa way too close and tantalizing for his own good. She smelled of his favorite perfume and her hair was tousled as if she'd just woken up. One strap of her nightgown slid off her shoulder and exposed her luscious breast, stopping just short of her nipple.

He forced himself not to stare at it and looked at her gun instead. Then at her, itching to touch her, kiss her, take her to bed.

"I'm fine. I hope you had the safety on." His voice came out hoarser than he'd intended. Hell, he hadn't intended any hoarseness at all.

"Safety?" Her voice was soft and concerned, seductive. "There is no safety, Rock. Not in my world."

Or his, either.

"Live with the safety on and you end up dead."

He could have told her she was living with the safety

on *against* their relationship, that she should let herself love him and damn the consequences because keeping them artificially apart would kill them both. But creating magic was all in the timing and the timing wasn't right. *Yet.*

She held the gun in her right hand as she braced herself against the mattress with her left. "You called out for me?"

"Did I? For you, specifically?" He pushed her for the truth. He couldn't remember calling her name. But then he'd been dreaming, so maybe he had. Maybe he was worse off than he thought.

"You called out for help. I'm help." She sounded disappointed.

So he hadn't screamed her name. And she wished he had. *Good.*

"Can't a guy have a nightmare around here without getting the third degree and having people react by bringing out the heavy guns?" He looked her in the eye and slid closer to her.

She stared back him, but didn't retreat. "Heavy guns?" She hefted her pistol, but neither of them looked at it. "This? This is nothing. This is a flyswatter. You should see my rocket launcher."

No, she should see his. Which this very minute was gunning to be deep inside her.

She frowned ever so slightly as if struggling to remember something. "The drowning dream?"

As he nodded, his hair fell over his eyes. Before he could brush it out of his eyes, she set her gun on the bed and, with a touch as light as a butterfly's, swept his hair back off his face. It was a gentle, loving, intimate gesture, like that of a mother comforting a child. Or a woman who couldn't resist touching her lover. The latter is what Rock wanted to believe anyway.

"It still haunts you? I'm sorry." Her touch trailed down his cheek to his jaw until she realized what she was doing and retracted her hand as if scorched. In the old days, she'd have held him in her arms, cooed to him, told him funny stories to put the dream in perspective. Not now.

Her lips were inches away from his, so close he could feel her breath as she spoke.

"And that wasn't the third degree," she said as if she was trying to create a diversion and take his attention away from the intimate way she'd just touched him. "A simple question isn't the third degree."

"Is that right? You mean I could have fired a few more at you?" Like why she was fighting what was between them.

She was so near it wouldn't take much to close the gap between them and he was tempted. Tempted to the point of frustration.

She shook her head and smiled. "Don't tease, Rock. The third degree is a spy term for a particular kind of interrogation and you know it."

"Is it?" He inched closer until their arms brushed. "Maybe you should teach it to me."

She laughed softly. "You want me to give you the third degree? You really think you can withstand my methods? If I torture you, you'll be at my mercy."

Maybe that's what he wanted, a little sweet torture. "Who says I'm going to be the victim?"

Her breathing became shallow and, even though the lighting was dim, he thought her eyes dilated even more. "You don't even know what it is."

"Then tell me," he said.

"You shine a very bright light in the subject's eyes as you question them. I'm very good with a light."

"I'm sure you are," Rock said.

She was good with a lot of things.

"But I'm a pro, too," he said. "I face bright, hot lights on stage during every act. I know how to handle myself around them. Lights don't sound like torture to me."

"They are if they're used properly." She held his gaze and damn if he didn't see desire flicker there.

"Anything can be torture if applied with the right technique." Like being so near her again and not touching her. Flirting like they used to.

Her lips moved a fraction of an inch closer to his. "I can teach you the proper technique."

He curled his fingers around her wrist. "As long as I get to be the interrogator." He shifted his weight on the bed as he put his arm around her. The gun slid into him. He picked it up. "It's a good thing we don't have children. This would scare the hell out of them. A simple glass of water is usually considered the best remedy for a bad dream."

Lani froze and a look passed over her face so quickly the average person would have missed it. But not Rock. *She feels guilty about something. The mention of children upsets her.*

As maybe it should have since the odds of them having any now were about nil.

"You're right." She took the gun from him and, without breaking eye contact, set it on the table next to the sofa bed. "But this isn't your average situation. You've already had one attempt on your life and there's a dangerous terrorist cell that wants you dead. Extra precaution seems warranted."

She was covering. Expertly. But still covering.

"Dreams of drowning aren't really about drowning," she said. "They usually mean you feel your life is out of control or your problems are figuratively drowning you." She traced a pattern on his arm and his breath caught. "I'm sorry, Rock. I am. You have to believe me—I didn't want to come back and disrupt your life—"

He cupped her face, "I'm pretty sure this one is a memory from the time I really did almost drown."

She continued to hold his gaze. "Yes, you told me about that. But not the details."

And he wasn't about to start now and give away that he owed Sol his life. "I never talk about the details. They aren't important." He cradled the back of her head, put an arm around her waist, pulled her close, and kissed her.

There wasn't much harm in a kiss, was there? As the saying goes, a kiss is just a kiss. Lani had played femme fatale and used her charms to get intel throughout her spy career. She'd started that way with Rock in the beginning of the Hoover Dam caper. Before she'd lost her professional control and fallen in love with him.

She walked a thin line. String him along just enough to get him to trust her again and keep him cooperative, but not get so close that he'd guess the secret she was keeping from him. And damn, how did she keep a son a secret from one of the world's best mentalists? Neither RIOT nor Rock knew about Stone. She couldn't risk her baby's safety by letting Rock find out he had a son. Both he and Stone would be at risk, and the country as well.

Being this intimately close to Rock was a supreme test of her spy capabilities. In the past, in a situation like this, she locked up her heart and concentrated on the lust, the animalistic physical pleasure. The private, vulnerable Lani was far away. The spy Lani was in control. To the spy, the man didn't matter except as a means to an orgasmic end and the intelligence she wanted. But Rock had never let her get away with resorting to impersonal animal instincts. Only he had ever penetrated her soul.

Rock slid her nightgown off her shoulder, exposing her breast fully.

"So you think you know me well enough for this now?" she whispered. "Even after seeing me with Tate?"

"Especially after seeing you with Tate." He sucked her breast until she gasped and threw her head back.

No emotions, just lust. She repeated the mantra as if it were a magical spell that could protect her heart from Rock's sensual assault. As if he wasn't the man she'd loved enough to inadvertently marry. As if the bonds of creating a baby together didn't exist. As if he wasn't the father of the baby she'd die to protect.

He laid her back on the bed. Trailed kisses down her neck as she ran her fingers through his hair. *Still in control. Just lust.*

He pressed himself between her legs until she wanted to release him from the confines of his boxers and slide him into her.

Rock conveniently wore very little to bed—a pair of tight boxer briefs that showcased his erection straining to get free and nothing else. No inconvenient shirt to remove. Nothing to hastily pull over his head and toss aside while she couldn't wait to get at him. Just his hard, tattooed chest to stroke and caress, lit by the strobe of colorful neon lights filtering in through the window making him appear as if he really were enchanted. His shoulder to gently bite and nibble until he groaned.

Very much in control, she thought.

She traced her finger around his nipple until it budded. But as she reached up to lick and taste his wonderfully hard pecs, she stopped short. Hidden in the complicated tapestry that covered his chest, just over his heart, was a new tattoo, an intricate web of words.

She ran her fingers through his hair, hoping he wouldn't notice as she read the inscription.

Lani in omne tempus.

The words spiraled into a cleverly subtle heart shape, so understated it was almost as if it was trying to fool the viewer. An optical illusion. One of Rock's magic tricks, the secret of the trick hidden in plain view. It was woven into the pattern of dragons and magic lore already in action across his toned frame.

Lani's Latin was rusty to nonexistent, but these words were an inside joke between them. Rock's was a playful jest at adolescent girls and yet full of meaning at the same time—*Lani until all time*. In the immortal words of mooning girls everywhere—*Lani forever*.

And the spiral heart? The heart was obvious enough. The spiral was a symbol of magic and energy.

Her spy resolve cracked, simply shattered. The real Lani broke through—

"Halt or I'll shoot!" With a perfect sense of timing, Tate stood at the top of the stairs, dressed in the fluffy, white, terry, hotel bathrobe, holding a gun on them and wearing an expression very much like a father who'd just discovered his daughter caught in flagrante delicto.

Lani slid from beneath Rock, made herself decent, and grabbed her gun. Next to her Rock had managed to pull his boxers up. He looked stunned, frustrated, and highly pissed at Tate. No doubt if he'd been capable of real magic, he'd have disappeared Tate for good.

"Sorry. My mistake." Tate grinned, but he was smart enough not to drop the gun. "I heard a noise and came to the rescue. RIOT assassins can be such pesky creatures. Tenacious, too. And capable of scaling tall buildings and cutting through penthouse windows."

"It took you long enough. Rock called out in his sleep ten minutes ago," Lani said. "We could have both been killed in the time I've been down here."

"I can see that." Tate slipped his hand into his pocket and smirked.

Lani frowned at Tate. Sometimes he could be a real

ass. "Rock had a bad dream. I came down to see if he was okay."

"And I see you were just about to give him something to make him sleep soundly again." Tate winked.

She didn't need to be a mind reader to know what he was implying—a good screw and a mind-blowing climax were the most effective soporifics around.

"Now that everything's all locked up nice and tight and everyone's safely tucked in, I can turn back in." Tate rested his hand on the light switch.

"Hold on!" Lani said. "I'm coming up, too." The mood was ruined and she was regaining to her senses.

"Lani—"

Lani aimed her palm at Rock to stop him from protesting, and turned and stormed up the stairs.

"Next time try a glass of warm milk," Tate said to no one in particular and laughed to himself.

At the top of the stairs, Lani brushed past him.

"Don't glare at me," Tate whispered to her. "You asked me to have your back and save you from yourself. I gave you plenty of time to back off."

He smiled. "You'll thank me in the morning."

CHAPTER NINE

*L*ani *is different*, Rock thought as he sat across the breakfast table from Tate and Lani, studying her and listening to Tate as they ate scrambled eggs. *Softer*. Something had dulled her hard, tough edge. He hadn't noticed it until last night in bed. The way she'd come to him and comforted him. The way she'd dropped her guard and almost let him make love to her. As if she needed him. If only Tate hadn't interrupted . . .

Rock liked the new softness. And at the same time, he didn't. Whatever had changed her had made her less impenetrable, vulnerable, even if only slightly. Vulnerability couldn't be good for a spy. Isn't that why Bond's true love interests always had to die?

Lani was dressed for breakfast in the big, white, cotton hotel robe. Even as bundled up as she was, Rock couldn't stop staring at her.

"Now that we've vanquished one small head of the Hydra that's RIOT, it's time to get down to the business of Outlandish Marauders," Tate said.

"It's just too bad Bancroft apparently doesn't know anything about it," Lani said. "At least not that our friends at the Bureau could find out overnight."

Tate shrugged. "They should have let us have Bancroft." He winked. "Nothing we can do for now. Back to our business. First things first. Talented young magicians, I hear you need some."

Rock perked up and looked at Tate. "Yeah. I have a list of the kinds of talents I need."

"I know." Tate grinned. "And I have a group of candidates lined up to audition for you."

"You know a lot about magicians?" Rock said.

"Lani helped screen them."

Just as Nelson had said, this plan had obviously been in the works a while. Rock turned his gaze on Lani again.

She gently shrugged. "I know what you look for in your onstage help."

"You mean like loyalty?" Rock helped himself to a plate of eggs.

Lani fired back. "I'm loyal, to the right people."

Rock ignored her. "What time do auditions start? Do I have time for a cup of coffee with my eggs?"

"Tonight," Tate said.

"Tonight?"

"Eager?" Tate took a sip of coffee.

"Yeah, we need every minute of rehearsal time we can get. We've already wasted a day. In the meantime, we'll have to go over my equipment needs, check into rehearsal space—"

"Not so fast." Tate set down his fork. "You won't find the kind of talent we need in Vegas. This requires a road trip to Los Angeles."

"Okay." Rock shrugged. The CIA was impossible to fight. He had to trust they'd allowed him enough time to get the illusion into shape. "Are we taking your plane?"

"Plane? What part of road trip don't you understand?" Tate said. "We'll get to LA just as fast, and have a hell of a lot more fun driving. With the added bonus of not having to drag out my corporate pilot and file a highly traceable flight plan."

"You mean if *you're* driving, don't you, Tate?" Lani spoke to Rock. "Tate loves driving. Fast."

Tate grinned. "I don't drive fast. I just fly low. We'll leave after breakfast."

"I'd better go put my face on then." Lani pushed back from the table.

For most women, that was a figure of speech. But Lani was literally going to put another face on and become another woman.

"All right, Gillian, baby," Tate said. "But don't take too long."

"She's going to be Gillian again today?" Rock didn't think he could stomach another day of Tate and Lani falling all over each other.

"I can't very well parade around as myself," Lani said. "Besides, I was seen going into Tate's hotel room last night with the two of you. Think of the rumors that will be flying!" She winked and pushed back from the table.

"Good point. You can show me a little public affection today, too," Rock said.

"Sorry, but regardless of the rumors, Gillian's a one-man undercover woman." She laughed and shook her head before disappearing upstairs.

"You're never going to win Lani back by being that way," Tate said after Lani left. He was still sitting at the table finishing the last of his coffee. "That's what you want, isn't it?" Tate said when Rock didn't reply. He was grinning. "What else could there be in it for you?"

"The thrill. Duty to my country. The cash. Getting to perform the illusion of a lifetime. Should I go on?" Rock said.

Tate laughed loudly, calling Rock on his outright lie, and shook his head. "Come on, you can lie better than that. I can help you, you know."

Rock stared back at him. Tate didn't blink. Neither did

Rock. They were locked in a kind of playboy, macho man game of who will blink first.

"Really," Rock said. "What do you know about women other than how to bed them? I don't need your help. I do pretty damn well in that department myself."

Tate laughed again. "You're such a sucker. Don't believe what Lani told you earlier about my ex-wife. Our decision to divorce was mutual. We both wanted different things. When we were together, I made her extremely happy.

"But that's neither here nor there. Women like me because I like them and know how to treat them. I know what women want."

Rock let out a loud snort of disbelief at Tate's incredibly egotistical statement, causing him to blink and probably lose the damn competition and alpha-male edge. "What? Wait! Don't tell me. This is where you spout pabulum you've skimmed from women's magazines and online help articles. Save your breath. I know how to read."

Tate shook his head. "Rock, Rock, Rock. You need to trust me, man. I know of which I speak. You want Lani back. You not only want her back, you want her back madly, passionately in love with you." Tate's gaze was steady and piercing.

Right then, Tate looked too much like a mind reader for Rock's tastes. And felt like one, too. Rock kept forgetting these secret agents were as adept, or nearly so, at reading people as he was.

"Genius observation. For the last two years I've made that pretty clear pretty publicly. Hell, I've literally put up a billboard."

Tate was unperturbed. "Yes, you wanted her back. But you don't really have her back, do you? Not in the way you'd imagined. You can bluff and bluster all you like, but I can see right through you, my friend. You want Lani back, Lani the loving wife. Lani forever. And I can help you. Not just because I know women, but because I know Lani.

"It's been written all over your face since I met you. You want her and you want the magic of what you had. The magic of love." Tate winked. "I'm not a master magician, but I do know about love. I can give you the love potion you're looking for. Of course, I'll want something in return.

"That's the way it works with love potions and secret agents. There's always a price."

Rock was interested now, if for no other reason than he'd like the amusement of hearing what the pompous ass had to say. "And what would that be?"

"It'll be obvious when I give you what you want—the secret of making Lani fall in love with you again."

Rock resisted the urge to purse his lips or furrow his brow in thought. He put on his poker face. "I don't make blind deals—what will this priceless information cost me?"

"I'll need your complete allegiance for the duration of this mission—I'll have your back and you'll have mine. No hesitation. No enemy lines between us."

"Fair enough." He could use someone watching his back. He held out his hand to shake.

Tate took it and shook firmly.

"Amaze me with the secret to Lani's heart," Rock said.

"Also fair enough." Tate stood and poured himself a third cup of coffee. He carried it to the couch and took a seat.

Rock followed him and plunked down in a chair across from him.

"Lani, like all the female agents in NCS, is an alpha woman. She likes to think she's tough and independent, but deep down she's still a woman. And what all women want are two things—to be appreciated for who they are, who they really are, and for their men to protect them and meet their innermost needs."

Rock rolled his eyes. "I hope there's more."

"I'm just getting started," Tate said. "Besides a certain quirk of personality, what makes a woman an alpha?"

Rock frowned. "I've never thought about it."

Tate grinned. "And that's your first mistake. You're in love with a strong, independent woman, an alpha, and you haven't bothered to wonder what made her that way?" He shook his head. "A need to prove herself," Tate answered for Rock. "A need to protect herself so she can't be hurt again."

"Lani? Hurt?" Rock was angry and thinking now, imagining all kinds of things like child abuse. "She never mentioned anything."

"When she was young and impressionable," Tate said. "Oh, come on, man. This is easy. All you have to do is look at Lani."

"She's beautiful and confident—"

"And she's a complete mutt. She has no community," Tate said. "No ethnic heritage to relate to. She's a quarter black, a quarter white, a quarter Hispanic, and a quarter Asian. She's not anything. She belongs nowhere. Each group makes fun of her, tells her she can't relate to them. Her parents were both half-breeds. They had no real sense of community, either.

"All that wounds a child. Children are joiners, belongers. Anyone who doesn't fit in with the mainstream is an outcast. Made fun of. Teased. Bullied."

Rock swallowed hard, imagining a little Lani being pushed around and bullied. Just the thought of Lani being tormented made him want to punch someone.

Tate paused, studying him. "Have you guessed the secret key yet, Mr. Wise and Mighty Oz?"

Rock didn't answer. He didn't have one.

"Lani has a burning need to belong. Make her feel like she does and she'll be yours forever. That's the first part, the internal obstacle you have to overcome. Impressed yet? Worth your pledge?"

Tate was a fricking genius. Though Rock would never say so out loud.

"That's why Lani loves the Agency so much; why she'll never give it up. We're a collection of like-minded people. A collection of fakers and freaks, actors and liars. A place where a woman of her unique ethnic background is an asset, not a liability. We give her the chance to pick an ethnic group and relate. She'll never leave us, no matter what it costs her to stay."

Rock's mouth went dry.

"There was another place she felt she belonged," Tate continued, almost too casually. "She told me herself. Another place where all those assets of hers fit in—in the magic community with you."

Rock felt suddenly cold, as if Tate had hit him with a sledgehammer. Why hadn't he seen it himself? Maybe he was afraid she'd been faking that, too.

"Deer in the headlights!" Tate was obviously enjoying himself. "You are such a neophyte where women are concerned. A rank amateur. You really didn't know. I told you. I'm worth my weight in platinum when you need advice with women."

"But she left me—"

"For us. Because she had to. Because NCS put her in an impossible situation—lose you or lose us. She can't have both. And she knew us better. Knew what we offered. We can protect her."

"Then I'm screwed," Rock said.

Tate shook his head. "Not necessarily. You have two choices staring you right in the face—give her a stronger sense of belonging with you than with us. Show her you can keep her safe. After all, you can give her something we can't, true love." Tate grinned. "Does that sound corny? Sorry."

"And behind door number two?" Rock said.

"That's obvious, too. Join us permanently. I'm living proof that marriage between Agency employees is allowed with the chief's blessing."

Rock must have looked as stunned as he felt because Tate's grin spread from ear to ear. He looked as if he was having the time of his life.

"Oh, come on," Tate said. "We have great benefits. And a pension plan." He took a sip of coffee and set the cup on the stand next to him.

"You have time to think it over. I'm not pressing you for any kind of decision. See how this mission goes. See if you like it. You asked for your love potion, for the key to winning Lani's love, and I gave it to you. Is it worth the price now?"

"But how do I—"

Tate held his palm up to Rock to stop him. "The execution is up to you. I only promised the secret."

"Tricky bastard," Rock muttered, lost in thought. Everything Tate had said made perfect sense.

"I'll give you one more piece of intel to help you out. Lani was picked for the original mission for many reasons, but a big part of it was her familiarity with magic. You may not know this, but her African-American grandfather was a magician. One of the first men of color to be inducted into the International Brotherhood of Magicians' Hall of Fame."

"What?" So that's where Lani learned her rudimentary knowledge of magic.

"You never wondered why a dancer took to magic so easily?"

No, Rock hadn't thought about it at all. "Was her grandpa anyone famous?"

Tate shrugged. "He was a local club magician. He did gigs everywhere, including department stores. But was he famous like you are? No. Just small-time stuff.

"But Lani loved him. She was his little assistant. Magic holds good memories for her. It's homey and reminds her of the best aspects of that miserable childhood of hers." Tate gave Rock a minute to digest the news. "Time to pay the piper. Why does Sol Blackledge hate you so much?"

"Wait a minute—when did I agree to answer questions about Sol?" Rock said.

"It falls under the allegiance clause. It's in the fine print."

Rock shook his head and smiled. "Okay, you got me there. This could take a while. How long do we have?"

"Until Lani comes back downstairs."

"You'll need the short version then," Rock said. "We were roommates and pals when we were both starting out and taking classes at the Magic Castle.

"Back in those days, we were cocky, ambitious young guys. Full of ourselves and certain we'd be big stars." Rock grinned. "Come to think of it, we haven't changed, just aged. Anyway, Sol was good, just not as good as I am. He had flair and showmanship, but not creativity. He could copy, but he couldn't create.

"I've always been creative. I see tricks in my head and envision how to work them, how to stage them, the costumes, every detail.

"People started noticing me and my act. I got buzz. Filled small venues and got booked at bigger ones. I was doing better than Sol. Surpassing him. With an ego twice the size of his talent, he couldn't stand it. It didn't make any sense to him. It wasn't fair.

"Sol's a chronically jealous bastard. The more I succeeded, the angrier and more vindictive he became. Behind my back, he started bad-mouthing me, spreading rumors, sabotaging tricks, leaking some of my secrets.

"I put up with a lot of shit from him until he got so crazy, I couldn't take it anymore. We got into a fistfight one night. I broke his pretty-boy nose." Rock laughed. "That was it. We parted ways.

"But we've never stopped competing."

Tate nodded. "You were RIOT's first choice, too, weren't you?"

Rock frowned, taking a trip down memory lane. "Yeah. I realized that once Nelson dragged me into this mission. About the time Sol and I parted ways. I had bigger ideas than my bank account could afford. A group of investors, venture capitalists they said, approached me about backing me. Or rather their representative did. I never met the actual big guys behind it. I turned them down."

"Why?" Tate asked.

"They wanted an equity stake in my show and tricks." The memories came flooding back. "The assholes wanted creative control, too. They wanted to dictate what tricks I could and could not perform. I told them to go to hell. No one tells me what to do as an artist. The money wasn't worth the loss of control and artistic direction. Looks like I made a lucky escape."

Rock frowned and snorted to himself. "Shortly after that Sol came into a pot of cash and started performing some of his large-scale illusions, the ones that launched his career.

"Including one he stole from me. One I was trying to finance on my own. I always figured the little shit took those big shits' money. He sold out." Rock stared at Tate. "Why am I telling you this? You know at least the basics already."

Tate didn't answer.

"I never knew how Sol got that trick," Rock said, still thinking about it. "I'd kept it top secret. Told no one. It was one of those illusions I'd had no money to set up and perform. I knew it was a winner and I was right. He got his first TV appearance because of it. It launched Sol's career.

"Sol has always claimed he came up with it independently. A case of great minds thinking alike. But that's pure bullshit and he knows it. The execution was identical to what I'd planned. He wasn't even smart enough to make a few changes to throw me off."

"Were you working on Outlandish Marauders while you lived with Sol?" Tate leaned forward.

"I've been working on and dreaming of Outlandish Marauders since I was sixteen. I have notebooks filled with doodles and notes." Rock stopped short. "Sol stole Outlandish Marauders that long ago? But it wasn't finished—" Rock cursed beneath his breath. "You mean RIOT has been spying on me all these years?"

Tate nodded. "It appears so."

Rock swore some more. "I stepped up security after I realized what Sol had done. And since I've gotten famous, I've hired the best security experts. If RIOT got past them, they're very good."

"They are," Tate said. "Almost as good as we are."

Lani came downstairs dressed in a sleeveless, short, flirty, casual dress with black, white, and gray horizontal stripes and enough spandex to hug her curves. She wore black platform peep-toe pumps and the blond wig and carried an oversized white purse. She was Gillian again, but she still turned Rock's head and turned him on.

"Ready to go, boys?"

Rock couldn't stop staring at her. "We could take one

of my cars, but the Lamborghinis only fit two. In fact, except for the SUV my staff uses, they pretty much all only fit two."

Tate shrugged. "Looks like we're stuck with the rented Audi S8."

CHAPTER TEN

The valet brought the gray Audi S8 sedan around.

"It's not as sleek as a coup, but for a sedan it's pretty hot. With three of us, it'll have to do." Tate was staring at it as if it were a woman he'd like to sleep with.

Rock admired it, too, but he wasn't the car buff Tate apparently was.

The valet parking attendant reluctantly got out of the Audi and held the front passenger door open for Lani. She slid in, giving him a view of her long, lean legs. Rock admired them, too. Lani caught him in the act and frowned at him.

Rock balled his fist and climbed into the backseat as Tate grabbed the keys from the attendant and climbed into the driver's seat. Seconds later, they peeled out of the lot and darted through traffic toward I-15 and the open road.

"Rock, buddy, as my friend," Tate said, "you're going to have to stop ogling my girl so openly." Tate laughed.

Lani made a kissing motion at Rock in the rearview mirror and laughed. "I hope you don't get motion sickness. The way Tate drives, riding in the backseat can be hell."

"What are you, saying, baby?" Tate laughed. "I drive smooth."

Lani ran her fingers along Tate's jaw and laughed. "I have Dramamine," she said to Rock.

Rock just clenched his fist.

The open road wasn't really all that open. But it didn't seem to faze Tate, or slow him down. He took the car up to 120 mph. Slow-moving traffic, meaning anything traveling under a hundred mph, was nothing to Tate. He dodged and wove through traffic without cursing or calling people idiots, and without slowing down. He was completely unperturbed. Rock would have felt more comfortable if he'd been in the driver's seat. He sure as hell wouldn't have been going 120.

"What does this thing top out at?" Rock asked to be conversational. If he'd been a woman this might have been construed as a hint to slow down.

For her part, Lani looked as if she was enjoying the ride.

"Top end is so yesterday. No one talks about red line," Tate said as he darted into the right lane to pass a slow-moving car in the left and the guy in the car he passed gave him the finger. "It's all about acceleration. This baby can go zero to sixty in four seconds. Not bad for a sedan."

"The trip's about three hundred miles," Rock said, doing the math. "You're planning on getting us there in two to three hours?"

"Less if we hit an open stretch of road and no one needs to stop to take a piss."

"Sure you don't want that Dramamine?" Lani said with a tease in her voice.

Rock ignored her. "Is that ETA with or without the automatic jail time you'll get if you get stopped?"

"Not to worry," Tate said. "I have a radar detector and an official *get out of jail* card from the CIA." He laughed and stole a quick look in the mirror at Rock. "Worried about my driving? I'm a pro. I've taken so many extreme driving courses I'm certified to teach."

"No, not at all worried about you. Just a bit concerned about stray dogs, potholes, bumps, blowouts, and little old ladies with slow reflexes who pull out for a Sunday drive."

"None of that's a problem. I can dodge all that in my sleep. Besides, it's not Sunday." He winked at Rock.

Rock arched a brow. "I hope you have a pilot's license, buddy, because we're flying." Done with his civic duty and pleading for his life, Rock settled back to enjoy the trip.

Two and a half hours later, they pulled to a stop along Malibu Beach.

"Are we holding auditions at the beach?" Rock said, looking out the window.

"Sorry, man, forgot to mention we have to pick up a friend." Tate turned off the engine and jumped out of the car, followed by Lani.

Rock trailed after them. "Friend or fellow agent?"

Tate shrugged. "Both." He took off his sunglasses, glanced at his watch, and looked around. "We're two minutes early." He sounded disgusted, like he should have lingered at the last stop sign just so he could arrive precisely on time.

"I could have told you not to drive so fast," Lani said with a smirk. "We had plenty of time."

"You timed this whole trip down to the two-minute mark?" Rock couldn't believe it.

"The spy game is all about precision. And I know my shit."

Just then a bronzed surfer dude with rippling abs, sun-bleached brown hair, and dressed in board shorts flipped his hair out of his eyes as he walked toward them. Three women in his path sighed.

"Ah, there he is now." Tate waved to the approaching surfer.

"Now that's magical timing." Rock couldn't help being impressed.

"Ty, dude!" Tate grabbed the approaching surfer and the two shook hands and slapped each other on the back.

Rock got a whiff of coconut and suntan lotion on the stiff breeze that was blowing.

The surfer saw Lani and pulled her into a hug. "Good to see you, Magic." He took a step back and looked her over. "You look terrific. Good to be back in the field, huh?"

It irked Rock that this new guy immediately recognized Lani in disguise and called her Magic.

"How's the surfing today? Epic as always? There's a nice wind blowing," Tate said.

Ty shook his head. "Too many geeks and poseurs out. And the heavies are getting out of control. In a minute they'll fly the meatball."

Rock had no idea what Ty was talking about, probably, again, because he was speaking in code. It was all Greek, make that surfer slang, to him. While Tate nodded along as if he understood, Rock pondered the sight of flying meatballs. He hoped it wasn't code for bullets whizzing by. In the company of spies, you just never knew.

Tate made introductions. "Ty, meet my man Rock Powers. Rock, Ty."

"Dude, like the magician?" Ty said as he shook Rock's hand.

"The same."

"Mondo."

Rock looked at Tate with a *what the hell does mondo mean* expression. Tate smiled and shrugged as if it didn't matter.

"Ty, you up for joining us for some drinks and a little magic? Rock here's our ticket into the Magic Castle."

"Awesome!" Ty said.

"Magic Castle?" Rock said.

Lani leaned over and cooed in his ear, "You mean you

didn't guess? It seems the obvious place. Where else would we hold auditions for magicians?"

"Just about any auditorium would do," he said.

"But it wouldn't be nearly as much fun. Besides, we're all dying to get into the Castle."

Spies!

Rock looked Ty over, wondering if the surfer even owned a suit. "You'll have to change first. We'll all have to change. Suits and ties are required." He looked down at Ty's bare feet. "And shoes."

"No problem. We can change at the bungalow."

Rock speared Tate with a look. "You should have let me in on the plan. I would have grabbed my tux. I hope you packed us a change of clothes."

Tate winked. "I'm sure Ty has something for us at the bungalow."

There wasn't room in the Audi for the surfboard. Ty headed out on foot, saying he'd meet them there. Tate seemed to know the way without needing directions. The bungalow was only a few blocks from the beach, but they had to wait nearly ten minutes for Ty to show up on foot, carrying his board over his head. It had taken Tate, Lani, and Rock mere seconds to reach it in the airplane Tate called a car.

Ty unlocked the bungalow door and held Tate, Lani, and Rock back with his board. Not horribly hospitable of him, but nothing surprised Rock anymore. As Ty scanned the small premises, he aimed the board like a weapon from point to point around the room. "Disabling the security system," Ty whispered. Finally, he nodded, held the board out of the way, and extended his arm in a gesture of welcome. "All clear."

When they were all in and the door closed behind them, Tate grinned and ribbed Ty. "A surfer cover, again? At this rate you're going to be typecast."

Ty shrugged. "Says the man who never goes undercover as anyone other than himself." He punched Tate playfully in the arm and set his surfboard down in the corner. "I'm a damn awesome surfer, dude. The best in the Agency. I have the looks." He winked as if making fun of himself. "I know the lingo. There are worse covers. I could be a dishwasher." He grinned at Rock and winked. "Or a magician."

Ah, the Popov reference again, Rock thought, ignoring the jibe at magicians.

"So how's the wife? How's Treflee doing these days?" Tate asked Ty.

"Crabby. Big as a blimp and ready to pop. The kid's due in less than a month. If we don't get this mission wrapped up so I can get my butt back for that birth, I'm in deep shit."

"Poor Treflee. It's horribly uncomfortable to be pregnant in the heat," Lani said.

What does Lani know about being pregnant? Rock thought.

"She loves the car seat you gave her for the shower," Ty said to her.

"Oh, I'm so glad. I knew she'd get a kick out of the tropical beach print of the seat cover. But really, with the speeds you drive, Ty, your baby needed the safest one on the market—"

"Wait a minute," Rock said, interrupting the banal baby banter. "You're married and expecting a kid?"

Ty nodded. "Our first."

Rock frowned. "Your wife is a spy then, too?"

Ty shook his head and snorted. "Of a sort. She thinks she is, anyway."

Now this was really too much. Rock glared at Tate and Lani. This no-wife stuff was bullshit to keep him in line. "I thought you said agents aren't supposed to marry outside the Agency and no one is supposed to have kids."

Tate slapped Rock on the back. "Ty was already engaged when we recruited him and stubborn enough to insist he wouldn't join unless he could marry the wench. There wasn't much the chief could do about it."

"And now we're expecting our first little agent," Ty said. "It's a risk. But the wife wanted kids." He shrugged. "The chief doesn't like it, but that's life."

Rock glowered at Tate.

Tate shrugged. "Don't blame me. I only said the Agency frowns on marriage."

Ty walked to the fridge, pulled out three beers, and shot one each to Rock and Tate. Good thing Rock had quick reflexes. He caught his and popped it open. Ty handed Lani a flavored water. He evidently knew Lani well.

"Ah shit, that's right," Ty said, with a tease in his voice. "You're Magic's old man." He turned to Lani. "I keep forgetting you took the plunge." He was obviously ribbing her now. "Did I ever send you a wedding present?"

"Shut up." Lani glared at Rock and back to Ty. "Treflee's been threatening to. I told her not to bother."

Rock scowled.

Ty pulled a shirt on. "I can't believe you had an Elvis wedding, Lani. Tref says you're a girlie girl at heart. We always pegged you for a big, fancy, princess-style wedding."

Lani shrugged. "Next time around." She glanced at Rock as he tried to keep his cool. "I know. I'm not a fan of the King. Not even the 1970's one with the white spandex and the fringes."

How did these two know so much about Lani that he didn't?

"You never mentioned you didn't like Elvis," Rock said to her. "We could have gone somewhere else. If I'd known—"

She shrugged. "What does it matter?"

"It matters because I would have found another chapel. Anything to make you happy and give you the wedding you'd dreamed of."

"It was a quickie thing," she said. "I didn't even want to get married."

"She told us you drugged her," Ty said with twinkle in his eye.

"I did not drug her." Rock looked to Lani for help. "Tell them."

"Hypnotized her, then," Ty said.

"You can't hypnotize someone and make them do something against their will. Especially not if they're drunk. Lani married me because she *wanted* to." He stared her in the eye. "The rest is all bullshit denial on her part. I didn't have to do any coercing. And I didn't."

Lani didn't defend him.

Ty exchanged a look with Tate. "I'm pretty sure we can hypnotize someone while they're drugged, can't we? Or drunk? Or drugged and drunk?"

"And tied up," Tate said. "Or not. Hell, we have drugs that we slip to people to *aid* with the hypnosis process. For those highly resistant subjects. It's all part of our intel gathering, interrogation war chest. The conspiracy theory nuts are always accusing us of that very thing. Like hypnotizing entire crowds, thousands at once."

Tate shook his head. "Yeah, that crowd theory thing is over the top. We can't do that. I mean, maybe a dozen willing subjects, like in a show. But thousands?"

"Exactly," Ty said. "I think I've seen a few hypnosis-induced marriages in the case files. Am I wrong?"

"No," Tate said. "You're right. You're very right."

Rock couldn't tell whether they were messing with him or not, but he was tired of the conversation. "Enough of this bullshit. What's the plan at the Castle? Do these kids think they're just auditioning for me? I assume you haven't told them they're actually auditioning for the CIA."

Tate laughed. "Of course we have. How could we get them to do this mission without letting them know they're working for us while working for you?

"They all applied via our online job application. They've been carefully screened with background checks, and signed nondisclosure agreements just to get the opportunity to audition. The Agency has been watching some of them for years, hoping to recruit them. Part of the test is whether they can keep a secret. Anyone who couldn't keep quiet was eliminated."

"Not literally, I hope," Rock said.

"From the competition for the jobs." Tate winked.

"Yes, but doesn't advertising for magicians give the mission away to RIOT?" Rock didn't understand secret agents.

"Why would it? Our online application is completely secure," Tate said. "Otherwise, how would we ever get new recruits? We can't track and invite everyone we need. And besides, RIOT knows we've been looking for a John Mulholland replacement for years."

Rock shook his head. "Whatever you say. I guess this means I'm sponsoring the event and your night at the Castle. You three are just coming along for the ride while I hire for my top-secret NUFO show, that's the cover?"

"Exactly," Tate said.

"I hope I made reservations for dinner and booked an audition stage," Rock said. "Otherwise we'll be auditioning at Taco Bell."

"Naturally," Tate said.

Rock grinned. "Good to know the people at the Castle don't hold a grudge. Last time I was there a few of my guests got out of hand. Sawed some furniture in half and couldn't put it back together, if you know what I mean."

"We're the CIA," Tate said. "We have powers of persuasion. And apps that handle everything."

"Lani, I mean, Gillian, is your arm candy." Rock hitched his thumb toward Ty. "What's surfer boy's story for tonight? How is he part of our party?"

Tate laughed. "He's an old college bud of mine I ran into and you invited along."

Ty glanced at the clock. "I'd better hit the showers if we're going to make it to our reservation on time."

Rock turned to Tate. "I assume you have our tuxes in the trunk?"

"I have mine."

"You're slipping in the mind-reading polls." Ty strode to a closet near the entryway and threw the doors open. "Formalwear, anyone? Malene sent them over."

"I hope she sent my dress chains." Rock eyed a fabulous nude evening gown that hung in the closet, imagining how Lani would look in and out of it.

Tate scowled. "I never let the ex dress me. I won't give her the power, the satisfaction, or the opportunity to dress me in a suit dowsed with itching powder. I have my own tux in the back of the Audi."

Ty pulled a package from the closet and tossed it to Rock. "This came for you."

Rock caught it, pulled the open tab on the box, opened it, and pulled out a wand. "I'm not some dumb-ass old-school magician. I don't use wands."

Ty came over and inspected it. "That's not really a wand. That's your backup gun."

Lani took it and gave it a look, too. "A six-shot automatic number. Sleek. Stylish. Very nice. I want one. I could use one if Sol gets out of hand."

Rock crossed his arms. "I don't want it."

"You don't have a choice—the wand picks you." Tate laughed again.

"I have my thumb gun and the poison ring. That's plenty."

Ty and Tate exchanged a look.

"Sometimes one shot is not enough," Tate said. "You'll take the wand." He forced it back on Rock.

"I hope your R and D guy is as good as Britain's MI6's Q. Q's always giving Bond exactly the right weapon for the right Bond movie. A breathing apparatus when he needs one. A protective ball in an avalanche."

"Our guy is good, but he can't predict the future like Q seems to," Tate said reasonably. "Still, you never want to be in a position where you say, *'I should have taken the wand gun.'*"

CHAPTER ELEVEN

"A surfer, a billionaire, and a magician walk into a bar," Tate said as the four of them got out of the Audi in front of the Magic Castle and turned the car over to the valet.

Ty wore a white linen suit, dark blue shirt, and shoes with no socks. Lani thought he looked like an updated version of Sonny Crockett from *Miami Vice*. Tate wore an expensive designer Italian tux and looked as if he were Bond himself, which was so very Tate. Rock wore a midnight-black tux, snowy-white shirt open to his chest, with a bow tie loosely holding it together that made Lani want to run her hands all over that fabulous chest, kiss that *Lani forever* tattoo that was showing and melting her hard spy heart, and completely divest him of every stitch he wore.

Mal had sent a nude, curve-enhancing, skintight, mermaid-cut gown for Lani that on first look made her appear naked as she hung on Tate's arm. The only touch of color she wore was a deep red shade of lipstick. If the way Rock was shooting daggers at Tate and stealing glances at her was any indication, the dress was practically lethal.

She experienced a momentary flash of guilt. It seemed almost cruel to be hanging on Tate's arm, cooing to him, laughing with him, and playing up to him right before Rock's eyes.

She had to stop thinking like that and feeling guilty. Being around Rock again, she was losing her professional cool. If he still wanted to be in her life once he saw all that she really was, he'd just have to get used to her being undercover and doing what the job required.

"That's a nice beginning," Rock said. "What's the punch line?"

"I haven't worked that out yet."

"You'd never make it on the comedy circuit," Rock said.

"I guess that rules out being the comic magician." Tate's tone was dry as he opened the door to the Castle and held it for Lani, then let the other two in in front of him.

"Something about putting on a tux turns a guy into a gentleman," Ty said. "Or an asshole alpha dog. His mom would be proud."

"Of being an asshole?" Rock said.

"No, the alpha dog," Tate said. "Mom's a typical former senator's wife—power hungry to her core. She would have made a great First Lady."

For years, Lani had dreamed of going to the Magic Castle. If she'd stayed with Rock, she was sure he would have taken her. It was bittersweet seeing it now as Tate's date rather than being on Rock's arm. She was sure Rock would have shown her the innermost workings of the Castle and taken advantage of the enchanted surroundings to impress and seduce her. The thought sent tingles through her. She forced herself to stop thinking about how exquisitely sensual and seductive an evening at the Magic Castle with Rock could have been.

The lobby of the Magic Castle looked like a nineteenth-century magician's library—the walls were papered in deep, dark red wallpaper with a filigreed pattern, the woodwork was dark, a fireplace with heavy wrought iron was on one wall, a framed aerial map of the Castle above it, and dark wooden bookcases, the shelves adorned with ornate patterns and filled with dusty leather-bound books of magic filled the rest. To the uninitiated, it looked like they'd hit a dead end. There was no hallway into the building.

"A one-room castle. Nice," Ty said.

In his element, Rock shook his head and strode to the shelf where a bookend in the shape of an owl sat. "Open Sesame."

The bookcase opened, revealing a secret passage.

Tate rolled his eyes. "Rather obvious, isn't it? You guys need a consultation with a security expert."

Rock shook his head and grinned. "We have security cameras inside. If by chance the riffraff sneak in, and they're always trying, we turn them into newts. Or saw them in half. Or disappear them forever. Or turn them over to the cops as trespassers."

Tate laughed. "Nice. You have a fine collection of newts, I assume?"

Rock grinned. "Where are we meeting our cadre of talented young performers?"

"On one of the small stages." Tate rattled off the name of the room. "You'll have to lead the way."

Rock nodded. "This way."

They walked past a collection of rabbit collectibles— ceramic, glass, and stuffed—past the Victorian dining room where they'd dine later to a small auditorium.

Thirty-five carefully screened hopefuls filled the room, joking and talking. When Lani walked in with Tate, the kids—none of the young CIA magician hopefuls were older than twenty-eight—quieted. Some looked and subtly pointed. When Rock strode in, they went completely awestruck silent. Rock read surprise on all their faces.

"Fellow magicians, I'm Rock Powers. You'll be auditioning for me tonight. Thanks for coming. Welcome and good luck!" Rock held his arms out. A ball of fire appeared in his right hand. He tossed it toward the crowd.

The crowd of them stepped back. The ball of fire turned into confetti and rained down on them.

As the young hopefuls applauded, Rock leaned in and whispered to Tate, "So they know this is really an audition for the CIA. But did they know I'm the one who'd be selecting them?"

"Of course not." Tate grinned. "The element of surprise is a useful weapon. Never hesitate to wield it."

"And do they know the rest of you are secret agents?" Rock asked.

"No. They think Tate's here as an Agency consultant. His company does quite a bit of software work for the government. I'm his guest, and Ty is an Agency recruiter." Lani kept smiling as she spoke. "Only those we choose will find out the truth."

Rock nodded, turned on the charm, and dove into the crowd, shaking hands, performing little tricks, letting the kids do small tricks for him.

Tate leaned in and whispered to Lani, "Stop staring at him like you want to eat him. You're supposed to be with me tonight. I'm your fantasy man, remember?"

"Right." Lani laughed, but she was duly chastised. Why was it so hard to stay in character around Rock? "Just appreciating his showmanship. He knows how to work a crowd." Lani pasted a smile on her face. "Look, he's singled out our top contenders. Very good."

There were seven of them Lani thought would be right for the job. Odd numbers were good for magic. Lucky. Especially seven. Two girls and five guys. There were another four or five who would do. She wondered whether Rock would see things the same way.

"A hip-hop street dancer; a geek; a fashion model in a short, skintight, hot-pink dress; a gamer; a guy in a hoodie over his tux; and a girl with a smartphone attached to her ear walk into a magic club," Tate joked.

"I have to hand it to these young magicians," Lani said, studying them. "Their choices of tuxes are interesting and distinctive enough to give their stage personalities away."

Lani followed Tate's line of sight. If anything, he was eying the fashion model, a leggy, blond stunner. "Hey," she said to Tate. "Follow your own advice. You're here with me tonight."

Tate grinned. "Spoilsport."

Rock worked his way back through the crowd to them and whispered to Ty. "Make sure that girl with the cell phone doesn't take any pictures. They're prohibited back here in the top-secret part of the club."

Ty looked as if he wanted to roll his eyes. "Everything's jammed."

The group of entertainers was staring at them. Rock took over and made introductions. "Let me introduce my guests tonight. Software magnate Tate Cox."

There was polite applause.

"His lady friend, Gillian."

Someone hooted.

"And Ty Smith."

More polite applause.

Before Rock could say more, the hip-hop guy broke into a break-dance, spinning on his head and levitating.

Head levitation. Now that's good, Lani thought. He was more impressive in person than on his audition video.

The hip-hopper did a flip and righted himself into a stand inches in front of Rock.

"Smokz. The break-dancing, hip-hopping magician. Magic was never so—"

Rock's cell phone rang in his pocket.

"Take the call, man," Ty said.

"What the hell? I thought you guys were jamming.

And who gave out my number?" Rock said, looking at the fashion model.

Lani looked at her, too. She wore a flowing, strapless, calf-length dress with sparkles that caught the light from the candelabra overhead.

"Wasn't she in pink?" Rock said as he pulled the phone from his pocket. A text popped up. Lani read it over his should.

Britt, social media magic like you won't believe. You're a Sagittarius or I miss my guess.

Fashion Girl pushed the others aside and extended a beautifully manicured hand. Each of her pink fingernails had a magic symbol painted on them. "Ashley, the fashion magician. I can change in a flash."

She tossed something at the floor. Ty and Tate looked about ready to reach for their guns, but Lani knew flash powder when she saw it. And so did Rock.

When the puff of smoke around Ashley cleared seconds later, she was wearing a brilliant coral dress with a plunging neckline.

"Impressive." Tate winked at the girl.

Lani clutched his arm and curled tighter into him as if she were jealous. Someone had to keep up the act and she didn't like the way the fashion model was eyeing Tate back and a couple of the girls in the crowd were drooling over Rock.

The video gamer shook his head. "Zach. I need a stage to do my shit."

A regular-looking guy spoke. "Daniel. The same."

"Will. Me, too."

A chorus of them followed.

Rock held up his hands and silenced the crowd. "Everyone will get their turn. Let's get these auditions started."

* * *

Lasers bounced around the stage, controlled by Will as if by magic. They'd already watched more of Smokz's hip-hop rapper magic. Seen the quick-change artist go through an entire season of fashion in her allotted ten-minute act. Watched Daniel doing amazing tricks with models, making them believe he'd destroyed the Parthenon, toppled the Eiffel Tower, and disappeared the Statue of Liberty. Seen Zach manipulate video games and use them to read people's minds. Watched as Britt manipulated social media sites at will and used them to predict the future. And now Will was shooting lasers into the audience. Bending laser beams. Cutting them. Disappearing behind them and reappearing on another part of the stage. And watched the rest of the thirty-five contestants, except for one, Jake.

To watch him, they'd have to head to the alley. But Rock was pretty sure of what they'd see—a man who could jump off tall buildings and disappear into thin air. Reappear where he wanted. Hard to perform on stage, but genius.

Rock had already decided who he wanted on his team. He leaned in and whispered his choices to Lani, who sat next to him, "Will, Smokz, Daniel, Zach, Ashley, and Britt. I still need my alien. I'm hoping Jake's our guy."

Lani nodded. "They were my top picks as far as their illusions and expertise with magic. Ashley's a little weak with her shooting skills and Daniel's written test indicated his verbal skills were on the low side. He isn't much good with languages. But we can work around all that. Tate? Ty?"

"Britt has a bit of a tell," Ty said. "Nothing we can't train out of her."

"And Smokz looks like a hothead," Tate said.

"Jake, our parkour wizard, I assume he jumps from

buildings and disappears? That he does what appear to be superhuman stunts?" Rock said.

Ty nodded. "Yeah."

Rock turned to Tate again. "How deep are your pockets? I need those seven young magicians."

CHAPTER TWELVE

Ty, Tate, Lani, and Rock settled in for the night at the Enchanted Castle Inn, conveniently located less than a block from the Castle. It didn't have quite the same ambience, and it wasn't exclusive, but it was convenient.

They met in Tate's room for a post–magic audition conference. Ty finished setting up jammers. The CIA guys had jamming and security on the brain.

Rock watched Ty's preparations. "Kind of gives *jam pants* a new meaning, doesn't it?"

Tate gave him a quizzical look.

"Old Eddie Izzard joke about a gadget for Bond—jam pants. You know how Q always makes Bond the exact right gadget for the right time? Izzard imagined Q giving Bond jam pants. And Bond's thinking, *What the hell am I supposed to do with these*? It's a funny routine.

"Though I think the comedian really meant pants made of jam, as in jelly that you spread on toast. Maybe a more correct term for ours would be *jamming pants*." He paused. "That doesn't sound quite right, either. Jammer pants?" Rock shook his head side to side as if weighing the idea. "Could be a new trend. If we got the right designer."

Rock watched Ty set up the last of the jammers. "Maybe our billionaire here would like to invest?"

Tate laughed and shook his head. "No. Too much of a niche item. I put my money on mass appeal."

"Jammer pants, I'll suggest that to our version of Q." Ty took a seat in a chair across from Rock.

Tate walked to the minibar and poured himself a glass of bourbon. "Drink, anyone? Rock, money aside, why haven't you tried staging a smaller version of your Space Invaders illusion?"

"Are you kidding?" Rock said. "I don't do anything half-assed. Until I had full capabilities, I wasn't risking it.

"Besides, the last thing I needed was the government watching me." He realized what he'd said and laughed. "With the airport hangar to Area 51 across the street from the hotel I perform at? I'd be branded a nutcase if word got out before I was ready. Or a threat to the U.S. government's top-secret military installation.

"Hell, it's bad enough already. With my fame, money, and apparently psychic abilities and magical tendencies, people might start to believe I'm part of MJ-12. Or a half-breed alien myself. After all, the identity of my biological old man is pretty much a mystery, even to me."

The secret agents stared at him as if he were a little touched. Maybe it was *already* too late to save his reputation.

MJ-12 was supposedly a top-secret organization made up of powerful, rich, influential men who were keeping aliens a secret from society. Theories varied as to whether these men were using alien technology to make fortunes. Whether they were behind disappearances of people who were never heard from again only to be mashed up as alien food, or used to mate with aliens and create a super-human, superpowerful alien-human half-breed. Evidently, according to urban legend, anyway, aliens had lost the ability to reproduce on their own. MJ-12 would then be raising these half-breeds to rise as rulers under the control of MJ-12. The first half-human, half-alien U.S. president would be quite a coup.

"All those acts we saw tonight," Rock said. "The core of the illusion. All needed for setting up Outlandish Marauders. Ten years ago, it wasn't possible to perform. But now with social media and readily available lasers . . ." He shrugged. "Even though it'll be dicey whether I can pull a convincing illusion together with novices so quickly, it's exciting.

"I hate to say that, knowing what's at stake. But this illusion has been my dream since I was a teenager. Although I'd always planned it as an illusion, not a vehicle for evil.

"I'll get to perform it, a version of it, anyway. But it won't be a spectacular like I planned. A major television event."

"I wouldn't say it won't be spectacular." Ty grinned. "And you'll still get your reveal.

"As for the timetable, in an ideal world, we would have involved you earlier. We've had the basics of your Outlandish Marauders illusion since Lani lifted it two years ago."

Lani shrugged.

"We didn't know RIOT had complete enough plans or access to the technology they needed until just a few weeks ago. Or how they were planning to use the trick to get into Area 51. We called you up, so to speak, as soon as we could.

"Now our problem is making sure RIOT knows we're planning to perform it at the NUFO conference. That's Lani's job. She has to feed that intel to Sol for him to pass on."

Rock shook his head, imagining how Sol would feel once he found out the illusion had been snatched from him. "He'll be furious that I'm planning to steal his trick.

He's relishing the thrill of performing it as much as I am. Watch for him to retaliate."

Rock frowned. "I've been thinking a lot about the illusion and RIOT's plans for it.

"The way they're planning to use Outlandish Marauders is really nothing more than performing a modern version of the 1938 radio broadcast of *War of the Worlds*. The reason that worked so well was twofold. One, Americans were already primed for an invasion.

"And two, Orson Welles timed the broadcast so that the part where the Martians emerge from their spaceship coincided with a commercial break on the other, large commercial stations. The station he was broadcasting on scheduled their commercial breaks to be at different times from the big stations. So like with TV today, listeners flipped stations. And so they happened to tune in late, without hearing the caveat that it was fictional at the start of the program.

"They were already primed to be listening for a German invasion. A large segment of the audience didn't hear the reference to Martians or spaceships and thought the Germans were invading.

"So you got two kinds of people panicking—those who believed in aliens and those who believed the Germans were attacking. That's what Sol and RIOT would want to do today—play to those who believe in aliens and those who are afraid of a terrorist attack."

"That worked then because there was no instant replay," Ty said. "Today you can go back and read through hashtag streams or Facebook posts."

Rock nodded. "You can. But you can also cause a lot of confusion and diversion in the short term. Or rather, someone like Ashley can. Diversion is the soul of magic. All you need are a few hours. By the time the truth is sorted out, the trick, and the damage, is done."

"As you've already determined, the NUFO convention picnic at the black mailbox provides a supply of true believers ready to panic."

Lani was still wearing the blond wig and the nude-colored dress. "Personally, a picnic sounds like fun. The clothes are more comfy than dressing for the Magic Castle, anyway." She sighed. "I can't wait to get out of these body shapers."

Rock would happily volunteer for that job.

"By all means, go ahead," Tate said.

"And miss being in on the plans?" She shook her head. "No, thanks. So, about the second set of panickers—how do we get those?"

"If it were me, and I had all the time in the world," Rock said, "I'd wait for an opportunity when the public's attention is focused on another major event of some kind. When they're jumpy and easily susceptible to believing they're being attacked."

Rock felt dazed as he realized the implications of what he was saying. "If I were RIOT, I'd stage a real terrorist attack somewhere in Nevada shortly before performing the alien attack illusion. That will cause confusion, tension, and apprehension like the *War of the Worlds* broadcast did. Cover for the illusion."

"It will also divert our resources," Tate said.

Rock took a deep breath. "What they're planning is diabolical. It makes me sick to think of them using my trick for evil. All I ever wanted to do was entertain and maybe debunk some of this alien invasion conspiracy theory. I never intended to use it for evil. I never even considered trying the *War of the Worlds* approach. It was supposed to be a show that people paid to see, not a tactical event to scare people." Rock looked at Tate. "I think I need that drink now."

Tate poured him one.

Rock took it from him and swirled it in the glass in front of him. "But using human nature to do their work for them. Appealing to the nut jobs, the conspiracy guys. Making sure they hear about the invasion and storm the place to get a look for themselves.

"Frothing up the general populace and adding them to the mix. Getting the patriots out to defend the territory. Getting others racing to the area for help. Overwhelming the outer security . . . It's heinous."

Ty nodded. "Random is brilliant in his way. Who else would have thought of courting magicians in the hope of using an illusion to get what they want five to ten years in the future?"

Rock shook his head. "It is brilliant. The notices on the property state that deadly force can be used against trespassers, but shooting dozens of innocent civilians who were duped by an illusion? That's some bad press brewing. No president wants that shit on his political record.

"What's to say RIOT can't manipulate our illusion to its advantage? Whip up some kind of other panic there that will overwhelm security and cause an incident? A fake camo dude firing into the crowd, for instance?"

Ty nodded. "We're already taking precautions against it. But it's a risk we'll have to take.

"This NUFO conference with their specialists in debunking sightings and fakes, and their believers trying to prove aliens exist is what we've been handed. Their picnic at the black mailbox, the reported prime alien viewing spot, is what we have to deal with."

"Isn't the black mailbox white now?" Tate said.

"Yeah, come to think of it, I think it is," Ty said.

"Gentlemen, the color of the mailbox is neither here nor there," Rock said. "The real problem is that RIOT must be planning that attack that makes the general public jumpy. Whether they perform the illusion, or we do, it plays to their hand. We have to stop it."

"Or use our considerable talents, our camoufleurs and sonic deception engineers to create and stage a fake attack." Ty grinned. "A thwarted one, of course. But we have to beat RIOT to that one, too. Fortunately, we have a gullible, easily manipulated media on our side."

"And one talented social media magician," Rock added.

The meeting wound down. Lani yawned. "It's been a long day and tomorrow we have an early morning. I think I'll turn in."

Rock popped to his feet. "I'll walk you to your room."

"I'm still Gillian. I think that's Tate's job." She moved toward the door and grinned at Tate.

Tate waved her off. "I think Gillian can manage on her own. Her room's just across the hall."

Rock wasn't backing down. "I insist."

She gave a graceful shrug of her creamy shoulders as if acquiescing. Everything she did turned him on, even when she spurned him. He had to talk to her.

"Good night, boys." She blew a kiss to Tate, winked at Ty, and let Rock follow her out of the room without further objection.

At her door, she swiped her key card and turned the handle when the door clicked unlocked. "I think I can handle it from here."

As she opened the door, Rock caught her arm. "We have to talk."

She studied him. "Do we?"

He refused to back down.

"All right then." She let him in just inside the door. "Stay here while I make sure the room is clear."

Spies were a paranoid variety, but he enjoyed the view of her in her skin-colored gown, imagining her really naked, as she cleared the room. Finally she nodded to him. "Close the door."

He did as she requested, but she stopped him from coming in any farther than the entry. "That's far enough."

"Don't trust me, or don't trust yourself around me?" He took a step into her. They stood only inches apart.

"You're full of yourself, Rock Powers. But that's part of what I like about you." She took a baby step toward him, standing so close her breasts nearly brushed his chest and they were toe to toe. She looked up into his eyes. "So talk."

"Can you take off the wig and stop being Gillain for just a minute?" He knew all too well how easy it was to play a role when a person was in costume. He somehow had to reach the real Lani, the one he knew and loved.

She pulled the wig off, unpinned her hair, and shook it out, brushing up against him as she tossed the wig away, egging on his desire and getting a rise out of him. He'd been too long without her.

"Better?" She smiled up at him.

"Much." He held his ground, though he ached to take her in his arms. He imagined the feel of her pressed up against him, slim and firm, soft in all the right places.

"So?" she said again. "Talk."

"If you're trying to intimidate me, it won't work."

She held his gaze. "Why would I try to intimidate you?"

"Because you don't want to admit that you love me."

She stared at him and then laughed as she ran a finger over his bare chest that showed through his open shirt. "You are bold."

"If I'm wrong, look me in the eye and tell me I am. Tell me you never loved me." His lips were just inches from hers. "And remember that I'm trained to read facial expressions. I'm so good people think I'm a real mind reader and a psychic. So lie to me, baby, if you dare. I'll know the truth one way or another."

"Maybe I did love you, a little." Her eyes were lit with excitement as if she was enjoying their game, too.

He felt the brush of her breath against his lips as she spoke. He was so close to her, just a breath away. Her heady, sensual perfume filled his senses. Her cold calm only turned him on further.

She was a clever little femme fatale. She knew how to read people, too, and cover her true feelings. Admit the truth, but mask it in a little lie. It was a brilliant strategy and threw him off. He was having a hard time determining just how much truth she told.

"But it was foolish," she said. "And dangerous to both of us."

"And now?" He held himself still though he ached to touch her. But it was clear they were playing a game of chicken, each daring the other to break.

"It's my turn to ask a question." She moved her lips a fraction of an inch closer to his, teasing him with her nearness. "How do you know you really love me?"

He frowned. "What kind of question is that?"

She laughed. She'd won this round and thrown him off his strategy. "My colleagues call me Magic for a reason, and it has nothing to do with what you do." She smiled. "Well, maybe just the tiniest bit.

"I'm magic because I can be whoever I want to be, whoever I have to be. I have a master's degree in psychology. I'm a trained hypnotist. And I trained with the best and was a star pupil in neuro-linguistic programing. I read people, particularly men with the ease most people breathe.

"Do you know what my specialty at the Agency is?" Her words were sensually spoken, slinky.

He shuddered beneath her touch as she pressed her

warm palm over his heart. He had a horrible feeling he knew the answer. But he couldn't force himself to say it.

She kept smiling. "You know the answer. I see it on your face. But since you won't say it, I'll spell it out—I have a particular talent for manipulating men and making them fall in love with me. I study their profiles. I study them. I know what will turn my marks on and melt their hearts and I exploit it. I can look however I want, be whatever race I choose at the moment. Act however I want. I'm a man's fantasy. Whatever fantasy they want.

"Men in love part with their secrets amazingly easily." She paused. "How do you know I didn't manipulate you?" She was breathing hard.

And so was he. As if this punishing game excited them both. She thought she had him. She thought she'd bested him. He read it on her face.

"How do you know I care?" he said. "I love you and that's enough."

She snorted, gently, almost seductively. Her eyes were still lit with the lust of the game. If she was surprised, she didn't give it away. "That's what they all say, Rock. I've heard this before. You fell in love with someone, but she wasn't me. She was just a character I created to suit your needs, a figment of your imagination and desire."

"No, Lani, that may have been your MO in the past. But with me, you slipped up and let the real Lani show. The little girl whose grandpa thrilled her with magic. The girl who never belonged. The woman who'd never met her match in deception.

"You belong with me. In my community where your looks are an asset and make you invaluable. Where your acting skills make magic, too. Stay with me, Lani. When this is over." He was pleading with her, he knew it. That gave her the upper hand, but he didn't care.

She put a finger to his lips and looked almost sad,

though she masked it well. "I'm a spy, Rock. That's who I am. I get my thrills and my joy from protecting this country and its people. It gives my life meaning. I can't leave this life. And I don't think you can stand back and watch me live it. What I do sometimes calls for infidelity. I never should have married. That's not a lie. It wasn't fair to you."

Damn, she was good, speaking truth again to cover the truth of her feelings.

"Why did you come back, really?" he asked.

"It's a mission. I'm under orders."

He held her gaze. She didn't flinch.

Finally, she sighed. "To protect you, Rock. And because I owed you closure."

He took her fingers in his hand. "I love you, Lani. I'm not giving up. I will win you over." He gently kissed her fingers and squeezed them before releasing them. "I'd better be going." He turned to leave.

He stopped at the door and looked back at her. "One more thing, Lani, since you owe me."

She gave him a quizzical look and waited for him to speak.

He swallowed hard. "Don't sleep with Sol. Not to save me and not to save this country. Don't sleep with that slime bag. Drug him. Manipulate him, but don't debase yourself for him."

Lani had no intention of sleeping with Sol. Ever. The very thought repulsed her. Her heart broke every time she pictured Rock's face last night in LA as he professed his love for her. He was right, dead-on, about what he'd said. She did belong with him, if she really belonged with any man.

She'd longed to fall into his arms and tell him everything. But she couldn't. To tell him why she really couldn't love him or let him get too close was to put their baby in danger.

Once RIOT realized that Rock was planning to perform Outlandish Marauders, his life would be in even more danger than it had been. Rock may not have realized it, but NCS had stepped up their security of him. RIOT would be angling to bend Rock toward their will and looking for anything that would give them that leverage and an edge for getting into Area 51. They already knew Rock was beyond being bribed or enticed with money.

RIOT might still figure that putting her in peril would turn him. But now that she'd aligned herself with Sol, she was hoping it mitigated that danger at least somewhat.

RIOT would dump Sol for Rock in a second. And once Sol discovered he'd been usurped by Rock's trick, he was likely to retaliate.

As she waited at the rehearsal hall for the choreographer and Sol to show up, she reviewed her plans. She was going to use her own brand of magic to lead Sol to the edge and make him *think* they'd had mind-blowing sex. Rock was right about one thing—she was planning to engage in some hypnosis-induced pillow talk with Sol.

Rock thought he'd taught Lani all the magic she knew, that she was merely assistant material. He had no idea of the real depths of her talents.

As she'd told him, she held a master's degree in psychology and was a board-certified hypnotist. She could implant a thought or a whole false memory at will. If she could get close enough to the subject. That was key.

That's why the Agency had her go after Rock the first time around, during the Dam episode, as she referred to it. Though it had quickly turned into the Damn caper.

She'd told Rock the truth. She'd played with his mind during that mission. Just as she was planning to play with Sol's. Suggested to Rock's subconscious that he fall in love with her, was in love with her. And then she'd played the role of the woman Rock had always dreamed of.

Only she'd realized, as Rock had said, the role she was playing was really who she was. And what a relief it was to be with someone and not have to pretend to be someone else. As she was implanting the thoughts in him that he was in love with her, she was falling in love with him. And no one was using any love spells on her.

It's true you can't hypnotize a person and get them to do something they're absolutely set against. But if they have the inclination? Anything's fair game.

And now she wondered—would Rock have fallen for her without her help? And was he right that it didn't matter?

Around Sol she was playing another role, that of his ideal woman—a dark, deceitful girl who couldn't be trusted. If she got the chance, she'd plant that same *you're in love with me* thought in Sol. It was a dangerous game to play. Magicians were notoriously hard to hypnotize. They recognized the techniques. And love could turn to obsession. Men like Sol were prone to dark obsession and lethal jealousy.

Sol walked into the studio just then. "Ah, there's my new star." He looked around the room. "No one saw you come in?"

She gave him the smile she used to enchant men. "I'm a spook, Sol. You know that." For once she was actually telling the truth.

Sol laughed and walked up to her, standing in her personal space.

"I was very careful." She took his arm. "Believe me. I'm taking no chances with my big break."

"I tried to reach you last night," Sol said almost too casually. "You weren't in the hotel room I reserved for you. Where were you?"

She'd expected he'd have her followed. But she refused to be his prisoner. Sol wouldn't like it, but he'd respect her more if she could best him and disappear beneath his nose.

"Why didn't you call me on my cell?" she said, playing his game.

"I wanted to know where you were," he said.

"With a friend," she said, equally casually. "Hiding out." She gave his arm a squeeze and made eyes at him. "Like I said, I'm taking no chances. Making sure there's no connection between us. Using extreme caution."

"I appreciate that, Lani, my dear. I do. But we could have had a pleasant evening together."

"Oh, there's plenty of time for that. *Plenty.*"

The door to the studio flew open. A young, cute man with his hair stylishly highlighted and messily spiked strolled in dressed in dance tights and a tight T-shirt. The choreographer had arrived.

"My place. Tonight," Sol said.

CHAPTER THIRTEEN

The view from Sol's hotel penthouse suite was a breath-taking combination of neon and nature. The setting was intimate and the dinner catered. Lani had dressed for the occasion in a sexy, short, clingy black dress with a slightly exotic Asian cut to the bodice and skirt. She'd played up the slight almond shape of her eyes with liquid eyeliner and heavy plum makeup, going for smoky bed-room eyes. Her sandals were spiky and her jewelry gold, a Japanese crane pendant hung around her neck.

Asian women turned Sol on. They were his one big weakness. At least that's what his dossier said and her personal experience confirmed.

Candles flickered. The wine was the most expensive the hotel offered. Soft romantic music played in the back-ground.

"You were fantastic at practice." Sol sat next to her on the sofa, swirling and sniffing an after-dinner glass of deep, red wine, his arm looped casually around her shoul-ders.

"You picked up the dance moves quickly and handled the reappearance and escape moves expertly." He raised his glass to her. "It's a shame Rock's tastes run toward Hispanic women and you have to wear that gaudy wed-ding dress costume he designed for you." He nuzzled her neck and ran a finger down her collarbone and between her breasts. "The dress you're wearing tonight suits you *so* much better."

Lani forced a smile and nestled her head into the crook of Sol's neck, resisting the urge to slam her head back and break his nose. "Rock's tastes run toward the showy."

Sol wore an expensive, delicious-smelling cologne. Lani had the feeling that after tonight, the scent would make her gag.

"The way you've done your makeup suits you better, too. Plays up your gorgeous eyes." He set his crystal wine goblet down on an end table next to the sofa and gently guided her chin until she faced him. "Maybe . . ."

She shook her head and pretended to be transfixed by the look in his eyes. In actuality, the lust reflected there repulsed her. "We've been over this, Sol. For the reappearance to work, I have to look *exactly* as I did that night. Top of my head to tiny baby toe. The same. Otherwise, how will the audience recognize me?"

"You're too modest, Lani. How could anyone ever forget you?" Sol rubbed her shoulder with one hand. "You're tense, baby. Let me help you loosen up. I'm *very* good with my hands."

I bet you are. She was good with hers, too. She knew how to kill with them and if he pushed her too far . . .

She set her wine goblet down and turned her back to him for him to massage. Or pummel, as the case may be. Sol liked to be obeyed and tonight it was her job to humor him. Until she bent him to her will using trickery and deceit. And hormones. Once she had him at her mercy—

Suffice it to say she wished there weren't rules and policy and guidelines that restricted her from doing what she really wanted to do to the pompous, egotistical, illusion-stealing enemy of the state. Of course any regular licensed hypnotherapist would be thrown out of the profession for what she was about to do. Fortunately, NCS wholeheartedly approved of her methods. Torture may be out, but abusing hypnotherapy and implanting false memories were still approved methods of interrogation. And a lot of fun, too, if a tad on the dangerous side.

Sol rubbed both of her shoulders with enough force she almost winced. Which she was sure was his intention. Despite his clean-cut looks, Sol was brutal and brutish to his core.

When he was finished abusing her shoulders, he lifted her hair and bit the nape of her neck with the vigor of an angry toddler, stopping just short of breaking the skin. She let out an involuntary yelp, which only seemed to turn him on. He trailed kisses and semi-gentle gnaws down her back.

She was leery of him now. On edge, which she was sure was what he intended. Tense and ready to arch away if he bit again. The last thing she needed was a trail of his dental records down her spine. She'd already let him inflict one mouth-shaped bruise she'd have to hide from Rock and the world.

But she wasn't most women. She'd pay him back for that bite. *Sol, baby, you just earned yourself a bout of erectile dysfunction.*

Word on the street was that Sol liked his sex hard, abusive, and punishing. She'd like to disabuse him of his thoughts that he was a great lover. And deliver a nice karate chop to his groin.

Sol's hot breath, followed by the long stroke of his reptilian tongue on the back of her neck, made her skin crawl. She involuntarily shuddered. Fortunately, Sol took it wrong and thought his finesse had turned her on.

If only he knew. Each nip and lick pushed her one step closer to removing him of his manhood—permanently. Only years of training and the thought of another two years of desk duty kept her in line. She let out a small gasp, mostly of disgust, and tipped her head back, letting Sol stroke her hair.

He yanked her head back by her hair until she was looking back at him upside down. He kissed her, brutally thrusting his tongue down her throat as he slid a hand down her dress to fondle her breast and squeeze her nipple, hard enough that she suppressed a yelp of pain.

He pulled back and grinned down at her, looking just as evil upside down as right side up. She half expected his eyeballs to start spinning like a mesmerizing snake's, demonic and trance inducing. "How do I know you won't betray me to Rock?"

"If I had any loyalty to Rock, would I be here with you?" she whispered back as she reached up to stroke his face. "Besides, I have something to tell you about Rock. Some secret information that will prove my loyalty to you."

Sol froze. "What could you possibly know?"

"I still have friends here. Girls who hear things and like to share. Word on the street is that Rock went to LA yesterday with his new pal, that software guy, Tate something?"

"Cox."

She had Sol's attention. She nodded. "Yeah, that's the guy. Him and some blonde. They went to the Magic Castle and interviewed a bunch of magicians for a top-secret new act Rock is planning."

Sol's eyes grew hard. He was definitely interested now. "What kind of act?"

Lani shrugged. "I don't know. But one of the girls at the hotel said she's seen him hanging with one of those alien-believing nuts, a bigwig of some sort with them. They have a conference coming up next week and he's been in town making arrangements. Another one of her friends partied with that bigwig and he was bragging about a big surprise they're planning for their attendees. Something that will blow them away." Lani shrugged. "So I put two and two together. I bet he's hired Rock to do a show for them.

"Trust me now?" She was getting a crick in her neck from the awkward position. But she put on a sexy pout for his sake.

He laughed softly. "I've always trusted you."

"You are such a wicked liar." She pulled free of his grasp, slid off the sofa to kneel between his legs, and ran her hands up the inside of his thighs toward his crotch. "Prove it." She rested one hand on the bulge in his pants and gently rubbed with a touch that made him shudder.

"Prove it?" He was cynical and laughing at her. "Trust can't be proven, only built over years."

She shook her head. "We both know that's not true. Give me a shot at hypnotizing you. Let me let loose all your deepest desires."

He laughed again and shook his head, looking at her as if she was crazy. "Lani, baby, you ask the impossible. I'm not susceptible. I'm part of the twenty percent who can't be hypnotized."

She grabbed the zipper to his pants and slid it down slowly, one notch at a time. His eyes dilated and his breath grew rapid.

"Being hypnotized is a matter of trust. Like trusting I'm not going to catch your cock in this zipper." She leaned forward and untucked his shirt with her mouth, still holding the zipper and the fly of his pants. "Let me try. Let me take you to new heights, to pleasure you've only imagined.

"I know how to hypnotize a man to heighten the experience. Let me work *my* magic." She let go of the zipper, pulled him onto the sofa, and climbed onto his lap, cupping his face in her hand.

"Don't tell me you're afraid?" She kissed him lightly.

"Are you afraid of ecstasy? Are you afraid to let the beast in you go?"

He grabbed her dress, pulled it over her head, and dropped it on the floor, leaving her exposed in her see-through lace bra and matching thong panties. "Is that a challenge?" Sol's pupils dilated until the brown rims of his irises were barely visible.

The large blue topaz ring on her right hand sparkled in the candlelight. Her lips were inches from his. "Absolutely, baby."

She moved his hands to her breasts and stroked his cheek with the back of her fingers, running her hand right next to his nose just as she hit a hidden button on the ring. The ring released an invisible, odorless burst of the hormone oxytocin, which stimulates trust and generosity to strangers. It was a hypnotist's dream drug.

She cupped his chin and released another burst of the oxytocin. "Trust me, baby. I can make you very, *very* happy."

He thrust his pelvis into hers so she could feel him hard against her. "You can make me happier than this?"

"I can make you happier than *ever*."

His black eyes stared back at her. "I'm game. But when this fails, we play my way."

"You have to promise to try to fall under my spell."

"I'm already under your spell. But I'll try harder." He thrust up against her again.

She kissed him lightly again and waved her hand in front of his face as she released another burst of oxytocin. "You're getting very sleepy."

Sol grinned. "You're going to have to do better than that."

"I've only just begun." She stared deeply into his eyes and went into her patter in her smooth, calm, seductive voice, releasing bursts of oxytocin at regular intervals until his body relaxed and his head lolled back.

"Sol, Sol, can you hear me? Your left hand is heavy. Very heavy. Dead weight. Too heavy to lift. Can you lift it for me, Sol?"

Sol struggled, even grabbed it with his right hand and tried to lift it. But it wouldn't move.

He's under.

"That's good, Sol. You can stop trying to move it now."

Sol had hidden cameras watching everything. Lani leaned back and pretended to remove a shoe, hitting a secret button in the heel that activated a camera jammer.

"You're a brilliant man." She stroked his cheek again, releasing another burst of the hormone. "Brilliant men are sexy," she cooed. "But you don't get to brag, do you? Such a shame. The world should know how great you are. You're planning a big illusion. Something so fantastic and brilliant you can't tell anyone. Except me, Sol. Telling me will give you a sexual high.

"Imagine kissing me, tasting me, running your hands over my body, experiencing every inch of me, knowing we share a secret so dangerous and brilliant it unites us as one. Telling me releases you from your bonds, makes you whole and powerful. It will show them who's in control." As she stroked his cheek, he gasped and writhed beneath her.

If only she could stop straddling him, jump off, get dressed, and head home to shower. But she couldn't take the chance of breaking his trance.

"When you tell me your secrets, you'll feel a tremendous sense of relief, and a rush of sexual excitement like you've never felt before."

She unbuttoned his shirt and stroked his chest. "You're turned on. Throbbing. Pushing to the point of release.

Feel strong. Feel the power of sharing. What are you planning, baby? Tell me about your next grand illusion."

Sol was breathing heavily. "Outlandish Marauders."

She already knew that. "Give me the details. Who's involved? Who are you working with?"

He tensed and became agitated and silent. He was afraid.

No one ever got out of bed with RIOT alive. Or screwed up and lived to tell about it. She had to proceed carefully or risk pushing him out of the hypnotic state.

"I can bring you great pleasure." She leaned into him and whispered in his ear, "But you have to trust me with your secrets."

He shook his head and muttered, "People." His fear was too great and deeply rooted to overcome. She tried several more times, but he didn't spill any intel.

"Sol, listen to me. Relax. Just relax. Everything is okay. Go back to that deep place inside yourself where you feel safe. Are you there, Sol? Are you safe?"

He nodded.

"Good. Good. I'm going to put you to bed. But first, you're going to tell me a bedtime story—all your lovely, sexy fantasies. What turns you on. Your favorite positions, what you love for your women to say, how you like to be touched. How you imagine making love to me.

"When you wake in the morning, you won't remember a thing about what we talked about. But you'll remember everything you describe in your story to me as real, so make it detailed and explicit, imagine it as a movie, as if we pleasured each other in all the ways you describe.

"You'll feel so close to me you'll never want to hurt me, ever. No matter who orders it. You'll protect me. Understand?"

He nodded. "Never hurt you."

"You'll never speak of this to anyone. Telling *anyone* could cost you your life."

He nodded. "Never speak."

She gave Sol a last dose of the oxytocin. "After you tell me your story, I'll tell you mine." A little story about a magician who developed a sudden case of erectile dysfunction.

Later that night, Lani cuddled up in the ultra-comfy king-size bed in Rock's guest bedroom suite at his mansion, still trembling with disgust from having had to listen to Sol's base fantasies. She'd managed to avoid Rock when she came in. He was in what he and Tate were calling the war room where they mapped out the illusion.

The illusion. Rumors, of course, abounded about the U.S. military installation, Area 51, or Dreamland as some called it, located about a hundred miles outside Las Vegas. Many Americans believed it's where the U.S. government housed captured aliens for study and flying saucers and other UFOs. As far as Lani knew, Area 51 was simply a top-secret weapons and R&D facility. Even she didn't have clearance to know what it was RIOT was planning to steal from there.

Lani's cell phone buzzed on the nightstand next to her. Her heart raced as she grabbed the phone, typed in her password, and hit view to see her text. Her little Stone smiled back at her, his dark hair flopping over his toddler eyes so like his father's as he held a toy wand. Her weekly picture.

Nanny sent one a week, but only after Lani sent the code word that it was all clear. Until the mission was over and RIOT no longer had a need for Rock, or any leverage against him, once-a-week e-mails were all the contact she was allowed.

She stroked the phone as gently as if she was stroking her fifteen-month-old's cheek. He looked so much like his daddy. She wished Rock could see him. She wished . . . for a lot of nearly impossible things.

It's showtime, Lani thought as she waited in the dark just offstage for her cue to reappear after her two-year absence. Finally, the audience, an audience, anyway, would get their prestige. In Sol's act. *Damn, Sol.*

For two days Sol had punishingly worked her butt off in overly long rehearsals. Bending her into pretzels and contortions, trying everything to get just the right, most dramatic reveal. He'd finally settled on reenacting Rock's act, with himself cast as the groom. This time successfully reappearing the bride.

It was clear Sol wouldn't rest until he'd completely humiliated Rock. If it weren't for this mission, and its importance, Lani would never have agreed to be a part of it.

Sol didn't work just her. He'd worked the entire cast with an almost demonic energy. He was a dark magician with a mission—revenge and one-upmanship. And evil.

Sol had micromanaged everything, including the repair and cleaning of the original bride costume from Rock's show that Lani had brought back with her. The shoes had been a bit of a problem. The one had a broken heel and both were covered in blood. As everyone knows, blood is impossible to get out of white satin.

There was no way Lani could ever bring the originals back to show Sol. But Malene had worked her brand of magic and managed to get an identical replacement pair. Even making them look slightly worn.

In the meantime, Sol's PR firm had worked with equal furor ginning up publicity and fervor for this show, aided behind the scenes with help from NCS. Hinting at a stunning surprise, a great feat never before performed on stage, they'd managed to fill the audience with paparazzi, gossip rag reporters, and Rock. Which delighted Sol beyond measure. So much so, that Lani was more suspicious than usual of Sol's motives, worried that he had a sinister something else up his sleeve.

These last two days, Sol had watched her so closely he bordered on obsessed. And a sociopath obsessed was nothing to mess with. Hypnotizing him had been a dangerous, and perhaps foolhardy, move. At times, she wondered whether he'd succeeded in fooling her by faking the hypnotic state.

She would have doubted her success even now. But Sol had made several passes at her during rehearsals and after. He'd grabbed her, held her close, and pressed his aroused advantage. Only to quickly wilt.

It saved her from having to fend off his advances. But she felt that he somehow blamed his male problems on her. Which, of course, he should. But he didn't know that. A sexually frustrated sociopath, however, was an exceptionally dangerous animal.

Sol and his minions watched her every move. She was never left alone and she'd collected little to no new intelligence.

And Sol's cast and crew? Tight-lipped or knew nothing. They gossiped innocuously and seemed genuinely happy and excited for the act. She was completely stymied.

Meanwhile Rock worked long hours in secret with his troupe of young magicians, locked behind closed doors in his private rehearsal space. He hadn't made good on his promise to win her love. Hadn't even made any halfway valiant attempts. And she'd so been looking forward to the game. But then he was as much a liar as she was.

Maybe she should have been relieved, but she'd expected more tenacity from him, And fun. He'd disappointed her.

But he was sweet in his concern for her safety, insisting on devising a signal, a parade wave aimed at him and Tate, if she felt in any danger on stage during the performance. If she gave the signal, he and Tate would rush to the rescue. They evidently had contingency plans for everything. Rock believed that Sol would stop at nothing to get revenge. Killing Lani was an effective way to do it.

Lani blew out a breath as she waited for her cue.

Lani agreed with Rock in theory. But she was convinced Sol would never do anything to ruin his act. Despite Rock's fears, she was confident she'd be perfectly safe on stage. For the duration of the show.

The show's choreographer came by and rested a hand on her shoulder. She jumped.

"You okay?" he asked. "Got a case of jitters tonight?"

She gave him a wobbly smile. "Just a bit of stage fright. It's been a few years." She paused. "You have to admit—this is a pretty dramatic comeback. What will Rock do when he sees me again?" She laughed nervously. And she didn't even have to fake it. "My mouth is dry as cotton."

The choreographer gave her shoulder a squeeze, twisted the top off a bottle of flavored water he'd been carrying, and handed it to her. "Here. Wet your whistle. You'll be fine. Sol will protect you."

Sure he will. She nodded, took the water, and gratefully took a sip. But only a sip. That's all her nerves and costume would allow. The water was overly sweet with just a hint of bitter aftertaste. Or maybe that was just the bad taste in her mouth from working with Sol.

She needed to get her head in the show and calm down. As it was she could barely breathe in the tightly corseted white bodice of her costume. She was sure Sol had ordered it laced extra tight.

Before the mission began, Malene had altered the costume so that it still went on like second skin. Lani looked down at the wedding gown with a diaphanous skirt that would catch the laser light bouncing around the stage. The sheer material showed off her tanned legs and the tiny white-sequined bikini panties she wore. Just like it had the first time she'd worn it. She was even more nervous now.

On stage, Sol was performing the pledge, the setup of the trick. "Ladies and gentlemen, behold my beautiful assistant. Isn't she lovely?" Sol's voice boomed through the theater, silken and husky, a clear imitation of Rock's.

The assistant, who vaguely resembled Lani, was dressed as the sexy vixen in red who'd reappeared instead of Lani in Rock's act. A close-up of the red lady's face flashed on a giant video screen behind Sol. The sequins of her costume caught the stage light and flashed sparkles of red, looking as if she was shooting sparks. Sol was making it clear he was performing Rock's trick in reverse, disappearing the red girl. But could he reappear the bride?

The audience had already begun to suspect something special was about to happen and grew hushed in anticipation.

Rock and Tate sat in the third row. Close enough to come to Lani's aid. Up front to be directly in the spotlight so the press could find them and take in Rock's reaction. She hoped he acted according to plan and the script they'd all laid out and agreed upon.

Lani peeked through the curtain, though it was fruitless trying to get a look at Rock and gauge his reaction in the darkened audience. The video of Rock disappearing Lani that final time had gone viral and been splashed all over the news for weeks. Sol was copying it bit for bit. Lani hoped Rock's handler, Tal, had trained him well enough to maintain his cool.

Sol, who always wore a tux on stage, was looking slightly disheveled and grinning widely, euphoric he was finally about to upstage the great Rock Powers. Sol wore tight black tux pants. His gauzy white shirt fell open to his waist. His bow tie was untied, hanging loose on either side of his chest.

He pulled the red assistant into his embrace. "They say that love makes you feel as if your feet don't touch the ground."

That was Rock's line. The audience recognized it. They were on the edge of their seats. It was so quiet, Lani could have heard a silencer go off.

Slowly, the two began to levitate together. The audience wasn't impressed. Not yet. Sol was just heading into the turn of the trick. Another sexy, scantily clad assistant tossed him a shiny silver hoop.

As Sol spun it all around the two of them, proving there were no strings attached, the audience applauded. But they were still tense with anticipation for the real magic.

The red-clad woman wrapped herself around Sol. Touched his cheek. Ran her fingers through his hair. Watching a parody of herself, a mockery of how she and Rock had been on stage, a fake, Lani felt sick and a little light-headed.

The couple levitated higher into the air. The crowd went wild. Lani screwed the lid on the bottle of water she was still holding and set it on the floor out of the way.

Curls of smoke wafted up over the curtain. The music on stage rose to a crescendo. That was her cue to get into place. The choreographer gave her a gentle shove. "Break a leg."

She slid behind the black curtain that was part of the trick and let the stagehands lock her into the cabinet that was part of the illusion. She felt a wave of panic. She'd been in some tight situations and never been claustrophobic before. It was thinking about Rock, how this would hurt him, even though he knew about it.

In a second, the other assistant would glide behind the

curtain. The stagehands would switch the cabinet Lani crouched in with the one on stage. When Sol opened it, Lani would jump out like a stripper popping out of a cake and take the other girl's place in the act.

Lani listened intently to the music, waiting for her cue and trying to remain calm and not hyperventilate in the tight space. She couldn't seem to catch a deep breath. The feeling of being light-headed grew. She'd never had this much stage fright before, but she was beginning to feel thickheaded. She practiced a moment of meditation, an old stress-relieving technique they taught at the Farm, and a more pleasant floating sensation washed over her.

The motion of the cabinet being moved momentarily gave her vertigo. This had never happened in rehearsal.

There was a tap on the top of the cabinet. Lani loosened the latch from the inside. The lid snapped open. Lani sprang to a stand and threw her arms in the air in a triumphant pose.

Her long dark hair blew in the breeze created by fans at the other end of the stage. She felt disoriented. The music was louder and more pulsing than she remembered and the laser and lights bothered her as if she was getting a migraine. She had to resist the urge to turn to the audience, find Rock, and stare at him.

Sol faked a surprised, stunned expression. He took a step back and threw up his hands. His jaw dropped. "This isn't the girl I just made disappear." He leaned in for a closer look and then broke into a grin as her face flashed on the screen behind them, eight feet tall and unmistakable side by side with a picture of her from Rock's act.

Sol extended a hand to help her out of the box. As they'd rehearsed, she took it and stepped out of the box. And stumbled. She felt oddly clumsy and unable to control her body.

Sol held her hand, steadying her.

"Ladies and gentlemen, if I'm not mistaken, a miracle has just occurred. I've just completed another magician's prestige from a trick that began two years ago.

"May I present, Mrs. Rock Powers!"

Sol held her hand in the air, entwined tightly with his. The audience went pin-drop silent and burst into applause. Sol grinned into the auditorium directly at Rock. "I believe you owe me one hundred thousand dollars, Rock."

CHAPTER FOURTEEN

A spotlight highlighted Rock where he sat in the third row of the audience next to Tate, staring at Lani. Something was wrong. She was clumsy and the fingers of her free hand were twitching.

Out of the corner of his eye, Rock saw a muscle in Tate's jaw tic. Tate was realizing the same thing as Rock. Sol had drugged Lani.

"Damn the signal," Rock said beneath his breath to Tate.

"Go." Tate whipped out his phone and initiated the rescue sequence.

Rock bolted out of his chair, jumped the two rows of seats in front of him as Jake had taught him how to do in practice, and bounded onto the stage almost as if he flew.

Rock dislodged Lani's hand from Sol's, shoved Sol out of the way, and pulled Lani into an embrace. One hand around her waist, he tipped her chin up so her eyes met his. Her pupils were pinpoints and her eyes unfocused.

He kissed her for the crowd's benefit, to throw Sol off the scent, and give his team time to spring into action. Kissed her as he'd imagined kissing her for two years, willing her to hang on. Kissed her deeply as if he'd never let her go again, hoping it wasn't too late to save her.

The crowd erupted in cheers.

Rock pulled out of the kiss, and leaned into Sol's mic. "I'll drop the check in the mail. Thanks, man. Now, if you'll excuse us, we have a honeymoon to make up."

Rock got a glimpse of Tate getting to his feet in the crowd.

As Sol took a step toward them, Rock let loose a hefty dose of flash powder. The fancy stuff with the sparks and glitter the guys had made fun of.

While Sol was stunned and disoriented, Rock grabbed Lani's hand and pulled her with him behind the black velvet vanishing curtain. With the roar of approval from the crowd masking his exit, Rock dragged Lani past the stunned backstage crew.

Lani stumbled, clumsy on her feet as he pulled her toward a hotel service entrance to the backstage maze of hallways the hotel staff used. Two of Sol's thugs hung fast on their tail, closing Rock's meager lead.

Rock had to get Lani out of danger and give her the antidote before it was too late. She was breathing shallowly and her reflexes were slow. He recognized these particular symptoms—narcotic poisoning. He'd seen them before. In layman's terms, a drug overdose.

Rock aimed his thumb gun at the men pursuing them. He looked like an inept hitchhiker trying to thumb a ride. But his thumb was deadly and he had the element of surprise. No one expected a thumb gun. Only one problem—he had one shot to take down two pursuers. And with his curved thumb, his aim wasn't that good.

Should have brought the wand gun. Six shots would even the odds.

One of the thugs pulled out a semiautomatic pistol and drew a bead on them.

First rule of dying another day—don't let the bad guys apprehend you.

Lani was dragging, barely staying on her feet. Rock scooped Lani into his arms and charged around a corner out of sight of their two pursuers as a bullet whizzed past them. "Hang with me, baby."

The service entrance loomed before them. Rock pointed his finger at it. "Alakazam!"

The door required a key card to open, but Will, his geek-boy magician's apprentice, had made Rock a jammer finger. The door clicked and unlocked. Rock threw his shoulder into it and barreled through with Lani still in his arms.

A stick to jam the door was leaning up against the wall just where Rock had instructed Will to leave it. Rock set Lani down for a second, propped her against the wall, and jammed the door just as Sol's guy thudded against it. Rock also jammed the security cameras with a gizmo he'd borrowed from Tate.

Even trying to use the wall to steady herself, Lani was wobbling on her feet. "I'm so sleepy, Rock." She gasped for breath as her skin started turning blue. "I'm OD'ing. Sol put something in my bottled water." She gasped again as her arms and head twitched.

In another few minutes she'd convulse and go into a coma.

"I know, baby. I know." Rock pulled a syringe from his pocket and jabbed it into her thigh.

Her eyes went wide and she tried to smile, but the shakes were engulfing her entire body. "Naloxone? Are you a closet addict?"

"I've heard rumors Sol dopes his assistants with narcotics to help them stay calm in tight spaces. Usually he uses small doses of codeine. I came prepared in case he tried something, like making it look like you took your own life or accidentally ODed." Rock took her in his arms and held her tight, kissing the top of her head. "Hang in there. It'll take effect in a few minutes and then I'm gonna get us out of here."

As her shakes started subsiding, Rock picked her up and carried her along the corridor.

Her color started coming back and her breathing became more regular. "They'll be waiting for us at the exits."

"Let them. If everything's gone to plan, my decoy's already leading them on a merry rabbit chase."

"Decoy?" The pupils of Lani's eyes were returning to normal.

Rock almost felt like he could breathe again, too. "Ashley."

"No, Rock! It's too dangerous—"

He laughed and fought back a wave of emotion. Lani was going to be okay. "Worried about others? You must be feeling better. Don't worry. Ashley's damn good. She'll dart here and there, throwing them off, changing outfits in between and mysteriously reappearing.

"I warned all the kids this would be dangerous shit. No one objected. NCS recruited them for more than their magic. You want them to be agents, then it's time they started acting like agents."

Rock propped Lani up against a wall again and reached into his pocket to pull out one of Ashley's ingeniously designed quick-change outfits. It was so compact and lightweight, he'd even managed to carry the shoes—a pair of ballet flats—on him.

"How big is that pocket?" Lani was trying to smile. "What else are you going to pull out of there?"

He grinned. "Britt's got us covered with social media magic. She's whipping up a frenzy of support for us right now. There will be a crowd waiting for us in the driveway in front of the lobby. We're going to walk right out the lobby beneath Sol's nose. I don't believe even Sol is dumb enough to strike us in the middle of a mob of fans.

"Think how angry he'll be when he sees the footage of you walking out of this joint on my arm, very much alive." His voice broke with emotion.

He covered quickly by holding the clothes out to her. "Change into this? I want it to look as if we've changed into our honeymoon clothes and are trying to sneak away. And they'll provide cover in case anything goes wrong with my plan." He held the outfit out to Lani. "Do you need my help?"

Lani rolled her eyes as she reached for the change of outfit. "You've been trying to get me out of my costume since the first day you met me."

As she peeled off her bridal veil and kicked off her heels, Rock stripped off his jacket and unbuttoned his shirt, taking it off to reveal a T-shirt beneath. "Guilty as charged."

He took off his signature leather necklace and ear-rings and pulled on a hat. Then he grabbed the front of his pants, gave a quick tug reminiscent of the old pull-off-the-tablecloth trick and his pants came off, revealing a pair of skintight leather pants beneath.

"Whoa!" Lani smiled. "Stripper magician."

"Ashley's pure costuming magic."

"Quick change isn't as sexy as a slow, tantalizing strip-tease."

"Next time I'll bring the stripper pole in my pocket," he said.

"I'd like to see that." Lani turned her back to Rock. "Get me out of this corset. Fast. The stays are killing me. I can barely breathe."

Rock's fingers trembled as he untied the corset strings and clumsily loosened the back of the bodice holding her in. He hoped she didn't notice. Her back was bare and creamy beneath the bodice. In fact, except for the tiny panties, she was totally bare beneath the costume, period. Her color was returning. She was coming back to life, but he wanted to get her safely back to the mansion.

Lani took a deep breath and sighed as she shimmied, still somewhat awkwardly, but totally erotically to Rock's sex-starved brain, out of her costume.

He handed her the blouse to the disguise Ashley had created for Lani to Rock's specifications. Fortunately, he'd still had her measurements on file. As if he hadn't committed them to memory.

Although recovering, her motor skills were still off and clumsy. She couldn't get the blouse over her head and time was ticking dangerously away. Rock grabbed her hand. Helped her get it into the sleeve. Pulled the garment over her head. Got her other arm in. Still from behind her, he reached in front of her to pull the blouse down and got an accidental feel of her budded breasts.

His breath caught. *Damn.*

He expected her to slap him. Stomp on his foot. At the very least upbraid him. Instead, she relaxed into him, leaning her head back against his shoulder. "You're my hero, Rock."

"You won't think so if RIOT gets us." Rock had to tug to get the top over her breasts. She was bustier than she had been, and yet she looked no heavier otherwise.

He didn't have time to worry about it. From behind, he kneeled and held the tight red skirt out for her to step into. As she put a foot into it, she had to brace one hand on his shoulder to keep her balance. She laughed as she stumbled.

This wasn't funny. She'd had a close call.

She released his shoulder. He stood as she bent to tug

the skirt up, struggling once she reached her hips. She lost her balance and fell back into him, pressing herself against the rising bulge in his crotch.

This was no time to be aroused, yet Rock couldn't help himself. However magical, love and lust were involuntary reactions. The threat of danger and discovery only heightened them.

He reached behind her, grabbed the skirt, and yanked it up, struggling to get it over her hips, too. He mumbled, "This was supposed to be a quick-change operation."

Somehow he got the skirt in place. But not before he copped a feel of Lani's firm sexy stomach. He smoothed the skirt into place, running his hands over the curve of her hips, balling his fists against temptation. Finally, he kneeled before her like Prince Charming and helped her slide into the flats. He scooped up her clothes, grabbed her hand, and ran.

"There's a limo waiting for us in the driveway. Very good car service. They provide security detail and excellent drivers. And the glass is bulletproof."

"You've thought of everything."

Rock ditched Lani's clothes in the first laundry cart they came to. He pulled her along until they came to the door that let them into the end of the lobby nearest the exit.

Rock took a deep breath. "Showtime. Make it look like we're trying to sneak out unnoticed."

Rock slid the door open. The two of them slipped out.

A crowd of reporters, paparazzi, and hotel guests milled around the lobby and spilled out into the driveway and into the night.

As Rock led Lani toward the car, a bright young blonde turned in their direction. It took a second for recognition to dawn on her. "It's them—Rock and his reappeared wife!" She waved and squealed and bounced up on her toes.

They were immediately bombarded with flashing lights from paparazzi and a swirl of questions from reporters and fans alike.

A thousand mics, or so it seemed, were thrust in their faces.

Lani's head buzzed. A crash was coming. The lights hurt her eyes. She held her hand up to shield them. This may have been a brilliant plan, but she didn't like feeling so exposed. A well-trained sniper like her fellow agent Jack Pierce could have taken her out without hitting anyone else and disappeared into the night like the spook he was. A RIOT agent could do the same.

Someone stuck a mic nearly up her nose. "Why'd you come back, Lani? Where have you been?"

Rock shoved the mic away and took command. He was grinning like an idiot in the same way he had during their wedding ceremony. "I'm thrilled, thrilled to have Lani back. Many thanks to my old friend Sol for returning her in his typical showy fashion." Rock laughed. "But watch out, Sol. You owe me a prestige. If one of your girls turns up in my act, it's only fair play."

"Rock, you've maintained your innocence all along. Do you feel vindicated now?"

Rock was still grinning. "I have and I do. I think this clears my name now." He grinned for the cameras and stepped aside just enough to show Lani off. "Doesn't she look gorgeous?" His voice broke.

The man was a true showman.

"As you can all see, she's perfect. Not a hair harmed." Rock squeezed Lani to him. "I'm a damned awesome magician. And so is Sol. But neither of us can resurrect someone from the grave."

More flashes went off in their faces. The lights hurt Lani's eyes and she felt weak. She leaned on Rock for support.

More rapid-fire questions: "What's the full story, Rock?" "How did this happen?" "Where has Lani been?" "Did you plan this all along?"

"If I had planned this all along I would have reappeared her myself." He tried to guide Lani through the crush. "We promise we'll have a press release soon and explain everything we can. For now, please allow us a little privacy and time to get reacquainted. This is all very new to us, too."

"Lani! Lani!" someone yelled. "Are you glad to be back?"

The crowd wanted a showstopper. A brilliant sound bite, a delicious video clip. She slid her hand along Rock's cheek, turned his head toward her, and looked up into his eyes with all the longing and emotion she'd been keeping pent up for two very long years. She smiled at him, a genuine smile, a sappy almost hero-worship smile, and leaned up for a kiss, trying to keep the adrenaline flowing.

Her lips met his softly, delicately. This was just supposed to be a sweet kiss, nothing too vulgar, no over-the-top public display of affection. Just a tentative, romantic reunion between two people separated too long. And wasn't that the truth?

Rock seemed to sense it and kissed her back gently. And then, before she could react, he scooped her into his arms.

"Now, if you'll excuse us, my wife and I have a long-overdue honeymoon to take." Rock winked at the crowd.

Magically, like everything Rock did, the crowd parted for them and broke into simultaneous applause. The young woman, Rock's social media magician, disappeared.

At the limo, the driver opened the door. Rock gently placed Lani on the seat and slid in next to her, slipping his arm around her waist. He was still waving as the driver closed the door on the crowd.

The instant the privacy shield was up and the tinted bulletproof glass was between them and any RIOT thugs with murderous intent, Rock took Lani's face in his hands and stared into her eyes. "That was close."

He grabbed her wrist, felt her pulse, and relaxed. "Nice and strong."

And rapid because he was so near and she wanted him so badly.

"You've turned doctor on me now?" She shook her head, teasing him, flirting. The heat of his hand around her wrist and his confident, reassuring grip turned her on. An escape from death always gave her a high, and this one had been a close call.

"I know a thing or two about addicts and the signs of overdose." He slid his other arm around her and pulled her closer. "Your skin is flushed and hot again. Your eyes are dilated in the dark. All in all, you're responding well to treatment."

And his touch. He was describing a woman who was turned on, and from the look in his eyes, he knew it.

A cluster of paparazzi pulled out behind the limo, chasing and pulling up next to them, trying to get the picture of the moment. The limo driver took a quick right turn, trying to lose them. But they weren't fooled and quickly caught up. Though she couldn't see them, Lani imagined dozens of cameras were pointed at her and Rock.

Lani ignored them and took Rock's face in her hands. "You saved my life. There aren't words, but thank you."

He held her gaze. "You won't thank me when the naloxone wears off and your mood crashes."

"There are antidotes for that, too. Any good doctor knows an endorphin rush quells depression and withdrawal symptoms." She leaned into him until her lips were only inches from his.

"Damn, that's too bad. I don't have any dark chocolate

on me. Isn't that a woman's endorphin drug of choice?" He tightened his grip around her waist. "Maybe back at the mansion."

"By the time we arrive, the adrenaline rush from our little adventure will be wearing off. Everyone knows thrill seekers like us get a huge endorphin boost from adventure, especially after a narrow escape like this one.

"A double endorphin rush completely cures a post-high depression." She inched her lips closer to his. "And the next best thing to chocolate is sex. So . . ." She brushed his lips tantalizingly lightly and traced his chest with one finger. "We can either stop at a convenience store for chocolate and let the paparazzi harass us and snap pictures of us buying candy bars. I can just see the headlines on that one. Or you can make love to me now. Your choice."

But she wasn't really giving him a choice. She needed Rock *now*. Needed the comfort and love of holding him and making love with him. As she slid off her ballet flats and slid into Rock's lap, straddling him, her tiny red skirt slid up around her hips.

His breath caught as she settled herself on the straining bulge in his lap.

"I've missed you, Rock. Missed you so much, baby."

Very lightly, very softly, very slowly, she lowered her slightly parted lips to his until they just barely met. She knew Rock—he was a crazy romantic. He liked to be teased, tantalized, and eased slowly into passion.

His lips were slightly parted, too, warm, relaxed, and soft. Lani lightly touched the tip of her tongue to his through their parted lips.

Rock shuddered. She ran her tongue over his lips with the whisper-soft touch of a butterfly, ran her fingers through his hair with one hand, unbuttoned his shirt, pulled it open, and stroked his chest.

Next to them, a motorcycle pulled up.

He held her close, pressing her against his naked chest and kissing her neck. "Lani, Lani . . ."

Lani slid off him just enough to reach his fly where he was hard and wonderful and ready for her.

Rock grabbed her wrist and pulled her chin up to look her in the eye. "Not like this. Not in the backseat. Not after two years."

"Exactly like this," she whispered back and nibbled his ear. "In the dark. In the heat of passion. I want you desperately." She twisted her wrist to free it.

He clamped it tighter, so tightly she felt her pulse pounding through his grip.

"Do you love me?" he whispered back.

She held his gaze, unable to lie to him. So she told a half-truth. "In this moment, yes."

He let go of her wrist.

She leaned her forehead against his, looking him in the eye.

"Not with the paparazzi watching and ready to snap a picture with their night-vision lenses," he said. "The right lens can take a picture through tinted glass."

The neon lights from the strip filtered through the bulletproof glass, lighting the car in bursts of blue, green, red, pink, and violet.

"What do we do, then, Rock?" she whispered as she rubbed her palm against his nipple and imagined Rock sucking on hers. "I'm *so* desperate for you."

"Still have that fantasy where I disappear you in a puff of smoke on stage and we make love in the two minutes before the smoke dissipates?" His voice was ragged with desire. "Does the thrill of being caught still turn you on? Night cameras can't shoot through smoke."

She hadn't thought it was possible to get even hotter, but just the thought of acting out her fantasy made her wetter. "Don't tell me that magic pocket of yours holds even more tricks?"

He grinned. "The tricks I can do are endless. The smoke will be thick for only a few minutes. You'll have to hold your breath through the thick of it."

"I can hold my breath for three minutes." She traced his jawline. "Are you up to it?"

"I once held my breath for seven minutes during an illusion."

"But you weren't making love to me, baby," she cooed.

"I think I can make it for two. Ready?"

She kissed him lightly and unzipped his fly on the sly. "I'm wearing thong panties. They shouldn't be much of a barrier to entry for you."

His breath was shallow and rapid. "On the count of three. One."

Anticipation made her tingle.

Two."

She took a deep breath.

"Three. Disappear with me, Lani." Rock tossed a handful of vanishing powder onto the floor.

As smoke filled the limo, and the neon lights caught the sparkles, lighting the cab with glittering bursts of fireworks, Lani pulled Rock's wonderfully full and hard erection out of his pants and stroked him.

There was no time to linger. This was breath-holding, hard-on, fast-paced sex.

He caught her hand and removed it from his hard desire, kissed her fingers, and thrust up, past her panties, catching her off guard with the force and urgency of his entry. He felt so hard and wonderful, she almost lost her breath as the sparkles from the flash died out. Sheer force of will kept her from gasping or crying out as waves of pleasure built.

She wrapped her legs around Rock, clamped him

tightly and rode him mercilessly in the thinning smoke. Only touch mattered. Neither of them made a sound, not even heavy breathing.

As Rock bucked beneath her, she dug her heels into his back and pulled him deep into her, shutting out everything but the feel of him and the joy of being with him. With each thrust, he pushed her closer to the edge of climax.

With each thrust, the smoke became gauzier and thinner and her excitement at being caught built.

Their veil was rapidly lifting. But Lani held back, savoring the intimacy and pleasure until the last minute before she ran out of breath and smoke.

Rock thrust again and again, more insistent, more determined, more powerful. She gave him a breathless kiss and arched back as the most exquisite climax crashed over her, so powerful, she involuntarily gasped for breath and moaned.

Hearing her, Rock lost control, grunted, stiffened, and climaxed with her.

Breathing hard, Lani leaned her forehead against Rock's. "You really can hold your breath."

He grinned. "I'm breathing hard now." He stroked her hair and kissed the tip of her nose. Sweat beaded on his forehead and chest.

Her legs trembled around him. She kissed him again and slid off him, coughing on the last wisps of smoke as she adjusted her clothing.

Rock opened the window and clasped her tightly against him. He kissed the top of her head. "That was close."

"No, that was perfection," she said as half a dozen cameras flashed at them through the window.

CHAPTER FIFTEEN

Tate beat them back to the mansion. The rented Audi sat in the curved drive in front of the house.

Having expertly evaded the paparazzi at the gate, the driver stopped the limo and came around to open the door. Lani was exhausted and almost asleep. Rock scooped her into his arms and carried her inside. He liked it when she was like this, needing his help, letting him baby her. She was usually so alpha, take-charge. He would have spoiled her so much more, shown her so many more good things, taken care of her if only she'd let him.

Ty looked up from a tablet notebook he was reading and arched a brow.

Tate set down a glass of what looked like whiskey on the bar. "The kids made it back safe and sound. We were beginning to wonder about you two."

"The paparazzi slowed us down," Rock said.

Even Tal was there, popping in from out of nowhere after days of absence. "Welcome home."

"Where the hell have you been?" Rock asked him.

"Handling my other charges." Tal laughed. "You think you're my only one?"

Lani leaned her head into Rock's chest. "That's the way handlers operate. They pop in and out at will." She spoke softly and yawned.

"We need to talk," Tal said.

"After I put Lani to bed."

"Rock saved my life," she said and looked up and winked at him intimately. "With a shot of naloxone."

"I'm relieved to hear it," Tate said. "Good job."

Rock nodded. "I told you he'd try something."

"How are you feeling now?" Ty asked Lani. "Do you want us to send for a doctor?"

"I feel . . ." She looked at Rock again. "Fine. Tired. I've lived through worse. No need for a doc. I just need some rest."

Rock walked past them and carried her up the curved staircase to the master bedroom. No one made a move to stop him. Good thing, too, because he was pretty sure they could all outshoot him and his thumb gun.

As he carried Lani across the room, she slipped off her shoes. He managed to pull the covers back with one hand, barely disturbing the pillows on top. Those tablecloth-removing skills came in handy now and again.

As he slid her onto the sheets and pulled the covers up, she sighed and snuggled in. She looked young and re-laxed, with none of the tough edges she had when she was awake and in secret agent mode.

He supposed he should have undressed her. But she looked so comfortable and happy, he simply pulled the covers up. He smoothed her hair back from her face, kissed her lightly on the cheek, and walked across the room pre-paring to face the secret agent inquisition from the guys in the room below. Rock paused at the door to look back at Lani. *If she can love me in a moment, she can love me forever.*

He knew he'd been right to search for her all this time. He hadn't been mistaken. She may have been on a mis-sion then, as now, but she loved him despite orders not to.

Now he just had to figure out a way to convince her she was better off with him than without him.

He stepped out of the room and closed the door softly behind him.

Downstairs the three agents were exactly where he'd left them. They all looked up and gave him matching looks to those he'd received upon his first arrival. These guys needed to add some variety to their act. Maybe he'd suggest it.

"How'd you know to bring naloxone?" Ty asked.

Rock shrugged. "Elementary. Sol's rumored to give painkillers to his assistants before his act. It calms them and allows them to get into painful positions for his acts.

"I told you, Sol uses dangerous practices. Codeine has always been his drug of choice. It wouldn't be too hard for him to claim Lani took too many because of nerves or guilt and accidentally overdosed."

"But killing Lani like that?" Tate said. "I wonder if that went against RIOT orders. Lani is the only leverage they have against you. Why eliminate her?"

"So that when I commit suicide in a few days, despondent over her death, no one will suspect I've been murdered." Rock paused for dramatic effect. "For spies, you really don't watch enough cop shows.

"But I will have to say you were right about one thing." Rock held up his thumb. "I should have brought the wand gun. I had two thugs on my tail. One shot was not enough."

Tate grinned. "More firepower is always better."

"Yeah, I realized that too late." Rock walked to the bar and poured himself a drink. He pulled his cell phone from his pocket. "I should check in on my team and congratulate them on a job well done."

"Don't bother," Ty said. "We already have."

Rock grinned. "I did a damn fine job with those kids.

This was a dress rehearsal for the bigger show and they pulled it off without a hitch. Or a leak. Key for both magicians and secret agents."

Tate walked behind the bar as if he was going to mix himself another drink. Instead, he stooped, picked something up, and held it up for Rock to inspect. "Does this look familiar?"

Rock examined it. "One of the knives I use in my act." Rock frowned. "What does that have to do with anything?"

"It's distinctive and it shouts Rock Powers. And we pulled it off one of Sol's goons. You were wrong about the overdose," Tate said, drily. "After Lani's death, they were going to slit your wrists and make it look like suicide."

As Rock stared at them, he felt his jaw tic. "That's bloody."

"And painful," Tal added.

"I'm going to kill Sol when I get the chance," Rock said.

"I wouldn't go spouting that around in public," Tate said.

Ty, Tate, and Tal exchanged looks with each other. For a trio of spies, they looked decidedly uncomfortable and as if they were keeping something from Rock. He thought these guys were supposed to be kings of the poker face. Which made him just the tiniest bit suspicious—what garden path were they planning to walk him down now?

Tate looked at Ty. Ty shrugged. Tal was evidently no help.

"Ah, hell." Tate sighed. "You're probably going to hear this from Sol himself sooner or later, but he was bragging to his crew about sleeping with Lani."

Rock clenched his jaw so tightly he felt like he was about to break a tooth or pop a blood vessel or maybe both. "Sol's a liar! Lani would never—"

He cut himself off and looked at the three other men.

Tal cleared his throat. "She's a spy. She does what she has to do."

Ty nodded. "Yeah, we all did. In the pre–ball and chain days. Now Tate's the only one who gets to sleep around for the job. Treflee would kill me if I did."

"If she found out about it," Tal said.

"She'd know. Believe me, she'd find out about it. She has spies everywhere. Sometimes I think the Agency should hire her and her network," Ty said.

"Don't listen to them." Tate slapped Rock on the back. "It's not all that much fun sleeping with enemy agents. After the sex, when all you'd really rather do is sleep, they try to kill you. Nearly every time. And if not then, later. And don't even get me started about an enemy agent scorned . . ."

"Yeah, it's really tough duty," Tal said. He shut up when Tate shot him a look that said he wasn't helping matters.

Rock took a deep breath. "Why would you take Sol's word for it?"

"Lani was right there and didn't deny it," Tate said.

The master bedroom in Rock's mansion had blackout curtains on its 180-degree panoramic-view windows. The room was round, like a turret on a castle, a knight's abode. But the curtains were cracked open and the sunlight was streaming through when Lani was awakened from sleep by the gentle swoosh of the door skimming deep, plush carpet, and the smell of bacon and coffee.

She sat up, reached for her gun, which was missing, and swung her gaze toward the door, assessing her options. She realized then that she was still dressed in the red outfit Rock had had her change into last night when he stole her from Sol's show.

Rock stood in the doorway, carrying a breakfast tray complete with a red rose in a vase. "Morning, beautiful. No need to bring out the big weapons. It's just your ador-ing husband come to pamper you before a hard day of spying." He wore the trace of a smile, just a trace, and his voice was low and sexy, mesmerizing.

Lani glanced at the clock. "What time is it?"

"Nine." Rock walked over and set the tray over her legs.

Nine! Lani couldn't remember the last time she'd slept so late.

Rock sat down next to her on the bed. He smiled and swept the hair out of her eyes. "You were drugged, remember?" He laughed softly. "Maybe not." He laughed again. "I rescued you from Sol's clutches and certain death."

Rock looked perfectly delectable when he was bragging about his heroics. "Certain death? I thought you stole me away in the middle of his act. Just to foil him and steal his thunder. You always have liked to one-up him." She mocked a frown. "There goes my paycheck and my shot at black magic stardom."

Rock held a cup of coffee out to her. "The asshole deserves it. And you'll have your shot at stardom. With me. *If* you want it."

His words made her breath catch as she took the cup from him. She didn't know what to say. Oh, she knew what she should say. She knew she should stomp on his little old aorta and dash any hopes of an *until death do us part* little wife-and-husband duo. The odds didn't favor a family magic act for them and the son Rock didn't know he had.

Rock mistook her hesitation. His grin faded, replaced by a look of concern and consternation. "You don't remember the drugging?" He cocked a brow. "And what followed?"

Oh, she remembered that well enough. She was just pulling his chain.

She nodded and took a sip of coffee before speaking. "That bottle of water the stagehand gave me just before I went on. Never trust a sealed bottle of water, not from a magician, anyway. Or one of his crew."

"You can trust *this* magician." Rock pulled the linen napkin from the tray. "Nothing up my sleeve."

Nothing but rock-hard biceps. He was wearing a short-sleeved T-shirt that showed them off very nicely, thank you.

"No, I can see that." She set the coffee down on the tray. Knowing what was coming, she watched him closely.

"Empty napkin to begin with." He showed her and then grabbed the napkin and began rolling it from the center. When it was in a nice roll, with only a triangle of tail hanging out, he grabbed the tail and pulled. The napkin unrolled, revealing a table knife with a flourish.

Back in their happy good old days, Rock used to bring her breakfast in bed just like this. He'd set the tray down and make all kinds of things appear in the center of the napkin. Usually flatware. Sometimes a piece of jewelry or other small gift.

She knew how the trick was done, but as many times as Lani had watched him perform it, it still seemed like magic. He was that good. She never saw him working the reality behind it. It was a lot like being in love with Rock—somehow he worked his magic on her, even though she shouldn't have loved him.

"Dull cutlery, how lovely. I hear you pulled diamond jewelry out of thin air for Tate's latest bimbo, that awful blonde, Gillian." She winked.

"But, baby, you are Gillian." His voice was calm, deep, sexy. Almost mesmerizing. He stared at her with a look she couldn't quite pin down.

He was masking what he felt from her. He was good at masking, nearly as good as she was. It was disconcerting. She liked to be the one in control and able to read the other person with her considerable skill in reading microexpressions. Rock stymied her. But that was part of the attraction.

"You were there when I had to give it back." She pulled the knife from the napkin and used it to spread jam on her toast. Rock had brought her a nice pot of seedless raspberry jam, her favorite.

"Unborrowed jewelry. I'll keep that in mind for next time. Hard to spread jam with, though." Rock continued staring at her with his deep, penetrating gaze, his voice modulated and under control.

"Something the matter?" she asked him.

"No. Should there be?"

Last night had been fantastic, hot, exciting between them. But now there was a subtle distance between them. For whatever reason, Rock was trying to hide it. But it was still there. She couldn't think what she possibly could have done in the hours she'd been asleep. Best to ignore it. "Why did Sol want me dead? He doesn't suspect I'm an agent, does he?"

"No. It was his ultimate revenge against me." Then he went on to explain about the knife and the theory that Sol was trying to kill Rock and make it look like suicide because he was despondent over Lani's death.

"Not good about him wanting to kill us. But good news my cover isn't blown." She frowned. "For a minute there I thought he'd realized I'd hypnotized him. My hypnotic suggestions not to hurt you or me sure didn't stick.

"I should have known not to mess with a messed-up mind. I should have figured his sense of revenge would overcome my hypnotic suggestion to protect me. He is a sociopath, after all." She cursed beneath her breath, mumbling about a lapse in her spycraft.

"Don't tell me you tried to hypnotize him?" Rock's calm expression momentarily cracked again. A quick look of fear crossed his face before he regained control.

When he spoke, it was in that same soothing voice. "You *really* think you hypnotized Sol? Sol isn't hypnotizable. He knows all the tricks and he's one hundred percent resistant.

"But it explains why he tried to kill you. Now he *knows* you're not loyal. And if there's one thing Sol can't stand, it's unfaithfulness." A microexpression of anger crossed Rock's face at the word *unfaithfulness*. It, too, passed quickly.

Lani stared at Rock with the table knife in one hand and a piece of toast in the other. "You do realize I have a knife in my hand and I know a thousand lethal ways to use it, even though it barely slices through jam?" She pointed the knife at him as she spoke. "FYI, I'm a highly trained, certified, licensed master hypnotist—"

Rock shook his head, still totally tranquil and reassuring when he should have been at least at touch angry at her for trying something so risky. "I know, we've been over that. Sol was faking it, baby. Faking. Don't take it too hard. He can fake out the best of them."

"No one fakes it with me." She paused. "As a secret agent for the U.S. government I also have several powerful hypnosis-aiding drugs at my disposal. I hypnotized you once, too, magic man."

He arched a brow. "Oh, really? When?" He was almost too calm.

She set the knife down. It was no good pointing it at him, anyway. He didn't seem the slightest bit intimidated. "Just after we met. At the beginning of the Hoover Dam mission."

She paused for effect. "I hypnotized *you* to speed you along in the falling in love with me process." She set the toast down, too, next to the bacon and eggs that were growing cold. She'd lost her appetite.

Rock gave her a deadpan look. "Not this again. Not the

Aphrodite complex. We've been over this before. You can't make men fall in love with you left and right by looking deeply into your eyes. Can you make your eyes spin, too? Is that part of the trick?"

He leaned forward across the bed toward her. "Seriously. Lani, darling, you were so cute hypnotizing me that I went along with it."

He paused. "It was flattering in its way. I'd never had a girl so hot and desperate for me she resorted to hypnosis to get her way. Thrown panties at me, yes. Offered to be sawn in half or volunteered to be my able-bodied assistant, absolutely. But hypnosis? Now that was new and thrilling."

He continued to hold her gaze. "You could have been a little more creative, though. Maybe made me your sex slave. I could have gone for that."

"You flatter yourself, Rock."

He ignored her comment. "You really can't hypnotize someone into falling in love. You know that, right?"

She arched a brow.

He paused again, looking as if he was thinking about it for a minute. "Seduce them, possibly. Temporarily bend them into a crush, maybe. If they're already susceptible to your charms. But that's a big risk and a lot of work to go to when a little flirting would suffice."

"Flirty doesn't build loyalty," Lani said. "Flirty doesn't make the other person trust you enough to share secrets."

"I see," Rock said. "What secrets did you want from me?"

She ignored the question. "Why do you think you continued searching for me for two years?"

Rock took a deep breath, looked at her with a confident look of love, and shook his head. "Oh, I don't know. Because I really *do* love you? Because I wanted to clear my name and get the police off my tail? Because I missed you and wanted closure?

"Lani," he said softly. "I know love at first sight sounds stupid and sappy. But you caught my eye the moment you walked into the ice bar wearing that white faux fur coat and matching Russian hat. I knew right away you were the one for my act. *And* me."

"All the girls were wearing white fur coats and hats. It was part of the admission package."

Women wore white coats. Men wore black. Rock had looked particularly hot and handsome in his black faux fur coat, his eyes lined with eyeliner, a magic wand up his sleeve.

She'd gone to the bar ostensibly with friends for a girls' evening out on the prowl—for Rock. In reality, the other three girls with her were also agents, backup in case something went wrong or the Agency intel about Rock's taste in women proved inaccurate. And for cover. A lone girl in a bar was a bit too obvious.

The ice bar was like a modern rendering of the Snow Queen's winter palace. Everything from top to bottom, from wall to wall, was created out of ice—the couches, the bar counter, the floor, even the glasses. Practically everything but the deliciously cold vodka-based cocktails.

On the April day she met Rock, the temperature soared to over a hundred degrees outside. She still remembered with fondness the luxurious feeling of stepping into freezing temperatures and snuggling into a fur coat, even if it was fake fur.

Cold blue light, neon, illuminated the décor, shone through ice sofas, and reflected off polished ice walls so pure they'd turned into mirrors. Elaborately carved ice sculptures adorned the room—winter-white swans, rabbits, deer, and bears.

"You knew I'd be there that night," Rock said, bringing

her focus back to the present. "All my best memories of us and they're setups." He shook his head, but he didn't seem upset.

He looked almost amused and impressed by the deception. Deception was his trade, but—

"Yes, we knew. Of course we knew," she said, trying to figure him out. "Which is why I did my Hispanic impersonation of a Russian agent. I was playing a Bond girl, for your eyes only. We know you love danger. You're a thrill seeker. A Bond girl, a woman with a dangerous edge, has always been your ultimate fantasy."

"Is it? You know me well. Well enough to understand— you're my fantasy, Lani." He paused again. "Now that I think back, the four of you were a redhead, a blonde, an Asian girl with hair as dark as black magic, and you. A buffet, was that it?"

She nodded. "Sometimes it's best not to dwell on the past."

"Still, all dressed alike, all beautiful women, and you were the one who caught my eye." He sounded almost breathless.

"I was intended to. The rest were backup. They intentionally stayed in the background and showcased me. Think back, Rock. Picture it in your mind's eye. Do you have the image? You see what we were doing. You see the performance for what it was.

"The way I caught your eye. Smiled at you. I was practically begging you to send me that drink. If you hadn't, I'd have had to resort to something more obvious." She, too, now spoke in dulcet tones.

"Would you? I would have liked to have seen that. If only I'd known." He was so unflappable and good-humored.

"Still, it *was* impressive the way the drink appeared out of nowhere in a wisp of smoke in front of me. And then there you were, standing beside our table. Pulling an ice rose from up your sleeve was a nice touch, too. Too bad the rose didn't last long out of the bar in the Vegas heat.

"I'm not generally sentimental. But the first flower you ever gave me and there was no way to press it or dry it for posterity." She shrugged. "And here I like to keep souvenirs from my missions."

"You have your wedding ring. That should be souvenir enough for a lifetime." His gaze was intense, his tone soft. "I hope you brought it with you. People will expect you to wear it now that we're happily reunited."

Her wedding ring. *Crap.* "It's in the safe in Tate's hotel room."

Rock made a fist, rubbed his fingers together, and opened his hand palm-up. Her wedding set glistened in the sunlight in his open palm. "Is it?"

She gasped. "That Tate—"

"He had nothing to do with this. I requisitioned it on my own. Saved him a trip. May I?" He took her left hand in his and gently slid the ring on, holding her gaze as he did.

The ring slipped onto her finger as if it belonged there. He squeezed her hand.

She'd never tell him, but she often wore her wedding ring between missions when she was alone and wanted to remember who she really was. Or simply needed to think of him and feel him near her. Never long enough or regular enough to build up a ring imprint on her finger or gain a real sense of permanency. Her covers demanded she be decidedly single. Not a woman who'd removed her rings to go looking for love.

The ring was a gorgeous set with a princess-cut diamond worth nearly a quarter-million dollars. Not the kind of thing a girl could easily pawn. And distinctive enough to give her away if she'd tried. Yet the money would have come in handy, especially with the expense of keeping Stone hidden. If not for the Agency footing the bill . . .

Not that she could ever part with Rock's token of love.

She let Rock hold her hand in the intimate squeeze of his a moment too long. For her own good. She couldn't let herself latch onto Rock again. She had to think of their son. If she got too close to Rock, she'd be tempted to tell him about Stone. And that would never do.

She slipped her hand from his and resisted the urge to hold her hand up and admire the ring resting in its rightful place on her finger.

"Hypnosis is done in steps, Rock. I was drawing you in from the beginning, mesmerizing you, manipulating things. Bending your mind to my will. Love at first sight? Really, I'm surprised a respected member of the magic community would ever believe in such things." She may have been teasing him, but she was playful and trying to build his trust at the same time. She put a hint of flirt in her voice.

She waved her hand, admiring the sparkling ring on it. "Your love at first sight was smoke and mirrors. Nothing more than hormones and chemistry. Aided in your case by alcohol, ambience, your favorite perfume heavily laced with pheromones, and a carefully crafted persona of your fantasy girl.

"You loved how I looked. You loved how I made you feel because I flattered you and played up to you in a way I knew would impress you and turn you on. I'm very good with men." She watched him closely. He didn't flinch.

"You loved the fantasy. It was all pure animal attraction, not real love. That kind of thing doesn't last a lifetime. It melts quickly, like the ice rose you gave me.

"What happens when I'm old and gray? Stooped and walk with a walker. When I gain fifty pounds?" She smiled slightly, knowingly, and yet she laced her voice with seduction. "You're right, Rock. That was all an illusion."

"I'll give you that you looked like my fantasy girl. But it was *you* I fell in love with. Your soul, your personality, your essence."

She shook her head. "Really? You mean you love the girl who coincidentally likes your favorite comedians, TV shows, and movies? Who has so many of the same interests?"

She leaned into him. "We know everything about you and how to manipulate you with that knowledge. I already told you that's how I work. That's my specialty. That's part of what makes me a good spy."

She expected him to get up and storm out. Or maybe disappear in a puff of flash powder. But he sat on the edge of the bed and took her hand again, rubbing his thumb over her ring.

"Baby, I'm pretty good at reading people, too. And knowing what's genuine and what's an act. You have never given me enough credit for my mind-reading skills. Believe me when I tell you, I saw the real you. And that's the woman I love.

"Imagine," he said, "what our life could be like if you trusted me with your love. Think of the wonderful times we could have together. You and me, on stage together performing. Touring the world. Seeing places and people. Making love in all kinds of fabulous, romantic locations." He leaned even closer, so close their noses practically touched and there was no looking away from his gaze.

"You trusted me once, enough to show me your magic. Remember how you tried to one-up me with little magic tricks the evening we met? Pushing a coin through an ice table, now that's impressive and takes skill. And guts

Making your number appear on the bottom of my ice glass, that was awesome. Besides someone in the biz, no girl has ever impressed me with her magic like that.

"You have a real love for it. It takes practice to be as skilled as you are."

He was right. She did love magic. The life he painted for them was seductive and enticing.

"My grandpa was a magician," she said. "He taught me those tricks and a love for the art. Why do you think I was chosen for the assignment? Most of the girls could have come to Vegas and gone undercover as showgirls. I had skills that no one else had. Another example of how the Agency played you."

"Apparently the Agency is a better matchmaker than any online dating service. They matched our points of compatibility completely and perfectly. My compliments to whoever was in charge of the mission. If funding's ever low, you should suggest NCS make a little money on the side fixing lonely hearts." He sounded almost genuine with just a small, almost undetectable undertone of hurt in his voice. And maybe a touch of wounded pride. As if he should have sensed a setup, but missed it.

"You fell in love with the real me, too." He pushed a lock of hair back from her face. "You may as well admit it. It may have started as an assignment for you, but I turned you on the moment you met me.

"You didn't think NCS was finding you your soul mate. They probably didn't, either. They were so busy making sure you'd turn my head, they never considered what I'd do to you.

"They made a tactical mistake and forgot to think on all sides. So they completely overlooked the possibility that so closely matching an agent with a target could lead to a dangerous attraction.

"You should warn them to think about the impact on

their agents, Lani. You really should. Otherwise, a breach of national security is inevitable."

"It's a good thing the chief isn't listening to this little speech of yours," Lani said. "He'd be furious."

Although the chief did fancy himself something of a matchmaker. But never an inadvertent one.

"Good to know we're not bugged here in the bedroom." Rock was serious. "I see now why I couldn't resist inviting you to try out for the show. Did you get rid of my other girl so there'd be an opening? Suzie had been with me for over five years."

"You make it sound like we offed her." Lani didn't break eye contact with him. "Her pregnancy was convenient timing for us. But we would have found some way to get me into your show."

He bent over and whispered in her ear. "You're a girl after my own heart. You know, baby, how much successful illusion turns me on. There's something seductive about it, even when I'm the victim." He leaned back and looked at her tray. "You aren't eating?"

"Our conversation's been too diverting."

He smiled slowly. "Cook will be insulted. Do you remember your first rehearsal with me?"

"How could I forget? You ordered me into that impossible little box so you could saw me in two. Two very unequal parts—my head and the rest of me."

"Everyone these days knows how the illusion is done. That Masked Magician has given away all the basic tricks. I had to put my own new spin on it. Or try. You trusted me enough to give it a try. I'm still impressed when I think of the way you wedged yourself in like you were a master yogi."

"You also made me wear an impossibly tiny outfit."

"I never said I didn't like how you looked. Or that your looks aren't part of the attraction."

She shook her head. "It was all a test, wasn't it? I thought it was a joke. An impossible task. I only wanted to prove you wrong and show you what an arrogant ass you were. Get into that box or lose the gig—right. Still, I couldn't blow the mission. What would I tell Emmett?

"Getting out, of course, was the real trick. And the joke was on both of us." She still remembered the panic of being wedged in that small space, unable to get out. She'd never felt claustrophobic before, even though she'd been in some tight spots during her career.

The buzz of the saw coming at her didn't even make her pulse rise. But at the end of the trick, when she was supposed to be put back together, she couldn't get out of the box. First the latch stuck. And then she was wedged in so tightly she panicked and couldn't get out.

The crew tugged on her so hard it felt as if they were wrenching her shoulders out of their sockets. She winced in pain and her legs began to cramp. Someone suggested getting a sledgehammer and smashing the box. Someone thought they could soap her up and squirt her out.

Rock rushed forward. "Leave her alone!" He shooed the crew away. "Oh, baby, this is all my fault," he whispered to her. "Look, you got in. You can get out."

He took her hand, which was flopping like a fish out of the box and turning blue from lack of blood flow. It was cold. She was cold.

She'd never forget his tone—confident, reassuring, calm. His hand holding hers was so warm and strong. She wanted to get out of the box, but she didn't want to lose the connection to him.

"You can do this. Really." He'd stared into her eyes and spoken in that confident, mesmerizing tone of his. "Just breathe calmly. Relax."

She studied Rock closely. "Do you remember what you told me?"

He laughed. "That next time I'd try a new trick—sawing you in half vertically?"

"Terrible thing to say. Really bad joke. And yet it worked."

"You laughed and relaxed and simply stepped out." His gaze held hers.

"Right into your arms."

"Perfectly safe. And we did that act time after time without a problem. Admit it. Challenge excites you."

"I'm not admitting anything. But if that box had been half an inch smaller . . ." She set the tray of cold breakfast aside.

He took her hand again and held her gaze. "Imagine trusting me like that again, Lani. Remember the feeling of comfort and peace as I held your hand. Just like I am now. Take a deep breath, baby. Relax."

She felt the tension leaving her body. A sense of peace washed over her. He was right. She should trust him and relax.

He squeezed her hand again and held it tightly. "There you are. Let the tension flow out of your body. Picture yourself in a pleasant spring meadow. Blue skies. Flowers. The peaceful sounds of birds chirping.

"Do you feel relaxed, Lani?"

She nodded. She did. She felt more relaxed and peaceful than she had in ages.

"Good. Good. You trust me?"

She nodded again.

"Yes? Good. Keep picturing that meadow and how freeing it is. How light you feel there. Telling the truth makes you feel light and free."

She nodded again.

"There's something you want to tell me, isn't there?" Rock's voice sounded far away and soothing. "A burden you're carrying, a dark secret. Share it with me now, baby. Free yourself. What are you keeping from me?"

The doorbell rang, piercing irritatingly through her calm meadow.

"Son of a bitch!" She threw her arm back and slapped Rock with all her might.

CHAPTER SIXTEEN

Rock rubbed his cheek, which stung like hell. Almost as badly as his pride. Lani had really whacked him. Caught him off guard, damn it. He'd gotten too cocky and forgotten how astute she was. If it hadn't been for that damn doorbell—

"Damn it, Rock, you're good." Lani's face was red and her eyes hard and snapping. "Building rapport, establishing trust, switching off my critical mind with *imagines* and *what ifs*, and then making the irresistible command. You were using covert hypnosis on me, you bastard."

"Turnabout is fair play," he said. "Don't think I didn't notice you doing the same thing."

She glared at him. "What is it you want to know? Why don't you just ask me?"

He glared back. He had to proceed carefully here. He couldn't tell her the most important thing he'd been trying to get out of her, which was whatever she'd been hiding from him from the beginning. He still hoped to seduce that out of her somehow or hope his PI found something out. Which left him only one believable option. He was going to have to look like an asshole and ask the other thing straight out. "Fine. You want blunt questions, here goes—did you sleep with Sol the night before the show?"

She held his gaze, but she looked amazingly unsurprised

by the question. "No. Now was that so hard? Really, Rock, we're going to have to learn how to communicate. Without subterfuge and trickery."

"Where's the fun in that?" he said. "I don't believe you, baby. You're too damn good with a lie."

She cocked her head. She didn't look the least bit sorry for slapping him. If anything, she looked as if she wished she'd hit him harder and a bit like a cobra ready to strike again.

He involuntarily leaned back out of her arm's reach.

She sighed. "See, trust issues. This is exactly one of the problems with the secret agent profession. No one believes you when you're telling the truth." She pursed her lips. "What even gave you that idea? Has Sol been bragging?"

Rock stared at her. Why would she ask the question if she wasn't guilty?

"He has." She sounded resigned. "Let me reiterate—I did not sleep with that piece of human debris. Nor would I ever. I, and you're not going to believe me, you didn't believe me the first time, but I hypnotized him and implanted the suggestion that we'd done the deed. Very pleasurably and to his slimy, perverted tastes." She shuddered. "I guess he's like a lot of men. Promise a woman anything to get her into bed and then discard her after. Or kill her. Well, what do you expect from maniacal villains, after all?"

Rock studied her. She sounded sincere. She looked genuine. Her involuntary reactions all spoke of truth. But hypnotizing Sol?

Lani leaned toward Rock. He lurched backward, nearly losing his perch on the bed.

She laughed and shook her head. "I have my revenge, though. Sol will be unable to perform next time he's in the mood. And every time after. Until I remove the hypnotic suggestion of impotence. Fortunately, that suggestion seemed to stick. He must really have impotency issues."

Lani reached out and this time very gently stroked Rock's stinging cheek. "Don't listen to rumors, Rock. Memories and gossip can be so unreliable."

There was a knock on the door. Rock swung around to look. Tate stood in the doorway. "Everything okay up here?"

"Fine," Lani said. "No thanks to you."

Tate grinned and ignored her complaint. "Great. Time to get cracking on the big mission. Oh, and Lani, better freshen up a bit. Maybe put on clothes that don't look like you slept in them. There's a cop downstairs who wants to talk about what you saw that night two years ago."

While Lani was being grilled by the cop, and playing the innocent, Rock got a text from Davo, his PI guy.

I found something. Meet me at my office.

Finally. Rock texted back that he was on his way. He slid off his spy ring, replaced it with the original non-spy version, and stashed the one NCS had given him in his drawer before heading downstairs. He didn't need Tate following him where he was going.

Tate caught Rock in the entryway just as Rock was about to leave. "Going somewhere?"

"Business calls."

"And you weren't going to tell us?"

"I wasn't aware I was under house arrest." Rock grinned at Tate, trying not to show how excited he was by Davo's text and hoping to divert Tate's suspicions. "Would you believe I have a show to plan for? Business managers to meet. Contracts to sign. Contractors to speak with?"

"No." Tate sounded serious, but his eyes twinkled.

Rock cocked a brow and played along. Tate was teasing and using a bit of Maxwell Smart's *would you believe* humor. "How about just a show to run, managers to meet, and contracts to sign?"

"Fine, Max. Get out of here." Tate put a hand on Rock's shoulder. "But be careful. Do you remember what Tal taught you about evasive action and losing a tail?"

"Yeah, I do. And if that doesn't work, I'm pretty good with flash powder."

Tate laughed. "Good man. Just remember, this isn't a game. RIOT is watching you and wants you dead."

"Got it." Rock pulled his keys from his pocket. "I'll be back in a few hours."

Tate handed him the long-handled bomb-checking mirror that had been resting against the console table in the entry. "Don't forget to wand the car after your meeting." Tate paused. "You know, the problem these days— assassins can remotely activate bombs. Gone are the days when they had to rely on the ignition triggering it."

"Thanks for the reassurance." Rock grabbed the mirror. "Later."

As Rock pulled out of the driveway, he activated the GPS spoofing device he'd purchased on the black market from one of his shadier casino friends on a lark way before Lani had come back. Never know when a gadget like that will come in handy. Let NCS believe he was at the hotel. The last thing Rock needed was them finding him across town at a PI's office.

Fifteen minutes later, after doing a little evasive action driving just for fun, Rock parked on the street in front of Davo's office. The PI's business was located in a flat, one-story building next to a popular and busy pawnshop. There was absolutely nothing remarkable looking about the building on the best of days. A few palms provided shade along the street. You were lucky if you found a shady spot. Rock wasn't.

Davo's car was in its customary spot next to the

building beneath a RESERVED FOR PRIVATE DICKS sign. The usual blast of hot air hit Rock as he got out of his car. Temperatures were already climbing toward one hundred.

Being associated with spies had made Rock jumpy. He looked over his shoulder. As a magician, he was trained to watch for tricks and shadows, subtle movements, and diversionary tactics. Everything looked clear to him and there was nowhere for an enemy agent to hide between Rock's car and the door. A sniper, of course, was another matter.

Davo's administrative assistant only worked two days a week. She wasn't in and the office was terrifyingly quiet as Rock entered.

"Davo, buddy? Where are you man—" Rock froze on the edge of a sticky puddle on the floor that oozed out from behind Davo's desk. It took a second for it to register what the puddle was.

Blood? Shit!

He had to get the hell out of here. Someone was on to him.

As Rock turned on his heel to beat a retreat, a great big former linebacker slammed into him from behind, hitting Rock in the kidneys with his elbow. Rock gasped and doubled over with shock and pain. *Damn, that hurts. This asshole knows what he's doing.*

The big guy grabbed Rock and slid a bag like an executioner's hood over Rock's head before Rock could right himself.

As Rock struggled, another assailant subdued him, grabbed his arms, and bound Rock's hands behind him with an industrial-strength zip tie. Making sure to cinch it tightly enough to nearly cut off the blood flow in Rock's wrists. His wrists throbbed immediately and he felt his fingers going numb.

"Well, Houdini, let's see you get out of this one." The

thug laughed as Rock cursed. "Not so powerful and impressive without your trick handcuffs."

"I'm an illusionist, not an escape artist." The bag over his head muffled Rock's words. *Show no fear.* James Bond never showed fear and it seemed to work for him.

"Yeah, no shit. We can see that. You big-shot magicians are all the same without your stage crew—ordinary guys." The guy grabbed Rock by the elbow and propelled him toward the door.

"Let me guess—this kidnapping is my engraved invitation to the kind of event I wouldn't ordinarily agree to on such short notice. What's the occasion and who are we going to see?"

"The boss would like to talk to you. That's all I need to know. That's all you need to know for now. I just do as he says. And so should you." The guy had a deep, bad voice that was almost a cliché for a villain.

"Talking? Sounds pleasant. It would be easier without the hood, though. It's muffling my stage voice."

The thug shoved Rock. "Get moving, wiseass, before I turn your stage voice into a permanent falsetto."

Damn. Tate was right about the spy ring—Rock should never have left home without it. With its GPS tracking and poisoned surgical steel switchblade, it would have evened up the odds. Which right now Rock calculated were running about a hundred to one against him. Living in Vegas all these years, he was pretty good with odds. *Shit.*

The two thugs took Rock by the arms and roughly propelled him into the back alley. Being taken to a different location made the odds of survival even worse. Maybe two hundred to one he'd get out of this alive. Rock wasn't wearing his thumb gun, either. And the wand gun was in the glove compartment of his car. He was left with his wits. The two heavies had even disarmed his sleight-of-hand advantage.

"This boss of yours," Rock said as one of the goons shoved his head down and pushed him into the car. "He's a fan of magic?"

A host of suspects flashed through Rock's mind. Vegas didn't have a reputation as Sin City for nothing. Rock had made fools of a few crime bosses during his shows. And won some big pots in backroom poker games. Then there was that incident with Tate and the high-stakes game. Any of the non-RIOT losers could have decided they wanted their money back and were going to get it the old-fashioned way from him. But top of the list was RIOT. Playing with fire had never frightened Rock before. Maybe it should have.

One of the two goons laughed. "He likes disappearing acts. He's not so big on reappearances. He's good with making people and problems disappear, permanently. Buckle up, magician."

The door slammed shut. One kidnapper got in beside him. The other slipped into the driver's seat and started the car. The air conditioner mercifully came on full blast. The hood was hot and stuffy. And the radio belted out smooth jazz.

"Calming music," Rock said. "How thoughtful."

As they turned out of the alley, Rock registered they'd turned left. He had a nearly photographic memory and had trained himself to count cards. Now he concentrated on counting turns so he could reconstruct the path. Which would come in handy, should he actually be turned loose alive. Back to those bad odds. Maybe he should spend his last few moments alive engaged in more pleasant thoughts. But hope springs eternal, as they say.

Rock couldn't let the goons suspect what he was up to, so he kept talking. "What does the boss want from me? If this is about a gig, he should contact my booking agent directly."

"The boss doesn't deal with middlemen." The thug laughed.

Rock leaned back in his seat, counting turns and trying to plan an escape. And pretty much failing. Falling from a moving vehicle hooded and with hands bound would have been a good trick. If he'd been able to open the door without using his hands or getting shot.

All too soon, they arrived. One of his captors pulled Rock out of the car, dragged him through the heat of the day and into the air-conditioned comfort of a house that smelled of jasmine and gardenia. Jasmine and gardenia were now toast as far as comfort scents.

The two beefs propelled Rock across a cool tile floor, as Rock tried to push images of bleeding out on it from his mind. They wound through the house to the back. One of them opened a door and Rock was back in the heat again. He could smell chlorine and suntan lotion. Alcohol and dust. He was standing on aggregate concrete.

"Welcome, Mr. Powers. So nice of you to stop by for a visit."

The voice stopped Rock cold, so cold he almost shivered. It took a force of sheer willpower to keep his mouth shut and not gasp his surprise. Even though he was hooded, he steadied his expression. Fortunately all his magic training had taught him how to use a poker face to his advantage, even through a mask.

"Take the hood off. I like to see a man's eyes when I'm talking to him."

One of the two heavies removed the hood. Rock took a deep breath, thankful for the fresh air. It was so much easier to fend off panic and think when he could actually breathe.

Rock stood in the shade on a patio in front of an expansive, irregularly shaped, sky-blue pool. A quality misting system emitted fine spray, cooling the area to what should have been a comfortable temperature—for a man not in fear for his life or worried about the security of his country.

He was at an obviously pricey mansion with a view of the mountains and a private backyard surrounded by palm trees and green, watered foliage. Rock was almost afraid to look at his captor for fear of who he'd see. A motion in the pool, like a fish jumping, flashed in the corner of his eye. Cowardice was not Rock's forte.

He steeled himself, fixed his expression against surprise, and turned his gaze on his captor. Sure enough, lounging at a patio table in front of him, sipping a martini, with two big, buff bodyguards behind him, sat Emmett Nelson, NCS chief. And traitor?

There was that moment, that second when time stood still and flashed by all too quickly as Rock assessed his next move as if this was some big, spying game of chess. Acknowledge the chief? What if this was a trick? What if the man in front of him was an imposter?

It seemed improbable. But wasn't everything in the spying business?

Rock paused, as if he was in no hurry to speak, and studied his adversary closely. His captor had subtle scarring around the ears, evidence of plastic surgery, maybe a face-lift. Or something more extreme, like changing his look completely. It could even be a very convincing mask-and-makeup job.

The Emmett before him was the right height and build and his voice was similar enough to be eerie. Rock had only seen the chief the one time, and that was under duress, but he was certain the chief didn't have the scar.

Rock played dumb. If this was a RIOT imposter, then as far as RIOT was concerned, Rock shouldn't know the chief. It would be suicide for both him and the mission to reveal that he did.

"To whom do I have the pleasure?" Rock said in as smooth a voice as possible. "I'd offer to shake, but my hands are currently bound."

The chief clone smiled. "My apologies, Powers." His tone was totally insincere and made it clear he enjoyed seeing Rock sweat. "My men are thorough and exceptionally protective. They won't take the chance of you producing a gun from thin air." He laughed. "A man in my position has many enemies. " He didn't rise to his feet. He merely lifted his glass. "Archibald Random."

Damn! The RIOT chief himself.

Rock forced his expression to remain blank of recognition, even as his pulse quickened with excitement. Here was the spying opportunity of a lifetime. He, Rock Powers, magician extraordinaire, could be the first magical double agent in history. If he played his cards and tricks very carefully.

"Well, Mr. Random, you have the advantage on me. I'm sorry to say your name doesn't ring a bell. Have we met? I meet so many people—"

Random took a sip of his martini and belted out a laugh. "Not in person, no. You don't remember? I made a generous offer to bankroll your show early in your career."

"I remember an offer, yes. That was you?" Rock's arms were going numb behind him. With his arms bound, performing any feats of prestidigitation or Houdini-like escapes seemed out of the question. Which was undoubtedly Random's intent.

"The very same." Random's tone and manner were friendly only on the surface. The undertones of his behavior stank of pure ice and were more effective than his expensive misting system.

A fan blew the overhead water vapor across the patio. It carried with it a hint of Random's cologne. Rock had the feeling that if he survived, the scent of that cologne would forever make him break out in a sweat.

"I hope you weren't offended when I turned you down. It was a generous offer. But I'm an individualist and a perfectionist. Always have been. I like having complete control." Rock was stalling, hoping for a blinding bit of inspiration to save him. Or a CIA helicopter.

Damn, why had he taken that ring off? He could only hope Tate or Tal noticed the GPS signal coming from Rock's closet, got suspicious, investigated, and tracked him the old-fashioned way. Did they still know the old-fashioned way?

Random nodded. "I understand completely. I'm the same myself. It's an admirable trait. In moderation.

"I'm prepared now to make you another offer. One you can't refuse. I'm afraid, though, you won't find it quite as generous as my previous one. In financial terms, at least."

Rock shrugged. He couldn't look too eager to join forces with Random, even though that was his intent. If he got into Random's inner circle, or at least got access to his plans, what a coup that would be. "That's kind of you. But, to be honest, I've been extremely successful and am well set. I don't need any backers. I prefer to maintain full control."

Random paused, studying Rock, burning him the way an audience watching his hands for the secret of a trick does. "That may be. Don't make any hasty decisions until you hear me out. First, though, I have a bone to pick with you. You cost me a pile of money last night when you swooped in and stole your wife away from my magician Sol in the middle of his act.

"Not the smartest move on your part. But then, maybe you didn't know who you were dealing with." Random smiled with all the warmth of Boreas.

Rock shrugged. "I hate to say it, but that's what you get when you hire second-rate performers like Sol. It's always been way too easy to steal Sol's thunder." Rock knew he shouldn't taunt Random, but he couldn't help himself. The man was an arrogant prick.

"But I'm good for the reward money. I said no strings attached and I meant it. I just wanted Lani back. I posted the funds in a certificate of deposit two years ago. It should cover any perceived losses." Rock paused and stared Random in the eye.

"However, we're both businessmen and I think you know my little stunt just boosted stock in Sol's act. Have you seen the gossip rags this morning?

"I did you a favor. Lani's reappearance is the celeb news of the day. Sol's getting more publicity than he has in years. Everyone wants to know how he pulled it off and whether we colluded. Are we back to being old friends again? Or not?"

Rock held Random's gaze, wondering whether he should give covert hypnosis a try or whether that would definitely be signing his death warrant. "Did the temperature just drop out here? I thought I just felt a dip in your cordial manner."

Random laughed outright. He looked so eerily like the chief, Rock had to remind himself he wasn't. Probably.

"I don't care about money. I have plenty of that, too," Random said. "But I crave power. And I don't like to be made the fool. It's a bit of a coincidence you were in the audience that night, isn't it?

"What is your game, Rock? Why were you looking into where your wife had been two days before she reappeared?"

"ESP, tips, hunches, prophetic dreams, ever heard of those?" Rock forced himself to breathe evenly.

"Don't play me for a fool, Powers. I know you're a de-bunker, not a believer."

Hell, it had been worth a shot.

"After two years, my PI finally had a lead. Nothing sinister about that. And there was nothing coincidental about my being in the audience that night. Sol invited me."

If Rock hadn't exactly warmed up to his host before, now he was filled with cold fury, fear, and dread. Cold to his core. The blood in Davo's office . . .

"Speaking of my PI—where's Davo? You can release him now. He can't tell you anything I can't."

"That's certainly true. Boys!" Random snapped his fingers and two buff thugs behind him opened a large cooler sitting in the shade.

Rock hadn't paid any attention to the cooler before, assuming it was full of beer or soda. Maybe bottles of iced tea. Now a sickening sense of dread turned Rock's gut as one of the heavies tossed the lid aside and two blue fingers came into view.

Rock's stomach seized. He swallowed his bile and sense of guilt. The two pulled Davo's beaten, blue body from it. Rock stared at Davo's lifeless, obviously tortured remains and fought to control his rage. Davo had been a good guy. After two years, he was a friend of sorts.

Random's men carried Davo's body to the edge of the pool and dropped it with a thud.

Rock looked away. What had Davo told Random? And how long had he held out?

"Get Mr. Powers a glass of water," Random said. "He looks suddenly peaked."

"I don't need water. I'm not squeamish. I've driven stakes through my wrists on stage and slit my arms and pulled coins from my veins." He was bluffing. He felt sick as hell.

Random laughed. "Smoke and mirrors and fake blood. But I admire your bravado. Now, to business. I have an irresistible offer for you."

"No deal. As I said, I work alone. I do only what I want." Rock shook loose of the two men holding him.

Random had finished his martini. He motioned for another one. "Oh, I think you'll take my offer, once you hear it. I hear you're planning to perform Outlandish Marauders for the NUFOs at their annual picnic."

Rock let loose a string of curses. "How do you know about Outlandish Marauders? That's a top-secret gig."

Rock tried not to look at Davo's body poolside where flies were beginning to collect.

Random laughed. "I know everything. And what I want, I get."

Rock let out a breath. "I don't work for crime bosses. And it's just a hunch, given the way you issued my invitation for this little poolside visit, that you're one. A very powerful one. So save yourself some trouble—kill me now or let me go."

"You're very direct and decisive. Brave. Good qualities. Attributes I'm happy to have on my team." Random shook his head. "But unoriginal with your demand. Some people can be so selfless, almost cavalier, when it comes to their own lives and personal safety." He paused. "Aren't you the tiniest bit curious what Davo was going to tell you?"

Negotiations were delicate now. Just how much should Rock protest before accepting would seem reasonable? He didn't want to lose the opportunity. Though, to be honest, he doubted he really had any choice in the matter. Rock shook his head. "No."

"That's a shame. Considering Davo gave his life for it." A laptop sat on a table next to Random. He pulled it toward him and opened it. "Your lovely Lani has indeed been keeping something from you, just as you suspected. Why remains to be seen. I imagine that's your own business. What goes on in a marriage is a private matter. But I think you'll agree that knowing what it is changes everything."

Random slowly slid the laptop screen around until it faced Rock. Rock frowned. A toddler of about one and a half, a smiling little dark-haired boy looked back at Rock. He had a round face and chubby baby cheeks. His eyes were Lani's, but the rest of him was the spitting image of Rock as a baby.

Rock felt as if he'd taken another blow to his kidneys. He struggled to hold onto his poker face and shrugged. "A baby, so what?"

Random pulled a cigar with a blue band from his pocket and waved it in front of Rock. "*Your* baby, Rock. Your son. Congratulations, Daddy." He grinned, but only an evil light lit his eyes.

"That's what Lani's been hiding and Davo was going to tell you." Random rattled off the boy's birth date and held up one of Davo's reports for Rock to see.

"Nine months from the quickie wedding. Perfect timing. He's yours, Rock. Surely you see the resemblance?" Random held the cigar out toward Rock, though he knew perfectly well Rock couldn't take it with his hands zipped behind his back. "Celebration cigar? Exploding, just for fun." He laughed cruelly.

Rock scanned the report. It looked authentic, what he could make sense of through his shock. The intelligence it contained was damning. Of all the things Rock had imagined Random could hold over him, he'd never dreamed of this. A son? His own boy? How could Lani? And did Random have the child? Rock's mouth went dry at the thought.

Behind his back, Rock clenched and unclenched his fists, stretching his numb fingers as he tried to make sense of the situation and maintain some semblance of cool. The existence of his son put a wrinkle in his plans. Rock couldn't see a way out. Of course he was going to agree to this deal and then he was going to double-cross and stick it to Random. After he got his baby back.

As Rock processed his shock, Random set the cigar down, snapped his fingers, and pressed a button on the laptop, making a show of his power. "Boys, get rid of that body. It's attracting flies and distracting Mr. Powers as he tries to think."

One of the thugs rolled Davo's body into the pool. Dozens of fish suddenly swarmed out of nowhere, jumping and snapping at the body. Rock hadn't imagined seeing a fish jump. There were fish in that pool—hungry, pack-hunting fish. Random must have been keeping them penned at the far end.

Rock averted his gaze and stared directly at Random. Never let a bully see you flinch. "How very Blofeld of you."

Random grinned. "Bond fan, are you?"

Rock shrugged. "I've seen most of the movies."

"Well then, you know Blofeld only had tiny piranhas. These are tiger fish," Random said, though Rock hadn't asked. "They're five to eight times larger than piranhas. Even more deadly and vicious." Random was obviously proud of one-upping the fictional villain.

Random paused again. "Imagine how frightening and painful it would be to be eaten alive. A little boy would be terrified."

"You sick bastard! Leave the boy alone. Where is he? Before I agree to anything, I want to see him. In person."

Random shook his head. "Not possible. Not now. Co-operate with me and I'll guarantee his safety for life.

Refuse me, and I'll send his mother the video of him playing with my tiger fish."

Rock swallowed hard, defeated. "What do you want me to do? I'll do anything you say. Just don't hurt my boy."

CHAPTER SEVENTEEN

Rock was in a fury. At Random. At Lani. At himself. At the world in general. He'd the same as killed Davo. And now the world's worst terrorist organization had Rock's son. How in the hell could Lani keep that from him? How could she be so cold and collected that she'd go on a mission while RIOT had her baby—

He stopped short. A cold chill washed over him. Unless they were blackmailing her, too. Or she thought her baby was safe and didn't know he'd been snatched.

Rock ran a hand through his hair and winced at the movement. His back was bruised and felt like hell. His ego was pierced. And he was sick at heart and stymied.

What did he do now? Who did he trust?

Did he confront Lani? Tell Tate, Ty, and Tal? Do Random's bidding and hope Random kept his word and gave his boy to him unharmed? Betray his country and sign the death warrants of who knew how many innocent people?

Whatever Random wanted with Area 51, it couldn't be good. Area 51 was the development site of the Oxcart airplane and the SR-71 Blackbird spy plane. Whatever the CIA was trying to protect there was a matter of national security. In the hands of an enemy . . .

Whom to turn to? Who could he trust? Could the CIA

get his boy back for him? Could Rock take the chance? He needed to think.

When he was in a temper and needed to clear his head, Rock headed to his studio stage. He stood in the stage wings after heading there on autopilot, hardly aware of making the drive. He turned on a couple of spotlights before walking to the center of the stage.

Daggers of Death was the perfect trick for his mood. He'd love to shower some real daggers at Random. For now, all Rock could do was perform the act and pretend.

He stabbed a handful of gleaming, sharp silver daggers into the soft wood of his show table, imagining plunging them into Random's smug heart. He donned his magician's vest, turned on his fog machine and the red laser lights, and positioned the target wheel ten paces in front of him.

Usually one of his beautiful assistants would be strapped to it. Today he wished he could strap Random and his goons on it and see just how good his real aim was. Next to the wheels stood Rock's cones of tantalizing, awe-inspiring fire. Rock gave the wheel a hard spin and stepped back.

Lasers lit the fog, casting eerie, devilish wisps of flame. Rock crossed his arms in front of him and dramatically flung them into the air above his head. Fire shot to the ceiling from his cones. *The power*. If only it were real and not controlled by a pedal at his feet.

He called up the fire again and grabbed a dagger. "This one's for you, asshole." He let it fly at the spinning board.

Really let it fly.

He was actually pretty decent and accurate with a knife. In the show, of course, he never actually threw the daggers. No matter how good his aim was, really letting them fly was too dangerous. He pocketed them in his coat while a stagehand used a special device that shot knives through the back of the wheel to make it look like the pocketed knives were hitting the board and outlining his assistant.

Rock let out a growl like that of a wounded tiger, grabbed one of his stage knives, and tossed it at the board across the room where it landed with a satisfying thud. He tossed another and another and another, watching them slice into the board across the room.

Lani had dished him the ultimate betrayal. How could she have kept his son from him? And what had Rock done now by looking for Lani's secret?

He should have known that secrets revealed always destroyed the magic. Now he wasn't sure he could ever forgive her. All he knew for certain was that he'd wanted his wife, and eventually a family, and now his boy was in danger. And it was because of his own actions.

The boy. The question was, did Random really have him? It was a haunting question, a chilling question. But Rock was thinking of illusions and diversions. If Random had the kid, why not show him to Rock? Why not flaunt him right in Rock's face? Make the kid cry? Have Rock ache to hold him? Threaten him right in front of Rock?

The fact that Random didn't made Rock think there was a chance Random was bluffing. That he didn't have Rock's son. No doubt he was trying to get his hands on him. But he was probably still searching for him. Lani, being who she was, would have hidden him well. Which would explain why she could be confident on the mission. But was that an acceptable risk to take? Could Rock chance it?

He'd have to confront Lani and warn her, just in case. Would she panic? Or could they work together to get the child back, even if she was being blackmailed, too? And what about the chief? Was Random impersonating him?

Or was he a double-crosser? What game was Random playing?

Rock tossed another knife, engrossed in his own world.

"Whoa! Hold your fire."

Rock froze. He stabbed the dagger he held back into the table and turned around to find Tate staring at him.

"And here I always thought there was a trick to this trick, that you didn't actually throw the knives." Tate eyed the board and cocked a brow. "Next time I'll be more impressed. Assuming your aim improves." Tate held up Rock's spy ring. "You went off the grid. Keeping secrets, are we?"

Rock held his breath. Only one spy would have known where to look for him. She was either here, or she'd told Tate where to find him. Just as the thought crossed his mind, Lani stepped from the fog.

"And remind me not to let myself be strapped there again, not with Rock in a temper." Her words were light, but her tone was concerned. She watched him closely. "What's the matter? What happened, Rock?"

It took Rock a minute to compose himself enough to even think semirationally. Even then, words hardly came. He was suddenly paranoid. He couldn't trust that they weren't being spied on even here. Instead, he turned his back to them and held up his shirt to reveal the black-and-blue, fist-shaped bruises.

Lani gasped and started toward him.

Tate restrained her. "Rock?"

Rock let his shirt down and turned back to face them. "The walls have ears," he mouthed.

Tate pulled a device out of his pocket and switched it on. "Combination bug, phone, and video jammer. The modern spy's cone of silence." Tate still had Lani by the arm. "What happened?"

Rock glared at Lani, love, hate, and betrayal warring within him. "I went off the grid to meet with my PI. I had the feeling my wife was keeping something from me. Turns out I was right."

In the ghostly, foggy light, it was hard to tell whether Lani paled beneath her beautiful caramel skin. Rock imagined she did. Her eyes went wide, at least. Rock cracked and lost control.

"You underestimate me, baby," Rock said. "I may not be a spy, but I know how to read people and spot lies and diversions.

"But back to my story. I was intercepted, by RIOT. Turns out I had an audience with their chief, Archibald Random."

Tate dropped Lani's arm, but she remained frozen in place. Tate's jaw was set. "He roughed you up? What did he want?"

Rock gingerly touched his bruised back and ignored the second question for the moment. "This? This is nothing. You should have seen what they did to my PI, Davo. He's not just swimming with the fish. He's been eaten by them. Your buddy Random has a Blofeld complex. And a swimming pool full of tiger fish."

"What did Random want with your PI?" There was real, genuine fear in Lani's eyes.

If Rock hadn't been in such an angry, hurt mood, he might have felt some sympathy. Instead, his heart was hard. Rock approached the two spies until he stood directly in front of his wife and stared her in the eye. "He handed me an exploding cigar with a blue band and congratulated me on being a daddy."

Tate cursed beneath his breath.

"My baby!" Lani grabbed Tate's arm. "RIOT has my baby!" She pulled her cell phone out of her purse.

Tate grabbed it out of her hand before she could dial

and held it out of her reach as she lunged for it. "No, Lani! Think clearly. RIOT can't possibly have him. If they did, we'd know. But if RIOT's looking for him, you'll give away Stone's location."

Stone. She named their son Stone. After him?

"We have to use emergency procedures," Tate was saying.

Rock was barely listening. He was too busy watching Lani worry about their kid. She was so distraught and distracted, she hadn't even paused to consider how Rock might feel about her betrayal. Didn't she realize that she'd stabbed him in the gut?

"Rock!"

Hearing Tate call his name broke Rock out of his stupor. "Does Random have Stone?"

"I don't know. He refused to show him to me." Rock told them everything he knew. He related every detail, including his memory map of the left and right turns and times between them from Davo's office to the undisclosed RIOT location.

"We have to move!" Lani glared at Rock. "How could you stop by here to play with your fire and knives when your son's life is in danger?"

Rock stared back at her. "Is that what you believe about me?" He shook his head, numb. "I haven't answered Tate's other question yet, what Random wants from me. In return for Stone's safety, Random wants me not to perform the prestige and let the crowd storm the Area 51 perimeters.

"And there's a complication I had to think about before I acted. One more thing I haven't told you—Random looks and sounds like the chief. Either he's the chief's twin, or he's altered himself to look like the chief, or the chief's a double agent. Take your pick."

Rock stared into his wife's eyes. "I'm going to get my boy back safely. I promise."

* * *

Lani was furious at Tate for restraining her, even though he was in the right. Her motherly instincts interfered with her spy sense and all she could think about was making certain her precious baby Stone was safe.

Tate took out his phone and called HQ to initiate the safety precautions regarding Stone. For the first time in her life Lani was so scared she couldn't think. Foreign agents and terrorists could do anything to her, but if they harmed her baby she'd fall apart.

She'd really screwed up her life and career. First by marrying Rock and then by accidentally getting pregnant. She'd been on birth control. She still wasn't sure what had happened.

As Tate talked to HQ, Lani unleashed her fury at Rock. "Damn it, Rock. You couldn't leave well enough alone. You couldn't keep your nose out of the secrets of the last two years. You didn't trust me or that I had good reason to keep those years a blank from you. Look what you've done with your prying!" At that moment, she hated him.

"Don't look at me like that." She glared at Rock. "Like I'm unreasonable for protecting my child—"

He glared back. "Your child? Don't you mean *our* child?"

"My child, Rock. Mine. If you'd left well enough alone that's all he'd be." She glared at him, wanting to hurt him. "It had to be that way. It has to be that way. Or maybe it doesn't matter now that you've ruined everything." She took a deep breath to stave off tears and try to keep her voice from shaking.

"I'm the bad guy for wanting to know what my wife was up to for two years? Yeah, that's real nasty of me." He stared right back at her. "Blame me if you like. I feel shitty enough for stumbling into the discovery and making Random aware of him. But it's not my job that put him in danger in the first place."

"Wasn't it?" She glared back at him. "You don't understand, do you?" she said. "Yes, my job makes it dangerous to have children. But as long as Random had his sights set on you as being useful to him, which he has for over ten years, no child of yours would ever be safe.

"Think about it, Rock. What leverage did he have? Even when you were broke he couldn't buy you. You're not close to your family. You loved me, so you say, which put me in RIOT's crosshairs.

"I'm used to being a target. I can take care of myself. I removed myself from the situation in part to keep you safe and out of RIOT's reach.

"Without me, RIOT still had no bargaining chip. But a child, Rock? That's a weapon they're free to wield. As long as RIOT wanted you, you couldn't have a child.

"So think about why I couldn't come back, Rock. Give it a good, long think. I had to protect my baby. As long as you didn't know about him, he was safe. But once you went digging, you handed RIOT the opportunity they've been looking for for the last ten years."

Tate got off the phone. He flicked a glance at Lani as her heart pounded in her ears. He shook his head. "Nanny's not communicating. We've sent a team out to investigate. We'll know the minute they know anything."

Lani gasped, all manner of horrific scenarios running through her mind. If RIOT had her baby, she was off the operation. Nothing would stop her from hunting down the RIOT bastards who'd taken him.

Rock was cursing and making all kinds of threats. Tate had to restrain him to keep him from charging out.

Rock struggled against Tate's vise grip on him as Tate

spoke. "Calm down, you two. Nanny's the best. If RIOT has them, Nanny will escape.

"You know Nanny, Lani. Nanny's sharp and well-trained as an agent and great with kids. Nanny will protect Stone, no matter what."

Rock calmed down and stopped struggling to get free. Tate released him. Lani couldn't look at him. She'd underestimated Rock. She should have known he'd see through her ruse. It was part of her attraction to him that he seemed to get to the real her no matter what façade she put on. She should have known he'd try to find out where she'd been and what she'd been up to for those two years. She'd made a tactical mistake and now she was paying for it. She swallowed hard and took a deep breath.

"There's only one thing to do now." Tate's gaze bounced between Rock and Lani. "Let our rescue team handle it. They're specialists in rescuing hostages and agents in trouble. We have to go on with the mission and pretend that Rock will do Random's bidding.

"We'll foil Random's master plan and make sure he has no further use of Rock's talents. Once Rock isn't valuable to him anymore, he and Stone will be safe."

"Assuming he doesn't come after us out of revenge," Rock said.

Tate shook his head. "I'm not saying Random doesn't like his revenge served cold. But in this case I believe your celebrity will save you. Your death would generate too much interest."

"Not if I simply disappear. If that happens, my fans will be waiting for the ultimate prestige—when I reappear myself after a mysterious, prolonged absence," Rock argued. "And why shouldn't they think that? I've already done it with my wife." He flicked a glance toward Lani.

He blamed her, but she didn't feel guilty for protecting her child in the only way possible.

Tate shook his head again. "And all those millions would be looking for you. Random's a psychopath, but he's not crazy. Not that way. He doesn't need the scrutiny. RIOT operates in the shadows until Random decides otherwise. When he goes public, it will be with a real sensation and a show of power. We've foiled his attempts before. We know what he wants.

"His goal is to terrify and control. No offense, but he won't waste his one big splash on you."

"None taken," Rock said.

Tate stepped away from Rock. "Once you're of no use to Random, he'll leave you alone. Our best chance of getting Stone back safely now is to defang and neuter Random. At least as far as magic is concerned."

Lani stared at Tate. He was right. She knew he was right. But it didn't make her feel any better. Her arms ached for her baby boy. And crazily, for her husband's warm, strong, tattooed arms around her, too.

Rock frowned. "There's still the little matter of Emmett Nelson—is he also Archibald Random or not? Who do we trust?"

CHAPTER EIGHTEEN

Random's not the chief. He can't be the chief." Lani's protests were purely reactionary. A world where the chief was a traitor wasn't worth living in. And it meant her baby boy was in more danger than anyone could imagine.

Tate, however, shook his head adamantly as he leaned casually against Rock's magician's box, the box where a beautiful assistant was usually sawn in half. He crossed his arms and legs and smiled. "Emmett is *not* Random."

"Do you know how esoteric that sounds?" Rock looked doubtful. "How can you be sure? I saw him *in person* and I have doubts. I don't think he is. There's that tiny scar around his ears that indicates plastic surgery. But even using my highly trained powers of observation, I can't be one hundred percent certain."

"I can," Tate said.

Lani stared at Tate. He could be an arrogant bastard. He was born to privilege and played hard. But he was an amazingly talented spy and loyal. The rule in the spy business was to trust no one. Sometimes you had to break the rule. Her gut told her to trust Tate. At least in this instance.

Tate's gaze bounced between Rock and Lani. He sighed, somewhat dramatically. But that was Tate for you. He laughed, even though Lani couldn't find anything funny in the situation. "It's obvious I'm going to have to prove it to you. Let's just give the chief a call and see what he has to say for himself, shall we?"

"No!" Lani protested. "What if—"

"What if Emmett's a double agent? Sounds like the plot of *Tinker Tailor Soldier Spy*. We can't perform our mission without confidence in our chief. He'll want to be apprised of this latest wrinkle in the plans.

"Rock, hand over that laptop you're using to control the lights. Let's Skype Emmett and see what he has to say for himself."

Rock grabbed the laptop and held it out to Tate.

"If the chief isn't Random, you're committing career suicide," Lani said. "And if he is, you've just betrayed your country. Either way, it's your hide."

Tate took the laptop from Rock. "The Kobayashi Maru scenario. Bring it on."

Lani shook her head. "Didn't know you were a *Star Trek* geek, Tate. Who would have thought?"

Tate put in a Skype call to the chief on his top-secret, for-emergency-use-only Skype address—Chief Among Problems.

Lani shook her head. "You're calling on the equivalent of the red phone. Hope the chief doesn't chew your head off."

Tate ignored her. "Look closely for that scar," he whispered to Rock. "If he's an imposter, we hang up and call the director. Or the head of the Senate Intelligence Committee."

Lani rolled her eyes.

"Oh, hell, what now?" Emmett picked up holding a putter in one hand and an expensive golf ball in the other. He wore a navy-blue golf shirt with the distinctive CIA emblem on the left where a pocket would ordinarily be. He looked directly into the camera.

"See any scar?" Tate whispered to Rock.

Rock tilted his head back and forth. "Hard to tell. The angle's bad. It was more evident by his ears."

The chief frowned into the camera. "What are you two whispering about?"

"Security protocol. Just verifying your identity. Chief, can you give us a profile from each side?" Tate said.

Emmett rolled his eyes and complied.

"He has good features," Rock said.

"Yeah, a nice, dominant profile. Just what you want in a chief."

"And no discernible scars." Rock looked as relieved as Lani felt.

"Satisfied?" the chief said. "This had better be important. I have a game with the commander in chief, the chief justice, and the joint chiefs in less than an hour. I need to get the hang of this ball R and D gave me before I head out." Emmett's gleeful grin was positively evil.

"It's not time for the chiefs' tournament again, already?" Tate shook his head.

"It is indeed that time of year already. After suffering through the tight budget debacle these last years, I'm going to make sure Intelligence wins on points this time." Emmett tossed his ball in the air and caught it.

"On points?" Rock looked confused. "Isn't the point of golf to make as few points as possible?"

Tate shook his head. "That's a roundabout way of saying the president and the chief justice have to win the actual game of golf.

"The points are figurative and depend on how much sport you can make of the president and chief justice while at the same time currying as much of their good favor for the Agency as possible. You want a kind eye during budget proposals and Supreme Court decisions."

Emmett was swinging his putter. "I really got the rest

of those so-called chiefs last year with that self-destructing ball. The vice chairman of the joint chiefs spent a good half hour looking in the rough for it. Then I handed him another and detonated it once it hit the green. You'd think a military man would be more savvy about weaponry.

"This year I expect one of the joint chiefs to play dirty with a drone ball. It would be just like them." Emmett laughed again.

"What do you have for them this year?" Tate asked. "Anything special about your putter?"

Emmett looked at his putter and shrugged. "It's top of the line. And has a nice semiautomatic rifle feature. For emergencies only if the Secret Service doesn't do their job."

Emmett leaned the putter against his desk and picked up his ball again. "This is our real secret weapon—a remote-controlled ball with GPS. It flies out of sand traps. Literally. With this baby," he shook the ball at the camera, "I'm unbeatable."

Emmett grinned. "And so is the commander in chief. I'm going to gift him some for the game. The guys at Langley will be playing his balls remotely and making sure they fly where they need to to guarantee the president lowers his handicap and comes out victorious. It allows me time to network without worrying about the president's game."

"Yeah," Tate said with a twinkle in his eye. "That explains why the guys at HQ have been playing so much Wii golf on the job. They've been practicing for the chiefs' tourney. You'll be playing your own ball, sir?"

Emmett gave Tate a serious *shut your trap* look. "Naturally." He scowled at Tate. "Enough of this bullshit. What's up?"

"Not much," Tate said.

He must have had a career death wish.

"Just thought you'd like to know Archibald Random is impersonating you. So if you run into yourself, don't freak out. Reach for your gun."

The chief cocked a brow. "How reliable is your source?"

Tate hitched a thumb at Rock. "Rock, tell the chief what you saw during your little audience with the RIOT chief."

"You met with Random?" The chief sounded suddenly interested.

"You could say he issued an invitation I couldn't resist," Rock said.

"You mean he kidnapped you," the chief said.

Rock nodded and explained about Random's likeness to the chief and what had happened to PI Davo.

"Still using tiger fish and mansions." The chief shook his head. "Someone should tell Archie to get a good villain's cave like all maniacal supervillains. Have you located the mansion?"

"We're on it, sir," Lani said.

"Ah, Lani, you're there, too. Good. Hang in there, kiddo. We'll get your boy back safely. I promise."

The chief's promise made Lani feel marginally better. The chief kept his promises and if Stone was on the chief's radar, he had at least a fighting chance.

Emmett turned his gaze back to the boys. "The mansion will be empty before you get there."

The chief cursed beneath his breath and showed them his jawline and ears to erase any lingering doubts. "It was only a matter of time until Archie tried something like this." The chief set his ball down. "With the high-tech state of makeup and plastic surgery, I'm surprised he hasn't tried it sooner."

The chief shrugged. "Damn. It appears I'm banned from Area 51 until we can clear this matter up. I'll send out the memo and notify the appropriate authorities. If anyone bearing any resemblance to me is caught anywhere near the perimeters of Area 51, let alone inside, they're to be arrested and confined immediately."

The chief rolled his ball back and forth on his desk. It zigged and zagged in an unnatural manner. The chief was stealthily controlling it somehow. The man was a skilled magician. His sleight of hand was undetectable. "Good work, Rock. We've been waiting for a chance to apprehend Archie and catch him red-handed. You've just given us the golden opportunity.

"No doubt he plans to use this magical mission to get into 51 and personally retrieve what he's looking for."

As the chief spoke, Lani watched Rock. As angry as she was with him, she couldn't really blame him for what he'd done. He wasn't a seasoned spy. Curiosity was in his soul. And she'd hurt him terribly. Even so, he looked strong, stoic, and determined. The non-spy part of her, the purely womanly part, wanted to throw herself in his arms and feel his strength. As much as she craved the contact and the comfort, she pushed it below the surface and acted indifferent.

"What, exactly, does Random want you to do?" the chief asked.

Rock looked Lani directly in the eye. If she hadn't known better, she'd have suspected he was trying to hypnotize her again. The truth was he'd had her under his spell from the beginning.

He turned his attention to the chief. "Random wants me to throw the prestige, bungle it or not perform it in time so the crowd panics and storms the perimeters of Dreamland, just like they'd planned for Sol to do when he was orchestrating this tactical illusion."

"Predictable," the chief said.

"How are the plans for the terror attack we need coming along?" Tate asked.

"We have an elevated terror alert out at Hoover Dam, Area 51, the casinos, anyplace that would be advantageous for Random to attack. I'm going to elevate it even further. We'll make it nearly impossible for RIOT to strike.

"We have the intel leak to the media in the works. We'll publicly raise the terror alert level to red.

"My theory is that people will still be expecting an attack, primed for one, even though there hasn't been one. It's safer this time than calling out the sonic illusion team."

"Archie won't order an attack unless he has to. It's risky and expensive."

"Expensive, Chief?" Rock asked.

The chief laughed. "Yeah, believe it or not, even dastardly villains have budgets." The chief leaned back in his chair. "How close are you to being ready to perform, Rock, realizing this is the performance of your life? Are your baby magicians ready and up to the task?"

Rock flicked his hand and one of the flame cones behind them shot fire. "Sorry," he said. "Just letting off a little steam.

"My young apprentices will be ready. They're all hard workers, talented, and dedicated. How about my flying saucer—will it be ready?"

The chief grinned. "You'll have your spy plane. The camofleurs are working night and day to make it even more UFO-like. The schedule's tight. But they'll have it ready."

Rock whistled and mumbled something beneath his breath about spy planes being the ultimate flying saucers. "I hope it's impressive."

"It'll blow your socks off."

Rock tented his fingers in front of him, looking as if he was suddenly itching to get going. "We generate the crowd and the panic as we planned. We impress the NUFO group. But now . . ." He swallowed hard. "With this new wrinkle, do I still reveal the illusion for what it is—a trick? If my boy's still in any danger then—"

"Yes," the chief said. "If we're smart about this, we'll take down some of RIOT's most wanted. If we get lucky, we'll take the ace of spades, Random himself."

"It's risky, Chief," Lani protested. "My baby—"

"Everything we do is risky," the chief said. "Our rescue team will have your baby back before the big show."

"I don't like this." Something felt off to Lani. "Random's a forked-tongued monster who's incapable of speaking the truth. He could just as easily be setting us up."

"Like we're setting him up?" the chief said. "You know the way the game is played. Spying is more a chess match than anything. The best we can do is guess and anticipate our opponent's next move. If it's any consolation—he's at the same disadvantage. We proceed as discussed."

The chief glanced at his watch. "I have to run. Good luck, all of you. Keep me informed. Oh, and Rock, wear the spy ring and keep the thumb gun and wand gun on you. We don't just invent these devices willy-nilly, you know. There'll come another time when you need them. Count on it."

CHAPTER NINETEEN

Rock was staring out the window of his master bedroom suite into the darkness of midnight when the door softly opened and Lani slid in almost silently. He sensed her hesitation as she hovered just inside the door. He could almost feel her gaze boring into his back. But he didn't turn around or invite her in. Call him a coward, but he wasn't sure he could face her. Why the hell had he thought he was smarter than the CIA?

From the time he'd first fallen in love with her, he'd believed she loved him back, deeply, passionately, with every part of her that she allowed herself to love with. She was an outsider, someone who'd never really belonged, someone like him. They belonged together, and that was all that mattered. He knew there was a part of Lani she didn't, or couldn't, share with him. Or anyone else.

But everyone had secrets, including him, and he'd have been a hypocrite to hold it against her. In time, when she was ready, if there was a need, she'd share hers with him. Yeah, that she was a CIA agent. Now that had been a shock.

And later, after her return, after the big secret agent reveal, he knew she kept another secret, as it turned out, his son. He should have trusted her with that secret, trusted her enough to act to protect those she loved. He should have waited for her to come to him with it. Trust was the true magic of a relationship.

If he'd only left well enough alone, waited out the mission, and wooed his way back into Lani's life, he believed she would have told him about Stone. Once the mission was over and the danger was past. Once RIOT no longer had a use for him.

Rock saw it all clearly now, the reason Lani had risked everything to come on this mission. It was their only chance to be a family.

And he'd messed up royally, proving he didn't trust her and putting their baby's life in danger. He wanted nothing more than to see his son, hold him in his arms, see the look of forgiveness in Lani's eyes. He'd do anything to make it right. "Any news?"

He pictured her shaking her head, could almost hear the movement in the silent room.

"RIOT has them," she said. "Our team is tracking them down, but they believe both Nanny and Stone are alive and safe for now. RIOT needs them alive at least until the illusion goes off as they want." She paused. "You okay?"

What could he say? Hell no, he wasn't okay. He wondered whether he'd ever be okay again. If Random killed Stone, nothing would ever be the same again.

"I'm sorry, Lani," he said instead. She didn't need him laying his guilt trip on her. He didn't feel like talking about it anyway. "This Nanny person, is she undercover?"

Lani nodded. "As an old friend of mine who's watching Stone until I bring him out and use him to extort money from you. That was the cover story we planned.

"Of course, when you rescued me and we had a happy reunion, the story had to change. Now Nanny is keeping Stone until I can find a good way to tell you about him." She snorted. "I guess I blew that one."

"Yeah." Rock paused. "Sol's all over the papers and

social media taking credit for finding you and saying he's worried about you, that he fears you were becoming addicted to prescription painkillers. You were acting strangely just before the act." Rock snorted. "He must be sweating bullets not knowing how you survived and what accusations we might make against him."

"I've seen them. I've also seen the picture of us in the limo with the window open and the flash powder smoke pouring out. *Smokin' Hot Reunion,* I think was the headline."

"Sol won't take this quietly. He'll retaliate again if he can. He was dangerous before, but now he's terrifying. If he can find a way to mess up our illusion, he will. And if we fail—" His voice broke.

They both knew what Rock meant.

She came up behind him so close he could feel her heat behind him. He saw her hesitation reflected in the window glass before him.

"We're watching Sol." She laid a hand on his shoulder and squeezed softly, not saying anything. "Don't blame yourself. You didn't know."

"I should have trusted you. I should have left well enough alone. You would have told me. *Eventually.* When the time was right."

He spun around to face her and took her gently by the arms. "Stone, the baby, that's why you resisted making love with me. That's why you pushed me away.

"You were afraid you'd be tempted to tell me about him. The closer we got, the more tempted you'd be. You were afraid you might even slip up."

"You're too observant, Rock. That's always been your curse. You're exactly right." She bowed her head. "I was afraid, all along, you'd find out about him. I almost turned down this mission. But the chief made it impossible.

"Becoming a mother does something to a woman's

soul, makes her into a different person. I was never afraid before. Not for myself. Now I'm afraid all the time. For Stone. I've become softer. More vulnerable." Her voice went very soft. "Fear isn't good for a spy."

Rock swallowed hard and let go of her arms. To his surprise, she slid her arms around him and pressed her head against his chest, tucking her head beneath his chin. He held her tightly, afraid she'd pull away and he'd lose her forever. He kissed the top of her head.

"If you could see him, Rock. He's so precious, so precocious. Like you." Her voice caught. "His hair is the coarsest baby hair I've ever felt, and yet as soft as anything you could imagine. It stands straight up like a buzz cut and sometimes I want nothing more than to run my hands lightly over it.

"He laughs all the time and when he does it comes from deep in his belly, a real baby chortle that can't help but make me smile, even on the worst of days. He walked before he crawled and he rolled everywhere before he walked. He has tiny stubby legs, and dimples in his hand, and his diaper gives him a big bubble butt he's always falling over on. And yet, when he wants he can practically outrun me.

"He sleeps with a stuffed rabbit that lights up at night and projects magical stars on the ceiling. During the day he carries it around by the ears, along with a toy magic wand he likes to wave around as he says something that sounds kind of like abracadabra. But his first word was daddy . . ." Lani grabbed Rock's shirt in her fist and squeezed it tight. Her body trembled in his arms as if she was trying not to cry.

He kissed the top of her head again and tipped her chin up to meet her eye. "We have to trust Nanny. You told me she's a top agent. She'll protect him. We have to believe that."

He paused. "We'll get him back." Rock set his jaw. "I'll get him back if I have to give my life for his."

"Rock—"

"No, I mean it. I'll do anything to make this right again and get our baby back. Without him, we're lost and you and I are doomed. We'll never forgive ourselves. I'll never forgive myself." He tightened his grip on her.

"I love you, Lani. Like I've never loved anyone before and don't expect to ever love again." He gently stroked her cheek, brushing a tear away.

He'd made his brave spy wife cry. Shit, he was an asshole.

"This will be the illusion of our lives, baby," he said. "We'll give the show of a generation, fool RIOT, and we'll get our baby back. Promise."

Her mouth was inches from his. Her lips quivered. He wanted her, wanted one last time to be with her while they were still whole. Because if their world fell apart, things would never be the same again and he'd lose her.

She stared into his eyes, holding him as if she'd never let go.

He held her tight. She was worth fighting for. Their baby, their life together, he'd never stop fighting for them.

She looked up at him, took his face in her hands, and very gently pulled him down into a kiss.

Rock could make barren rosebushes bloom before her eyes, pull coins from out of nowhere and make them disappear again, levitate, and even walk on water. But his real magic was the way he made Lani feel—safe, secure, comforted, and loved. All of those emotions swept over her as she pulled Rock's face into hers for a kiss. He'd been suddenly distant, tentative, as if afraid she'd reject him, as if she blamed him. She had to show him she didn't. Words were one thing, actions another.

The blame was hers for keeping Stone from him. And now she was panicked and frightened she'd blown things for them forever, stolen Rock's chance to ever know his son. Rock was right. They had to remain calm and trust Nanny. Nanny was the best. But RIOT was a foe worthy of fear.

Lani's lips met Rock's tender, tentative kiss and another magic was revealed—the comfort of his embrace, the powerful quake of chemistry between them, and the way they belonged together. Rock made her feel like she belonged, and if that belonging was only to him, that was fine by her.

She slid her arms around his neck and ran her fingers through the tangle of hair at the nape of his neck as she leaned into him and kissed him with the intensity she'd been holding back for far too long.

Rock responded in kind, kissing her so deeply he nearly took her breath away. Lani wanted Rock in the worst way. Needed the urgency of his lovemaking and the union of their souls. She unwrapped her arms from his neck, slid her hands down his chest and up under his shirt to stroke his bare chest.

Rock's muscles flexed beneath her touch. His chest was hard and strong, and she could feel his heart racing.

In the movies, impediments like clothing just disappear or are tantalizingly removed in suggestive stripteases. Lani's scramble to get Rock naked and him to strip her bare were more like those of a quick-change artist—desperate and fast, clothes flying everywhere until they stood naked staring at each other and breathing hard.

She ran her gaze over his lean, hard chest and arms, admiring the design of his tattoos as they covered his sculpted body. *Lani in omne tempus.* She leaned forward and sucked his nipple, placing her hand over the words of his pledge and his heart. She slid her tongue over the words, licking her way to his other nipple while he stood perfectly still. She sucked it until he whispered her name.

She ran her tongue down his body, licking him gently across the heart and the dragon on his torso as she slid to her knees, stroking his hard-on with her free hand. Just as she was prepared to lick and tease him and take him into her mouth, he pulled her chin up.

"Damn it, Lani. I don't have that much control." He swept her into his arms and carried her to the bed where he gently laid her down. He came down on top of her, kissing her, stroking her, driving her wild with need.

Poised over her, Rock was long and hard and ready for action. She and Rock had never been poetic. They'd always opted for fun. She ran her gaze down the length of him, fixed her sights on his arousal, and arched a brow, aching for him to be inside.

"Now you see it," she whispered to him, as she had so many times before.

He leaned down, nibbled her neck, and whispered, "Now you don't."

With a thrust so powerful it made her gasp, he was inside her. She locked her legs around his waist and rode him in the way she'd imagined doing too many lonely nights over the last years. She made love to him like the scared, desperate woman she was.

They rocked the bed and banged the headboard against the wall. He thrust. She held on and arched back to his rhythm. She could lead, but this time she found comfort in letting him take control. She let him work his magic, moaning, and arching back as Rock wound every thread of passion and fear together in her, tightened, and amplified into a tapestry of ecstasy. Rock made music with her body in a pulsing crescendo beat until she thought the build couldn't last a minute longer.

He toyed with her, pushing her almost to the edge and pulling back at the last minute to restring the bow and begin tightening her strings again.

She looked him in the eye. "Take me there, Rock. *Now*."

He grinned. And then he did what no other magician had ever done for her—pulled an orgasm out of her with an intensity she'd never known.

As she gasped and arched up, Rock thrust twice more and followed her to climax, grunting and collapsing on top of her.

They were sweaty and breathing hard as she released the lock she held him in with her legs.

He pushed up as if he was about to roll off her. She held him a moment longer, looking up at him and letting everything she felt shine in her eyes. This may be the last opportunity to let Rock know what he meant to her. "I love you, Rock."

As he stared down at her, the corners of his mouth curled up very slightly, but not quite into a smile. There was nothing really to smile about. He knew what she was saying. She saw the realization in his eyes.

If they didn't get Stone back safely, if something went wrong with the illusion, or Nanny screwed up, then this was good-bye. Lani planned to disappear into the shadowy ether of the spy world and throw herself into destroying RIOT with every part of her being. She'd no longer care whether they killed her or not. She'd give her life to take out as many RIOT operatives as possible.

Yes, she'd disappear so deeply Rock would never find her again. She'd have to if she was going to do the work she planned to do. She couldn't endanger Rock again, or risk creating another child that could be used against her, not for what she had in mind. No, if things went wrong, she'd be a woman bent on justice and she'd be damned if she'd ever give RIOT anything to use against her.

Further, from now until the mission was over, Lani couldn't afford the distraction of letting her façade crack again or her motherly and womanly emotions to shine through. Back to being a warrior, back into mission mode. This was the mission of their lives and she wouldn't allow anything inside her to get in the way of success.

"I love you, too, Lani. More than you can imagine." Rock brushed her lips with a soft kiss. "I won't let you down. Promise."

The tone of his voice said it all. He knew the stakes they were playing for.

CHAPTER TWENTY

The black mailbox, address Rachel, Nevada, sat in the middle of a gravel lot, with two large boulders nearby, possibly placed by locals to be used as seats during any alien-watching sessions. The black mailbox, which was really white, was covered with graffiti and had a small slot next to a picture of a flying saucer for alien mail. Though why a sophisticated alien culture would need to send snail mail remained unexplained, at least to Rock's way of thinking. That mailbox was a relic of the 1950s.

Hell, even our relatively low-tech, completely backwoods culture compared to theirs, doesn't use the USPS much.

Usually picturesquely quaint and out of the way, isolated even, the mailbox was now surrounded by kegs of beer, coolers of soft drinks, bags of chips, bonfires, iPods blasting music that would have scared any self-respecting aliens away, live bands, and about a thousand NUFO partiers. Maybe more.

Rock had never seen anything like the spectacle before Ty and him and wasn't about to start counting the NUFOs now. Rock wondered just how many unbalanced loonies Random had peppered that crowd with. From what he'd heard about RIOT, they didn't leave anything to chance.

The deck, or in this case, the crowd, was always stacked in their favor.

The alien watchers toasted marshmallows and barbecued hot dogs and burgers. They danced to music provided by bands with names like Alien Fusion. They pointed their telescopes to the sky and aimed lasers.

Some wore sophisticated night-vision goggles or wielded night-vision binoculars. A small percentage of the NUFOs dressed in costume. Most wore shorts, T-shirts, or sweatshirts. The NUFO logo was the fashion statement of choice and appeared on a sea of hats, shirts, and sweatshirts. It was so prevalent Rock wondered whether a real alien force would mistake it for the uniform of an attacking audience.

This swarming mass of alien-watching, extraterrestrial-believing, UFO-sighting hopefuls was his audience, *the* audience that would crown Rock's already stellar career or end his son's life. The stakes had never been higher.

Tal had coached him to keep his head and perform the mission complete with the reveal, as planned. Rock really had no choice. The rest of the team would carry it out without him.

If Rock could manipulate the NUFOs into believing his illusion, and then marvel in his reveal, he would indeed be the world's greatest magician. And if NCS hadn't gotten Stone back, that would seal Stone's and Nanny's death warrants.

However crazy these NUFOs may have seemed to some people, their sophistication in watching for alien and UFO sightings should not be underestimated. When Rock had originally imagined Outlandish Marauders, most of the technology the NUFOs now so casually wielded had not been invented.

Then again, neither had the spy plane Emmett had

promised. Or the lasers Will had set up. Or the social media networks Britt would use. They were in virgin, unmarked territory now with much more than Rock's personal reputation on the line.

Rock and the hard place. Nice pun.

Next to Rock, Ty, his CIA bodyguard for this mission, received a text. "They've found them," he said simply.

As Rock's heart raced out of control, Ty clapped him on the shoulder. "Stone and Nanny are alive. The rescue and sniper teams are in place. Our best sniper, an old friend of mine, is on it. We'll have Stone back before it's time for the reveal."

Rock took a deep breath, trying not to break down. It wasn't quite time for relief yet. But there was hope.

"Don't think about it," Ty said. "Stay focused on the mission and let our agents do their job while you do yours. That's the best way to help them."

"Yeah." Rock nodded as he fought to control the odd, adrenaline-induced cocktail of emotions that coursed through him—anxiety, fear, excitement, expectation. Had Rock thought of everything? What could go wrong?

There were a dozen things, maybe more. There hadn't been time to perform and refine the trick to Rock's liking. To work the bugs out. And in Rock's experience, there were always bugs. Usually too damned many.

The need for secrecy had prevented them from performing Outlandish Marauders in its entirety on set here even once. The setting also was not to Rock's tastes and wouldn't have been to his choosing if there'd been a choice of locales. The barren landscape with little brush and no trees added difficulty points to this maneuver. Rock would have preferred a forest with plenty of cover for Ashley, his quick-changing alien, Zach, his video gaming magician, and Jake, his parkour illusionist.

Here in the open, the chance of being caught or found out was magnified.

Somewhere in the audience, Britt, Rock's social media wizard, wound her way innocuously among the NUFO, mixing with the crowd as she awaited the UFO and her cue to drum up the hysteria and panic he needed to pull this off.

The mailbox was a good two and a half to three hours from the traffic and crowds of Las Vegas. It would take that long for anyone who responded to Britt's Tweets to reach them. That was all according to both RIOT's and NCS's plans. For RIOT, that meant a second wave of mischief and mayhem in case the first wave of NUFO panic didn't produce the desired result. For NCS that gave them time to do the reveal and head off that second wave. If all went according to plan, the illusion would be long over and the reveal performed before anyone from Vegas could respond.

The mailbox and the party were a good ten miles down a dirt road from the warning signs and camo guys at the Area 51 main gate. To get to Area 51, a person had to cruise down Mailbox Road, past the Crescent Reservoir to Groom Lake Road and from there along the dirt road to the gates.

There was no fence that protected the perimeter of Area 51, just security cameras and camo dudes who appeared out of nowhere to confiscate video and pictures and turn back intruders. And plenty of speculation about all kinds of high-tech security devices, like sniffing machines that could tell the scent of a human from an animal, that may or may not really exist. Sensors that can hear a footstep past the gates.

One thing was real—signs warning that deadly force may be used against trespassers.

Rock had never heard of anyone being shot. There

were no records of it. But there were no records of Area 51, either. Officially it didn't exist. Some even said it was a cover for another, even more top-secret facility. The thought of an innocent person, a panicked, excited person rushing to the rescue of their planet being shot worried Rock, even if it seemed like a remote possibility. At his core, Rock was not a violent man and he didn't like playing with people's lives.

He'd had no need to know about the directives Emmett had issued to the camo dudes or the other security forces inside Area 51. So he had no real way of knowing how safe any panicked NUFOs would be if they chose to ignore the warning signs. And what of Edwards Air Force Base? What were their standing orders? What had the CIA told them, if anything? Would a squadron of aircraft suddenly buzz them from the base?

This illusion had so much potential for failure and screwups it blew the mind. What would the president do with the black eye of a few dozen dead NUFOs on his record? How would the press spin Rock's actions? Would the CIA throw Rock under the alien spaceship, so to speak, and toss him in jail for this "prank"? How would they spin it so that no one else ever dared even imagining trying such a trick again?

Faced with the reality of the illusion, Rock had all kinds of doubts and second thoughts. This scheme seemed crazy, even for him.

Plan to fail half the time. Who had told him that? The chief? Rock sure as hell hoped this wasn't the half where he failed.

The weather had cooperated for the NUFO's annual party and Rock's illusion. The starry night, far away from the light pollution of the city, seemed to stretch to infinity and beyond to the far reaches of the universe. To that place where the aliens supposedly lived.

There was no wind. None. Good for Rock in that it wouldn't blow away his smoke screens. Not so great for air-pollution conditions. The occasional howl of a coyote, when it could be heard over a pause in the live music, lent atmosphere.

The stage, the vast canvas of the Nevada desert, was set.

The plan was deceptively simple—fool the crowds with an alien invasion and drive them toward the gates of Area 51. The devil was in the execution.

In just a few minutes, Emmett's spacecraft would buzz the mailbox. He'd guaranteed something spectacular and convincingly UFO. It would then disappear in the direction of Area 51. Translated into truth, that meant land there. While the plane was in the air above them, Will would work his magic with his lasers, aiming them so that they looked like energy streams coming from the UFO above. To do that, he needed a literal smoke screen to illuminate the laser light.

Ashley and Jake would then "materialize" dressed as aliens on the ground at the end of the light beam. In the meantime, Britt would spot the aliens and get the message to the entire crowd, along with confusing and panicked messages about what was happening. Messages that would encourage the crowd to rally toward Area 51, if they weren't already so inclined. She'd also spread the word online to the mainstream medias and legions of other alien watchers.

This is where the timing got tricky. Ashley and Jake would bound and fly through the air toward Area 51, encouraging the crowd to follow them. At one point, Jake would disappear and reappear hundreds of yards away as if by . . . magic.

Actually, it would be Zach who did the reappearing. Then Jake would leapfrog him and repeat the magical feat, leading the crowd to the front gate of Area 51.

At the same time, Ashley would split off in another direction and lead as much of the crowd as she could toward the back entrance of Area 51. RIOT had specified they wanted as much breach capability as possible.

Ashley, though, was supposed to disappear long before the crowd caught up with her. She'd accomplish this by doing one of her quick changes and then hiding out to join the crowd once it caught up with her. From there she'd join Britt in guiding the masses toward Area 51. This is where the lack of cover made the illusion riskier than Rock liked. It was devoid of even a decent-size cactus. This is also where it got so fun that if Stone hadn't been in danger, Rock would have been barely able to contain himself.

The aerial acrobatics had to look real. Rock was in essence trying to reproduce the effects of flying, as an actor does with a wire on stage. But hang a wire from the sky? Even Rock wasn't that good. So he'd asked the CIA for a jet pack or two to help him out, even though he hadn't been optimistic about convincingly camouflaging them. Rock had wanted it to look like the creatures were flying on their own power. A jet pack–powered alien was just too earthly and could be too easily proven to be a fake.

The CIA had done Rock one better and provided him with top-secret developmental hovercrafts—one for Rock and Ty, one for Will, one for Jake, and one for Zach so he and Jake could leapfrog. Ashley had been jealous, but she had a different role to fulfill.

Will would move with Jake and Zach and provide more smoke screens and laser magic to add to the effects.

Even with the hovercrafts, it was risky, dangerous work done without a harness. With his knowledge of video games, Zach had choreographed the effects, which at times required Jake to jump between hovercrafts, which were being controlled remotely by engineers deep within Area 51. Timing, timing, timing.

Rock's version of extraterrestrials were sexy and scary, not funny-looking, long-necked creatures like ET. So he'd incorporated many of the traditional alien features into a handsome, athletic, warrior alien and his warrior lady companion.

Masking the sound of the hovercrafts moving had been another obstacle, one that had been overcome by issuing Britt a muffler-free dirt bike, which she was immediately supposed to fire up once the alien was spotted. After that, Rock figured any hovercraft noise would be drowned out by the plethora of dirt bikes, motorcycles, and all-terrain vehicles that gave chase.

Rock didn't like performing stunts without built-in safety features, but he was up against it. The feats had to look real and Jake insisted he could do it. Rock, Zach, Will, and Jake had incorporated as many safety features and procedures as they could.

As soon as the aliens landed, Rock was supposed to jump in the hovercraft with Ty and head for the main gate of Area 51 ahead of the pack. When they arrived, he'd be waiting for them, ready to reveal the illusion and stop the crowd from entering the perimeters. He just hoped he could go through with it.

In the meantime, Lani, Tate, and Tal were stationed inside Area 51 waiting to apprehend Random, and any other RIOT agents, if they made an attempt to infiltrate the area.

Randomly roaming cows were a problem in the surrounding area, especially at night. If you hit a cow, local law stipulated that you had to reimburse the owner. To give everyone more time, a herd of cows was going to be driven between the aliens and the alien watchers. Followed by a bunch of angry ranchers.

Timing, timing, timing. It all came down to timing.

Rock looked at his watch and then through his binoculars at the crowd in front of him. He took a deep breath and looked up just as a gigantic flying saucer appeared on the horizon.

Tate, Tal, and Lani waited inside one of the security stations inside the Area 51 compound with one of the area's senior security officers, watching the security feeds of the installation and surrounding area and awaiting further commands. Now they knew everything the camo dudes did and more.

Lani had dressed to once again alter her appearance. If anyone from RIOT saw her, or any of Rock's fans that might be among the crowd of NUFOs, she couldn't risk being recognized. A master with makeup, she'd deemphasized her Asian and African-American features, playing up her white characteristics. She wore a shoulder-length wig that hid her long, wavy hair. Dressed in camo dude gear, she looked like a camo dudette of Mediterranean descent. An Italian or possibly a Greek.

"Front row seats for the show," Tate said and laughed, leaning back in his chair and taking a swig of nonalcoholic beer. Nonalcoholic wasn't Tate's style, but real life wasn't like Bond. He couldn't just swill martinis until the ground rose up to smack him in the face. He, too, was dressed in the camo dude uniform. His eyes were blackened and he wore a fake beard for the occasion. "Now all we need is some popcorn."

Lani scowled at him. "Since when do you eat popcorn, caviar boy?" She hated being out of the magical action. Her fingers tingled with energy and she had a hard time forcing herself to stay seated and focused on the feed. She wasn't audience material. She was a showman to her core, a performer even when she had a gun in her hand. Waiting was for cowards and expectant fathers. Now more than ever, with her baby's life on the line, she wanted to be in the heart of the action where she could do the most damage. She much preferred performing sleight of hand and illusions and front-of-the-stage action.

Her gaze bounced between the feeds before her—the all-night party the NUFOs were throwing, the various hangars and secure areas of Dreamland, as Area 51 was colloquially known, and Rock and his operation and team.

She resisted biting her lip. Everything hung on Rock and the rescue team poised to save Stone. She tried not to think about what was going on in upstate New York. Jack Pierce, the CIA assassin she'd helped recover after he'd been blown up, was the sniper on the rescue site charged with taking out Stone's captors. He was the best in the world. If anyone could do it, Jack could. She had complete confidence in him. But it was her baby's life on the line and she was a mother and she was worried.

She tried to focus on her mission. She should be with Rock. She was his able-bodied assistant and his superior in the intelligence community. She *wanted* to be with him more than anything. Until death did they part. If something went wrong today, parting was going to happen one way or another. She hoped death wasn't part of the equation, but it was a real possibility.

As a showman, she trusted and respected Rock above anyone else. She never doubted he could pull off the illusion. If RIOT or Sol didn't somehow interfere. She had a bad feeling about things. RIOT *was* involved. Rock was an entertainer, not a secret agent, not a fighter. If he got into trouble . . .

And so she cooled her jets, surrounded on all sides by technology that put jets to shame. And waited with Tate and Tal for Archibald Random, and any other RIOT agents who showed up, to make RIOT's next chess move.

Given the chance, she'd gladly grab Random. Whether she could restrain herself from killing him once she had him and forced him to order Stone's release was the question. With Random dead, Lani's problems would be over. Except for maybe her court-martial and a lifetime jail sentence for screwing up national security. The Agency would have her head for not allowing them the opportunity to mine Random's brain for all his twisted plots.

The camo dudes and the internal security squads throughout Dreamland were on high alert. As Lani watched the screens, she could almost feel their nervous anticipation. Despite the warning signs that trespassers would be shot, when was the last time one of them had actually fired their weapon?

Tate's cell phone buzzed. "From the tower." He picked it up, listened, made a few murmurs, covered the mouthpiece with his hand, and relayed the news. "A plane just left Vegas bound for Dreamland. It has clearance." His gaze bounced between his fellow agents.

Lani's heart raced. "Now? In the middle of our operation? That's quite a coincidence. What's the explanation? Midnight contractors who want to get a jump on the day shift?" She was being sarcastic and from the looks on their faces, her fellow agents knew it. "Random?"

Tate shrugged. "Could be."

Damn it all, does Tate always have to understate things and be so calm?

Lani didn't like this, not at all. It was too bold. As the senior field agents for this mission, they had command authority. She meant to use it. "Instruct the tower to call out the guard planes. Have them escort the plane out of our airspace to Edwards and let the air force deal with it there. If the plane's legit, they'll comply without complaint."

Tate nodded. "My thoughts exactly."

Tal just grinned and nodded.

Tate removed his hand from the phone's mouthpiece and was just opening his mouth to relay the orders to the tower when the chief appeared on their top-secret command stream security feed, which also appeared in the tower, stopping Tate before he could issue the order.

"Hang on," Tate said into the phone. Though he didn't need to. The tower would be watching the chief, too.

Emmett was seated in his office with his shirtsleeves rolled up, looking calm and relaxed. Then again, the chief never lost his cool. He was unflappable and indefatigable.

"Sorry to be so late to the party." The chief laughed, sounding like the chief. "Given the excitable state of those NUFOs partying in the desert, I'm sending in a team of riot squad specialists. Just in case. They'll arrive within the half hour.

"We don't want an incident on our hands. Give them a friendly welcome." He blipped off and the direct line command screen went dark.

Tate went back to the phone. He was scowling as he hung up. "The tower says they have their orders. The chief outranks us."

"Shit." Tal swore beneath his breath. "If that really was the chief. Anyone else notice he was kind of vague and didn't directly acknowledge us?

"On the other hand, if that was Random, damn that was too easy. A mask or a bit of plastic surgery, steal a few fingerprints, maybe fake a retina scan, and he's in, impersonating the chief and giving orders. He even sounded enough like the chief to fool us. Of course, he could have been using sophisticated voice-altering software to imitate the chief's voice."

"What I want to know is, if that was Random, how did he get the chief's clearance code and break into our feed?" Ty was scowling.

"Exactly the question on my mind," Tal said. "If that's the case, we have a traitor in our midst." He paused.

"Let's get the chief on the horn and straighten this out, find out whether that was really him we just saw."

Tate's jaw was set and his eyes hard and serious for once. He shook his head. "If Random has the capability to break into our telecommunications system, what's to say he doesn't have the ability to intercept and reroute our calls back to himself? How can we trust that we'll get the real chief?"

Tate continued frowning. "I say we revert to our standing orders and consider ourselves chiefless until this mission is over. Remember—the chief gave strict orders that if he should appear at Area 51, to ignore any commands he gave and immediately arrest him. I'd say a video feed is the same thing as an appearance.

"We may not be able to get the tower to comply, but we ignore orders and proceed."

Lani nodded her agreement. Tal agreed, too.

"What if that plane is carrying a bomb or weaponry that can be used to take control of Dreamland?" Lani asked the question that was on all of their minds.

"Tal and I will go to the tower to wait for the plane and arrest anyone on board until we can get a bomb squad to clear the plane," Tate said.

"And if they come in firing?" Lani asked.

Tal shook his head. "They won't. Not if their goal is to steal something from inside here. We'll fake a welcome and then nab them."

The boys were right. Lani reluctantly agreed with them. "Does it bother anyone else that Emmett seems to be on a first-name basis with Random? And they're both very familiar with each other. Too familiar. How could an imposter know, and mimic, the chief's mannerisms so uncannily? It's not like the chief's a high-profile public figure." Lani stared at her fellow agents, watching their reactions to her question carefully.

Tate was shaking his head. "No, it doesn't bother me. Don't let this imposter get to you or disrupt your loyalties, Lani. He's trying to mess with our heads.

"Remember this, Emmett has had personal run-ins with that bastard over the years. Rumors abound that they were once friends. Until Random stole the chief's girl, the love of the chief's life."

Lani frowned. How in the world did Tate know all this stuff? He was better at ferreting out gossip and intel than any woman Lani had ever known, including her mother.

Tate, though, was a different kind of agent. Privileged and from a well-connected and powerful family. His father had been a senator and the head of the Senate Intelligence Committee. And a spy who'd served with Emmett's predecessor. Tate had known Emmett since he'd been a boy. Their families were friends.

Connections! Lani thought with some scorn. She'd worked her way up and into the Agency on her own, with no help from anyone else. She was proud of her accomplishments, but she wasn't a true insider like Tate.

The thought, though, of Emmett scorned in love was both preposterous and funny. She had to fight not to smile or laugh out loud at the ludicrousness of it. Emmett in lust, sure. He liked women. He'd had his share. He'd been a notorious womanizer during his spying days. These days he kept his affairs under wraps.

But vulnerable and in love? And losing out to another man? No way.

No matter how Lani tried, she couldn't imagine any woman preferring the villainous Random to the chief. Not unless she was a blackheart of the darkest kind herself. The chief would never fall for an evil woman, would he?

If this purported woman existed, and wasn't some bit

of urban CIA espionage myth, it was unthinkable that she could have fooled the master mind reader into believing she was on the side of good. Not unless she was a genius herself and a supervillain. Or had somehow changed course from good to evil midstream.

There would be a great story in that, if it were true. The human mind was a delicate machine. It reacted to pain and stress and loss in unexpected ways and tipped toward mania at the slightest provocation. At least some people did. Then there was always greed as a motive for change.

"That has to be pure fiction. Emmett in love? Can you imagine?"

From the looks on their faces, none of the boys could, nor wanted to.

As entertaining as the story of Emmett's love life might have been, Lani forced her thoughts back to the mission at hand. "The plane will be here soon. We'd better move. You boys have guests to greet."

Tal nodded and picked up his gear, including his sniper rifle.

"I have a bad feeling about this." Lani couldn't help it. Call it a woman's intuition, but she had the feeling something was going to go wrong. She just hoped Rock could handle it if it did.

"We have an advantage, Lani. Random doesn't know we know he's trying to impersonate the chief." Ty's logic was sound.

But Lani remained uneasy. "I still don't like it." Lani shook her head. "What is Random's real goal? What is he trying to steal?"

Tate shook his head. "None of us have a need to know, therefore, none of us does."

"Yes, but aren't you curious?" she asked Tate.

He shrugged. "You know what they say about the cat? And curiosity didn't work out so well for Pandora, either.

"Here at Area 51 you check that kind of curiosity at the door. Hell, everyone here has the highest clearances in the country. But that doesn't mean squat as far as broad knowledge of an operation.

"The reason Area 51 has been so successful at keeping and being kept secret all these years is because no one asks questions. Pilots fly planes and report the data without knowing why. The guy who designs the engines has no idea who's designing the navigation systems or what the payload is. No one ever writes anything down and only a handful of people have the whole plan in their heads.

"It's best that way. No one person can give away the operation."

Yes, Lani knew how security worked. She knew the rationale and it was all logical. Still . . .

She smiled at Tate and teased, "You don't think there really are aliens here, do you?"

He shrugged and arched a brow. "I just told you—only a handful of people know the whole plan for this place."

Tate received a message from the tower.

"Our UFO has arrived. It's buzzing the mailbox as we speak. Let's hope our young magician makes it to the gates before the crowd gets him."

Lani's breath caught. The illusion Rock was performing with his protégés was more dangerous with more potential to go wrong than any of them liked to admit. Jake and Ashley were as brave as any war heroes. If the crowd, which was supposed to be worked into a frenzy, caught them and discovered their deception, there was no telling what they'd do. In all likelihood, it wouldn't be good. Think lynch mob.

Let the illusion begin.

Rock was good, the best magician around, but the

stakes and the degree of difficulty for this illusion were just too high. And no matter how hard she tried, Lani couldn't get rid of her feeling of apprehension or keep her mind off the rescue that was going on on the other side of the country.

CHAPTER TWENTY-ONE

D *amn, that UFO is awesome.*
      Rock stared, actually gaped with his mouth open, as the UFO appeared out of nowhere from the distant horizon, sneaking up on the partying NUFOs and the desert without a sound. How fast did that thing have to be flying to just suddenly materialize? Rock was no aerospace engineer, but he knew it had to be damned fast.

At first glance, the thing was a literal flying saucer. Radiating, pulsating lights. Emmett had not been joking when he'd said he would give them exactly what they needed and it would be impressive.

Rock stared at the hovering monstrosity, dumbstruck. That man could build something like this was almost incomprehensible. He had an instant of doubt. *What if the chief is lying? What if this is a* real *alien craft? What if Area 51 really is an alien testing site?*

The saucer shape is not the ideal aerodynamic shape for flying, not in a gravity environment, anyway. And not for a craft using a propulsion engine. Ever seen a saucer-shaped bird, for example?

And everyone knows you need a pointy rocket to pierce the atmosphere and get into outer space. At least, man has traditionally needed one.

The beauty of the saucer, however, was that it was

aerodynamic in any direction, assuming propulsion could be from any direction and not from a rear-mounted engine or the flapping of wings. Perfect for outer space.

Long before anyone had thought of this, though, UFO spotters had reported the saucer-shaped crafts. Rock had never been able to decide whether the crazy shape of flying saucers validated or invalidated reports of extraterrestrial ships. Let's face it, not one piece of transportation on earth, from ships to bicycles, was saucer-shaped.

Which gave Rock pause for just a minute as he stared in awe at the craft above him wondering whether it had a Romulan cloaking device as well. Which would explain the sudden appearance. Or could mask the real shape of the aircraft, which to his knowledge would need a propulsion engine.

Rock aimed his binoculars toward it. Black and unearthly, with spinning rims of light shooting outward from it, it was impressive. Rock wondered whether it was an optical illusion, because the thing looked big enough to house a small city. What was it made of? A composite, like the new airplanes being manufactured? Radar-absorbent materials?

The way it had sneaked up on the now hushed and frozen NUFO crowd in front of Rock, the craft had to have reduced acoustic, infrared, visual, and radar signatures. Full of a fair share of serious scientists who were determined to find alien life and ferret out fakes, the NUFO crowd was armed with radar and infrared detecting equipment. And everyone had ears. The NUFOs wouldn't be easily fooled.

Rock glanced at the crowd. They were entranced by the flying machine above them. The scene reminded him of a dozen alien movies. No one was moving. Mouths hung open. Eyes were wide and it was as if everyone held their collective breath.

This was a sight that had never been witnessed before. It didn't take a mind reader to know what everyone was thinking. Would the ship attack? Suck the crowd up into its portals? Perform hideous alien experiments and then dump the victims back on earth with their memories wiped clean? Or worse yet, disappear before it could be documented?

Rock, of course, was thinking something altogether different. *This is the illusion of the century. Or is it? Maybe that thing really is an alien ship. Or one of ours reverse-engineered from one.*

Rock's pulse roared in his ears, even though he knew the truth of the ship's origins. Or thought he did. You couldn't trust those bastards from the CIA. They were as much liars and illusionists as he was.

Suddenly, the crowd of NUFOs, as if realizing the craft wouldn't hover above them forever, jumped into action. Hundreds of flashes of light penetrated the darkness as people snapped photos of the craft from their cell phones and cameras. Pieces of scientific equipment were aimed at it and the collective hush of the crowd broke into an excited murmur.

Only Rock held his breath as he waited for the perfect moment to signal to his crew to act. *Timing, timing, timing.*

Adrenaline and the thrill of performing overshadowed Rock's desert stage fright. As a beam of light shot from the craft's belly to earth, to the precise coordinates where Jake and Ashley hid, ready to appear as aliens, Rock pressed a button on his cell phone and set their part of the illusion in motion.

Will set off a series of flash powder explosions to mask Ashley and Jake and aimed his lasers to add to the illusion.

Rock held his breath again, watching as closely as the

NUFOs would be for any sign of fakeness. Faking an alien landing wasn't as simple as dressing in a big, hairy suit and staging a Bigfoot sighting. The technology involved. The movements required.

Jake materialized from the smoke on cue, looking as if he'd been beamed from the ship rather than popping up from the ground, as was the reality. Ashley appeared a second later.

As the crowd of NUFOs gasped and pointed, Rock congratulated himself on choreographing the illusion so well. *Yes, I'm a genius.*

And only a magical genius would have thought of all the details that Rock had. Only two highly talented young people could have pulled off his instructions.

The "alien" spaceship hovered a second longer, and with a sudden burst, blew past the crowd toward Area 51, disappearing as suddenly as it had appeared.

Beside him, Ty swore beneath his breath.

Will shook his head in amazement. "Does that thing have a cloaking device or what?"

The crowd let out a collective gasp.

Rock watched the crowd for signs that Britt had also sprung into action. Any second now the masses should begin pursuing the two newly beamed-down aliens.

They'd reached the part of the illusion that Rock thought of like a movie. A movie can lead the audience down a path that seems logical as it unfolds, exciting, stimulating. But if the viewer pauses, the inconsistencies and illogical nature of the movie can be seen.

Rock hoped the crowd would be too frenzied to wonder why a highly sophisticated alien culture, with technology that surpasses ours by light years of scientific discovery, would make the mistake of beaming two of its life-forms right onto the edge of a mass of earthlings.

Of course, there were explanations. Like the two aliens were being punished for some hideous crime or another. Banished to be captured and tortured by earthlings.

Still, if that were the case, was it reasonable to go after hardened alien criminals? Who knew what lethal-force technology they might possess?

Rock had insisted his aliens not be armed with any obvious weaponry. He felt semiconfident the NUFOs wouldn't shoot unarmed aliens. After all, their stated goal was to take aliens alive and try to communicate with them.

Semi being the operative word. One can never tell what a drunk UFO watcher might do. For safety, both Jake and Ashley wore bulletproof vests. Even though the vests had made costuming harder and weighed Jake down, making his job more difficult.

The crowd suddenly surged forward, as if controlled by a single mind.

"Get in!" Ty screamed at Rock.

Rock jumped into the hovercraft, night-vision goggles trained on his magicians. Ty fired up the engine and took off toward the gates of Area 51. At the same time, a large part of the crowd decided Area 51 was the place to go, too, and jumped on their motorcycles, or into their vehicles to join the chase.

Rock's pulse pounded, beating a rhythm that matched the march of the crowd of people and vehicles surging toward them as they kept just ahead of Jake and Ashley.

Right on cue, Ashley veered right and took off toward the back gates, which were still miles away. This was delicate, so delicate. Ashley was on foot and running for her life while still executing the moves Jake and Zach had taught her. She leaped and darted, sprinted and jumped, looking natural and believably alien.

Rock had his fingers crossed. If Ashley, Jake, or Zach, when he appeared, made the slightest threatening movement or apparently reached for a weapon, all hell and gunfire could break out.

Rock and Ty were in the only manned, nonremote-controlled hovercraft. Ty was grinning like a kid with his first car as he piloted them toward the front gates and the big finale. "Finally, a hot vehicle. This makes up for a lot of crap."

Rock barely heard him as he watched the crowd closing in on Ashley. Damn, they were taking chances with this illusion. If anything went wrong, if anyone got hurt, it was all on his head.

Ashley stumbled. Rock cursed. The crowd closed to within fifty yards of her as Ashley sprinted to her vanishing point.

Rock held his breath, hoping Will was on with his timing as he provided smoke and laser cover. Will was heavily camouflaged in the hovercraft, code-named the duck blind, so well hidden that Rock couldn't see him even using the goggles. Because the NUFOs also had night-vision goggles, it had to be this way. Rock was trusting the engineers at the home base to pilot Will into position. And he was trusting Will to perform accurately and on cue to cover Ashley.

If the NUFOs realized they were being punked, the show was over.

This was just like a stage production. All his magicians were used to working with precision timing. But this was open country. Rock prayed a wind wouldn't kick up or that a new gopher hole hadn't opened up overnight since they'd plotted and cleared Ashley's path and planted stage markers as guides.

Ashley was running in the dark. She was wearing night-vision goggles, true, but they didn't provide the same visibility as bright daylight.

Rock counted the paces as he watched Ashley run. *Now, now, now!*

Rock held his breath. Ashley raised her arm and tossed a pot of flash powder onto the ground. Will ignited a larger cache of smoke and lit the scene with eerie alien-looking lights, as if Ashley glowed.

Rock crossed his fingers, which was highly unmagicianlike. Use every diversionary mind trick possible, but never rely on luck was a cardinal rule of magic. But, hell, for once no one was watching Rock, who was used to being the center of attention and taking all the heat. Rock was experienced enough to recover from an unexpected snag or snafu, but these kids? He crossed his fingers tighter, hating the feeling of not being in total control.

The crowd reached Ashley's location and paused, waving their hands to clear the smoke and looking around in confusion. Ashley had obviously disappeared.

Beside Rock, Ty was also scanning the crowd, looking for Ashley to reappear. He wore an expression of complete seriousness. Could it be that one of those unflappable NCS agents was as nervous as Rock was?

Ty pointed. "She did it! I have a visual. She's part of the crowd now. Look!"

Rock followed the direction of Ty's finger, squinted, and just made Ashley out. She was wearing a distinctly marked NUFO T-shirt that glowed in the night-vision goggles so they could easily spot her.

Rock and Ty watched as Ashley gestured and pointed. She was wearing a wire so she could communicate with them.

"There!" they heard her say. "It went that way!" She pointed.

Roughly a third of the crowd had followed Ashley. They were now committed to chasing her alien.

Yeah, you guys chose wrong, Rock thought, feeling almost disappointed for them. *Almost*. He could feel those unfortunate NUFOs wishing they'd decided to chase the other alien, the one who was still visible, but too far away for them to catch.

"It's heading to the back gate of Area 51!" Ashley screamed. "If it gets there, we'll lose it forever. Follow it!"

The crowd, moving like a free-flowing, irregularly shaped amoeba drifted, and then surged in a charge toward the back gate where Daniel and Smokz would perform the reveal as assistants to the holographically projected Rock, who would be performing live at the front gate. Smokz would be on dressed as an alien to do a little head levitation. Yeah, it was going to be awesome. Epic. Record breaking. Wasn't CIA technology grand?

In the meantime, Jake was leading his part of the crowd, more and more of whom were jumping into cars, ATVs, and motorcycles, toward Area 51. His movements were fluid and so convincing, he nearly fooled Rock. As Jake stood on the hidden hovercraft, he looked as if he was running on his own steam and pulling away from the crowd, but not so far that they would lose hope that they could catch him.

The first big "jump" was coming up. Rock held his breath again and counted down, whispering his mantra— timing, timing, timing!

Jake leaped, arms pumping, feet striding in the air like a triple jumper. The boy could fly. He got good height and was a beauty to behold. Just at the height of his jump, he disappeared.

Beside Rock, Ty was silent, watching with the same intensity as Rock was.

Off in the distance, Zach appeared in a beam of light provided by Will, dressed identically to Jake so that he appeared to be the same alien creature. His timing was perfect as well. He, too, was striding through the air, looking as if he was the same creature completing a hundred yard jump on his own power.

"Impressive, like Superman." Ty laughed as if this mission was the most fun he'd had in a long time. "Only half a dozen more jumps and nine more miles of performance to go until we reach the gates."

Ty threw the hovercraft into warp speed, the earthly approximation at least, throwing Rock backward as they surged forward just ahead of the crowd.

Back at Dreamland HQ and security control, Lani watched the security feed as Emmett's UFO cruised into its hangar. Stunning. That's the only way to describe the aircraft she watched fly in, looking as if it belonged in a sci-fi movie or the twenty-fifth century or something. Even knowing it was of this twenty-first-century world and one of theirs, it struck terror in her, along with a swell of pride and awe.

Imagine being attacked by that thing. She shuddered. *Imagine it in the wrong hands.* At the same time, the plane from Vegas taxied onto runway five. Lani went cold. *Random, is that you? Or one of your agents?*

If it wasn't, she, Tate, and Tal were in deep space doodoo. Emmett would be furious at them for ignoring orders.

The Vegas plane coasted to a stop. Tate and Tal were in position, hiding and ready to make their surprise move. Both men were excellent shots and had nerves of steel. But Lani couldn't help wishing the Agency's top assassin, Jack Pierce, could be in two places at once—saving her baby and here. Even after coming back from a near-fatal accident and having to retrain, Jack never missed. He was so calm and calculated, sometimes she swore he didn't have a heartbeat.

Jack had taught her an assassin's trick or two and helped her improve her shooting. But now she was stuck in the observation booth. What, exactly, was she supposed to do if Tate and Tal got into trouble? Run to their aid? A lone gun against everyone, friend and/or foe? There was no way she'd be able to get backup.

And what happened if Ty and Rock and the young guns ran afoul? What did she do then?

The door to the plane opened. A uniformed Dreamland employee pushed a set of mobile stairs to the door. Lani held her breath as a man emerged from the jet.

Jake and Zach leapfrogged and appeared and disappeared at will. With Will's laser and smoke cover, everything was going according to plan. The crowd chased after them, eager, yelling greetings in Klingon and gibberish that must have been other alien tongues as they hung out of their cars and waved. Why Klingon? Who knew? Sounded alien, Rock imagined. They signaled the aliens with flashing lights that mimicked Morse code and waved banners with crazy-looking characters.

Rock had to hand it to the NUFOs. They came prepared for every kind of alien sighting.

Less than a mile to the gates. Rock wasn't exactly superstitious except about opening nights like this one. Rehearsals had gone too well. There was always a bug, and opening night usually found it. If he was very lucky, it was something small that the audience wouldn't notice. Tonight, though, he couldn't afford anything to go wrong at all.

He went over everything in his mind. He'd planned the illusion so the audience would be so diverted by the alien craft and the aliens themselves that they'd overlook the mechanics of what was really going on. No one would notice the hovercrafts.

Now that part of the performance was nearly over and the most dangerous part, his part, stopping the crowd, was almost upon them. And there was still no word from the rescue team.

The hovercraft cooked along, skimming above the earth, and providing the smoothest ride Rock had ever had. He was going to be spoiled for life now. And from the look on his face, so was Ty.

The ride was so smooth and bump-free that Rock had stopped holding on and stood watching the crowd without bracing himself as he might have in a regular land vehicle.

The mind is an amazing thing. When it's fully concentrated, it can be so single-minded of purpose that it blocks out all other stimuli. A person deeply engaged in reading a novel won't hear their spouse call their name. Deep in the heart and world of his illusion, concentrating on details, Rock didn't hear Ty speaking to him until Ty shook his arm.

"Do you hear that?" Ty's voice was urgent. A second later, he began cursing and shoved the hovercraft into full throttle.

Rock was still coming out of the fog of concentration. The sudden movement of the hovercraft sent him sprawling backward on his ass. "What the hell?"

A second too late, he heard the distinctive whistle of a missile coming at them. Ty dodged and weaved as Rock tried to get his bearings.

Ty swerved to the right, throwing Rock against the hovercraft wall. "Hold tight. It's locked onto us."

"That can't be good." Rock's right arm throbbed from banging against the side of the hovercraft. "Can we outrun it? Force the missile to blow something else up?"

Ty shook his head as he concentrated on steering the craft. "Hell, no."

Ty pulled a lever and the hovercraft suddenly lost altitude. "I'm taking us down. When I get near enough to the ground, I'm going to throttle way back. We'll have a short window to abandon the craft before the missile hits it. Tuck and roll when you hit the ground. On my signal, bail. And run like hell when you get your feet beneath you."

Rock pushed to a stand. Here was his bug. And it was worse than he'd ever imagined—a bomb. The last thing he wanted was a bomb in *any* sense of the word.

"Ready." Ty veered the craft sideways.

Rock climbed the wall of the craft, balancing on it as if he was on a high-wire. Good thing he'd seen so many Cirque du Soleil shows.

"On three," Ty said. "One . . . two . . . now!"

Rock threw himself over the edge of the craft.

The pilot emerged from the plane with his hands raised, strapped to a bomb.

Lani leaned back in her chair and held a hand up to the security section chief next to her in the security booth. Tate emerged from his cover and approached the pilot. A squad of armed military guards appeared from nowhere to back Tate up.

"Don't come any closer! Any movement could set the bomb off." The pilot sounded calm enough, but the look in his eyes said he was terrified.

Tate's voice came over the TV in Lani's security room. "Send the bomb squad."

"I'm on it." Lani hardly needed to contact them. They were already on their way.

"What about the plane?" Tate asked the pilot.

"Clean, as far as I know."

"Who's on board?" Tate had his gun aimed at the pilot.

Trust no one. For all they knew this could be a double-cross. A plot to lure more soldiers onto the plane to meet their deaths.

"No one. My passengers bailed over the desert."

What? Lani's heart stopped. How had they missed that? She had to contact Ty and Rock immediately.

As she reached for her cell phone to contact Ty, a movement on the screen monitoring the illusion caught her attention. Lani frowned and paused with the phone in her hand.

"What in the world is Ty doing?" Lani whispered to herself, heart pounding as she watched the hovercraft carrying Rock and Ty fly erratically, as if Ty was drunk at the helm. It bounced around so much she lost visual contact with Rock and Ty.

She hit a switch in front of her and called engineering. "Something's wrong with craft one. Take control—"

An explosion rocked the screen where just a second before the plane from Vegas had arrived. The plane was completely engulfed in flames and sirens were going off. She couldn't see Tate in the mayhem.

As Lani pulled up Tate's number to call him, Ty's hovercraft exploded before her on the other screen, turning into a great fireball.

CHAPTER TWENTY-TWO

An aerial acrobat, Rock was not. He jumped, tucked, and rolled right onto the hardest patch of ground in the entire desert. Or so it felt. He knocked his head pretty good against a boulder, too, as he came to a full and complete stop with a mouthful of dust. Damn, rocky landscape. He had to work on sticking his landing next time. He spat the dirt out and wiped his mouth with the back of his hand.

Ty, however, had made a perfect stuntman landing next to him, and rolled to his feet while Rock was still struggling to catch his breath.

An explosion nearby nearly blinded Rock and sent his ears back to ringing mode. Next to him, Ty shielded his eyes with his arm.

Rock's first thought was that the bomb had blown up the hovercraft. But as his eyes adjusted to the dark again and his night-vision goggles kicked in, bits of shrapnel rained down on him, and Rock realized the bomb had exploded in midair.

"Damn, they missed it. Great job, man." Rock punched the air and bounced to his feet.

Ten feet from them the hovercraft wobbled and floated unmanned, looking precariously close to crashing.

"Damn is right. RIOT doesn't miss. They exploded that

bomb on purpose. Don't you see? They want the hover-craft. It's experimental and top secret. I'm sure we're guinea pigs for the boys at Dreamland who are probably testing it out in a real-time environment—our mission.

"Unless I miss my guess, which I don't, it's what RIOT's been after all along. Or part of what they want, anyway. A bonus, maybe." Ty shook his head and stared at the craft. "Shit! If we wreck that vehicle, we're toast. Come on, we're gonna take our ship back, dude.

"Get your weapons ready, set your wand gun to kill, and watch your back. RIOT will be coming after us with everything they've got." Ty took off at a run for the hover-craft.

Rock pulled his wand gun from his pocket, and took the safety off. He took out his thumb gun and his spy ring and pounded after him.

Ty, with his washboard surfing-dude abs, was in shape and faster than Rock. The surfing spy dude pulled away from Rock and in no time was hanging on the edge of the hovercraft, trying to pull himself aboard.

Unfortunately, two intruders in night camo beat Ty to the hovercraft by seconds. They tossed themselves over the edge with athletic ease and into the craft just ahead of Ty. One of them was a big, burly brute holding an auto-matic pistol that he aimed at Ty's head.

"Shit!" Rock had to do something. As he ran, he took aim with his thumb gun, praying for a little accuracy. The closer he was to the target, the better his chances of hitting him.

Ever tried to aim your thumb while running, and shoot for accuracy without using a site when there was abso-lutely no time for hesitation?

As Rock took aim, a red laser beam spotted the kill zone on the intruder. Yes! Will was on the job, backing them up.

Seeing himself marked for death, the intruder froze. Rock ran, pointed, and shot just as the intruder ducked.

The shot went wide and missed his intended target. Back to the thumb gun practice range for him. Next time he was going to ask for a bomb-piercing bullet. Fortunately, his shot pinged off something in the hovercraft, startling the other RIOT thug, giving Ty time to let go of the craft and roll for cover. The CIA would just have to forgive Rock for the hole he may have put in their vehicle.

Ty came up shooting, but the hovercraft, which could move in any direction—front or back or sideways—leaped into warp speed, as Ty had jokingly called it, and feinted sideways. Warp speed wasn't really the speed of light. But it was a hell of a lot faster than Rock could run.

Behind them in the desert, the NUFO crowd had temporarily paused when the bomb went off. Good plan on RIOT's part to create a real panic. The crowd recovered and raced full bore toward them.

"Cows! Where are the damn cows we requested?" Ty was on his feet yelling into his mouthpiece.

On cue, a herd of cattle, which had been penned nearby waiting for their stage call, suddenly stampeded out of a cattle shoot, cutting the crowd of vehicles off from the spies and the hovercrafts, creating mayhem worthy of a Western movie. In seconds, Ty and Rock were surrounded by worked-up bovine.

Cows, dust, aliens, lasers, hovercrafts. It was like a scene out of *Cowboys & Aliens*.

Rock pulled off his spent one-shot thumb gun and stuffed it into his pocket. Now, armed only with flash powder, a poison spy ring that required close range to kill, and his six-shooter wand gun, Rock felt decidedly outgunned. Next time he was going to demand a rocket-launching magic hat.

Rock was not a rancher, not a cattle person at all. He

had no idea how to handle a confused mass of Daisy the cows. Were these milk cows or meat on the hoof?

He just stood there a second in the midst of the mooing madness, trying not to further upset the cattle or turn them against him, too.

The confiscated hovercraft had halted and was hovering on the edge of the cow crowd. *Damn, it's looking for us.*

In all the madness, Rock had temporarily lost visual contact with Ty as the herd swallowed him up.

"We need hovercrafts," Ty said into his mouthpiece, nearly being drowned out by mooing.

Good. Ty hasn't been trampled to death.

A movement a few cows away caught Rock's eye. Ty was commandeering a cow and climbing aboard with surprising confidence. Ty threw his leg over the cow and seated himself, somehow managing, while riding bareback, to hang on as it bucked and kicked like it thought it was a rodeo star. As Rock watched, Ty actually managed to point his bovine steed toward Area 51.

Impressive. Ride 'em, cowboy!

"You're never going to catch a hovercraft on a cow," Rock replied.

"Cattle can travel faster than horses in the short run. Until we get some wheels, do you have a better idea?" Ty's words were nearly drowned out by the earsplitting mooing and the sounds of pounding hooves. Not to mention the new round of alien signals and music emanating from the NUFO crowd.

"What the hell has the crowd so worked up again?" Rock asked.

"You mean besides the bomb exploding?" Ty said.

Rock glanced up to see an alien warrior rising out of the hovercraft.

Ty saw it at the same time. "Shit!" they said into their mouthpieces in unison as it became clearer what the

LICENSE TO LOVE 313

game was. RIOT had taken control of Rock's illusion and it was obvious they were intent on further panicking the crowd. "Where the hell did that thing come from?"

RIOT's alien was a scarier, less sexy version of Rock's. It had Sol's nasty, copycatting stamp all over it. Worse, it carried an ugly, impressive, highly lethal-looking weapon, holding it threateningly. Which explained the NUFOs' sudden urge to communicate with the aliens. They were trying to convince it they were friendly. *We come in peace.*

Good luck with that, Rock thought.

Unfortunately, the NUFO music was not calming the savage, or even domesticated, beast. The NUFO calls intended to make contact with aliens only upset the cattle more. Rock didn't think the music was *that* bad.

Ty cursed some more, a jolted, choppy sort of cursing made so by his bucking bovine steed. "Like dogs, cattle can hear higher frequencies than we can. The NUFOs must be broadcasting high-frequency sound waves. We have to get out of this herd before the cattle go crazy and trample us to death."

Death by alien, RIOT, or cattle. Not good choices.

Rock yelled into his mouthpiece. "Will, Zach, Jake, forget the illusion. Get over here with your hovercrafts and pick us up. *Now.*"

Ty was yelling more commands, trying to reach HQ inside Area 51. His calls went unanswered. "Damn, RIOT must somehow be jamming our signals from inside Area 51. We're on our own, boys." He sounded breathless as he rode his bucking cow. "Hey, bossie, bossie, calm down, girl."

"We've already dropped Jake at the gates," Will answered.

Zach cut in. "We're still being remotely controlled from inside Area 51. They're sending us through our preapproved illusion pattern. Give me a sec. I'm trying to wrestle control away and switch to manual operation."

"Can you do that?" Rock asked. "Do you know how?"

"I don't just play games. I have an engineering degree from MIT," Zach said. "I'll give it all I've got, Captain."

Rock rolled his eyes as the cow next to him cuddled up to him and began making eyes at him. He didn't know what she suddenly saw in him, but it appeared to be love at first sight. "Nice, girl." Rock reached out, cautiously, and stroked her forehead.

She let out a loud moo, but at least it sounded happy.

"Sounds like you have a new friend. Where are you guys?" Will said. "Your GPS is down and I can't see you in the dust and dark. Can you give us a signal?"

Rock had magic up his sleeve in preparation for the big reveal. Hell, he always had magic up his sleeve. But once he shot a sparkling flare up and gave away their location, RIOT would be after them again, too. Under the cover of cow, they'd been fairly safe. "We're less than a mile from the gates on the Area 51 side of the stampede.

"As soon as Zach gets control of your crafts, let me know and I'll send up a flare. And when I do, you two get your butts over here as fast as if you'd just been teleported. RIOT is looking for us, too. You better believe they'll see the flare and come firing."

"Roger," Will said.

An eternity seemed to pass while the cow next to Rock continued to make eyes at him and the cow on the other side let loose a large, unpleasant-smelling cow pie. Rock dodged out of the way just in time to save his shoes. Meanwhile, Ty had his cow under control and was maneuvering her to the edge of the crowd to make a dash for Dreamland. Rock hoped Ty had some badass weaponry on him, something more powerful than a six-shooter wand.

"Got it, boss!" Zach's voice rang with excitement. "We have control."

"But do you know how to drive?" Rock replied.

"I've played video games all my life. Piece of cake," Zach said.

"Will?"

"I'm no slouch, either," Will said. "Send up the signal and be prepared to board ship when we hover above you."

"Here goes nothing." Rock shot a sparkling flare straight up into the dust cloud above them. The flare startled his new friend Daisy the cow. She kicked and let out a loud moo, sending Rock back a step into that fresh, steaming cow pie her buddy had made minutes before.

He was still cursing and wiping his shoe in the sparse desert grass as a shot whizzed past him.

The hovercrafts had a low noise signature, which was part of the genius of using them for the illusion. Unfortunately, that meant Rock and Ty couldn't hear a now enemy-controlled one coming after them. Or hear the friendly ones approach.

Rock ducked back into the herd of cattle, trying not to get kicked or trampled. The cattle had seemed to realize he was the source of that frightening flare and now they didn't trust him. They gave him a wide berth. Even Daisy turned her back on him, leaving Rock in the open like a sitting cow thief as the lynch mob approached.

Ty had reached the edge of the herd. Will's hovercraft spotted him and swooped in to pluck him off his somewhat trusty steed. By hovering ten feet off the ground, the crafts were high enough to cruise above the cattle. The engineers had warned them not to hover at that height too long. It was a strain on the fans and engines.

The fans blew stiff breezes below the craft, providing the cushion of air the hoverers floated on. The cattle didn't like the late-night burst of wind and quickly cleared a path beneath the crafts. Ty's cow didn't like the wind from the fans any better than the rest of the herd did. As Will leaned over to grab Ty, and Ty pushed himself to a stand on the cow's back to pull himself into the craft, the cow bolted from beneath his feet. Ty dangled from the vehicle as bullets whizzed past him.

Off balance, the craft tipped precariously to the left. Zach pulled up in his craft on their flank. Ty shouted at him to rescue Rock. Zach ignored the orders and came around in his craft to give Ty a boost into Will's vehicle.

Meanwhile, Rock was surrounded by cow dung and the equally unpleasant odor of sweating cattle. Those were not the worst of his problems, however. Now that the cows had abandoned him, the commandeered hovercraft had spotted him and was headed directly at him.

CHAPTER TWENTY-THREE

It was utter mayhem on the tarmac—fire, gunfire, fire engines, smoke. Area 51 had been breached and was going into lockdown. Lani couldn't reach either Tate or Tal. And she'd lost contact with the magic crew and Ty on the outside, too.

But she still had a visual on the main craft. To her great surprise, Rock's hovercraft had not exploded. Instead, it was now being piloted by Sol dressed as an alien king and his RIOT henchman.

A flicker of hope crashed through her—where were Rock and Tate? Was it possible they were still alive? Had they somehow managed to escape?

The crowd of NUFOs was in full panic mode now as Sol made threatening gestures, almost taunting them.

It was clear to Lani that RIOT had taken control of the illusion, twisting it to fit Sol's warped sense of magic, and was intent on driving the NUFOs into Area 51, causing more mayhem while RIOT stole the developmental hovercraft and whatever else they could cart out of Dreamland.

Lani studied the feed with a trained eye, putting herself in professional spy mode to hold her emotions at bay. There was no sign of Rock or Tate. At least she hadn't seen their bodies. Yet.

A message from engineering cut into her thoughts.

"We have a problem. We've lost control of the hovercrafts. They've somehow been switched to manual and gone rogue."

The video feeds from the two auxiliary hovercrafts had been cut off. Lani couldn't bring up their cameras. "Looks like we've lost them, too. Do what you can to regain control."

There was only one thing to do—take back control of the illusion and stop the panicked hordes from storming past the point of no return. Already camo dudes were massing at the entrance, aided this time by soldiers with battle experience under their belts. If Lani didn't act, innocent people would die, and more damage done to intelligence and national security matters. She had to perform the reveal. And trust Jack and his crew to rescue her baby and Nanny.

She got on her mouthpiece. "I'm going out to end this illusion. I need backup."

She grabbed a rocket launcher and headed out.

Ty toppled into the craft and Zach headed out for Rock. Zach had the advantage of being closer to Rock than the enemy hovercraft. And all that high-performance video game driving paid off. Zach zipped in, hovered above Daisy, and threw Rock a rope. Yes, a rope. Low tech, but efficient. Since junior high PE Rock had been a rope-climbing champ.

He scrambled up the rope and fell into the hovercraft with Zach just as the enemy craft got close enough to see the enemy's eyes.

"Rock, how thoughtful of you to show up at another one of my performances." Beneath the creepy alien costume, Sol's eyes gleamed with malice in the moonlight. "Not planning to upstage me again, I hope."

"Really, Sol? Stealing another of my illusions?

Originality isn't your strong suit." Rock pointed his wand gun at the evil magician. "Now, you're standing in something that's mine and I'd like it back. If you'd kindly exit the vehicle, we can do this all without bloodshed."

Sol's laugh was positively bloodcurdlingly maniacal. He was obviously off his mind and out for revenge. "Make me, Rock. What's your plan, exactly? Are you going to hit me with the death curse?"

Rock smiled back, trying to keep his anger under control. "You know I don't believe in real magic. I have a reputation as a debunker to maintain. Now, don't make me shoot you. Jump out and take your goon with you."

Around them, the cattle were lowing and spreading out into the desert. And the NUFOs were winding their way through the herd on foot and in a slow-moving menagerie of vehicles. Rock could only imagine what the NUFO crowd must think of a magician holding an alien at bay with a wand. The cows didn't look too thrilled about it, either.

Rock had to get to the gates and head off the NUFOs with the big illusion reveal before the NUFOs crossed the line and someone got killed. He had to trust NCS to save Stone at the same time. But first Rock had to dispatch Sol.

Rock whispered to Zach. "Get me close enough that I can jump on that hovercraft. Then take out the thug and let me deal with Sol."

"Come and get me, Rock." Sol hit a button and his alien helmet lit up, emitting a blinding light show directly into Rock's eyes. At the same time, he pointed a laser saber at Rock.

Damn it! Rock pulled the wand gun trigger and fired into the light just as Sol's craft surged forward and rammed into them.

Sol let out a scream. For an instant, Rock thought he'd delivered a fatal shot. The laser saber dropped and

Rock could sort of see again through the spots in his vision. Sol was holding his arm and cursing.

Now, Rock thought. *I should shoot Sol now and end this all for good.*

He aimed his wand, but somehow he couldn't make himself fire on the wounded man. "That was just a warning shot, Sol. Because you saved my life once years ago in Lake Tahoe and I owe you. I won't miss again."

"Owe me." Sol laughed again. "You've always been naïve, Rock. I'm the one who was responsible for you taking the spill and nearly drowning in the first place. To cover my tracks so no one would know that I'd stolen your trick.

"I let you suffer as long as I could and only changed my mind about killing you at the last second. And that was only because you hadn't finished Outlandish Marauders yet. That was a good call. Without that, where would my career be today?

"That trick is what convinced Archibald Random to fund my show. So I could perform the first illusion I stole from you.

"Now, however, I think you've finally outworn your usefulness." Sol signaled the goon behind him.

The goon raised a rocket launcher to his shoulder. Rock reacted by pointing his wand.

Ty and Will were silently sneaking up behind Sol's craft. At the last second, the RIOT goon heard something. He spun around and fired at Ty's craft.

Ty returned fire, hitting the goon directly in the forehead just before Ty's hovercraft caught fire and went down. The thug dropped the launcher and fell forward, dead.

Sol grabbed the launcher. Rock pulled a handful of heavy-duty flash powder from his pocket and threw it onto the craft. "Get us out of here! Now!" he yelled to Zach. "We have to help Ty and Will."

Zach was already on it. Within seconds they zoomed around Sol's craft toward Ty and Will's now-fallen hover-craft.

The night was dark and the hovercraft was camou-flaged. To the crowd it probably looked as if Rock and Zach had simply disappeared in a burst of magic.

The gunfire and flash powder scared the herd. The cattle lowed and stampeded away from the area.

As Sol tried to figure out how to operate his hovercraft, Rock searched the area around the fallen hovercraft. Ty appeared, holding a fire extinguisher. Will was beside him.

Rock let out a breath of relief. "We're coming to pick you up."

Ty waved him on and spoke to him via their headgear. "No way. Leave this to us. Get out of here. Get to the gates and perform the reveal. We have to stop this mad-ness. That's an order, dude."

Lani arrived at the front gate with a battalion of soldiers and camo dudes and began issuing orders. How in the world was she going to operate the lights and the lasers and do the reveal without Rock and the others?

"Over there!" One of the camo dudes pointed to an alien leaning against the guard shack.

"Jake!" Lani ran toward him. "Oh, thank goodness." She turned back over her shoulder and shouted to the camo dudes, "We have our alien. We can do the reveal. Get the engineers and the stage crew in place. The crowd's approaching. Hurry!"

The need for secrecy had forced Rock to use Area 51 personnel for his crew. His regular stage crew couldn't be kept under tight enough wraps. She hoped these Dream-land guys could perform magic.

Jake stood.

Lani paused in front of him. "Are you okay?" Her voice shook involuntarily. One of the young magicians had survived. That was something. She may have lost Rock, but she still had a chance at getting her son back alive. She had a shot at making a hero out of Rock and she was damned well going to take it.

She never should have wasted these last two years. She should have been with Rock. They should have been a family. She couldn't undo all that, but she could ensure his memory and his magic lived on. And she could thwart RIOT. She had to.

Jake was nodding. "I'm fine."

Lani looked around, afraid to ask. "Where are the others? We lost contact. What happened to Will and Zach?"

"Rock called for them to bring their hovercrafts to him and Ty so they took off into the middle of that raging herd."

Lani felt so happy that for a second she couldn't speak and her eyes misted over. *Damn feminine emotions.* She pushed them aside. If Rock was still out there, he'd find a way to make it back to her. For now she had a job to do. "You know the old saying—the show must go on. In this case, right now. Before the NUFOs swarm us and breach the barrier. Can you perform?"

Jake grinned. "On with the show."

"Excellent," she said. "Prepare for your stage entrance. It's time for our prestige."

Unfortunately, Sol quickly figured out how to drive the hovercraft and his was bigger, faster, and more maneuverable than the two smaller previously remote-controlled crafts. Zach pushed their hover vehicle to the limit, but Sol was quickly gaining on them.

The crowd, too, had managed to breach the herd and

close the gap. The NUFOs were now hot on their tail, so close that Rock didn't dare fire his wand gun for fear of hitting an innocent bystander or making an instant side of beef.

Rock and Zach may have been able to go stealth and sneak away, but Sol insisted on showing alien theatrics and bathing both vehicles in light.

Rock looked over his shoulder. "Sol wants the NUFOs to catch us."

Though for the life of him, Rock couldn't figure out why. In the excited state they were in, they'd tear Sol as the alien king apart and ask questions later. But Sol didn't appear to care. He radiated anger and wrath. It was blinding him.

Rock pulled up his sleeve, wound up like a pitcher on the mound, and hurled a ball of fire at Sol. It was good theatrics, but completely harmless.

The leaders of the NUFO crowd fell back for a second, but not Sol. He retaliated by blinding them with the hovercraft lights and trying to ram them.

Zach anticipated his move and hovered up another few feet just out of range. He punched the air. "Yes! That bastard forgets we can move in three dimensions. He should play more video games."

"We need crowd control." Rock didn't know why he hadn't thought of it before. He called Britt and gave her an order to try to manipulate the crowd and get them to back off from the area. Lie. Tell them a horror story. Scare them. Whatever it took.

Sol came at them again with the rocket launcher trained on them.

Rock had to act. "Hold steady. Let Sol come within jumping distance of us."

"Too bad Jake's not here. Your command would have

been a lot easier to execute. That guy could jump the English Channel." Zach raised an eyebrow. "Your jumping distance or mine, boss?"

"Mine. And what we could really use is that jet pack I sent back. Seems I'm not as good at predicting what we needed for this mission as MI6's Q. At the very least, I could use a few of Jake's tips."

Sol's craft was closing on them.

"No time now." Rock stared at Sol's craft. Damn, if he hit that rocket launcher wrong, it was going to hurt like hell.

"Pump with your arms and jump like you mean it," Zach said, grinning as he reversed, flying toward the RIOT-controlled craft. "I think that's all Jake would tell you. That's the sum of the advice he gave me. For my part, hit the bad dude when you land and get rid of that fucking rocket launcher."

Rock made some mental calculations and bent his knees. Just a few seconds now. "Once I jump, make a run for the gates. Find Jake and start the reveal without me." Rock cleared his throat. "If I don't make it back, finish the show without me. And tell Lani she's always been my magic."

Rock watched as the gap between crafts closed. Fifteen feet. Twelve. He'd always sucked at the long jump. Ten feet. Eight.

He saw the whites of Sol's eyes. Sol pointed the rocket launcher directly at Rock.

Rock swung his arms and jumped.

"Now!" Lani screamed and gave the signal to the sound engineers and the guys in charge of the light show. *Where is Will when we need him?*

The NUFO crowd, mixed with several dozen head of cattle, was surging toward them, screaming in a mad mixture of English and purported alien and blasting across loudspeakers. Behind Lani, the camo dudes had made a barricade across the road and ringed the immediate perimeter of Area 51. They were no match for the crowd, though. None.

Megawatts' worth of pulsating light, the kind of lights and laser displays you'd see at the best Vegas shows, like Rock's, came to life, illuminating the stage that Daniel had designed to look realistically like a large starship. At the same time, strains of popular music blasted from loudspeakers.

Lani burst on stage in a blaze of flash powder and light, dressed in skintight spandex. "Ladies and gentlemen, alien watchers and scientists, NUFO conventiongoers and camo dudes, welcome to the grand prestige of Rock Powers's most magnificent, ambitious, astounding illusion yet.

"David Copperfield disappeared the Statue of Liberty. But has any magician ever appeared an alien ship? Given us such convincing aliens? Manifested hovercrafts? Fooled such a savvy crowd?

"I give you tonight's show—Outlandish Marauders!"

Rock missed Sol by that much as he hit the deck of the hovercraft just as the lights and music of the show lit up the gates of Area 51.

Sol swung the rocket launcher at Rock like a club. Rock ducked out of the way. Shit, he had to get that thing away from Sol before he did some serious damage with it. He reached for the nearest thing handy to use as a weapon—a fire extinguisher.

Rock meant to swing it, but Sol went on the offensive, stabbing and jabbing with the rocket launcher, which had been modified with a lethal looking knife at the end like a bayonet.

Rock used the extinguisher as a shield, backing up to avoid being impaled. Until he ran out of hovercraft and found himself literally against the wall. Sol grinned and aimed the pointy end of the rocket launcher at Rock's gut.

A gut wound was no way for a world-class magician to meet his end. But there was no way Rock was abandoning ship without neutralizing Sol and his dark magic.

Rock glanced at the meager weapon in his hands. What was he thinking? *Use the force, Rock. The force you have in your hand, idiot.* Rock pulled the extinguisher pin, and aimed at Sol's eyes, and fired.

Sol screamed and fell back, hitting the hovercraft controls and sending them at warp speed toward the stage as he dropped the launcher and pawed at his eyes.

The forward surge nearly sent Rock backward over the edge of the ship. Counteracting his momentum, he threw himself at Sol, grabbed the launcher, and tossed it overboard.

Sol roared and took a swing at Rock, with his bloodshot, foamy eyes blazing with hatred and killing rage. He connected with Rock's jaw, sending his head snapping around.

"Shit!" Rock yelled as he took Sol by his alien-costume shirt collar and smacked him with a right hook.

Sol staggered back, dazed, and wobbly on his feet.

Yeah, take that!

Rock had never been a fighter, but he was damn proud of that blow. Though his fist smarted. Rock shook his hand out, made a fist again, cocked his arm, and prepared to wallop Sol again as Sol seemed to come out of his dazed state.

Sol roared and cocked his arm, ready to take another swing. His eyes blazed with fury. He was foaming at the mouth—literally. And it wasn't from the fire extinguisher.

What the hell?

Sol gasped and fell to his knees. His body contorted and he began to spasm as foam poured out of his mouth and dripped down his neck.

Rock stared in horror, imagining an alien would soon pop out of him. He swallowed his revulsion and kneeled to help him. Which is when Rock looked down and saw that his spy ring had popped open.

Oh, shit! That single dose of poison . . .

"Rock! Rock, slow up before you crash the stage."

Rock looked up to see Will and Ty pulling up beside him on their partially toasted hovercraft.

"Turns out it was just superficial damage," Ty said as he climbed aboard. "Nothing a little space-rated duct tape couldn't fix."

Rock barely heard him as he watched Sol twitch in his final death throes.

"How are you doing, dude?" Ty took over the helm and the driving. Someone had to. Rock and Sol had been on unofficial autopilot. Which was taking them on a collision course with the stage.

Ty flicked a glance at Sol on the floor as Sol's eyes went blank, the life went out of him, and his body went still. "Nice work."

Rock felt pale. He'd never killed anyone before.

Ty glanced at Rock's hand. "Ah, the spy ring. Excellent. The chief is always right. Good thing he told you to take it along. See, the Agency doesn't just invent junk gadgets for no reason."

Rock flipped the secret compartment closed.

"Better dispose of the evidence." Ty held his hand out for the ring.

Rock slid it off and dropped it into Ty's hand without comment.

Ty put it into his pocket just as his cell phone buzzed. He grabbed it and read a text, then he broke into a huge grin. "They just rescued Stone and Nanny. Both are safe now."

Rock teared up. He was just so damned happy and relieved. He wiped his hand across his eyes as Ty gave him a one-armed hug.

"Okay, magic boy," Ty said. "It's time for the big Bond finish to this mission."

Rock stared at him with a blank look.

Ty shook his head. "We're really going to have to bring you up to speed on the spy stuff. That's where Bond gets the girl, idiot. And then gets a little action. You look like you could use some."

Ty nodded toward the hovercraft next to them that Will was patiently piloting. "Hop on over there with Will and let me take care of the mess here. You two go finish the illusion. Your audience is calling for you."

It wasn't until that moment that Rock realized the crowd was no longer screaming out alien messages for *We come in peace*, but his name.

Well, hell, who am I to pass up a big Bond finish? Rock slapped Ty on the back and stepped into Will's craft. "Take us to the stage."

They arrived to hover above the stage just as Smokz was levitating and Jake leaped on stage in his alien gear with his alien moves and revealed himself as an ordinary parkour expert magician.

Lani looked up to see Rock hovering above her. "And here he is, alien watchers, the grand master of the illusion, Rock Powers."

As the crowd went wild, Rock nodded toward the hovercraft, and mimed what he wanted her to do. He took a bow from the craft. Held up his arms and bowed his head. Then, on cue, let loose the last of his flash powder, and leaned down and pulled Lani up into the craft. The smoke cleared in a flash and the audience gasped.

Yeah, Rock still had it. To the crowd it appeared as if he'd materialized her there. Not only that, but Lani had quick-changed into a replica of that wedding dress costume, the one she'd disappeared in two years ago.

"Stone and Nanny are safe," he said. "It's over. They got them out."

She let out a cry of joy and nearly collapsed with relief. He caught her in his arms as tears appeared in her eyes.

She stared into his eyes and cupped his face in her hands. "I always meant to come back."

"Good," Rock said. "Because I was never going to stop looking for you."

Then he pulled her into a kiss that made the audience sigh.

STINGER

Nanny really is a wonder, Emmett thought as he watched Rock—his head of the newly formed NCS Department of Counter Magic and Cover Illusions—take his son in his arms for the first time. Lani hung over Rock's shoulder, beaming with love and pride, and out-and-out joy.

And Nanny, well, that big, burly guy and former Navy SEAL, just stood off to the side smiling, too. Emmett made a note to give him a commendation.

The Agency really is just one big, happy family.

That was a mission well done. Rock's reveal had stopped the NUFOs cold from forcing their way onto Area 51 property. Tate and Tal apprehended a top-level RIOT agent who'd escaped from the plane before it blew up and had been sent in to steal top-secret plans. The RIOT bastard was the queen of diamonds. Not a bad catch. The bastard was being interrogated in a CIA facility even as Emmett watched the happy family scene before him unfold.

They'd foiled RIOT's attempt to steal a hovercraft. And now that Rock was no longer any use to RIOT, his baby son and wife were safe.

Only Random had slipped through their fingers *again*. That slippery bastard. Emmett would get him one day.

Speaking of him, Emmett wasn't happy with Random's impersonation of him. How had Random managed to fool the Area 51 staff? Emmett's own voice was really much deeper and commanding. At least his agents had followed his orders.

Emmett knew what this meant—he had to develop a top-secret identifying mark or tic known only to those in his command. Something small, like a mole that moved around and only CIA personnel knew where it would appear. Like the code word of the day.

The only other loose end, or maybe he should say, loose cannon, was Tate's ex wife, Malene, the Agency's cover life artist. She was fit to be tied that Tate had prevailed and prevented her from designing those alien costumes. She'd cornered Emmett and let him know in no uncertain terms what she felt about the situation and how she was just as senior as Tate. Tate should not, repeat, should not be able to dictate what projects she did and did not work on.

It was going to be hell placating her.

Read on for an excerpt from
Gina Robinson's next novel

LOVE ANOTHER DAY

Coming soon from St. Martin's Paperbacks

Tate sat in Dulles International Airport, outside the security check, waiting for his ex-wife, Mal, to arrive. They were traveling together to Cheltenham, England, as mathematics professor Tate Stevens, PhD, and his trusty graduate student and research assistant sidekick, Mallie Green.

What the hell had Emmett been thinking assigning her as his cover life artist for this mission? And insisting she go into the field with him—lunacy. First of all, Tate worked alone. He certainly didn't need Mal, or any woman for that matter, tagging along to scare Sophia off. It was going to be dicey enough convincing her he was falling in love with her so he could bring her in. He didn't want to give her any reason to bolt.

Secondly, he and Mal got along now about as well as the Agency got along with RIOT—they generally wanted to kill each other.

Thirdly, while Mal was an excellent cover life artist, she wasn't a trained agent. Oh, she could shoot with the best of them, but a gun wasn't her most efficient weapon. No, she wielded words like a pro, cutting as efficiently as if using a stiletto. He knew—he'd been the recipient of her knife's edge too many times. He didn't want her sharp tongue anywhere near Sophia.

And lastly—she was a horror at math. Could barely balance a checkbook. He wasn't a math genius, but he had a degree in computer science and knew math as well as any engineer. What he didn't know, his eidetic memory would help him fake his way through. Without one, how was Mal going to convincingly play a mathematics grad student? He shuddered as he thought about how he'd have to cover for her. Could he claim she was mute?

Tate had reasoned, begged, and even pleaded with the chief to let him go solo. He didn't need a cover life artist. He didn't do disguises when he went undercover. He was an *out in the open* agent.

"You do this time," Emmett had said. "Our contact in London says Sophia insisted she will contact you. Not the other way around. She's nervous about being discovered and killed. Very skittish.

"You're to go to Cheltenham undercover as Dr. Tate Stevens, professor of mathematics. She specified the name. That way she'll know whom to contact. She says you're too well known in RIOT circles as yourself. She can't be seen anywhere near you. You'll have to go undercover and in disguise."

Emmett had given him an up-and-down look and scowled. "It's too damn bad you've never taken the trouble to learn how to use a disguise. They can be extremely useful."

Emmett was a master of them.

"She also said everyone at this science festival will be a geek of some kind. You're to dress the part." Emmett shook his head. "I need you to be a handsome, sexy geek. There's no way you can carry that off without help. Malene's your only hope."

Tate had sighed deeply and resisted pounding the arm of the chair he sat in. "Let her pack me a bag, but does she have to come with?"

"She does. She's your master of disguise in case things go wrong and you need to escape without attracting notice. Malene can get you new IDs, new costumes, new identities by wiggling her little finger. You need her on-site this time." Emmett looked amused at Tate's discomfort.

"Then assign someone else for the fieldwork. *Anyone else.* Call Kendra back from her mommy leave. Tell her I need her. Offer to give her a nice bonus, whatever it takes."

"And be slapped with a lawsuit?" Emmett's eyes twinkled. "She's not leaving her weeks-old baby to dash off to England, no matter what I offer her. I can guarantee that.

"This is a delicate operation. I need my best personnel on it and Malene is it."

Tate had scowled. "How am I supposed to seduce a twenty-four-year RIOT agent with Mal watching my every move?"

For reasons he didn't want to admit to, the thought made him uncomfortable, and he was anxious enough as it was. This mission was a conundrum wrapped in enigma.

"I doubt she'll be watching you that closely," Emmett had laughed. "Learn how to use a disguise. Get some fashion sense. And maybe next time I'll think about letting you go solo." And then Emmett had dismissed him, sending him to Research and Development to pick up his gizmos.

Tate had an uneasy feeling about this whole operation and setup. He believed in his sex appeal—he had as healthy a male ego as the next guy—but a college girl falling in love with his picture and file? It seemed a little *too* fantastic to him. It could happen, he supposed. But he didn't trust RIOT. Were they behind this? And if so, what mayhem did they have up their sleeves?

The brass and intel and data crunchers at Langley had

run through all the intelligence and data. Done thorough background checks. Sophia checked out in every regard. Her father *had* recently passed away. It was the perfect time to break away and escape RIOT's death grip on her life.

If she was genuine, she was still taking a horrendous chance with her life. RIOT's assassin squad, SMASH, would track her down and kill her no matter how long it took. She could live to be one hundred, and they wouldn't give up. Was a life spent in constant fear of discovery worth living?

On the other hand, constant fear pretty much described a life in RIOT's service. Maybe it was a wash.

However, if she *was* part of a plot by RIOT, what could they be up to? If they wanted him dead, it was easy enough to send a SMASH assassin to take him out. They didn't need to lure him out with a girl. He knew intelligence secrets, true, but nothing he could think of that could be seduced out of him by a woman. They'd have to torture them out of him, and again, sending SMASH to kidnap him seemed like a more efficient plan. Neither he, nor Emmett, nor the director, nor any of the heads of departments could think of a reason to send a girl to get to him.

Tate could have refused the assignment. Emmett gave him every opportunity to turn it down, had even tried to talk him out of it. But the opportunity to get the one-time pad that would open up RIOT's entire encrypting algorithm was too tempting to pass up.

"Tate!"

Hearing his name being called startled him out of his thoughts. He looked up to see Mal wheeling a suitcase the size of a small travel-trailer behind her. Seeing her, his heart stopped. When it banged back into action, it beat infuriatingly fast.

She was dressed casually in a tight-fitting dark denim miniskirt, thick, opaque tights, ankle-high brown leather boots with a low heel, a loose cream blouse, a long, loopy gold necklace, and a loose, reddish-orange military style jacket with gold buttons and leather trim. Her blond hair fell in loose waves around her face. Her makeup was light, fresh, and natural-looking. Except for her lips, which were deep red-brown, moist and glossy, the very look and color he found so hot. The way they'd looked when they first met. Mal had the most kissable, perfect mouth—full and lush, with a delicate bow in the middle. She looked as if she were still in college herself. One of the hot college girls all the guys chased. Why hadn't Emmett commanded her to deemphasize her looks, to shoot for dowdy?

Now *he* was going to have to tell her to tone it down and give her the satisfaction of thinking he found her even the slightest bit attractive. Damn his body for reacting to her. He wasn't prepared for the impact a college-age Mal made on him. She looked so much like she had when they'd met. More updated college style, but still as young and tempting.

He tried not to scowl. Mal was the queen of putting together disguises and cover life personas. She could have downplayed her looks and gone for major nerd, too. But she'd let her pride get the better of her.

"Traveling light, I see." He stood as she approached.

She arched a brow, which transformed her into a cynical thirty-three-year-old. Thank goodness. His attraction evaporated. This was the Mal he knew and didn't love.

"Nice to see you, too, Dr. Stevens." She leaned in and whispered to him, "Stop daydreaming and pay attention. We're supposed to be undercover already.

"I called out to Dr. Stevens three times and only got your attention when I used your first name."

"What can I say? I'm an absentminded prof. And I just decided—we're casual at the university. First-name basis only." He cut her off. He didn't want her arguing.

"Works for me, Tate." She took him in with the look of a tailor eyeing her work. Finally she shrugged and smiled, obviously pleased with herself. "You look good in nerd glasses and three-day growth."

He appreciated not having to shave regularly. But he had perfect vision. He didn't need the damn heavy black plastic-rimmed glasses. The frames interfered with his vision. He wouldn't have worn them at all, but the tech department had outfitted them with a concealed camera and rearview coating that made them halfway acceptable.

"Where's your bag?" she asked. "Have you checked in already?" She smiled sweetly.

She'd picked out his suitcase, bought everything in it, packed it, and had it delivered to his place minutes before he had to leave for the airport. Worse yet—she'd locked and booby-trapped it so he wouldn't tamper with it. There was no trust in the Agency. He pulled his luggage receipt from his pocket and waved it for her to see.

"Good. Now you can help me with my suitcase. It's too heavy for me to lift onto the scale. I have our . . . research materials inside." She wheeled it toward the check-in stand and got in line.

Tate followed her. He could hardly imagine all the torturous things she had in there. He was certain she was going to try to exact some kind of revenge on him for any number of perceived slights over the years.

They walked right up to the check-in counter. "Dr. Stevens? I mean, Tate."

He sighed and hefted the behemoth onto the scale. The bag weighed more than it should have, even given its size. He hoped R&D hadn't given her anything too dangerous.

The casual leather laptop bag he had slung over his

shoulder housed a host of goodies. Two magazines of bullets were sewn into a clever hidden and shielded compartment. He also had a stash of gold coins and currency of various kinds in the false bottom. The handle contained two lethal, ceramic fighting knives. And, of course, he had his laptop, iPad, and iPod, along with an assortment of bugs and listening devices.

The baggage handler weighed Mal's bag and charged her for the overage. Within a few minutes she was finished checking in, and they were on their way to the security checkpoint. Tate had a special air marshal waiver to get him through security. Mal was on her own.

They were supposed to be undercover, but as they walked side by side toward security, he had to ask about Kayla, innocuously, of course. "How's the kid?"

"Great. She's with my mom for the duration."

Tate frowned. "Yeah, I heard."

He leaned in and whispered in her ear at an angle none of the security cameras could catch to read his lips. "My mom wasn't happy. She'd like her turn. Kay's her only grandchild, probably stay that way, the least you could do is let her see Kayla once in a while. Take her off your hands for a few days. She and your mom could share."

Tate was an expert at reading micro expressions, tiny, involuntary muscle movements that gave away emotions. Though Mal looked calm enough to the casual observer, she was pissed.

"You divorced me, not Mom," he said.

Mal looked at him and rolled her eyes. "I wish. When I divorced you, I was hoping to be done with that witch."

"Hey." Tate grabbed her arm and stopped, pulling her around to face him. He was sure there were no cameras that could catch what they were saying. "Show a little respect. Kay and I are all the family Mom has. All she wants is a little time with her."

Mal's eyes narrowed. She glared at him. "And to turn her against me.

"I'm always the bad guy. The girl who stole her little boy from her. The evil villain who keeps her from her granddaughter.

"If she showed me some respect, I'd show her some. As it is, she's threatening to petition the court for visitation rights. I suppose you put her up to that?"

He ran his hands through his hair. His mother could be a handful. She always had been. She and Mal had never gotten along, which put him in a horrible bind in the middle. "I tried to talk her out of that."

Mal shot him a look that said she didn't believe him.

He *had* tried. "I did."

"Dr. Stevens, you say the most amusing things." A look of hurt swept across her face. Then she pinched his cheek and kept walking.

Damn, he didn't want to fight with her. He'd never wanted to fight with her. But she never understood that he'd promised his dad he'd take care of his mother, no matter what. And he'd never understood the rivalry between his mom and Mal. His mom was one of their irreconcilable differences.

He couldn't fight with Mal now even if he had wanted to. In their cover story, Dr. Tate Stevens and Mallie Green got along famously, were a real team. He had to hustle to get back in step with her.

"Yeah, I'm a real card."

They reached the security line.

"This is where we part company." She smiled sweetly at him.

He wondered whether there was any way he could rig the security screening so she failed.

"Don't even think about it," she said as if she'd read his

mind. "I have Emmett on speed dial and permission to use his red phone number."

Shit.

"See you on the other side." She winked at him and joined the line.

That woman was enjoying this way too much. He wondered what delights she'd filled his suitcase with. He knew that gleam in her eyes and it meant trouble—for him.